Fortnight's
Anger

Fortnight's Anger

ROGER SCRUTON

Carcanet Press · Manchester

To an angel
...*so leben wir und nehmen immer Abschied*

Scruton, Roger
  Fortnight's anger.
  I. Title
  823' .914 [F] PR6069.L7

  ISBN 0-85635-376-0

First published in Great Britain in 1981
by Carcanet Press
330 Corn Exchange, Manchester M4 3BG
SBN 85635 376 0
(C) Copyright 1981 Roger Scruton
Printed in Great Britain
by Billing & Sons Ltd, Guildford and Worcester

Chapter One

KENNETH FORTNIGHT felt that he was dedicating himself, not to his mother's death, but to the Kid's. It was his mission, everything that had, by right or stealth, come down to him. Yet he loved the Kid, just as he loved in a queer way the whole arrangement that had thrown them together in that house, where he was always escaping, always returning, always lingering or moving on.

The mission began with the Kid's illness: he was seven at the time, and Kenneth fourteen. The Kid did not consult his brother, but took on complete responsibility for his derangements. He went alone to the headmaster of St Stephen's School to complain of the throbbing in Kenneth's head. He took it upon himself to upset the house-warming party by appearing in pyjamas and firing the Colonel's Colt 45 at the claret jugs. No one responded; he adopted more radical methods. Lord Gilroy came to dinner: the Kid asked him whether his ancestors were distinguished by anything other than treason to the King and Martyr. Mr Kruschev visited America, and Dr Castro came to power: the Kid marked each occasion by unfurling the red flag from the top of the portico, with an upside-down picture of the Queen pinned to its lower corner. At last Fortnight decided on the need for action. He provided his brother with a name.

Of all the foolish things to call a seven-year-old, studious, snobbish and arcane as he already was. It was wholly unenglish, without style or class — like 'Huck' or 'Chuck' or 'Hank' or 'Slim'. But Fortnight invented it, because he wanted his brother not to have a real name. 'Francis' suggested a definite character, a place in the order of things, a right to exist. Just to be 'the Kid': it was as though he was not to earn that right, he was forever to be some kind of abstraction, like the National Debt, the railways, or the number two. Their mother continued to call him Francis, but gently and hesitantly. Even she was happier when confined with him in some corner where names were no longer required. But the Colonel followed Fortnight's example. It was the one good idea, he said, that Kenneth ever had, and he would always remember with gratitude and appreciation this dispensation from the general grief of child-rearing, that one of his sons should have found the word with which to sum up and eliminate the other.

Once the Colonel began to use the name, it had to be adopted. Orders were orders. But the Kid soldiered on in spite of it. He refused to *be* an abstraction. On the contrary, he was unique, an *Eigentum*, always one step ahead of any general conception of his nature. In everything, therefore, he became a challenge. You had to confront him, be whole and complete in a world of fragmentary things. Even his mother adopted the name in time, feeling the common need to confine his peculiarities to some impersonal form. It was not the lusions which changed her (on the contrary, she seemed to treat them as natural, like a family tradition in which the Kid had been tacitly instructed from birth). What affected her were the silences. It did not matter how much the Colonel bellowed or chattered, how much he slipped his tongue round this or that oily sentence and slithered it from his favourite observation post at the top of the stairs into the lower house: whatever the Colonel could do, if the Kid was silent, then the house was silent. For days, stuffed with some invisible cotton wool that sucked up the noise. Then later would come the exasperated chatter, the Kid talking and gesturing to the unseen observers who surveyed and discouraged them all.

His eyes began to go wrong at the age of six. After consultation with a specialist it was agreed that this was not his fault. But as for the rest they all, in their various ways, harboured suspicions. By the time he was eight a routine had set in. He would begin his days by singing loudly over the house, sometimes impromptu nonsense, sometimes Pergolesi or Bach. It upset Fortnight that the Kid was so musical. He would interrupt every practice, saying, 'There should be an F sharp in that chord', or '*Mendelssohn* didn't write that'. But music, like all his talents, also drew Fortnight to him: it was part of that peculiar way he had, of being on the surface of things, quick to see the point, quick to find the appropriate word or gesture. Perhaps the oddest thing about him was the way he combined this intuitive authority in all important things with the utmost eccentricity and awkwardness in everything that did not really matter. For example, he would insist on eating his breakfast in the garden. Even in the coldest winter months he would eat nothing until he was allowed to go outside with his plate of congealing bacon and tomatoey beans and wander up and down, prodding it quizzically with his fork. His mornings at home were spent not in play but in exploration. He had drawn up a map which covered the area up to a mile from the kitchen sink; well-known landmarks were given private and inscrutable names and the Kid had recorded in red and blue ink episodes of which no one else had any conception. (Fortnight remembered the day after he first went to Barbara's house: by chance he noticed that the Kid had ringed the house in green, and named it Avalon.) And at lunch, when the Colonel was absent and the boys were home from school, the Kid behaved with a studied correctness, taking over from their mother every menial or unpleasant task and conversing rapidly in polite and topical vein, always experimenting with large words which he would have to look up in the dictionary. Then he would retire, to read, or to work at his Latin, which he loved above everything and read as fluently as any of the masters at St Stephen's School. But as evening approached the singing would begin again, more loudly now, and with a disconcerting urgency, as though there were some other, more persistent, more terrible noise that he wished to drown.

It was a damp spring night when Fortnight returned, with no hint of summer. Everything seemed cold and stunted. No one walked in the streets of Flackwell and the only sound was a faint hum coming from the telephone exchange beside the station. He imagined the voices skeltering along miles of fine wire, bubbling through valves, leaping across the chasms of transistors with their little bundles of grief and joy. He enjoyed such thoughts. They put reality at a distance. He no longer had to worry about the telephone exchange, which blocked the only pleasant view from the station and obliterated the cobbled yard where he had played soldiers with the Kid. He thought only of the voices, the little worm-like voices, one of which had leapt that morning from the telephone and announced that his mother was to die.

He stopped at the corner, by the Kid's favourite signal-box, with its fine framed windows and elegant iron stair. The Kid said he liked it because of its brass and steam patina. He always used phrases like that, because he believed in magic and thought that words could make things permanent. In this case the spell had not worked. The signal-box was abandoned, and on the side facing the path all the little windows had been smashed. The previous year, on the day after the Kid's fourteenth birthday, the branch line to Dutton had been closed. Now only a bright red coach linked the local villages, skirting housing estates with incongruously lovely names: Hyden's Hill, Kettle Bank, Marleys, The Herons, Spearywell. Their mother had explained what they meant. Kettle Bank, if you looked carefully, had the shape of an old farm kettle; Spearywell was a damp patch where a rush-fingered spring had watered a nearby farm. The farmhouse had gone; so too had the coppices where they went blackberrying in the summer.

After the signal-box the next stop was always the Baptist church, founded 1905, services 10, 11.30 and 6, preacher the Revd John Cottrill, MBE, MA, caretaker Mr G.H. Busby. From here he would have to cross the park, and at the end of the park was home. He sat down, as always, and tried to calm down. Across the park at this end he could see the circle of cobbles where the High Street ended, with its Rotary Club benches and conical rubbish bins. The last building was the old bookshop where he used to go with Barbara after school. They had bought Ruskin, Shelley, George Eliot, Cardinal Newman, all in battered, soft leather bindings, thrown from Victorian drawing-rooms in the wake of death. All the books were in their basement in South Hill Park.

He remembered Barbara with distress, since it seemed necessary to his mission that she should retire into non-existence. But he had lived with her in London for nearly three years. Her image was fragmented and the parts of her imperfectly joined. He insisted that he was blameless if she came apart when he pulled. Recently, Barbara had taken to wearing rough denim clothes, dirndl skirts and dun-coloured headscarves. It made her look as though she belonged to an underground militia. When she was eighteen she used to fry before a sunlamp and paint her face in blue and cherry-red. Now she was all seriousness. She was even writing a thesis, on 'The social significance of Fine Art in late capitalist society'. He asked her what she meant by 'late capitalist'; she said he would not understand, but that he should read Gramsci. He read Gramsci as he read everything she told him to, but it made no difference. So she took him along to weekly meetings at her friend Sarah's house, where they drank cheap Italian wine and agreed to agree about everything important that they might not agree about. He did not like it. He had said so that morning because suddenly she had got up from the desk with a strange gesture of defiance and accused him of being an 'unperson', which he thought was particularly unfair since he had applied the word to himself only the previous evening. To his surprise he had managed to feel angry, even though for months he had hated himself for what Barbara was suffering.

'It's all too easy for you,' he said. 'You pick up a book and you read. You sit at your desk and you write. You get yourself a degree, and you go on to research. Everything goes smoothly. Everything is comprehensible, a task. You settle down with me, and I become a task. I'm kept and cultivated like a beastly thing in a jar. I'm fed on little worms of thought, little theories about art and society. I'm fed and fed and fed until I'm bloated and bursting and unable to move a single limb.'

Fortnight became quite excited about this speech, and was pondering how to go on, and what and what not to mention, and how he might weave in something about getting a job and giving up the Bar and perhaps settling somewhere else, when suddenly it occurred to him that he had no idea whether these accusations were serious, no idea whether it was the truth he spoke or whether he had the right to utter it. Everything became terribly dark. He stopped speaking and went out into the garden.

The old ailanthus was beginning to bud, and three stray cats were dozing on the patch of lawn. The day before they had planted out seedlings of herbs: samphire, lovage, southernwood and rosemary, fennel, woodruff and camomile. The names were soft and remedial. No doubt that was why Barbara's father — who cultivated gentleness with heartless conviction — had given them John Evelyn's *Acetaria*; it was the only acknowledgement he had made of their living together. In the bravest salads, said Evelyn, every plant must play its part. They must fall into their places like the notes in music, and there must be nothing harsh or grating. Barbara had read the passage to him before they began. He looked at the pots of old-fashioned earthenware, which she had carefully collected because she hated ugly things. He saw another part of her, neat, orderly, unassuming, progressing down a path which would have been flowers had he not lumbered before her, trampling on every pleasant thing. But when he pulled at that part, wanting to unite with it, it came away from the rest of her, and left him with a lifeless relic, a cold simulacrum of the girl he had desired.

He returned inside. Barbara looked tired. They had been awake most of the night, sitting at their typewriters. She said she must finish a chapter for the morning. He said that he was starting work on his novel, and, while he knew that she did not believe him, he would occasionally clatter out nonsense on the keys so as to surprise her with the sound of inspiration.

Somehow Fortnight could not bring himself to feel proud of Barbara, though he knew that she deserved it. A degree from the Courtauld, research at the Warburg, poems in two of the weeklies and even a long review in a learned journal of a book about Constructivist art: every day advanced her from was to will be, in the same quiet rhythm that swallowed even the unhappiness he caused. She joined societies, discussed things, changed (or thought she changed) her views. She sang madrigals with a group that was soon to go on tour — her teacher thought she could make a professional *mezzo* if she tried, and was trying to get her a place in the chorus at Covent Garden. All this was amazing and commendable, and in comparison he was an unspeakable waste of time. He hardly knew what he was doing from day to day, whereas she was neat and professional in everything: at any moment the signal would come, that she, at least, would have to move to Paris, or to Greenwich Village, or to some other place where the life of the professional bohemian must be lived. Uncle Jonathan's little legacy would soon be finished, and he had hardly begun the course at the Bar. It really seemed to him that he forgot each day as it ended, and began the next as though it were already three years old. Watching her at work he felt he was dragging her down. And then, out of fairness to himself and his biographers, he would always try to think of some little way in which she turned her back on him. His biographers were very clear that he should clatter on the typewriter in the most aggressive manner possible. 'Oh for God's sake! Stop!' she had cried; and that is how their quarrel began. But he knew it was his fault; he kept forgetting that Barbara had antennae which would always discover his thoughts.

When the telephone had rung and the Colonel's cold crisp message had fallen into his ear, Fortnight turned to her. For some reason he could not tell her the news. He went across, lifted her arm from the desk, and kissed her thin white wrist. It was cool, soft, pliable, crossed with pale blue veins. Still she was a girl, just as on that summer afternoon five years ago, when, in the long grass on Tyler's Hill, they had lost their schoolbooks and their virginity. He envisaged the time when they had not been friends, and she a leggy hoyden playing hopscotch in her father's drive. He was sure at least of that part; her activity, her determination, her conviction that she was in the right, these were no more than the wilfulness of a girl. She looked up at him and her grey eyes were fixed and clear, not like a woman's. They said 'now' to his 'sometime', and 'you must' to his anxious 'perhaps'.

'I have to go home. Things not too good.'

'Will you stay long?'

'No. Not long. At least I don't think so.'

'I suppose that's meant to be encouraging.'

Because he could not match her clarity he averted his eyes. There was a law book on her desk — she had probably read more of it than he had. The other books were heavy catalogues of art, or slender red paperbacks on social reform. Somehow they were to be coagulated into a thesis: he wondered how.

'It's not meant to be anything in particular.'

She withdrew her hand and went over to the bed, on which the white Indian durry lay, stained with purple wine. But she did not sit down there. Curiously she took off the leather-topped clogs she was wearing and laid them on the bed, neatly, side by side; it made him think for some reason that they belonged to someone who had died. Then she walked back past the table, trailing her arms behind her as though she did not want to assume too much responsibility for anything they did. There was a paper-knife on the table, a stunted pewter object with an art-nouveau design. Barbara picked it up from behind her. Once they had collected art nouveau, mottled pottery, shapeless lumps of pewter and paste, leafy tiles and languid dollops of glass. Sometimes they had stayed out all Saturday on Portobello, looking for the stuff. That too seemed strange, and when his eyes encountered these objects his mind fell away in a swoon as though he were trying to remember something — something of the greatest importance — and somehow it just would not come back.

'Nothing in particular,' he repeated. She could go forward, but he must go back. Simple.

But why was she crying? That was not part of the agreement at all. Surely she must realize that it was on the strictest terms that they had contracted to live together. Barbara Langley was to be cheerful, industrious, placid, fair and changeless as an Aegean day. While Kenneth Fortnight, Kenneth Fortnight.... There was a strange pattern made by the cracks in the kitchen door. Why had he not noticed it before? From where he was standing it looked like a tiger; it seemed to be carrying something in its mouth. He thought of the Kid, who loved cracks and could read so many meanings into them that it was a wonder he ever paid attention to human speech. The school holidays had begun. He would be home. Suddenly Fortnight felt a wave of apprehension. He had to go. Besides he could not concentrate on their discussion. It did not seem to concern him. He left the house quietly and even forgot to slam the door.

Outside it was already beginning to be cold and wet. Sounds were muffled. It was eleven o'clock and the day had found its routine. Out of habit he entered Archer's, a tiny corner shop with a green painted architrave and classical lettering, a shop so full of odds and ends of merchandise that clients must enter one at a time and decide immediately what to buy. Sitting on the bench by the Baptist church, he remembered the shop more vividly than anything else in London. Newspapers, razor blades, nylons, sweets, milk, eggs, potatoes and bacon were there all heaped up in disorder, and the lump of tinned ham that lay on the bacon slicer was half wrapped round with a pair of women's gloves. He entered because he liked the smell, and also because Mr Archer had a special way of greeting him, a way of saying 'Out early this morning Mr F' which might be ironical, or laudatory, or sometimes even sharp, and yet which always persuaded him of his normality and removed the urgency from private things.

'Well Mr Archer', he said, not looking up but staring into a dark corner where packets of detergent were piled beside jars of yellow pickle. 'Off home today'.

'The husband's not here, Mr Fortnight. Bit poorly.'

Old Mrs Archer looked at him with suspicion from spectacles in which her eyes swam like pale green jellies.

'Sorry to hear that. Nothing serious I . . .'

'Took faint yesterday. Just bending to undo them spuds there, it being Monday and the sack come in.'

She gestured to a large bag of stiff brown paper that stood still out of place, in so far as anything there could be out of place, in the very centre of the floor, like a memorial to Mr Archer's final act. Fortnight felt confused by Mr Archer's illness. In fact he went so far as to hold that Mr Archer was under a positive obligation not to be ill. It was particularly important that day, what with the news about his mother, and now this trouble with Barbara, particularly important.

'Not serious though. Doctor give him some tablets, told him to stay indoors. Just my luck; bin the busiest day this week. And what's for you?'

It seemed inconceivable indeed that someone who worked in that cluttered shop, who had every opportunity to study the manifest complexity of contemporary existence, who saw spread around him on every side the mass products on which the lives of other men depend, the tins, jars and razor blades, the biros, laundry markers, hairbrushes and potatoes, the hand cream, writing paper, eggs, comics, curvy grips, salt beef and bibles which he had been appointed by fate to distribute, that such a man should so easily excuse himself. His mother's case was different, entirely different. She had no definite place in the scheme of things, and in all her acts was thoroughly dispensable, with a timid susceptibility that gave zest to ill-treatment. She was everything frail and contingent, the ghost of a sad Christian lady, lingering in an age beyond her comprehension. She was the old Anglican church, the institutes and societies, the outings and tea-parties, the quiet unassuming rituals of an undone provincial life. You could be touched by her, but it was like being touched by some bad poem about a flower in a woman's magazine; you felt that a softness had taken hold of you, that you had succumbed to nostalgia, that your feeling was not true. Fortnight thought of her embroidery, her patchworks, and most of all her garden, their garden. His mother hated the pink of carnations, the vulgar trumpetings of red, red roses perched like pompoms on their stringy stalks, the earth cheerless as a laboratory beneath them. It was always the delicate and winsome flowers that she planted, the prunella and larkspur, the candid blue poppy and the sorrowful cornflower. She used to lay aside for them long borders of their own, where they would dance, blue and tremulous, a pale string of virgins at a ball. He was not to be touched by her; he remembered all those cold hard precepts that told him not to give way. She was a bad poem; but he was touched. He was part of her, she part of him, even though they spoke to each other from far away, and even though the telephone was soon to splutter and go dead. Her soul already breathed the unnourishing air of George Bourne and Thomas Hardy, and stared at him from the terrible distant kingdom where they lay.

But then, just sometimes, and unexpectedly, she too had spoken out, flushed and excited, with a passion rising from he knew not where. He began to remember an occasion during her previous illness . . .

'Nothing you want Mr Fortnight?'

He glanced at Mrs Archer's eyes, as they struggled to unfocus him. She wore old National Health glasses, with spring grips curling round her ears. Somehow this made him think that life was especially easy for her.

'Can't make up yer mind?'

It was a dark November's day. Black, sudden mallards rose from the clump of nettles by the dyke, their colours sucked out of them into the twilight. They flew in the shape of an arrow, sticking the sky before the window where his mother sat. Her little feet were encased in furry slippers and a pale violet shawl of crochet-work hung from her arms. He thought she was asleep. All afternoon she had been in pain, frowning from moist blue eyes at the ragged rooks' nests in the elm-tree, and at the scattered people in the park. Now her head had fallen back. Its puzzled expression had gone, and her brow was smooth, white and clear as a girl's. A few locks of hair fell into her left eye. She looked still, almost like a statue. But from time to time her left hand twitched, and the little blue veins seemed to rearrange themselves beneath its alabaster surface. Suddenly she started forward.

'No,' she cried, 'no, I will *not*. No!'

And then she sank against the chair, her head cushioned in its velvet surface.

'What is it mother? What's wrong? Was it a dream?'

He heard the habitual questions, framed in Kenneth Fortnight's voice, distant, as though from another sphere. In the cold reaches of his soul were being prepared the trite consoling gestures, the unmeant offerings of hope. Why did she make him hate himself so? It seemed almost unjust.

'Is that you Ken? No. Not a dream. If only . . . I mean . . .'

Suddenly she began speaking in a hushed voice, rapidly.

'It was seeing those ducks reminded me. The way they shot in a line across the sky. That was how it was at Blackett's, when we were married. Don't you remember the cottage? Always at this time of year the ducks would be flying over the lake, widgeon, teal, mallard, all kinds, and your father used to shoot at them with the old shotgun in the hall. It reminded me. I loved our life there. We were poor, do you remember? But I liked that. I liked the cold. I liked the damp. I liked the isolation. I liked having to make ends meet. And he was so kind. You've no idea how kind he was. Because I did things, little things, that he couldn't do. I made all the rush mats in the cottage; I even began a tapestry. Only we had to move; the army wanted us to move. He was going to be made a captain. Now we're well off, and he's a colonel brackets retired. But I don't love that colonel. I'm afraid of him. I am so afraid of him. I should have refused to go. You see, Ken, that's the kind of failure I am.'

She settled back, with her old self-deprecating laugh. He watched Kenneth Fortnight refuse to help. Had he not his own life to lead? Was he a nurse or a counsellor? It seemed wrong of his mother to harbour these feelings. He suffered them like an outrage. Turning, Fortnight noticed the Kid standing in the doorway. Tears were slowly dropping from behind his spectacles. Remembering all this he began to panic.

'What's to become of him?' he asked aloud.

'Who? Mr A? *He's* all right,' said Mrs Archer. 'Be back in the shop in a day or two. Came over all queer he did,' she added, pointing meaningfully to his feet, 'right there where you're standing. They say it's the weather. Lot of people bin affected. Keep out of the wind if I were you.'

He stared at Mrs Archer for a few seconds, and then at the place of Mr Archer's collapse. Everything seemed very strange. He wondered if the Kid would be able to answer her. The Kid always had words, whereas Fortnight's thoughts were speechless. He left the shop quietly. He recalled the rain, and a sense of universal brightness, as though there were a light that would burst through from beneath the surface of things and make him blind. He wanted to close his eyes. He wanted not to be. But somehow he got to Paddington, caught the train, and here he was, sitting as ever at Station Two, the bench by the Baptist church. Soon he was to see them again, mother, the Colonel and the Kid.

A travelling funfair had set up its booths and engines in one corner of the park, and came into view as he walked across. Music and circus cries rose up into the air, as the lights on the big wheel came on. Slowly it began to turn. A girl squeaked hilariously, and then a squad of black motor-cycles buzzed across the corner into the fray. The distance seemed inordinately great, and the sounds were muffled as though they came from far over the hill.

He stood at the park's edge, facing the old house from across the road. All the curtains were drawn, but he noticed a light behind them in his mother's room. The cedar-tree in the forecourt had grown; now its branches touched the white frame of his mother's window, and stretched over the high wall into the road. Something compelled him, as it always did, to count the windows. This was not a sign of insanity, he remembered, since Bruckner used to do the same; that was how you explained (according to Barbara) the rhythm of his scherzos. He went from left to right, top to bottom, three under the roof, three on the first floor, and the tops of the two downstairs, just visible over the wall, with the moulding of the portico jutting half-way between. But when he had rehearsed the familiar proof five times *sotto voce*, beginning at the premise of the Colonel's bedroom and ending at the conclusion of the door, he turned away. He could not possibly go in there. He had lost his key. Perhaps he had never had a key; he could not remember. Probably they would not want him to come in. If he rang the bell they would stare at him in astonishment and then quietly shut the door.

He walked down the alley to the vicarage, and took the little gravel path which ran from there to the garden gate. He was surprised when it did not open. It seemed to be wedged from behind. At last, pushing hard, he opened a crack wide enough to squeeze through. He discovered his old bicycle leaning against the gate, a waterproof sheet thrown across the saddle. He removed it to one side. The cold wet metal and the smell of rust affected him strangely. Images crowded into his mind, the Kid yelling as they steered the toboggan down Wenbury Hill, their mother putting out seedlings in the spring, a huge omelette they had once made, with twenty-four eggs, a lobster and five glasses of brandy, Uncle Jonathan quietly sipping beer through his moustaches in the garden shed — fragment upon fragment of his childhood fell in disorder through his mind, until he felt that the task of understanding was beyond him.

The tendrils of shrubs snatched at his clothes and then gave way. Once or twice his feet stumbled against an obstacle; a root, a stone that rolled down from the herbaceous border, a jar full of some liquid that gushed in the grass. He tried to fix his mind on the first words he would say to her, but they would not come. And yet it seemed as though he had been rehearsing them for months, for years, ever since he last was home.

He knew the garden. It was his mother's garden, their garden, his garden. Everything that happened to him had secretly seemed to take place there, as though he were some leisured creature subject to the law of Elective Affinity, never straying from his castle grounds. Strangely, however, he kept stumbling on uncharted obstacles; dark forms rose before his eyes, peremptory creepers suddenly tugged at his arm. All at once, and without predicting it, he had stepped into the kitchen yard.

A figure moved in the shadows by the wall. Its gestures were slow, quiet, mysterious, as it bent over a patch of earth and shone a torch into the leaves of a stinging nettle. Its tufted head nodded slightly as it swayed on its stalk like a top-heavy plant. Suddenly it swung round.

'Hey! Who's there?'

It peered into the darkness.

'What are you? Are you real? Are you a lusion? Speak, I command thee. And don't be boring.'

'All right Kid, it's only me.'

His brother bounded forward into the light from the kitchen door.

'It's only Kenny! And it might easily have been the Prime Minister, or an elephant, or a thing!'

The Kid's voice was breaking and he moved in a queer graceless way, like a badly made automaton. His hand gestured wildly and his blue eyes swam in the depths of bulging spectacles like strange aquatic animals. He stopped just in front of Fortnight, his lips quivering. His mop of fair hair seemed damp, as though he had been sweating, and his thin legs shuddered as they scraped together like the legs of a restive insect. The Kid was seldom still, but would move from one angular posture to another, each bearing some obscure geometrical relation to the last. It was as though his body were continually rehearsing some difficult theorem out of Euclid, the conclusion of which (as when one day he got up from the dinner-table and spat five times accurately into the Colonel's soup) often came as a complete surprise to everyone. Fortnight waited without moving for his final QED.

'How jolly', the Kid said at last. 'I've been wanting you to come for aeons. There's a plot on, and I've rumbled it. Why've you been so long?'

The Kid had grown; or rather, he had expanded in a formless way. But the problematic centre of his being, which now stood within a sphere of mawkish movement, seemed at the same time to have shrunk, to have become a tiny atom in the middle of a vast cocoon. You could not possibly reach it through the electrostatic fire. Within ten seconds of meeting the Kid had dictated their terms. What Fortnight knew as death was in fact a plot, and grief the mere cunning of a private eye. Were the Kid's terms negotiable? He didn't know. He decided to affect normality.

'Well Turnip-tops, you can tell me about the plot later. And then I'll explain why I've been away. But just now I must go in and see . . .'

The Kid fixed him with a stare and all at once stopped his movements.

'See what you'll see. And explain *that* to me if you can. But first you can say why you are wearing that suit. It's at least ten years out of date; not to speak of those creepy suede shoes. And no hat. Like an abominable snowman, standing there with your penguin arms crying out for a pair of suitcases. My dear Kenneth,' he went on, imitating the Colonel's tones, 'I am most awfully worried about you. Most awfully, awfully worried. And just one thing before you go. My name isn't Turnip-tops. That is an Anglo-Saxon vulgarism. Say Elaemosynarius if you must. It sounds more dignified — at least to the educated ear.'

He turned away and began to poke at the nettles with his feet. They were his school shoes, brown, with protruding soles of waxy crepe. It was obvious that he was going to cry. Only five yards away stood the black half-open door of the kitchen. Inside there was safety. Correction: inside there was danger that was real, something you could measure, something you could overcome. Putting it that way made it possible to move out of the circle of this guilt into that of another. It even seemed right to ignore the Kid's outburst and enter the house.

But it was not easy. The familiar smell nauseated him. The light flickered in the kitchen; the blue and white china rested on the dresser; the jars of stale chutney and crystal-crusted jam stood to attention on the shelf where the Kid and he had ranged them, veterans of a war that had never really mattered. It was all unchanged. The cups were hanging from the hooks above the sink. Fortnight recognized the Kid's square mug with its Catullan motto painted on the side — *Ridete, quidquid est domi cachinnorum.* The tiles of the floor were clear and greaseless; someone had been coming to clean. Stepping past the long deal table he caught sight of a medicine bottle standing on the shelf among empty jars. It was the heroin mixture that she had refused to drink, colourless, with a powdery surface. He recalled a sweetish sip of it. Was it Kenneth Fortnight's face twisted in a mask of sympathy that had forewarned her? Perhaps the Kid had told her not to drink it. He wondered why the doctor had spoken in front of the boy. Heroin. Jennie Fortnight. Perhaps it was simply that the ideas did not mix.

He stepped down into the hallway. The poetry bookcase stood in shadow, brown, blue and purple volumes glimmering in the light from the fan above the door. Barbara's look as he left that morning suddenly came back to him; it tinctured the expression he imagined on his mother's face. They viewed his coldness with uncomprehending misery. He must find the words to console them, else he should never be free. Suppose he could find the right poem; perhaps he could read it and read it until the membrane of his mind burst inwards and he understood. But where to begin?

Suddenly there was a groan. He started. It was like the moaning of a cat, low, menacing, and then gradually rising to a shriek. There was a scuffle, a tread of feet, and then a girl's voice saying 'It's all right. Don't worry. All right'. Then silence. He found Kenneth Fortnight running on the stairs, greedy with compassion. But a tap was dripping slowly and he paused to listen to it, as though it were the continuation of his mother's cry. At the first turning the door to the bathroom stood open, and the dull grey twilight filtered in from the frosted window, falling faintly on the carpet of the stairs. He began to tremble, and could hear the heart beating violently within.

He was on the landing, gripping the rail; the house was quiet. He prayed that the Colonel was absent, dead, drunk or asleep. Slowly he pushed the door ajar. A yellow light fell through the crack on to the second flight of stairs, which disappeared above him into darkness. He thought he heard movements in the Colonel's study.

Angela Williams, the little nurse who had attended her the previous time, sat at the bedside, staring startled towards the door.

'Hello Angel. How is she?'

Angela relaxed, shrugged slightly, and lowered her eyes. The gesture was quiet, soothing, accomplished. It invited him to see what happened as lying within his competence, just as it lay within hers. Which was why they paid her. When he was finally able to look at his mother it was with the thought of the conscience money that she had cost.

How motionless were her features. Her grey skin cast no reflections, her eyes were walled up behind their heavy lids, and the coarse grey hair spread across the pillow like flotsam. She seemed already dead.

'Hello Ken. Your father said you would never come. But I knew you would.'

'Never' — the word seemed tactless; but Angela's clear grey eyes absolved her from any fault. They looked as though they had been washed clean of all impurities. Her skin was smooth, white, full of life, as his mother's once had been. He moved into the room and closed the door. Suddenly his mother's eyes sprang open, her hand moved slightly, clutching the sheet, and there was a noise in her throat as though something were lying there, waiting to escape. Her eyes closed again and all was still. He felt again the violent throbbing of his heart.

'How long has she been like this?'

'Since yesterday evening. The worst is over now. She's quiet, by and large. I've told her you're coming. Now she's asleep.'

He swallowed. How strange the room seemed now, with its gold-spattered leafy wallpaper, its damask curtains, and its frothy velvet chairs, all cast over with the spell of death. The pieces of furniture seemed unnatural, self-consciously feminine; they stood at random in the room, like props from a theatre left out in the rain, all their uses gone. He stepped across to the bed and sat beside it. Her face was grey, but strangely young, without a wrinkle.

'Mummy. How are you?'

He was startled when she again opened her eyes. The brown wax of sleep had gathered around them. She ran a dry yellow tongue over her dry lips. As he bent down to kiss her he tried to avoid the gaze of her live eye, which quivered wildly, and of her glass eye which seemed to pierce him with a more than human understanding. He kissed her cheek.

And then a terrible thing happened. Suddenly her arms were round his neck, clinging, pressing, squeezing him. He struggled to free himself. He pushed against the bed with his hands; he moved his head from side to side. But nothing prevailed against the strength of those shrivelled arms. A chill terror caused him to pull again; it was as though she sought to drag him with her into that abyss. He arched back from her, withdrawing his face as far as he could from hers. Only when he touched her shoulder with his hand did she fall back and let him free.

'Ken. Darling Ken.'

The voice was distant, but still there was something coarse in her tone, as though she were shouting to him, but from very far away.

'Can't you come closer?'

He seized her hand and pressed it in both of his, but his body sat up quickly and directed its gaze at the linen press against the wall. The old brass double bed, dismantled, stood beside the window.

'Mummy!'

A girlish shyness seemed to return to her face. She moved her head to one side.

'I only want to go.' She paused for breath, and then swallowed painfully. 'As soon as possible. Wish it were over now.'

He realized she was apologizing. He thought of the years of guilt, of the immeasurable injustice she had done to them in refusing to accept her death. But his reasoning was tired and feeble. Only love would exonerate. He signed to Angela and she went out on to the stairs. At length he asked her if she suffered pain.

'No. No pain. Not now.'

She looked up at him. 'Why?' she asked, and then closed her eyes. After a silence, she continued her question.

'Dressed like that? Shouldn't travel in your suit. Ruin it. Oh dear!'

She sighed, opened her eyes, and then closed them again.

'Always used to dress. So badly.'

'Well you see, Mummy, I'm better now; more settled now.'

He stared away. It was his funeral suit, the heraldry of a secret wish, and in wearing it he bannered her onward to extinction. Why had no one given him the words, the gestures, the feelings, to make up to her? Somewhere, sometime, a terrible mistake had been made. But whom should he blame? And who would now relieve this great embarrassment at her death? He felt that she too was embarrassed, and would have preferred the whole thing to have been arranged so that she did not take the central part.

They remained silent. The sense of calamity was irresistible; he felt himself carried along by waves of fear. His mother's eyelids were closed, and except for a short rapid breathing, and the movement of her tongue as it scraped the cracked surface of her lips, she was still. There was no pressure in her hand; it lay dry and motionless in his.

A little table-lamp of turned mahogany with a parchment shade stood on the bedside table, and its light fell across a photograph in a red morocco frame. It showed his parents standing on the sea front at Weymouth; the four-year-old Francis clung to their legs, and the sun flashed in the left lens of his glasses. In some imaginary novel there was a Kenneth Fortnight whose feelings were unlocked by the memories of childhood. That unreal Fortnight had seen the photograph. Already he was summoning up images of those idle weeks, when he read so many thrilling books in the sunlit bow-window of a seaside terrace. How vividly he saw now the Jubilee clock on the Esplanade, the white stucco houses with their brave white windows facing the sea, the White Horse, the wave-washed pier, and the wide white sea-spray on the Portland breakwater. He recalled his childish delight in the wet sand out beyond the deck-chairs, away from the dozing adults under the sea-wall, out where the donkeys stood and the Punch and Judy, where his mother came barefoot beside him and the whole bright world was bathed in love.

The style, he knew, was impossible. The real Fortnight spoke to his inner self only in the timid language of anxiety, his mother's language, the language they shared. He had taken the photograph with the box camera given on his twelfth birthday; his father's eyes seemed still to demand gratitude. Captain Fortnight's arm, stretching behind his mother's back, gripped the fabric of her short-sleeved dress, pinching a clump of creases at the shoulder. She smiled, a vague, wan smile, and her eyes looked past the camera into a distant space. The Captain had ordered them out along the

front. Fortnight had sensed his mother's resistance, and wanted
them to stay behind, reading together in the window. Out on the
Esplanade he had followed beside her. The Captain shot out sar-
casms, as was his habit, at the crowds adrift on the windy sands, at
the bright shop windows filled with worthless souvenirs, at the
shrieking infants on the pier. Fortnight knew that it was his
mother who was in some way the real object of this contempt. This
little seaside world was hers. He remembered suggesting that the
Captain go down with Francis to the rock-pools, to look at the
algae and anemones. He wanted to be with her, silent, timid and
alone. The photograph too was Fortnight's suggestion, the only
relief that lay within his power. He sensed her suffering, and
shared the frail velleities that met everywhere with a firm and just
negation. Had it been suggested that one day she might die, he
would have screamed in unbelief. But where was that feeling now?
The photograph presented it, as an accomplished fact, to be
studied, comprehended, and then cast away.

He began to stare down at her the way one stares into the bottom
of a clouded river in search of something lost. Then slowly her eyelids lifted and she looked at him, the glass eye keeping vigil
patiently, the other full of tenderness. At the time of the photograph, before the cancer struck and crippled her, the two blue eyes
fluttered always absently. Now only one eye remained; it was
strange and beautiful, and suddenly filled with life. Something different had entered it, something he had never seen before, or
perhaps only once or twice, in childhood, when for some reason
the wall of inhibition had cracked a little, and he pulled himself up
to where he could glimpse her lying, virginal, in a private place.
He felt her hand move a little. A wave of tenderness escaped and
went coursing in a warm flood towards her fingertips, which
caressed her dry hand rhythmically. He wanted to tell her that he
understood. He wanted to say that there were moments even now,
even this morning, moments of which no one else knew anything,
but the pain of which she would have guessed immediately as she
speechlessly guessed at all his moods, when he desired only to rest
his head against her. The three years were not important. He had
fled, not from her illness, but from the conspiracy of silence which
surrounded it. He could even accept the Kid's account of things.
There had been a plot. They had all joined in it, she most of all. But
all the cold indifference that he had poured on his feelings could
be cast away. He could tell her now. The words seemed ready,
waiting to be said, simple decent truths that he had kept for her
dying moments. He wanted to embrace her, and, leaning forwards, caught a glimpse in the corner of his eye of Angela's navy
jacket where she had left it, lustreless and still against the old grey

chair. His mother looked and looked into the face that inclined towards her, and then suddenly closed her eyes, so rapidly that he was startled, for all her movements until then had been deliberate and slow.

'Ken,' she said, speaking with a new strength. 'Why don't you marry her? Marry that girl? Make up your mind? I feel so . . . sorry for her. So worried about you.'

'Mother!'

He drew back from her. Suddenly her face was weary. Perhaps it was setting into its final shape. For a moment she let her mouth hang open, and breathed several times heavily. He closed his eyes; a snore slowly ravelled from his mother's throat, breaking off in a gasp as she snatched at the air for breath.

'Oh dear!' she cried.

Fortnight opened his eyes again, and saw her lying as before, as though asleep. He now had to contend with both of them. Thinking of Barbara, a kind of stale flat odour arose within him, as though she too were dying somewhere inside, and remembering her was like opening the door of a putrid chamber where she lay. He watched his mother's left hand, which had begun to claw at the sheet, moving very slowly, like a wounded creature. Her breast was heaving, as though oppressed by the heaviness of the air. Fourteen pounds per square inch. He wondered how she survived it; such a weight over every inch of her fragile body! At any moment she must collapse and die! Perhaps she was dead already.

'Mummy! Mummy!'

She seemed not to hear. Her movements had stopped altogether. She had said her last words to him, would never speak again. He shook her hand; it was limp and fragile. He was afraid to grasp it firmly.

'Angel! Come here! Is she all right? Is she. . . ?'

There was a faint rustle on the stairs and Angela materialized at the bedside.

'She can't hear me!'

'It's all right. Let her rest. Try not to tire her.'

Suddenly the sick woman swallowed and opened her eyes.

'You were speaking,' she said. It was as though she were answering a question. She closed her eyes and softly murmured to herself.

'Is there anything you want, Mummy? Shall I fetch you something?'

He could not believe that she heard him. Something had changed. It was as though she were being borne away by a ship that pulled along the quay, and the rope which she had thrown out to him slipped unhindered through his fingers. Soon she would be far out and his cries would be useless.

'Is that you Julien?'

She used the Colonel's name; it was the first time he had heard it on her lips. She must have returned in her wandering thoughts to days of courtship, reaching her hand to the ghost of a vanished man.

'Shall I fetch him, Mummy?'

'Julien!' she cried out with sudden fierceness. 'Why can't you help me? Why do you. Just sit there?'

She changed her tone and began again in a confiding whisper.

'You know he has really been very good to me. I've been such a nuisance. Such a. Nuisance.'

For a long moment she was quiet, the lids gummed over her unseeing eyes. Angela went to the chair, and Fortnight stood up, releasing his mother's hand. There was a noise on the stairway and he jumped like a gigged frog into the middle of the room.

'Julien! Julien!'

She started awake and her hand reached out convulsively.

'Yes, yes, I'm coming!'

He held his breath. The Colonel creaked on the bottom stair, his hooting voice tired and petulant. He came into the room haggard and unshaven, curatical in his flannel dressing-gown, and stopped short with a concentrated stare. Then pulling the white cord tighter about his waist he breathed, a quiet hissing noise, and marched with long elegant strides towards the bed. Somehow he had never before seemed so impossibly large. Perhaps it was on account of the hard stare of his gooseberry eyes with which he reviewed his son's appearance and then contemptuously dismissed it as a phantom or a dream. The sick woman was trying to lift her head, and muttering in a language incomprehensible to Fortnight. He approached, while Angela retreated to her corner. They both stared at the Colonel as he snatched out angrily his spam-coloured hands and grabbed the fabric of his wife's thin nightdress. Fortnight stepped forward and took her by the other arm. 'Oh! Oh!' she whispered, and the Colonel scolded her unceasingly as they lifted her from the bed. Despite her thinness she seemed to have gained in weight, and every limb of her body had to be separately shifted. The soft white legs were coaxed to the bed's rim, and then her body heaved across so that she was sittting upright, wailing and dangling her strengthless arms across their shoulders.

'Stop making such a fuss,' said the Colonel angrily. With a great jerk, in which Fortnight weakly aided him, he pulled his wife forward until she sat on the square commode. Her legs dangled uselessly beside it. The wailing was tentative and beseeching, as if she sought permission for her anguish and would begin to cry out more loudly as soon as this was given.

'Is it hurting, Mummy? Wouldn't you rather go back to bed?' A gangrel aped him, borrowing his voice. He knew that the Colonel's roughness offered more support in her misery than this cold disdaining charity. Her live eye was wide, but opaque now, like a clouded opal.

'No, Julien! Oh dear! No pain now. What a nuisance! If only. I didn't have this trouble! Nuisance. What's wrong with me? Oh dear!'

The Colonel gripped her by the arm and looked with grim dissatisfaction at her shapeless body. Fortnight was afraid to speak, after these three years which his angry countenance at last and suddenly made real to him. The Colonel's hostility to his wife's anguish proceeded not from fatigue so much as from principle, or rather, from an affectation of principle which he judged to be dramatically correct. Fortnight felt himself included beside her in the same histrionic condemnation. Carefully he shielded himself behind her body, stooping motionless beneath her dying arm until it was time to hoist and settle her. As the Colonel chided in a quiet but angry voice his wife moaned unceasingly. And yet there was a meekness and submission even in the tone of her despair, and it seemed as though she had found out the feeling with which she must die, and it was her husband, not her son, who had dictated it.

'The district nurse will be here in a few moments,' said the Colonel, to no one in particular, but giving to the words a kind of warning intonation, as though the nurse would at last bring justice where it had long been deserved. Fortnight arranged the blanket and the pillow, but his hands were trembling and he did it awkwardly.

'Are you going to get some sleep?' Angela asked. They turned to look at her. She had been crying.

'Sleep? Sleep now? Why bother to lie awake when there is so much to do? A week since I have rested. Can't be helped; work. Most damnedly behind with things.'

Fortnight knew that these words were spoken for his benefit, and consequently he stood quietly to attention waiting for the direct assault, watching his father as he smiled with a penetrating tenderness at Angela. The Colonel stood for a moment, his red jaws chewing slightly, as though there were something more he would have liked to say. But then suddenly he relaxed his expression, turned to his son, and held out his hand.

'Good evening, Kenneth. Very glad you could make it after all. Such a miserable night. Confess I thought you might try to dodge the column. Did you an injustice.'

Then, without waiting for a reply, he gripped the cord of his dressing-gown, jerking it so that it pressed against his body, and marched out through the door, like an automaton at the summons of a switch. The door stayed open, and the Colonel's slippers flapped on the stairway with an angry sound. Fortnight recalled the rhythm of his evenings here, alone upstairs, reading, his father constantly ascending and descending the stairs on inscrutable errands connected with money. A feeling of staleness overcame him, and he looked despondently towards his mother's bed. If only they had taken her somewhere else to die!

There was no noise now, except for the quiet rustle of Angela's movements as she prepared to leave. She clicked her bag shut and went to the window.

'Don't worry Angel. I don't think the Colonel meant to be rude to you.'

'Oh I'm used to it. He's had a difficult time.'

She stared as a car passed, swinging its white eyebeams through the darkness. The tyres swished on the wet road. A glow from the funfair spread across the green and filtered through the cedar-tree, falling in a dappled pattern on her neck. Fortnight thought for a moment that it was for the Colonel that she had cried. He had a way with women.

She must be seventeen now. Probably her mother still kept the sweet-shop on Gilbert's Corner, where he used to buy lozenges out of great glass jars, and sherbet for the Kid. The Kid had never learned to suck the powder through the licorice straw. He could not control his breathing, and always finished with a nose full of sneezy crystals. Mrs Williams had once laid him out on an arm-chair in the backroom and repeatedly slapped him between the shoulders. Fortnight remembered the serious little angel busying herself with towel and water, sometimes lifting towards them her smooth unspeaking features. When the Kid had stopped they all sat still for a minute, while Mrs Williams made tea. Somehow he remembered the scene, and the cluttered little room, with its bambi-covered mantel, its cartwheel carpet and walls spattered with pink hydrangea-patterned paper, and it seemed like an image of perfect peace.

'But poor Jennie. It's terrible. And she was . . . she's the nicest patient I've ever had. The sweetest person. She was . . . so kind, so . . . I don't know.'

'Angel, don't cry.'

Fortnight was confused again, and began to envy her tears. He thought of his mother's question. Perhaps she herself, deep in her delirium, was regretting it, regretting the mad anxieties that churned in her mind, regurgitating always the remnants of old reproaches. But he could not be angry. He was to blame. Once again, his thinking slid away in a dwindling tergiversation, presenting only worn excuses and the shreds of forsworn resolves.

'The nurse is here,' said Angela. She touched him lightly on the shoulder and went to the door.

'Goodbye Angel. And .. and thank you. Thank you for everything.'

She vanished. He heard the sound of subdued conversation on the stairs, and then the nurse came straight in without knocking, a robust fern-scented woman, neither young nor old, but pink in the face and shiny.

She greeted him quietly and began at once to make the bed, moving the sick body as though it were a sack containing things less precious than useful. She took a flask of alcohol from her bag and rubbed drops from it into the flesh where the red sores were forming. When she came to the buttocks, on which the skin was magically white and soft like a child's, she slapped them almost playfully. Soon she had finished and began to rearrange the bed.

'These sheets are dreadful.'

He looked at them. They seemed like any other sheets, crisp, white, irreproachable.

'Are they?'

'Of course they are. Feel them. Just bound to give sores. Is there no real linen?'

'Real linen? I expect so.'

An image of the airing cupboard in the hall, with its little brass knob on which the Kid had once stubbed his head, crying 'A lusion! A lusion! They're back again!' And then his mother standing at the cupboard door, handing out sheets on Sunday evening, like a distribution of alms, her white features, and the clean water smell of linen everywhere, surrounding her.

'But do we have to? Can't we just let her lie? She's so weary.'

'Well, all right. Yes, you can now. No real need to change.'

She beckoned him outside. In the dark hallway her face glowed with the sturdy life of a creature wholly animal. The soft veil of official grief drawn over her coal-black eyes could not disguise the impression, and when she took his elbow and drew him further down the hall, he was seized by a crazy desire to kiss her and put his hands on her breasts. Shocked, he tried to be uncivil as he asked for her opinion.

'She's going into a coma. It's the end now.'

He stood still.

'Will it be long?'

'Sometimes it's a matter of hours. Sometimes it takes days. You can't tell.'

She had said the words a thousand times, to a thousand people. Somehow this prevented him from believing her.

'What do you mean?' he asked.

'There's nothing for any of us to do except wait. I'm sorry. But at least the worst is over. She's comfortable now.'

The word seemed inept. Its opposite is uncomfortable. Had she been uncomfortable? It was as if his mother had privately decided on a *déménagement* to some more pleasant spot, and was leaving them with all her hopes renewed. He told the nurse that she need not come again.

'But do you know what to do? When she goes, I mean?'

'Yes', he said. The Colonel would know. He showed the nurse down and watched as she strode on her chubby legs towards the road. At the gate she paused to peer into her bag. She took out a sheaf of notes, flicked through and replaced them, clipping shut the gladstone bag. And then she walked off briskly towards the fun-fair. The big wheel was turning slowly, silently, like a twinkling zodiac.

At the first landing stood the Colonel, leaning his head against the wall. His hands moved back and forth across the wallpaper with a dry noise like sand. His sobbing was almost soundless. It resembled the panting of a wounded stag.

An hour later Fortnight saw his mother suddenly start from her deep unconsciousness and try to raise herself on the bed. Both her eyes were blind now, but they stared wildly in the direction of the wardrobe.

'Julien!' she cried. 'What are the cases for? Why have you packed the cases? Where are we going? Oh! You didn't tell me! And I don't *want* to go! I don't *want* to!'

She gasped and fell back on the pillow, from which she had risen no more than an inch or two. He sat at the bedside, sometimes clenching his fists in rage, at other times weeping like a child, his mind empty and his hands limp. It was more bearable then, to know that he suffered after all. At one moment he started forward.

'Mummy!' He spoke softly, afraid he might send her plummeting for refuge through the dark. 'It's Ken. I'm here. I want to talk to you. I've come to talk to you! Mummy! Can you hear me?'

But the face was still and lifeless, the eyes were closed. Her hands too had ceased to paw at the bedclothes. He leaned forward until he could catch the sound of her breathing. Then, angry with himself, with her, with everything, he got up and walked about the room. At last he became aware of another presence. The feeling was so strange and gradual that at first he thought it was his mother, come in with her faint girlish step to watch as her body died. He turned quickly. The Colonel stood at the foot of the bed smiling strangely, and beckoning him to go.

They did not speak, and when the Colonel tugged at the cord of his dressing-gown it was as though he were pulling himself in, so as to avoid any contact as they passed.

The sight of his room, the bed, the desk, the schoolbooks and outgrown clothes, the one or two objects that spoke of former tastes and dead ambitions, his mother's watercolour of Blackett's, the old print of a harbour scene — all this filled him with pain. He felt as though he had not been definitely born, was continually born anew into the world out of the same narrow box, with its stale and foetid life to which he was joined indissolubly, had constantly to return and seek confirmation of himself there, must always struggle forth afresh, gasping, sneezing, wailing like a helpless child. When this was over, he told himself, he would leave for ever. He had made up his mind. He would go somewhere new, away from family, from the Kid, away from Barbara. He would find a career, a place of his own, friends, influence. He threw up the sash of the window and a damp breeze brushed against his cheek. The air of this new world that wafted to him was full of the coolness of mosses, full of the faint fungus-laden scent of budding vegetation. The damp speckled night shone on the wet leaves of the garden, and as he watched from the window the whole place filled for him with phantoms, the hushed ecstatic forms of his childhood world. They seemed to hover on the lawn, the Colonel mercurial in his many incarnations, his mother detached and motionless, watching with amazement the Colonel's gaiety and rage. And now another figure. . . . He stared for a moment in astonishment. The Kid was out among the rhododendrons, pointing his torch into thickets of leaf, holding back branches and lifting up stones. He moved restlessly, anxiously, as though looking for something, and from time to time would take some little object from the ground and bury it in the pockets of his flannel trousers. He seemed to be talking to himself. Something about this sight frightened Fortnight, and he withdrew from the window, closing it as quietly as he could.

His sleep was troubled by dreams. In one he is walking on a mountain road, with the Colonel and the Kid. The décor has been borrowed from their holiday in Greece, a time when for some forgotten reason they had been happy together, and the Kid had learned to pluck at a bizouki and sing raucous songs in the taverna. The sun is painted in bright vermilion with purple streaks, and casts on the road long shadows of Prussian blue. After a while Fortnight falls back. His companions call out to him, the Colonel hooting imperiously, the Kid's voice raised in shrill squeaks of fear. He must come. It is dangerous where he stands. 'Hurry! Hurry! Hurry!' their voices cry in thrilling counterpoint. But his limbs are heavy, winnowed of vigour, and he collapses beside the road. The land slopes before him, and then plunges into a valley of restless shadows. Beneath a grey-leaved olive-tree his mother stands, looking at him sadly. She is absurdly overdressed, wearing the brown fur coat that had been provided for army functions, and a long floral dress. She pulls the fur collar close around her neck and her face is pale. She has made it up with lotion and lipstick, and in her ears hang the cut paste baubles which once as a child he gave her for her birthday. Suddenly her face seems to freeze in its smile. It has become a mask, unnaturally pale, with vivid high-lights of lips and eyes.

'Are you not coming, Mummy?'

He is on his feet, eager, impetuous. He is determined to challenge the mask.

'Come with us. A walk would be good for you. Please come. We want you to come!'

His words crackle uselessly in the air. He approaches, but she raises a hand as though to wave him on.

'Not now.' A hollow voice comes from her mouth, sounding from far away. 'No point now. Remember me. To Julien. Remember me.'

He awoke with a start, the pillow damp beneath him. The plank of the last stair had creaked and under the door a crack of light was widening. A large black ghost haunted the space beneath the lintel, and then began to walk carefully to the bed's edge, lifting its feet high as though expecting some hidden obstacle. Fortnight pulled back the sheet and watched its movements. After a little reflection the Colonel took up a chair from the bedside and sat immobile in the middle of the room.

He began to speak, and his hushed tone suggested a desire for familiarity. Fortnight dreaded these moments, which broke the calm of their disaffection.

'Your mother, as you know, was very anxious about your present way of life. She felt, we both felt, that you can do better than this continual drifting from plan to plan, this idleness, this whatever it is that palpably fails to occupy you. Not that I so very much mind. After all you have made clear your independence, and in a sense I am quite happy with things as they are. In a sense. However, that's all by the way. Your mother felt that you should put in order the rather strange arrangements that you have made with this Barbara Langley. Of course I don't cast judgement, nor do I pretend to understand. I believe your mother had the idea that you might marry, or at least, failing that, since I gather that marriage is becoming increasingly unfashionable among the *jeunesse dorée* to which I suppose you must aspire, that you should settle in some more permanent way. For example, you might move back here, take over some of the business, live in the flat upstairs — there are many possibilities. But these are details. I am sure that, in any case, you will try to respect your mother's wish; it was, as you can imagine, very dear to her heart.'

'Was?' Fortnight repeated. He recalled that they had not really spoken together for at least a year, maybe three. He did not know what the Colonel meant in referring to the 'business', nor did he remember the existence of a flat upstairs. The entire speech had an enigmatic character that profoundly disturbed him. He was wrong to break the silence, and the single word 'was' repeated again, echoed strangely and ominously in his own voice.

'A few minutes ago', said the Colonel, getting up and solemnly addressing the window, 'your mother, who had been sleeping, suddenly opened her eyes and looked at me. In that very second her heart stopped and I knew — as one does know these things — that she was dead.'

'Dead? No! She's not!'

The Colonel had reached the end of his prepared speech and stood at a loss, making large and comprehensive gestures. It seemed as though he too had begun to doubt under the contagion of his son's distrust. The proposition had been put again too crudely, and he could not gauge its truth, unprotected as he was by any ceremony. The words seemed to scuttle here and there before the Colonel's glance. Finally he opened the door and stood on the threshold in readiness to go down. 'Take it easy,' he said, after a moment's thought.

'Easy,' Fortnight muttered, and at once the nurse's 'comfortable' sprang to its side and supported gently the frail new word. They clasped each other, inanely smiling. And then slowly the words danced in his mind, trailing a smoke of oblivion around her suffering and her death. He shook himself, as though in a trance, and threw again and again into the arena of consciousness the great word 'dead', and again and again it dissolved, corroded by the other two. He knew it was useless. He must get up and see her where she lay. But for several minutes he shuffled at the bed's edge, toying with the slippers on the floor.

She was covered by a sheet; only a few strands of silver hair had not been packed away. Why had they wished to hide her? He approached the bed. It was hard to believe that his mother lay dead there. But suddenly he caught sight of a protruding hand, half open, the fine slim fingers delicately turned towards the palm. He felt a shock, and then snatched the sheet brusquely to the foot of the bed. The body lay very pale and dead, its white limbs sticking at unexpected angles from the nightdress like wax candles from a sack. The mouth was propped shut with a pillow, and little slits of opalescent whiteness glimmered under the lids. It was not his mother who lay there. Someone had removed her as she died, leaving this waxy simulacrum in her place.

Dead, dead. The word stood at the doors of his understanding, calling faintly. The Colonel was beside him now. Timidly they looked at each other from amazed and vacant faces, which said that they had not foreseen this calamity and therefore could not be held to blame. Slowly the Colonel replaced the sheet, and his fat hand trembled as it brushed the dead woman's hair.

He stepped back and extinguished the light. It became apparent that the dawn was breaking. A grey dead light spread from the window, and when the Colonel lifted the sash, cool air gushed across the room. They pulled their night clothes closer and then tiptoed on to the landing. The Kid came out of his room, ran past them on the stairs, and then stopped by the bathroom door, watching with frightened eyes. They spoke quietly, as though the dead woman could hear them only now.

'She's peaceful now,' the Colonel urged, turning to Fortnight. 'Didn't you see how peaceful she looked?'

Fortnight glanced at his brother. The Kid was motionless, transfixed.

'Please Kid', he whispered, 'Father's right. She's better now.'

'Yes,' the Colonel went on in impressive tones. 'She knew it must come to pass. She accepted it. After so much suffering she knew it was for the best. At least we stood by her to the end. At least she didn't have to pass on in hospital. That would have been too awful.'

Suddenly the Kid snorted.

'God!' he said, 'What a freak! Just listen to him. A real life drama, Ken, that's what it is, a tragi-comedy. Sheer hell with onions on it!'

He ran into the bathroom and bolted the door. There was a pause, and they looked at the floor in embarrassment. Finally the Colonel suggested sleep. It was to be a tiring day and they would need to regain some strength for it. Damned nuisance about the Kid. Bound to take it hard. Have to get on to the doctor in the morning. He paused, and then swung on his heels and went up to his study.

Fortnight waited until the noise had ceased in the Colonel's room, and then stole quietly to where his mother lay. He sat in the old grey armchair and slowly relaxed. Before long he was asleep and when he awoke a few hours later it was with a feeling of lightness.

He noticed that the sheet had moved. Perhaps someone else had come in to look at her, or perhaps the breeze had rustled across the bed. One corner was lifted, and the slit of his mother's blind left eye dully caught the daylight from the window.

He rose to his feet. From downstairs came the noise of plates, and then a short ding as the telephone lifted. He moved away, and as he opened the door a gust of the mild breeze that was wandering in the open house hurried across the room, ballooning the curtains in the open sashes of the window-frame.

'Mummy!' He looked at her. Going up to his room his troubles seemed unreal. Later there would be time enough and leisure to restore his grief. Later he would come across the words he had meant to speak that night, as one comes across a letter that was never posted, and he would see that it was best to have kept his peace. For years she had been a stranger to him, and as he passed her room on the way down he breathed her name, not as a valediction, but because he wished to weigh the sound and feel what significance was still contained in it. The word rolled lightly off his tongue, borne on the breeze towards the open window. And the curtains bellied outwards as though to let it pass.

Chapter Two

IT WAS ONLY when Fortnight closed the door of his mother's room that he was struck by the oddness of his final gesture. 'Poor Jennie,' Angela had said in tears. And 'Jennie' was the name he borrowed for his mother's corpse. It suddenly came home to him that Jennie was not his mother's name. She too was called Angela, was still called Angela by her cousins. Uncle Jonathan had called her Angela. Why had she been deprived of her name? When had it begun? There must be a birth certificate, perhaps an old family bible, something that would tell him who she was.

The Kid appeared, holding a mug of coffee.

'Here! Mug. Old Mug. Cracks intact. Forty-seven, of which you may notice three.'

'It smells good. Is it Javanese?'

The Kid, who hated irrelevant questions, laughed mirthlessly.

'Javanese! Isn't that the funniest word? Javanese. Jar Van Ease. Jarva Knees.'

He stopped laughing and let his mouth stay open as though it had been locked. He remained like that for several seconds, and then addressed his brother urgently.

'She's here.'

'Who?'

'Grabenaz.'

'Not . . .'

'No. She's for real. In a sense. His latest idyll. A well of loneliness. A pool of living tears. Probably about as real as the Celtic revival.'

He went quietly to his room, muttering the word 'Javanese' over and over beneath his breath. At the door he turned, and looked at Fortnight angrily.

'I might as well tell you that the lusions went away when you did. And why? Don't ask me, you scoundrel, you man of unsound principle, you perfunctory address to the nation on the subject of ceramics, you. . . .'

He closed the door on himself, lost in meaningless imprecations.

The Colonel stood in the hallway, conversing with a tall lank woman. She wore a plaid skirt and a wheat-coloured cottagey

33

pullover which flattened her breasts and gave her the shape of a
skittle as she rocked back and forth under the impact of the
Colonel's words. Her bun of fair hair and quiet blue eyes were
girlish, as was the virginal melancholy that played about her lips.
But there was also something accomplished in the sympathetic
gesture of her left arm as she touched the sleeve of the Colonel's
jacket, something which suggested year upon year of unprinci-
pled sympathy for men. Fortnight creaked on the bottom stair. At
once, without looking round, the Colonel began to speak more
loudly.

'Yes, you're right. An honest woman. In many ways. The vicar
you know, gentle man, good man after his fashion, kept saying
that her honesty was so touching, so natural, that she had a right to
her loss of faith.'

'He told me that too.'

'Did he now? The old fraud. And of course it suited his book to
forget that he was the cause of it. She might have been a perfectly
respectable, unassuming Anglican housewife if he had stayed at
his post. She might even have been happy. Yes, happy.'

The Colonel began to modulate his voice, imitating an
indignant man.

'What damage these fellows do, these vacant reformers, with
their disrespect for mystery! "For the leaders of the people" ', he
intoned, ' "cause them to err; and they that are led of them are
destroyed." Why did he do it? Why did he stuff her head with all
that claptrap about the church's social mission, instead of sending
her back to her knitting and her kids, as was his duty? And then,
being the woman she was, she actually *believed* it, stuck to it, right
to the end. Honest, yes, commonsensical even, but utterly bewildered. That's what she was, honest, obstinate and bewildered.'

He raised a handkerchief to his moist right eye. He had found the
phrase he needed. It contained just the right degree of respect for
her, and just enough contempt.

'Poor Julien,' the woman murmured.

Suddenly the Colonel pulled himself to attention.

'Ah, you don't know my son, mine own Telemachus, to whom I
leave the sceptre and the isle. . . .'

The Colonel smiled. It was always a pleasure to him abruptly to
change his tone.

'Catherine, this is Kenneth. Kenneth, this is Miss Catherine
Parkhurst, a business associate. Catherine was very good to your
mother.'

Fortnight took the cool slim hand which stretched to him, but
although he smiled, the Kid's description stuck in his mind and he
found no word of greeting.

'Do you know, my dear Catherine, that this is the first time this young man has appeared in Flackwell for three years? Remarkable. He leads, you know, an entirely inscrutable life, following ambitions too fine to be translated into words. You slept well, Kenneth? I've been on the blower to just about everyone, including the doctor.'

'The doctor?'

'Holtius', said the Colonel, feigning not to see his son's unspoken remonstrance. 'Do you know him, Catherine? Strange man, bit of a theory-monger, but said to be good. Thought we might give him a try. The Kid's to go round this afternoon. Perhaps you'll take him, Kenneth.'

'Why? He's just the same. We should leave him alone.'

'You think so? Very interesting. And of course, having been here so frequently during this difficult period, you are bound to know.'

The Colonel began to brush the thighs of his trousers with the back of one hand. Fortnight looked away until his father had again resumed the conversation, describing Mrs Fortnight's vagueness and her obstinate unbelief, but in a tone of increased bitterness, as though in some way they had spelled the greatest misery to himself.

Beyond the woman's shoulders lay the door of what used to be called the drawing-room, where Mrs Fortnight's few family portraits were hung. The Kid had the habit of sitting there, among the cushions of the long canapé, chuckling to himself for hours, his little body curled like a worm. After some years the name 'drawing-room' had ceased to make contact with reality. Now it was known as the laughing-room, and visitors were not allowed there. It was wrong that the door stood open. Staring beyond it, he noticed his grandmother's portrait, hanging askew above the walnut sideboard. The dress was Edwardian, and the smile photographic. But her young eyes stared flutterfully like his mother's eyes. Her soft white hand lay in a satin lap, fragile as a living hand. He pushed past his father, left the mug of coffee on the bookcase, and went to the door.

'Be back by twelve,' said the Colonel coldly.

He walked in circles about the park. A group of jackdaws waddled around, rooting in the wet grass, their feathers seared by wind. They reminded him of Holtius, who wore black velvet jackets, and pointed his features like a bird of prey. Increasing his pace, Fortnight veered down the alley of shining terracotta, which bordered the Baptist church. He decided not to think of the Kid's condition. He decided to be cheerful. He was full of hope. We insist on hope. But then he recalled the trouble over his mother's name, and the

36

Colonel's disdainful conversation.

The worst of it was that the Colonel was right. Honest, obstinate and bewildered. But why an atheist? What special catastrophe had left her with the one conviction that could not console?

Fortnight remembered the garden during summer, where he would find her after school. She turned the pages of a book, pure in her detachment, beyond the reach of thought, and the pages passed before her eyes like so many scattered Christmas wrappings from which the gifts had disappeared.

When she spoke it was usually to express the distance between herself and the woman who was reading. She seemed glad that Fortnight deplored her taste, since it established, in a negative way, a common cause between them. Together they observed and belittled the reader. That woman was not the one who had given birth to him, but another, a later experiment in freedom, who had been sent on a mission into metaphysical space. It was safe to disdain her, safe even for Mrs Fortnight, so long as it was also safe for her son.

He remembered some of the titles: *Mysteries of the East, The Lost Continent of Mu, Yoga for Everyman.* A soporific orientalism had sapped the spirit of her native world. Mostly it was yoga that commanded her inattention. The real Mrs Fortnight was confined, softly fitted to her former surroundings like a chick to the underbelly of its hen. The experimental Mrs Fortnight, however, was a woman of infinite resources, who had mastered strange techniques. Yoga presented the right degree of difficulty, and the right measure of reward. It enabled you to move between spheres with the ease that comes of belonging to none of them. This was the philosophy not of the chick, but of the hard-boiled egg. His mother laughed guiltily as she exposed it to view.

'It's a question,' she once said, 'of discovering the Universal Self. We all belong to a Universal Self. So it says.'

She looked at her son, who nodded, so giving the signal that it did not yet matter how she proceeded.

'And you see,' she began again, 'there is this energy in all of us — they call it Kundalini — and it resides in the spine. You've got to make it rise into the brain, by exercising the whole body. Because you see it can get blocked at any point. Then . . . well, I don't know the details. But in this book it says that a sudden accident can release Kundalini in a great rush all at once into the mind. If you're not ready for it, then you fall down in a faint. That's how they explain catalepsy. That's what *they* would say happened that time your father pointed the gun at Francis.'

Fortnight remembered the strange way she looked at him as she said this, her mouth half-open, on tenterhooks. Eventually she would laugh. But for a moment she seemed to imply that, were he to encourage her, she might believe what she said. Perhaps the Kid was at the root of it: she wanted to find an excuse for him, a permanent exoneration that would justify her love. Fortnight was disturbed by this thought. He remembered being angry with the Kid afterwards, over the wisdom of Napoleon's tactics at Austerlitz. He had made the Kid cry, and then, ashamed, taken him to the Odeon cinema, to see an episode of Superman, which they both vigorously deplored.

Fortnight turned towards the Bramhurst road, which led to the little parish where once they had lived. His mother had bought two cottages there, hoping to restore them, as she had helped to restore the church. Then the Colonel, suddenly wealthy, had snatched her away from these sad little dreams. As he walked towards his mother's country, Fortnight felt the anger rising within him.

The road to Bramhurst took him past Barbara's house. He walked there between wet hedges, pressing back from the passing cars, beyond the green duckpond and the cricket pitch, to the expensive houses of the new middle class. Barbara's place seemed abandoned. The shutters of the barn were closed, and the blinds had been pulled down to the floor in the grey stone studio. Mr Langley had designed the studio himself. Its concrete beams were exposed, and a sheet glass window rose from the terrace to a gable on the roof. On a grey day, with the blinds down and the terrace wet, it seemed like any other bungalow on that road, eccentric, uncomfortable, coldly individualistic. Mr Langley had often explained the subtleties of its design, based, so he claimed, on Palladian principles of spatial organization, adapted to some unrealized project of Frank Lloyd Wright. But even in the best of weather the north-facing window had a despairing look, and the grey stones of the wall seemed crushed and accidental, as though the beams had fallen on them from a height. Mr Langley's Landrover usually stood on the gravel drive, and sometimes his wife would be visible, moving with the slow sure steps of a Pyrenean peasant in the kitchen garden by the stream. But Fortnight did not see the Landrover; nor was there any sign of Mrs Langley.

As he neared the windows by the road, Fortnight slackened his pace. He glanced at the white interior of the kitchen, with its bare pinewood shelves stacked with old stone jars. It was impossible to tell whether the Langleys were there. Even at the busiest times, when Mr Langley was at work on a commission for a stained-glass window or an altar-cloth, the house preserved the same museum-like decorum. Every pot, every book, every statuette, every musical instrument, occupied its own allotted place, and Mr Langley moved among these quiet exhibits in a state of dreamlike detachment which it was absolutely forbidden to disturb. Nobody claimed that Mr Langley was an important artist, but he was the only artist to have lived in Flackwell since the early nineteenth century, when an obscure disciple of Thomas Bewick had set up a workshop in the High Street. Mr Langley was therefore respected, and granted unconditional licence to be harmlessly insane. His wife, and even his daughter — rebellious though they sometimes were — deferred to his meticulous mannerisms. In everything that surrounded him there was a right and wrong; a right which upheld the aesthetic order, and a wrong which denied it. Fortnight had the definite feeling, as he stared into the neat interior of the kitchen that, in not hurrying onwards to his destination, he was doing wrong. But he remained, staring solemnly into the place of their courtship. Slowly his anger subsided, and his mother's question arose to trouble his mind. 'Why don't you marry her, marry that girl?' The mystery of his mother, and the mystery of Barbara, were now one and the same.

Fortnight was prepared to countenance only two explanations of his attachment to Barbara. The first, the innocuous one, which could be offered to strangers and was believed by all except the Kid, was that they shared their interests. This was proved by the fact that they had met at the local literary society and afterwards performed *Lieder* together during the moments allotted to *Lieder* by Mr Langley's scrupulous timetable of domestic pleasures.

The second explanation, which was the one that satisfied Fortnight since it justified their life together, was that they had been united by an intense sexual passion. This passion had taken them both by surprise; it persisted not in spite of, but precisely because of, their having nothing genuine in common. It was proved by another meeting, at a party. Their host was a local poet, who took pleasure in stimulating adolescents to sensual pleasures beyond their emotional means. Fortnight and Barbara had looked at each other silently across the hashish-laden air; they resolved to retain virginity in honour of that look. An accident which brings about the fulfilment of desire is always regarded as fatal. So they began to meet, in order to speak in respectful tones of their fateful look. This led almost at once to a sensuality far more violent than the tittering peccadilloes that took place in the poet's cottage. Since the idea of his maturity depended on this second explanation, and since the Kid too accepted it, Fortnight would always try to persuade himself of its truth. But, although he had carried out the proof many times, extraneous elements kept creeping into it, and these elements, so dangerous to his self-image, had to be closely confined. The most sinister among them was Dr Holtius. For if

Fortnight allowed himself to be honest, then he had to admit that Holtius too had played a part in his move to London.

Nobody knew where Dr Holtius had come from, or why he chose to practise in Flackwell. It was rumoured that he belonged to an experimental hospital in Bristol; some said that he was an Oxford don, that his profession was literary criticism, and that he had turned to psychotherapy only to divert his mind. Some said that he was a fraud.

Dr Holtius had acquired a Georgian house in the centre of town. With the help of a brass plate, embellished with his name and certificates, and a silent lady dressed in the costume of a nurse, he had persuaded people to refer to it as his surgery. The doctor was available every Tuesday and every Thursday. To be available so little was to foster the belief in his necessity. Many unstable residents of Flackwell concluded therefore that their condition was unexceptional, and a few of them began to transfer money to Dr Holtius, in exchange for confirmation of this thought.

The literary society met every week in the Senior Common Room of St Stephen's School, and it was there that Fortnight had first seen Dr Holtius. The doctor's appearance made an instant impression. Holtius was thin, young, dark, with a small head that would have been handsome but for the birdlike nose and close-set eyes. His long fibrous neck was always swallowing, as though unable to hold back the words that he was also unwilling to utter. Often all eyes would turn to him, expecting him to speak, only to see his face embellished with the offer of a conditional smile. Then his features seemed ageless, existing more as a vision of judgement than as an expression of human life. As conversation dwindled, it would seem that the silence of Holtius had conquered it.

At times, when something displeased him, the doctor's expression would change. The left eye began to seem slightly larger, sunk more deeply than the right, and the mouth curled in an expression of distaste. The whole face took on an air of watchful distrust, as though some disappointed, angry creature had chosen this special point of vantage from which to survey the world. It was this expression which made the greatest impact on Fortnight. He felt certain that Dr Holtius had perceived something truly wrong. If he refrained from judgement it was in the hope that people would seek him out, so that he could correct them more kindly. One day, if he had the courage, he would ask the doctor about the Kid.

Barbara had a passionate dislike for Holtius, and this caused Fortnight to refrain from approaching the surgery. However, it happened one day that he came across the doctor, walking in a country lane. Rushing forward, he secured what he thought was an advantage in being the first to say 'hello'. Holtius turned slowly.

'Who are you?' he asked.

'I am Kenneth Fortnight. You see me at the literary society'.

Fortnight suddenly remembered that, at every society meeting, Dr Holtius had observed him. Not overtly, nor impertinently. But he knew that Holtius often stared at him with a kind of professional intensity, as though he fully expected the boy to come forward and confess. Yet now the doctor seemed to disown him. The thought of this impressed Fortnight deeply.

They walked on in silence until reaching the brow of the hill at Bramhurst. In the valley the spire of St Mary Magdalene rose from a mist of vegetation; the red roofs of his mother's cottages soaked up the sunlight, and the little fields slowly seemed to darken with the afternoon haze. The sweet sickly smell of cow parsley filled the air, and they both stopped, breathing quickly. At the foot of the far hill Fortnight could discern the bounds of Blackett's farm, and the tongue of water that licked round the hill to touch their former garden.

'People often wonder why I came to this place,' said Dr Holtius. 'There you see the reason.'

'That was where we lived,' said Fortnight. He noticed that he adopted a strange tone, as though expecting the doctor to deny it.

'We moved, you see, to Flackwell.'

Dr Holtius remained silent.

'You know, it won't remain beautiful here. My father wants to demolish those cottages. He wants to develop the village, and maybe even build a canary yellow petrol station.'

'Typical.'

'Do you know my father?' asked Fortnight in surprise.

'No, but I can see from your face that it is typical. He is, I take it, some kind of military man. A bully too, if I'm not mistaken. I suppose that you want to thwart his plans?'

'Oh . . . I . . . No. Though my brother . . . How did you know that my father was a military man?'

'Just the way that you are expecting orders.'

Dr Holtius looked at Fortnight, who was disconcerted.

'I should think it would be rather a good idea if you came to visit me.'

'Visit you? You mean at the surgery?'

'There, or wherever. I think that perhaps you have a lot to say.'

Dr Holtius relaxed his expression and began to smile.

'Well yes, as a matter of fact I have. It is about my brother you see. I am not saying that he needs treatment, but there is no doubt that he is eccentric, very eccentric. I wanted to ask your advice.'

The doctor was still smiling at him, and Fortnight found himself becoming animated. There were a hundred things that he wanted to say. He forgot all considerations of order and propriety, beginning every thought at the wrong end, advancing from conclusion to premises, from belief to evidence, so that, when he had finished, he recognized that his portrait of the Kid was entirely upside-down, starting from ill-formed speculations about the nature of dementia, and ending with descriptions of the Kid's St Vitus movements, his braid Scots and dog Latin, his inability to control his breath. Because the doctor continued to observe him, he began to add details about himself. Eventually he took refuge in an idea which had just occurred to him but which he felt certain would secure the doctor's sympathy.

'You see Doctor Holtius, I admire him. He is extremely clever, cleverer by far than myself. I don't want education, you understand. I've decided not to go to Oxford, even if they give me a place. I have other plans. But the Kid, my brother, he should be learning things, he should be a scholar. Yet everything prevents him. It is not his eccentricities. I am sure he is not mad, not really mad that is. Yesterday I was reading, it was a strange episode, in a book of Victorian anecdotes, about a boy who was dying of consumption. There was the usual deathbed scene, prayers, miracles, reconciliations. But in this case, instead of sinking blissfully into his last sleep, the child protested. He pushed himself with his arms away from the pillow, and raised his hot body from the bed, coughing all the while, and with a strange look of hostility that all the bystanders observed. From one to another the dark eyes travelled, and in each of their victims they seemed to discover some horrid secret: lies, treachery, thievings, murders. All the praying mantises withdrew in surprise, avoiding each other's glances. It was clear that the boy had received some vision which gave him intelligence of their sins. He raised himself further on the bed, blood and foam gathering in the corners of his mouth, and then began to tremble. Soon everyone else was trembling, thinking himself about to be accused. Then suddenly the little boy laughed — or rather, tried to laugh, but was of course at once overcome by exhaustion and lay back suffocating on the pillow. The onlookers felt comforted by this. They had been prepared, you see, only for his exhaustion. It was against all precedent that they should have to witness the birth of a soul. They settled back into their ritual, confident that all was now as it should be. But again the little boy raised himself, with a terrible effort that caused him to rock back and forth where he sat. He pointed his trembling finger. It was his father he pointed to, and everyone drew back in order to clear a space for the gesture. I like that image. It seems to me that's how it must be. Every accusation makes a space around itself into which others can't trespass.'

Fortnight stopped and looked at his companion. Dr Holtius seemed to have grown in size, and there was something penetrating, almost vulturelike, in the stare which he fixed on him. Fortnight resumed in nervous agitation.

'What he said to his father was this: "You made me, but you did not let me be." Then in convulsions, he fell down into the sweaty bedclothes and died. Of course, I know that's all a load of rubbish, but . . .'

'It is not rubbish. It is most instructive. It tells me a lot about you.'

'I wasn't speaking about myself, of course, I mean not intentionally.' Fortnight laughed nervously. 'I meant to say, that that is what my brother feels. It is how he sees things; not just my father, but everything, or almost everything. He is fighting against a prohibition; he has made up his mind to exist, even in the midst of this illness, while we all try to prevent him. But somehow it doesn't work.'

'I suppose you don't realize that you have not been speaking about your brother at all? It doesn't matter, of course. But I do insist that you come to see me. I want to help you. I think you must understand that.'

Fortnight looked at the doctor in amazement. He tried to remember what he had said that might have given the impression that he needed treatment. Now all his words seemed confused and gratuitous.

'I don't need help. I want you to tell me about my brother.'

'Oh, I shall do that too. I just want to see you. Perhaps you can come tomorrow, at about six? Yes? Then I shall expect you.'

Fortnight hurried on, while Dr Holtius stood at the crossroads watching him. Feeling the uncanny penetration of those eyes, and the force of a strange unhappiness which seemed to speak through them, Fortnight began to walk unsteadily. He tried to impose order on his movements, but his legs seemed to wander from him, as though controlled by invisible strings which joined them to the doctor's eyes.

When he recounted the episode to his mother she looked at him in alarm.

'You mustn't go. Please don't go. Why did you speak to him? Whatever you do, keep Francis out of his way. I am sure he is a charlatan. Promise me.'

He promised her, surprised at her passion. When he awoke the next morning it was with the conviction that he must never see Holtius again. At that moment he wanted above all to be with

Barbara. He was about to get up, in order to telephone her house, when the Kid came in and sat on his bed. Fortnight kicked him off, but he climbed back again, being in a delighted mood, and anxious to tease his brother about the cuff-links and collar-studs which Fortnight had (in order to appear more autonomous) taken to wearing. The Kid related a conversation that he had overheard between the Colonel and his stockbroker, in which the Colonel had accused the man of being a living offence to the whole idea of Empire. Fortnight listened, and when his irritation had subsided, the Kid abruptly changed course.

'By the way, I saw Barbara Langley at the choir yesterday — she's got a super voice, seedy as a muted trumpet. We're doing *L'Enfance du Christ* by Hectoring Berlioz, did you know? I'm getting a ticket for you. I told Miss Langley today's a holiday, which she knew of course, and that you'd be free, which she didn't. *I* suggested a picnic, *nos tres*, on Medham Hill. But I said I'd consult you first. In any case she's coming round in her old man's Landrover this morning, and, in anticipation, I thought I'd lay on some champers — it's in the fridge. Hope you don't mind, squire. I really feel quite bucolic. *Cras amet qui nunquam amavit, qui nunquam . . .*'

The Kid, who was now standing on his head against the wall, ceased speaking. All Fortnight could say was that the Kid ought not to spend his pocket money on champagne, and in any case how was he, a twelve-year-old, able to buy it? Fortnight sensed for the first time that his brother was in the habit of stealing things.

'I have my methods,' was all he would say.

They visited the church at Lower Misten, where Burne-Jones and William Morris had designed the altar. They drank the Kid's champagne during the drive, and arrived hilarious. But entering the church they were struck silent by the smell of beeswax, chalk and wildflowers, the smell they had known at Bramhurst. Even Barbara, who was a devout Christian only in those matters that did not concern religion, became quiet.

The church had been newly whitewashed; roses and foxgloves decorated the altar; a light summer breeze blew in at the door and circled the aisles. Garlands were stuck with white tape to the key-stones of the arches, and brushed against their hair. The soft light from the chancel lay like a sleeping verger on the choirstalls, and curled the pages of an open hymnal. The red and black lettering stood out sharp and beautiful against the India paper. A sound of breeze in the yew-trees filled the church, and they went about on tiptoe.

Barbara began to make sketches, while the Kid contented himself with transcribing the Gothic lettering of a text from St John.

Fortnight watched them, and then turned to the altar. He became interested in the upturned anguished faces, the wringing hands which seemed to tremble visibly as they aped the postures of prayer. The maenad hair, the billowing dresses, the hollow eyes, the penitential attitudes, all reminded him of something near to himself: a feeling of selfness, of irreplaceability. This feeling followed him into the breezy day. As he watched Barbara's white complexion, the Kid's dancing form, the dizzy motion of trees and bushes in the graveyard, he felt everywhere the presence of himself. And Kenneth Fortnight was pale as death in his imagination, an inconsolable ghost.

Mr Langley showed them books, sketches, photographs. He spoke in liquid tones of the tracery, the leaf-work along the mouldings, the play of light on the figure of St Agnes in the altar frieze. His mellifluous descriptions were punctuated by popping noises, as he sucked on a pipe of sweet Dutch tobacco. To Mr Langley this St Agnes was the finest of Morris's inspirations, frozen, timid, and yet challenged by the movement of her robe. The artist had contrasted her inner virginity with the rough compulsion of the heathen world. They were the active clothes of a Roman lady, played on by an ethereal breeze which united them at every point with the symbolic order of the tracery. Mr Langley stared as he spoke into the middle distance, at a point from which inspiration came. His words seemed to caress the world, hinting at experiences too deep or too personal for words. After a while the Kid began to imitate Mr Langley's accent. He spoke in the same affected way of the beauties of his Gothic lettering, and of a group of ruminating cows of which he had been reminded by the gravestones. Fortnight signalled to be quiet, but Barbara smiled. For it was clear, after a while, that Mr Langley's documentary was well rehearsed, and that there was no room for a genuine interruption, nothing that could be added to, or subtracted from, the text. Of everything but art Mr Langley remained meditatively silent, unable to bless it with luscious vocables, and so preferring to look as though the matter were one about which he had yet to make up his mind.

After tea they drove home. The Kid began to compose a poem about Mr Langley. It began:

> *It transpired upon a holiday*
> *That I should go to stay*
> *In a house of herbal remedies*
> *Of cloves and caraway.*

Fortnight stared away into the countryside, hoping that Barbara did not mind the Kid's nonsense. Suddenly he remembered his appointment with Holtius. He thought of the doctor's inescapable, melancholy eyes. What did he want? What did he think was wrong?

> *'Have you ever tasted samphire,*
> *Or pickled mushroom stalks?*
> *Or lilies of the valley*
> *Picked fresh on summer walks*
>
> *And laid a year in vinegar*
> *Then washed in raisin wine?*
> *Oh come now, have you never had*
> *Cold cucumbers in brine?'*

'Kid, please stop,' said Fortnight. 'You cause offence.'

'But I always cause offence. I am a mistake of nature. But harmless, Miss Langley, please believe me, quite harmless.'

'You can call me Barbara.'

'Oh I know I can. But I won't. You see it's more aesthetic to keep a slight distance from people you really like. *'I'll fly the moon by twilight, And dare the powers that keep Great Astur in the starry realms, And Cthulu in the deep . . .'*

Eventually the Kid quietened down, apologizing, saying that he had not met an artist before and it had all rather gone to his head.

They dropped him off, and then drove on into the twilight. Barbara worked the Landrover as though it were an extension of herself, her hands reaching unhesitatingly for the knobs and levers that cleared the path before them. Suddenly she smiled at him, showing all her teeth. Her grey eyes met his, and, when this happened, it was as though her quick wilful soul flowed into them and made a conditional present of itself. His own soul, afraid of those conditions, took refuge in some hasty gesture. He would touch her knee, pull her earlobes, or utter something irrelevant.

'You wouldn't believe it,' he said, 'but I had an appointment with Dr Holtius, for six.'

'You what?'

'Of course I didn't intend to go. The whole idea was absurd. It's just that I met him, and we started talking about the Kid, and he suggested that I come to see him.'

'To talk about the Kid?' Barbara's tone was ironical.

'Well, no, actually. About myself.'

'I thought so.'

'What do you mean?'

'I've got eyes. That man is evil, distorted, destructive, and a fraud.'

'So . . .'

'And he has designs on you.'

'On me?'

'Yes, on you. Haven't you seen the way he stares at you, as though he wants to eat you up? He's a vampire, I'm sure of it. He wants you, for some nefarious purpose.'

'And you think I can't look after myself?'

'It's not that. You can look after yourself. But there is more than one of you, and it rather depends which one you decide to look after. There's only one of me,' she added, with a little shake of the head, 'and that one is head over heels in love.'

A week later Fortnight was walking on the Bramhurst road. He saw the Doctor coming towards him in a brisk, stiff walk, with his hands clasped behind his back and his head held high. There was something agitated about him, and his neck jerked back and forth like the neck of a moorhen making for its pond.

'Hello,' said Fortnight, as they drew near.

The doctor made no answer, but walked on at the same agitated pace, in the direction of Flackwell. On an impulse Fortnight turned to follow him.

'Hello,' he said again.

Still Dr Holtius continued to walk, although his legs jerked slightly as though an order to slow down had been issued and then instantly repealed. Fortnight felt sure that Dr Holtius was in the habit of administering this punishment he had the image of a hundred souls being sucked by this means into a vacuum, where they withered and died.

'Dr Caligari,' he called out, 'Did you not recognize me?'

The doctor stopped and turned round. He wore an uncanny smile, that seemed to be painted on his features like a clown's. 'Why, of course. It's . . . you know I *have* forgotten your name.'

His voice was unnatural, the syllables sounded forced through a restricting nozzle. Fortnight stopped and blushed. 'I think you are angry with me,' he said.

The doctor mirthlessly chuckled. 'Angry with you? Why should I be angry with you?'

'For not coming when I said I would.'

Dr Holtius smiled more broadly. 'My dear fellow, if we allowed ourselves to get angry with a patient for missing an appointment . . .'

'Who's we?'

'Has somebody been talking to you?' said Dr Holtius, suddenly changing his tone. 'Or do you merely suspect a plot?'

Fortnight stared at the doctor for some time. And then, for some unaccountable reason, he began to feel frightened.

'Look, it was all a lot of rubbish what I said about my brother. I would rather forget the subject. I thought it best not to keep the appointment. There is nothing seriously wrong.'

'I admire your confidence. And what if I am a little hurt that you did not come to see me?'

'In that case I should be sorry.'

Suddenly the smile collapsed and the doctor's face became suffused with melancholy. 'I would like you to be sorry', he said. 'Believe it or not, I would. Even someone like me can be hurt. But now I do not really want to speak, you see. There is something on my mind.'

Dr Holtius's voice had softened, and a menacing emotion seethed beneath the words. His body remained poised like a dancer's, and the fluttering, effeminate gestures of his hands had come to a sudden stop. Such control did his whole posture exhibit that it seemed to Fortnight as though he were speaking lines from a play. The fear which Fortnight experienced seemed to involve no particular danger, no particular person. It was a premonition. He was being granted an angelic vision of catastrophe, not so that he would avoid it, but so that he would want it for himself. He did not try to outstare the doctor. Instead, he absorbed the poison of those deep sad eyes, lingered on the immobile lips as they affected a gentle disdain, and on the gathered-up limbs that would not strike but allowed themselves merely to choreograph the soul's deep affliction. And then he turned on his heel and walked away. Again he had the sense that his legs and arms were being forced into a movement that was foreign to them, as though invisible threads joined them to the doctor's eyes.

Barbara was sitting at the piano, in the long passage of the barn. 'Listen to this', she said, as he entered. She played a major chord, and then another chord which echoed it. Gradually the chord was compressed into dissonances, and then opened out into skeletal atonalities like Schoenberg. Finally the sequence stumbled back into the original harmony by a series of plangent classical suspensions. He watched her fingers, puzzled by the sounds, which seemed to be produced by accident and through some other medium.

'Know what it is?' she asked.

'Oh — no. Did you discover it?'

'Did Beethoven discover the Ninth Symphony?'

'I mean, compose it?'

'You wouldn't believe it, but Mrs Thurlow dug this stuff out of the library. It's Scriabin. But I can see that you are not really in the mood for it. Why so glum?'

'Am I?'

'Positively evaporated. Something's happened. You had better tell me.'

She got up quickly from the piano, and even closed the lid. It seemed like a precaution. He became aware that he was staring at her, allowing wild thoughts to pass unhindered through his mind.

'It's nothing, nothing at all. Except that, now you have finished your exams, you'll be going. It just occurred to me. You are going to London, and I can't stand it.'

Barbara smiled.

'Don't you care?' he went on. 'Won't you mind being there without me?'

Barbara kissed him, and then began to walk slowly about the patterns of the Afghan carpet. 'Well, this can't be a new thought,' she said. 'I assumed you were going to Oxford.'

'Oxford? I'm not going to university.'

'When was that decided?'

'Yesterday. No, a week ago.'

There was a silence.

'The Kid, you know . . .' Barbara hesitated and looked at him.

'What about the Kid?'

'You won't be angry? I told him that you had seen Dr Holtius.'

'Why did you do that?'

'I wanted to find out his reaction. In any case, he is worried that your father might try to put him into care.'

'That's a joke. So what did he say?'

'He was very upset. His view was that I should take you away. He claims to have seen your father and Holtius plotting together.'

'That's another joke.'

'But he suspects what is true, namely . . .'

'Namely . . .'

'That I could take you on. Make you safe. Only, if you come to London, what will *he* do?'

'Who?'

'The Kid.'

'Perhaps he can look after himself. Otherwise he'll start living his life through me, and I don't want that.'

'It's too late, I think, not to want that. And what will *you* do?'

'Me? I shall compose.'

'Compose what?'

'Myself.'

A moment later, when they were lying on the couch, Fortnight looked up for a moment over the flushed face and crumpled hair beneath him, and met the watery eyes of Mr Langley. The artist hovered like a ghost between the tapestries that flanked the door, stared at the tousled couple for a few seconds, and then, selecting a book in a leisurely manner from the opposite shelf, walked quietly away.

It was not the thought of living with Barbara that caused him pleasure, so much as the idea that he would free himself from incomprehensible demands. Dr Holtius's sudden emotion had come to symbolize them. And so at first Fortnight blamed his departure on the doctor; it would have hurt him too much to blame it on the Kid. Besides the Kid was ostensibly in favour of it, and hid all anxiety in a frenzy of preparation. The whole thing was to be a secret, with the Kid himself in charge.

'After all,' he reasoned, 'the Colonel is bound to stop it if he discovers, and only I know how to hide things from him. Also someone has got to make Mummy accept, and who is that someone if not me? I think you will both appreciate the logic of this.'

In truth the Colonel was keeping a close watch on Fortnight, or, to be more precise, on Barbara. Colonel Fortnight was irresistible to women, but it was not often that a young girl came within his orbit. Fortnight wondered for a while how the Colonel would approach this problem, but then he dismissed the subject as unreal.

The Kid was adamant that their mother should not be told. She would accept the result, for she had heard rumours of freedom, and contemplated its advantage for her sons. But since it was not in her nature to initiate change, she made no distinction between the right and the wrong ways to effect it. Hence it was best to reveal only the *fait accompli*; then she would be impressed by the organization, and would settle down uncomplainingly to contemplate its meaning.

The Kid transferred books, papers, clothes, and even sheet music to the garden shed, where he hid everything behind pots and boxes, awaiting Barbara's Landrover. All stages of the operation took place at night, except one, which was of such ingenuity that the Kid could not forbear revealing it to his brother beforehand. It happened that the Colonel had business dealings with a retired major in Banbury, who trusted only fellow officers, and would invest money only where he also placed his trust. The major entertained a profound dislike of the human species, and resented unnecessary communication. He had no telephone, and regarded letters as an impertinence. If communication were necessary he confined himself to military telegrams. The Kid had read one in the Colonel's study. It said: 'no deal stop decision next Thursday stop not lower than five thousand stop Carsdale'. Searching through the Colonel's papers, the Kid discovered that the telegram referred to the purchase of a plot of land, the money to be provided by Major Carsdale, the land to be developed by a company of the Colonel's. It was clearly an important deal. The land lay close to Blackett's farm; it had been the Kid's policy always to foil the plans to

develop Bramhurst, both for his mother's sake, and because of a
growing hatred of modern things. He therefore conceived a plan,
which would distract the Colonel from Fortnight's escape, and
afterwards make it look as though it were made possible by the
normal hostilities between the Colonel and his younger son. Fortnight did not like the word 'escape'; it suggested he was not free.
The Kid replied, using a favourite phrase, that his brother was a
slave of unconstituted authority. 'And besides, you have no choice
in the matter; it's too late. Tomorrow I go with Miss Langley in the
chariot to Banbury, and I send a telegram to the Colonel. I thought
you might go, but the Colonel is watching you, so it wouldn't be
safe.'

'How do you know he's watching me?'

'How do I know apart from the fact that he is crazy about Miss
Langley, you mean? Well, because he wants to trap you here. Look
at the way he refrains from mentioning the future. When the subject crops up, he seems almost benevolent. He treats you kindly, as
though you were something approximating to a human being. He
doesn't interrupt you in your room, or stare at you during dinner.
You've not been upbraided or downbraided for weeks. These are
all bad signs. He wants you to stay, so that he can go.'

'But don't you want him to go?'

The Kid hesitated, and then looked away.

'Not while Mummy still loves him. But then . . . well, that's all
irrelevant, and belongs to stage two of the plan. So: he knows I'm
loony and always off on the trail like a wolf-boy. There's no chance
that he'll think the telegram came from me, especially as it's going
to be an overnight telegram from Major Carsdale, about the next
day's deal. It will say "Come at once stop vital discussion stop
exceptional circumstances stop Carsdale". We'll all be sitting at the
breakfast table, innocent as pie, and off he'll go. Then we ring Miss
Langley, who brings the chariot, we pack up your things and away
with you.'

'But where?'

'To London. Miss Langley and you.'

'And where do we stay?'

'I've earmarked a flat in South Hill Park. It was on a list at
Higgins & Higgins. That is to say, they're keeping it for you, and
Miss Langley will collect the keys when you get there. I paid the
deposit.'

'How?' Fortnight was astonished. He imagined a huge sum,
perhaps five hundred pounds. The Kid looked away.

'There's no need for you to know. And if you are worried then let
me tell you that I shall pay it back, just as soon as you're away; I

shall persuade Mummy to sign out some of Uncle Jonathan's money for me. Lay off, will you? Slobbering adolescent. I haven't finished yet. As I say. I then go to the GPO, and send another telegram, this time to Banbury, saying "Problems with deal stop your presence urgently required stop meet Falcon Hotel noon stop Fortnight". So along comes the major to Flackwell, passing the Colonel on the road. Consequences: when they do meet, some time around six I should imagine, they are both in a towering rage. The old buffer will be offensive, the Colonel sarcastic, and the deal will be off. The Colonel will then know that it was me who did it, and he will have to stay in the Hotel, drinking, so as to get mellow: he wouldn't want to go home and be cross with me, for fear of a crisis. Then he will arrive, roll into bed, and realize only the next day that you're gone. By then he will be preoccupied as to how to purchase the land. He will have to be nice to Mummy, and therefore to me, in order to get her to sell the cottages at Bramhurst. He won't succeed, but he will try very hard. So he will feign acceptance of your departure. If we help him at it long enough, the acceptance will become real. Eventually we'll tell him what has happened, and by that time you'll be settled, and stage two will come into operation.'

'And what does that involve?'

'Well, a coup will be required, and it will start from London. This is where you can be useful . . .'

The Kid was beginning to croak with excitement, Fortnight was reluctant to hear what came next; all the Kid's schemes, however crazy, were based on an inflexible sense of justice, and a longing for moral order. So something would be required in exchange. He was about to cut his brother short when the telephone emitted a short ding, and the Colonel's voice suddenly boomed out loudly from the upper regions.

'Kenneth, Kenneth, I want a word with you!'

Fortnight went out on to the stairs. 'What is it?'

'Can you please come up?'

The Kid shook his head. There was distress in his eyes, and his mouth hung open in an expression of dismay.

'I'd better go.'

He ran upstairs with the impression of taking the easier option. What interest had he, after all, in stage two of the Kid's arrangements?

The Colonel was pacing up and down the study with large, interrupted strides, stopping every now and then beside a book, a file, or a pile of papers, and prodding it curiously as though wondering how it could have got there. When he turned to his son, there was no hint of malicious humour in his features; he simply stared blankly as though at a wall.

'Where is your mother?' he asked softly. His voice seemed to tremble slightly.

'In the garden I think. Why?'

'She is under sentence of death.'

Fortnight looked uncomprehendingly at his father. For the first time he noticed that the Colonel's hair was white. It was odd to be discovering such an important fact. He became lost in thought about it. The sun was shining across the Colonel's damp forehead. It would be good to be out in the garden now. If his mother were there, he was sure that the enigma of his father's hair could be solved quite painlessly.

'I was just speaking to my friend Dr Holtius.'

'Dr Holtius?'

'Oh yes, I believe you have met him. Interesting man. Not a real doctor of course. But you see, he has friends at the hospital. He found out.'

'Found out what?'

'The real results of Jennie's tests. And the operation that she is to have. Forgive me, I forgot to inform you. A delicate matter actually.'

The Colonel was silent for a while, picking at the backs of an encyclopedia. It was clear that he had thought deeply about the subject over which he appeared to hesitate, and that the present information was being carefully leaked in accordance with a pre-established plan. At the same time he was embarrassed: more embarrassed than Fortnight had ever seen him to be.

'The cancer has returned. They do not expect her to live. She will have the operation of course. Various fairly significant parts will have to be removed. She will have some kind of life, for a year or two, maybe three.'

Fortnight did not comprehend his father's words. All that he knew was that their indirect purpose was to prevent him from leaving home. He was determined to resist them.

'I don't understand.'

'No, I rather feared that you wouldn't. The difficulty, of course, is the Kid. I'm in a bit of a quandary, you see, Kenneth. I am rather counting on your cooperation. I have some business which will take me away, and while Jennie's in hospital, you will be alone together. I was wondering: could you find an opportunity to explain it to the Kid, in some suitable anodyne way? I take it that you have made no arrangements that will prevent this?'

He looked deeply at his son with one eyebrow raised, simulating a Nazi interrogator. Fortnight shook his pavlovian head.

'Good, well, if you don't mind, I am a little distressed at present and would like to be alone. Have you any questions?'

Fortnight stood for a while and then slowly went to the door. The Kid was standing where he had left him, reciting *odi profanum vulgi* to a vase of desiccated flowers. Seeing his brother he stopped, gave a knowing leer, and said, 'So he's discovered the plan has he? Managed to fabricate some obligation to keep you at home? Crafty old bugger!'

The Kid laughed, and began to tap his heels in a world-famous imitation of Fred Astaire. The vase began to rock.

'Will you come for a walk?'

'Sure thing boss.'

The Kid danced out on to the park. He spoke rapturously of his plan, ignoring all interruptions, and sometimes clapping his hands. Fortnight ceased to speak to him. His wandering thoughts touched here and there on his mother's death: the idea came to him as a personal insult. Obviously it was not true. But supposing it were? He would go just the same.

In retrospect he could discover no decision in the process that led to his establishment in London. He allowed the Kid to send the telegrams, and joined Barbara at the appointed hour behind the vicarage. He could not speak as they drove to London, and Barbara, responding to his mood, remained docile and silent. She left him in a strange flat, where he took up his station by the window. The hot sun filled the room with melancholy. She left almost at once, in order to return the Landrover to Flackwell.

There was a bed in the room, with a striped, stained mattress. He lay down on it and stared at the ceiling. A fly was playing in the sunlight above his head. It flew in perfect straight lines, delicate, unwavering, changing course suddenly and miraculously as though it had touched the circumference of an invisible sphere. On every side its flight was enclosed by this sphere, a barrier whose only substance was the fly's ceaseless deflection from a line of flight. It was strange that something insubstantial should be so resistant. Fortnight watched for several minutes. Thoughts slowly filtered from the holes in his skull; soon he felt his skeleton at rest within its sheath of skin.

Fortnight slept. In his dream he saw the Colonel acquainting his wife with the details of her fate, simulating for her benefit the feelings of a man who could bear so much, but no more. His face flushed as he struggled to keep within the confines of this false emotion, and then, after a suitable pause, he burst out: 'No good pretending. It's curtains. Didn't want to tell you. But Kenneth insisted I should. Sorry. I don't need to ask you to keep it secret from the Kid.' He turned away as though manfully to hide his pittance of tears.

When Fortnight awoke, Barbara stood over him, and their life together had begun. Very much later he told her about his mother; Barbara sent him home. The Colonel was away on business. Fortnight began by attempting to stay at his mother's side, interceding between her and the imperatives of pain. But she followed him with tender eyes, and recounted in broken syllables her childhood and courtship. He received her confidences as an outrage.

One morning the Kid came to see him, sitting on Fortnight's bed in the sunlight.

'I think you should go,' he said. 'You'd be better in London. I've got my five thousand from Uncle Jonathan now. I want you to be in London; it would make stage two much easier.'

'But what is stage two?'

The Kid shook his head, and then continued sadly. 'I could come to visit you. I had an idea I might take up merchant banking, travel to town every day. I wonder, which club should I join? Bucks, do you think? We could go to the opera.'

He was silent for a while, and then began sadly to sing:

> Poppa wouldn' 'low it,
> Poppa don' 'low nuttin' . . .

Fortnight left that day, taking the Kid's five thousand to London. He knew that his departure forced the Kid to pin his hopes on a lie. But he could not go back on the decision that he had never made. To do so would be to realize that he had not made it. His reality depended on a complex self-deception. He therefore forced on Barbara the image of himself as wilful, even ruthless. He was amazed at the persistence with which she clung to him. He tried every means to make himself unattractive. He became certain that he did not love her, so as to be able not to love her. He imposed on himself a fastidious discipline of idleness. He gave up his career as a composer, justifying himself at length in terms that made no reference to the fact that he had never written a note of music. She selflessly encouraged him to read for the Bar; she even took him to dine in the Temple, pretending against her convictions that the life of the legal establishment was compatible with the highest moral ideals. She did everything in her power to confirm the image that he needed. But the more she did, the more he seemed like her creation. So she could not succeed. He began to molest her innocent goodwill. 'How can I be a barrister,' he would say, 'when so many other questions need to be settled first. God, for example. Does He exist? Has He made us in His image? Has He granted us freewill?' For refuge, she flung herself into the deep shadow of the future, and he made a great point of the fact that, in his idleness, he was swanning visibly in the light of day. By the time he had spent half of the Kid's money she had begun to seek other friendships.

And then, one day, not long before his return, during a dinner-party at which he disdained to speak, he caught from her a look of pity. It was then that he went back on his unmade decision.

Suddenly the blind shot up in Mr Langley's studio, and the artist appeared fish-eyed at the wall of his aquarium. Fortnight hurried on, remembering to forget Barbara, as he had forgotten Dr Holtius until this morning. He reached Bramhurst, passing the little stream where they had fished for minnows, and which babbled below the graveyard. His mother's cottages had been demolished, and the canary-yellow garage stood in their place. Whatever stage two involved, it had not succeeded. He recalled how quiet the village had been, and how the jumbled houses on the green had seemed steadily to breathe as they slept in each other's arms. Old women stood out at the gates, and the church door was always open, scenting the air with plaster and roses.

When they had prayed, it was at the end of the afternoon, beside the tomb of Sir Richard Fanning, obiit MDCXXI, who knelt in effigy, his dead wife at his side, and all their little children stretched out beside them in diminishing sizes, like dolls that should fit one within the other so that the whole line could be returned to the womb of the woman who prayed. He remembered tea with Dr Chadwick in the vicarage, the dusty sunlight on abandoned books, the quiet attentive manner of the scholar as he doted on Mrs Fortnight.

Most of the houses on the green had been rebuilt. Even the vicarage had changed. Its mock Jacobean windows had been flattened, and the porch demolished. It was divided into flats, and the avenue of wellingtonias that led to the church had been felled. If there was a vicar now he must come by car from some other parish. Nothing of his mother was visible; yet Fortnight was certain that somewhere she lingered still, panting like Anticleia for a drink of blood.

He went into the church, to study the Fanning tombs. The family had advanced from knighthood to lordship at the Restoration, and then, in the frozen marble tears of a Regency monument, they appeared with the honours of a gartered earl. With a shock Fortnight recalled that his mother had worked for Lord Gilroy; she had been his secretary. He remembered seeing them together, laughing, at a garden party. She was young then, pretty, and with a beautiful bonnet of immortelles. He picked up a booklet, hoping to understand.

So the church was already venerable when William the Conqueror granted it by a Charter of 1075 to the Abbey of

56

Jumièges in his home Duchy, as part of a thank-offering for his victory of 1066. He mentions that the grant is to include all dues as Odo the Chaplain and his predecessors held them in the days of King Edward. Many distinguished archeologists have puzzled to work out what was the plan of the Norman church, and the theory which links the arch over the north door with the north side of the nave at the chancel entrance is the most likely solution. This was propounded recently (1954) at a meeting of the Flackwell and Eastapsley archeological society. The Very Reverend Prior Sheldrake of Cheadle said he felt sure that the Norman doorway in the north wall was not now in its original position. . . .

This innocent love of place and purposelessness filled him with grief. He turned the pages, in search of information about Lord Gilroy.

The seventeenth century produced some church furniture, including the Jacobean pulpit, now lost, fine and massive altar rails, matching the lectern, and the Bible of 1611 went with it. These altar rails are now in the Lady Chapel, along with the Jacobean altar. The Bible is known as a 'he' Bible, as there is a misprint in the third chapter of Ruth, at verse 15. The Bible is now kept in the vicarage and can be seen on application to Dr Chadwick.

The eighteenth century seems to have passed without event, and in the nineteenth and early twentieth century this church, like so many others, suffered from 'improvements'. A gallery at the west end, which had held the organ and instrumentalists, was pulled down. A visitor to the church at the beginning of this century remembered this gallery, and remembered also the lady who played the organ wearing a cap like that of a miner, with a candle stuck in the side to give light. . . .

Fortnight imagined the state of mind of someone who regarded the eighteenth century as passing without event, and who could still be struck by the appearance of an organist's cap. It was a mind without guile or malice, learned too, in its cranky way, able to write freely of canopied crosses, maniples, thuribles and inquisitions; seeming to distinguish between rectors, vicars, chaplains and curates, and writing with Trollopian passion of the offices of rural dean. He closed the little booklet and laid it again on the pile by the font. Then he noticed, in small print on the cover, beneath a rough engraving of the church, the words 'compiled by Mrs Julien Fortnight, August 1958'.

He picked up the booklet and crumpled it. He could find no coin in his pocket with which to make an offering, and this circum-

He flung out of the church and ran down the road to Flackwell. The best thing, he thought, would be to work as a conveyancing clerk in a provincial town. He would handle ancient deeds and documents, read of hereditaments, easements and gifts in remainder, of 'all that the land herein described and more particularly set forth in the schedule hereto'; some little aura of her would linger in those documents, and, poring over them with crabbed and nervous gestures, he would accord to his mother such small acknowledgement as she deserved.

Chapter Three

FOR THE FIRST time, Fortnight sat down to a lunch prepared and served by his father. It was cold, copious, and ill-assorted. But the Colonel presented it with an unusual formality, a kind of *gravitas*, like an old servant in a country house. Something stirred in Fortnight's memory, some remark, some episode, that he was not to forget. He did not belong in that house, he was temporary, a visitor, brought by an errand from outside. This made him uncomfortable, and sometimes he would look up at his surroundings with a kind of surprise. Was this his father sitting in the grey serge suit, his watery eyes askew? The sharp tang of a pickled onion filled Fortnight's mouth; the Kid looked at him and began to laugh.

'You know, Ken, that I've been booked in with a shrink? Dr Holtius is the name. I ask you, what kind of a name is that? Apparently I'm to see him this afternoon. The Colonel said so. Orders. Was he in your department, sir? Did he have occasion to hexamine you? Paranoia? Schizophrenia? Uncontrollable toenails? Of course you realize that I cannot go.'

The Colonel ignored him and spoke of family history. He was sure that the boys must remember more than he remembered of those charming holidays, the little Dorset villages, the once-fashionable resorts, the riverside hamlets, the nature-loving, health-enhancing rituals which would make sense no longer, now that she was gone. He himself remembered a specific occasion in Weymouth . . .

'What now is the matter, Kid?'

He studied the Kid with detachment and then dropped his fork.

'Do you now wish to lie down? It is perhaps time.'

'No sir. Cannot lie down. Must see the doctor don't you know. Slightly wrong in the head. My arse.'

'See if you can eat something.'

The Kid roared with laughter, and their father got up from the table, his eyes filled with tears. Fortnight watched with astonishment these antics in a man whose ironical formality had always repelled him. He tried to feel sympathy, but it would not come. Everything had changed in that house. The Kid had changed, everyone had changed.

The Colonel was now walking in the garden, clutching his right hand to his heart, murmuring quietly. Fortnight saw him stare at some object in the grass which he proceeded to kick half-heartedly before continuing his progress towards the border. It was the Kid who broke silence.

'Don't be taken in. You don't know what old Fist has been up to.'

'Old Fist?'

It was a new name. Britchell, he remembered, and Mr Fanfare; both of them had disappeared with some new drugs the Kid was taking.

'Him out there. That great man I don't think with his brain quotient lower than a Gobi rainfall. He's up to no good.'

'I think you'd better explain.'

'I like that! Yesterday I offered to explain, didn't I? I was all set to explain. But no: you had to see for yourself. So you are going to find out for yourself. *Favete linguis.*'

He got up from the table and went singing to his room. Fortnight noticed that he began to run as he reached the landing, and did not hesitate, as always he used to, by the knob of their mother's door.

A veil had fallen. Through it Fortnight dimly perceived the Colonel, back now in the dining-room, clearing dishes. It had been a point with his mother to have no servants. 'Strangers in the house'. He remembered her blue and white pinafore, her white arms sunk in dough. She used to sing

> *The water is wide, I cannot get o'er,*
> *And neither have I wings to fly . . .*

'Do you remember how she sang?'

The Colonel's voice startled him.

'She did not have music in her; but she could be affecting. When I was a child now, my mother used to sing to me — stuff about ploughboys and millers and turtle-doves. Some bore must have collected them by now, coffined them up in grubby harmonies. But my mother now. That was a memory. She had a *voice*. Pity you never knew her. A better generation. Certain of things; none of this fatuous obstinacy. Certainty and obstinacy, you know, are quite opposite things.'

Fortnight looked at the blue Spode plates on the dresser, at the white table-cloth (why had he brought it out?), at the blue and white vase in the centre of the table, at the blue cotton damask curtains. His eyes and mind were filled with blue and white.

'She never worked of course. Never did a thing. Housemaster's wife couldn't. But she somehow acquired a pair of interesting

hands. Tiny, so tiny she couldn't play the piano. But fat, puffy, full
of crevices. When she sang she would hold her hands in my hair.
Now why did she do that, you ask? It was because that was the way
we sang in chapel, lined up in the front row, the masters, their
wives, the children in front of them, starched collars making you
sore round the throat. Good discipline in a way —

> *Love Divine, all loves excelling,*
> *Joy of Heaven to Earth come down ...*

With Mama's great voice in the air above you, her creased hands
pushing the melody down through the top of your skull. As a
matter of fact, my dear Kenneth, I ought to tell you more about her.
Not that I give a fig for family traditions.'

Fortnight wondered again why the Colonel had put out the
white table-cloth, and why he now left it behind after all the dishes
had been cleared, as though intending it to remain there forever. A
winding sheet. The Kid had spilled something by his place. A sort
of grief came over him at the thought that they should see that stain
each day. He looked around. The house seemed cluttered with
furniture, with clocks and knick-knacks, prints, candlesticks,
wooden boxes, sonorous inanities. When had we acquired them?
he asked himself. Now there was no 'we'. Perhaps there never had
been.

'You see, my dear Kenneth, this generation gap is not your
invention. Your generation is uncreative, even of its own
mediocrity. It was we who first became conscious of these things.
Mama had no idea, no idea at all. Poor innocent. Her life chock
full of bonhomous laddies. Then dying, surrounded by offspring,
happily sinking into the arms of the church, blessed and blessing
with those small mechanical gestures that she had picked up in the
womb. How could she mind it? But for us you see, for your mother,
death is a full stop, silence in a room where a clock had ticked ...'

Suddenly he ripped away the table-cloth and crumpled it in
angry trembling hands.

'... and that's the reason for it, for all this idiocy. Death is final.
No beyond, no reward, no compensation. So the bastards hang on.
They refuse to leave without demanding satisfaction; their paltry
desires magnified into rights. My right to food, to education, to
work, to health, to life itself! Each of the buggers presenting his
little bill of demand to which society has added some condoning
signature. "I promise to pay the bearer on demand ..." All these
little bills, circulating quietly for centuries among gullible peace-
able creatures like Mama, suddenly picked up by a footloose rabble
and presented at the central bank. Every man jack of them screaming for his miserable share! I'd shoot the lot.'

He threw the table-cloth into the drawer of the sideboard and slammed it.

'Why are you talking like that?' asked Fortnight's voice.

'Me? Oh.' The Colonel turned round, smiling maliciously and rubbing his hands.

'Nothing you know, temporary explosion. Old buffer got to get it off his chest.'

And, having kicked the table extremely hard, so that a castor detached itself from the pedestal, he sat down to sing in mocking tones some verses of his old school song:

> Ah! How they'll rise to heart and eye
> That well-remembered room!
> That winning hit! That last wild try!
> Those days of gleam and gloom!
> The cloisters and the clump! The hall!
> The high Flag flying over all!

Ahem chorus,

> Sons of the mother forth we go
> To the tropic suns and the polar snow.
> Something something as our flame
> Burns inly to the end the same . . .

He laughed. Fortnight was afraid he would continue, as was customary, with a medley of patriotic songs. The Colonel poured scorn on everything that mattered to him, pre-empting each assault on his personality by running before the enemy to the place where he could trample his own standard to the ground. It was for such virtues that the Intelligence Corps had seen fit to promote him.

But he stopped singing. Instead he looked quizzically, almost tenderly at his son, and said: 'You know, Kenneth, I think you are right. We'll cancel the appointment with Holtius. The Kid has his own way of coping. You, who understand him so well, you are bound to be a great support at the present time. I appreciate it. It takes such a burden from my mind. Thank you, my dear boy, thank you . . .'

He got up and quietly left the room. A little later there was a clatter of feet on the stair, and a small half-strangled cry. Fortnight hid his face in his hands.

The Colonel had always been a powerful man. Looking at his big black Oxford shoes, the heavy cloth of his trousers, and the large fat hands clenched in his lap, Fortnight thought of the kick that he had given to the dining-table. He had the impression that the Colonel was humming to himself. The silent forms packed into the fumed oak benches stared away from the Colonel as though some deformity radiated guilt from his bowed bedraggled head. The Kid sat beside him. Further along was the woman, Catherine Parkhurst. Fortnight averted his eyes.

From the wide windows of the crematorium chapel you could see the long alleys of memorial roses planted on the buried ashes of the dead. Beyond, the downs stretched southwards, and he could make out a flock of sheep moving slowly towards the crescent of a hill. Friends and neighbours had gathered for the sacrifice, but none of his mother's family. Staring at the back of his father's head, he reached an explanation. The Colonel had written a forbidding letter. Fortnight envisaged his mother's relatives, remembering a house somewhere, box hedges in a garden, a sweet smell of brewing beer, dogs, photographs, perforated silver. Uncle Michael had white hair and a short white moustache. Since retiring from the Royal Corps of Signals, he had played the cornet each Sunday in a military band. Sometimes you could see him in Regent's Park, playing Suppé, Strauss and Glen Miller. Uncle Jonathan was dead; Aunt Caroline he could hardly remember. Like his mother they were fragile people, easily deterred. The Colonel had done them a service with his letter, alerting them beforehand to an experience that they could not contain. Fortnight imagined the words, and Uncle Michael reading them, sitting in the little room above the grocery, its dilapidated wallpaper spotted with yellow flowers, the kettle humming on the gas ring by the window. 'I am distressed to have to inform you that your niece / cousin / aunt / sister died last night, after a painful illness borne with fortitude. She expressly asked that her body be not buried but cremated, when her sufferings were concluded. The ceremony will take place on April 11th at the Wayside Crematorium, Dingleton. You may then have the opportunity to pay your last respects to my wife.' Poor Uncle Michael, staring away uncomprehendingly at his regimental photographs, and at the various records of his finest hour as leader of the Cadet School Band, stood proxy in that moment for all his class. Mrs Fortnight's relations were threatened by incomprehensible forces rising to extinguish them. An enfeebled army paraded before Fortnight's inner eye: tax inspectors with impish moustaches who each year made a splash at Monte Carlo, accountants with an open interest in roses and a secret interest in Brahms, private secretaries to unfashionable authors, who lived alone in cottages and cultivated bees. They were ghostly abstractions, defined only by his capacity to pity them. They had heard of his mother's illness and put it from their minds. He saw not only the particular face of Uncle Michael, but all their amalgamated faces reading with a single blank expression the Colonel's heartless letter. He saw their tawdry relief at his father's language, their fear at the sight of 'body', 'painful', 'suffering' and 'died'. Fortnight was so convinced by this image that he felt a kind of cold admiration. The Colonel managed everything with skill, bringing each human feeling to the point where it must choose between avoidance and catastrophe. And he managed always at that point, a deft impresario, to step aside.

The plain whitewood box stood on a plinth beside the lectern, and its far end was hidden in the folds of a curtain that hung like an altar cloth where no altar could be seen. The Revd and Hon John Apperley addressed Mrs Fortnight's frozen form through the wooden panels. His words were chosen in order to give least offence, distracting the body from every thought of what awaited it.

'Why? Why me? Why now? When we ask these questions — and I know that Angela, Jennie as she was to us — asked them often, then it is that a certain spiritual anxiety troubles us. The proximity of nothingness. Do I vanish? Do I disappear into thin air, do I become a vapour, a breath of wind, a memory? Or am I substantial in the hope of eternal life? We have no answer to these questions. Jennie had no answer. She confessed quite frankly to her lack of faith. It is for her honesty that we remember her. Where weaker spirits fail, take refuge in easy certainties, make themselves comfortable in borrowed convictions, Jennie dared to look the truth directly in the eye. The truth is not pleasant. She suffered it, and her family suffered with her. The truth is our weakness, our absolute inability to conjure up an idea of the beyond. Now, as she takes her last journey towards that unknowable mystery — God, as some call it, the Absolute spirit, eternal love — she takes with her a peculiar certificate of merit. She will be recognized for her honesty; and she will go forward into that other world — if world it be — with a peculiar claim to represent us. Her unbelief will be the symbol of all our unbelief, and her salvation the ground of our salvation. In some manner of which we can know nothing, she will be recompensed for her suffering. And now let us be thankful that rest and peace have come to Jennie, and pray that we who grieve for her may find comfort in her passing.'

Almost all had restrained their tears. Fortnight felt the effect of the cold disdaining words, which offered no certainties, no hopes, no passion, no despair. Grief was annihilated, and as they sang 'For all the saints' (chosen, the Colonel said, because the organist could play nothing else), everyone showed relief. The Kid was smiling, gently rocking back and forth on his heels, clutching his hands before him as though to prevent them flying around his head. He had been thus all morning, obedient, silent, wreathed in ironical expressions converging on a smile.

Something was happening. All eyes were directed to the plinth as the Vicar turned to press a button on the wall behind him, murmuring as he did so and staring into space. The box began to move, slowly, silently, brushing the curtains as it passed. As it gathered speed the Vicar too mumbled faster, so that his last amen came just as the coffin plunged from sight. A hidden door opened and closed with a quiet snap, like the entrance to a ghost train. Fortnight fancied the crackle of flames.

As they began to move, the Hammond organ changed to 'All things bright and beautiful', tremolando, at half speed. Outside, in the damp air, they surveyed the gathered wreaths spread on the concrete drive. The Kid's smile was wonderful, placid, transcendent, embracing his whole surroundings. Fortnight felt a strange chill, and turned away, unable to shake hands with the queue of friends and neighbours.

In life his mother had never much liked the laughing-room. She preferred the rear of the house, the kitchen, the long damp scullery with its cold red tiles and marble basins. It was there that she would busy herself with plants or sewing, there that she would sing, spreading her thin voice like a perfume through the air. In the laughing-room she was silent, uncertain, cowed by the heavy portraits of her ancestors, by the over-wrought formality of Carolingian furniture.

Yet it was here, on forbidden ground, that they gathered to celebrate her departure, and, as Fortnight moved among the guests pouring claret into glasses and watching fingers muddle the patterns of Mrs Williams's sandwiches, he could hear his mother distantly singing in the scullery, arias of Gounod, Auber and Massenet. Once he had heard her singing, 'Marguerite, ce n'est-ce toi', from those distant regions. Then he had wanted to cry. The Colonel had angrily locked him in, but he was too small to protest and suffered silently the punishment of that room. It had been more terrible than any dark cupboard, than any dungeon, more terrible even than a coffin on which hammers beat, to stand there alone among sharp disordered portraits, each with some shade of his mother's fugitive unhappiness in its features, among the ornaments and silhouettes which he dared neither touch nor turn from, held by invisible wires that threaded his limbs to painted fingers, watched by eyes that penetrated him with images of death. And all the while the sound of his mother's voice, timidly laughing to itself in the scullery, as she pretended to dress for a lover before the steaming glass.

Aunt Kate was proving to the Vicar the non-existence of God. Fortnight began to greet her.

'Don't interrupt.'

She threw back a wisp of grey hair from her creased brow and stared at the Vicar's nose. Aunt Kate was a liberal and a free-thinker, widow of a London academic who had represented the Labour Party in an old forlorn election. She and his father had been close, and regarded each other with a mutual admiration that expressed itself in ruthless honesty about each other's failings. She stared at the Vicar with some amusement, but left off speaking to him.

'I only meant to say, Aunt Kate, how glad I am that you could make it.'

'Make what? Must you speak in riddles?'

'That you could come, is what I mean.'

'Don't be ridiculous. You know perfectly well that I had to come. Had I cared a fig for your mother I would have had some excuse, grief, for example, a preoccupation with mortality, Lord knows what perfunctory emotion.'

The Vicar expostulated. 'My dear lady, . . .'

Aunt Kate ignored him.

'Naturally funerals are family occasions. My brother has a deter-mined sense of family. In so far, that is, as it exonerates him from other responsibilities. There's much to be said for the family as an institution. I am sure Mr Apperley would agree with me.'

'I . . .'

'It is vital, I always believe, to create the illusion that the sphere of responsibility is narrow. Confined, if possible, to those whose faces are the objects of familiar contempt. The word "familiar" is interesting. *Familiaris*, as that child will tell you, has the meaning of "belonging to household slaves" and hence by extension "to the household". The word "family" itself comes from *famulus*, meaning an intimate slave or servant. The whole concept has evolved from that fine complexity of domestic contempt with which the Romans transformed the world from universal weak-ness to little circles of despotic power . . .'

As he moved away Aunt Kate caught Fortnight's sleeve.

'Don't go. I want you to answer a question. Who do you think was the greater man, Malatesta, or John Stuart Mill?'

'Malatesta', he guessed.

'Correct.'

Aunt Kate stared at him with unconcealed amazement. And then she resumed her cross-examination of the Vicar, who dreaded every occasion upon which he was called to explain himself. His face bore the character of a failed waxwork, irrelevantly shiny in parts, smudged and obscure wherever meanings might be read in it. When pressed for an opinion on any significant subject (and in

..

matters of religion he was profoundly agnostic), his method was to stare fixedly to one side of his interlocutor and meet his gaze only when it could not be avoided. There was at those moments a curious anxiety in the Vicar's eye, like an indignant moral surprise. His eyes seemed, when they briefly rested on another's face, to protest against an outrage. They said that the Vicar had not expected this, that it really was quite monstrous that he should be so put upon, that it was all he could do to keep a polite exterior in the face of this surprising challenge to his moral life. For once his expression seemed justified, as Aunt Kate mercilessly itemized the essential articles of dogma that he had, in his funeral oration, denied.

Some years earlier the Vicar had chosen from a catalogue of many-coloured refugees a little battered African to bring up as his son. He thereby proved to his congregation, who preferred to see the priestly role as purely passive, that he was capable of a moral gesture. And it was the congregation who rebelled against the Vicar. His rooted Anglo-Catholicism thenceforth gave way to a kind of random nonconformity bordering on outright atheism, as secular preoccupations took hold of his spirit. It was the principal members of this congregation — among them the Vicar's old friend, Sir Meredith Umpleton, (who had continued to refer to 'John's black bastard' until timidly reprimanded by Mrs Fortnight) — who now, for no reason that Fortnight could readily understand, filled the house with their Christmas matinée laughter. Sir Meredith already had his hand on Fortnight's shoulder, and, while extending his glass for more claret, asked him genially what he was doing up in town.

'I, I think, I mean I am, well I am just preparing Bar finals.'

'Pupillage fixed? Want any help? Can I speak to . . ?'

Sir Meredith's red-veined eyes swam away in pursuit of a female form. Fortnight went rapidly to the door. He felt drunk.

In the hallway it was dark. He could hear their voices as though in a dream. Hilarity was spreading through the assembly, not the hilarity of a wake, but something more poised and self-conscious, as though they danced in slow motion on a field of mud. He saw John Higgins the estate agent, squat, red-faced and drunken in his purple tie. He saw Gwendolen, his mother's friend, drying her tears and smiling, the make-up crisping in rills on her rough complexion. The Colonel sat on the floor in one corner of the room, talking urgently to his woman; all around him the figures moved in a strange ballet of feigned distress, their laughter sudden, choked, like bursts of uncalled-for applause.

--Did you see her?

—I came once or twice, I thought . . .

—Yes, difficult. One never knows. Poor woman. But Catherine
was kind.
—Catherine!
The conversation moved on. Pockets of light seemed to gather
among their faces, and then softly explode into words. How had
his mother known them all? Her world was shrouded in mystery,
and yet the laughing-room was full of the remnants of an interest
in whether she lived or died.
—I wonder Jennie stood for it.
—No choice. Lying there, twisted in agony.
—Don't!
—Anyway, she wouldn't have noticed. Never did. Think of the
others.
Fortnight recalled her pruning something in the garden wear-
ing the grey rough gloves that still lay on the window-sill in the
scullery. Tears were dropping, very slowly, from her cheeks. He
had crept past holding his arms in front of him so as not to make a
noise.
—Did she never herself? I mean, wasn't there something with
Ken Blakeley a while back?
—Ken Blakeley! That quacking waddling creature up at the
school? Fantastic! All eighteen stone of him?
—There's no accounting for tastes. Even Julien has been
eccentric.
—*Even* Julien!
—But we're probably wrong. If there was anything I rather
think that it was with old Gilroy.
—Bob Gilroy?
—Well, you know Jennie was an awful snob.
—So that accounts for . . .
—Accounts for his absence.
—But what about the others? No Langleys, no Corbett-Wim-
poles — and that Doctor chap, the one, is he from Oxford . . .
—But didn't you hear?
Fortnight wanted to move away, but the darkness behind the
door concealed him. How are your studies? How is London? Do
you see much of our Barbara? In his dark retreat all these ques-
tions dissolved in a single image — Sarah Bernhardt, his mother's
favourite peony, its blood-veined flowers glistening in their
pockets like wads of gathered silk.
And then suddenly Mrs Thurlow appeared, her little olive face
creased with smiles, a sense of carnival in her dress of polyester.
'And how *are* we?'
She pecked his cheek, assumed a solemn expression, and then at
once began to froth and bubble like a glass of babycham. How their

faithless librarian could move her ogling eyes!

'We've missed you so terribly! Where have you been, wicked boy! Nothing's the same without you.'

'Julia. I don't believe you. How's the library?'

Leaving school early you could get there while it was still empty, and sit by the window, watching the rustle of leaves in the court-yard next door. He piled up unreadable volumes, on alchemy and runic script, while Mrs Thurlow busied about him, flashing smiles from between the bookshelves, and sometimes, when they were alone, presenting him silently with a cup of tasteless tea. Once, on a rainy afternoon, when suddenly the library darkened, he had jumped across to her before she could touch the light. Her kiss was smooth, professional, embellished with a feigned sur-prise, his hands clumsy, inexperienced, seeking her breast with trembling fingers and manoeuvring towards her ready palm the burning handle of his passion. It was over in a second, never re-sumed, despite 'some other time', and her demure unconscionable smile when the door swung open to let in Dr Holtius.

'Stinking awful. But what else could I do? Alfred has to stay here for the company. I need to have books around me. Books, more books. He thinks I'm ridiculous.' She paused. 'But I say, I really am sorry about your mother. Such a lovely person. God, do I sound phoney? You must be quite fed up, poor darling.'

She touched him lightly on the sleeve, her smile slow, cracked, pruinose. She had been pretty once, with her small round face, her hazel eyes, her midget vitality. Now her left hand played with a lock of hair, and he noticed the wedding ring dented with a hundred tiny marks, as though she had been biting it and biting it.

—She was wonderful at bazaars and things. But that's not enough for anyone. I mean she must often have wondered how much she *missed* . . .

—An incomplete person. But my own feeling is that we should really be thinking how best to replace her. She would have been just the job for Saturday. Who is going to do the flowers? . . .

Mrs Thurlow was still looking at him, expecting a reply.

'I don't know. Everyone sounds phoney. I expect it's just me.'

'Oh you should try the French. I've had so much of them lately, living with a beastly group in Grasse while Alfred was in America — took three months off, you see. Not a *mere* librarian.'

—I mean Jennie did it well, but it was after all *her* way. I don't think anyone could take over from her. We'll just have to organize things differently. Sir Henry!

—Oh drop the Sir can't you? Gives me the creeps.

—Well, we were just discussing the display for Saturday.

'Living with this awful Vîcomte, growing lilies and entertaining the most incredible druggies, gun-runners, painters, even that chap who got the Goncourt last year — what's his name? Mostly *pieds-noirs* of course, and some of them even protestants. Lot of army types, like your father, only much more violent. Really the French! Of course, one adores one's French friends, but — do you think I'm awfully immature? — I find the mass of them quite abominable . . .'

—Pity we have to meet in these dismal circs, but while we're here I'd like a word about the woods at Spearywell. I had a little proposition to make; I think I've got the Colonel interested . . .

—Such a sweet, honest person. You wouldn't have thought he would be able to.

—Well, you know, that child — enough to drive anyone off the rails.

'the language of course is adorable, those lovely onomatopoeias — is that the plural? — words like *clapotis*, and *roucoulement* . . . .'

—did she by God! Well you could blow me down . . .

—not a large patch of land at all, only there are those two acres, the ones that Jennie inherited, I suppose they go to the Colonel now, and you know they have been untouched for years, ever since the Fortnights came back from wherever it was, Bramhurst where they had that place . . .

'such adorable villages, the late winter light on the rocks, sometimes out among the stone pines on a blowy evening I wanted to cry it was so beautiful, and then I could forget the people, people all over the house, spluttering into their Rosé de Tavel, shouting angrily about horrid military things or quietly weeping for reasons they would never divulge. It was only for the old Vicomte that I stayed really. But you must come some time — you could take a holiday'

'Julia, you say the most ridiculous things. My life *is* a holiday.'

'And that means that you need a real one, with a real woman to look after you. At your age (not that I'm so very much older than you) I used to fall in love deliberately every spring, in order to go on a romantic binge about the islands, dancing in tavernas, dreaming on beaches, love among the ruins, and always with a bag of books to read. Reading, love, reading, love, that's all it was, then, until the last time when I went with Alfred. But there . . .'

She was suddenly sad, looking at him.

The Colonel stepped between them and began to talk, all the time addressing Mrs Thurlow with his heavy eyes, and moving the muscles of his face in obedience to her grimaces.

'It really is good of you to be here. I cannot tell you what a relief it is to find someone genuine among this houseful of frauds. Can't think why I invited them. I hear nothing but sickly reflections on Jennie's goodness, her sweetness, her endless self-denial. Pious cant. And old Gilliboe, for example, even went so far as to say — no don't go Kenneth, you would be interested — to say that Jennie was distinguished most of all for her insight. I ask you! Jennie, a woman of insight. Oh I grant that she had many qualities. I admired her very much. But insight! What would she have done with a quality like that? Jennie had no more need of insight than a bat of eyes! She sensed the contours of an obstacle and cunningly avoided it. It is amazing how closely she could sheer against a cliff-face and still stay twittering in empty air!' Suddenly his voice changed and he fixed Mrs Thurlow with a dark expression. 'Take that child, for example . . .'

Fortnight moved away and pulled himself up along the bannister-rail. The house was swimming, the voices cascading along the hall. Upstairs there was silence, and he went from room to room, opening doors and surveying the contents like an auctioneer. The walls of the Kid's room were covered in dollops of ice-cream, which the Kid was throwing from a bowl that he held between his knees. The yellowish muck was slipping down on to the little chest where he kept his clothes, and melting over its surface.

'What the hell is this?'

'Roughly speaking, Kenny, it is ice-cream. At present I am engaged in throwing it at the walls. Smears rather beautifully, don't you think? Caligula, of course, would have opted for human blood, but I don't seem to be able to lay my hands on any just at present.'

The Kid was crying as he spoke; his Latin books had been spread across the floor and trampled on.

'Why don't you stop a moment and help clear the mess?'

'Hardly appropriate actually, Ken. You see the mess has to stay. Part of the spell.'

'What spell?'

'The one I'm casting, obviously. In order to get rid of them.'

'Get rid of whom?'

'You are a daft booby and you know who I mean. I'm getting rid of Grabenaz, and I'm also getting rid of Fist. We have to have them out of the way.'

'And why is that?'

'So the investigations can begin.'

The kid dropped the bowl of ice-cream, and fell on his face along the bed, sobbing miserably, his twisted body contorting itself like a stricken animal. Fortnight left him, closing the door as quietly as possible, and descending the stairs. It now seemed as if he had to rejoin his father, almost as though to warn him of the Kid's intent. The Colonel still stood locked in conversation with Mrs Thurlow, but suddenly, as Fortnight passed, he clicked his heels and saluted. In the laughing-room people were moving jerkily, aimlessly, like chickens with severed necks, and hardly a noise seemed to emerge from them.

A cloud passed and the hallway darkened. A red face glowed before him, eyes like pinpoints glimmering beneath an overhanging brow. A few hairs flopped back and forth above the tall forehead, as though stirred by a wind driven from some secret duct in the top of the skull. The head seemed hardly to move, so fixed were the beams that issued from the sockets of its eyes. It was the Colonel, who chuckled and rubbed his hands.

'A great success,' he said, 'a great success', and nodded towards the door of the laughing-room. A serene smile broke across his features, as he drew Fortnight into a corner of the hall. Fortnight stared for so long, that a dark shutter seemed to be drawn across the Colonel's face, leaving only chinks through which to view the mottled skin. It was no longer his father's face but a mushroom patch spattered with sunlight in the darkness of a wood. Worms made their house there, and nothing was constant between the rapid decay of existing growths and the multiplication of spores.

The world receded from them, the Colonel turning over in his mind the important message he was about to impart. The funeral party proceeded silently and inconsequentially, like a dance of paper in a street.

'Are you comfortable in your room? Do you have what you need? You'll see that I tried to keep it as you left it. I think that it's very important for a young man to have a place he can call his own.'

The Colonel went on to explain, in a manner imbued with kindness, that he had intended at one stage himself to live in Fortnight's room, so soothing was it, so well supplied with books, and with such a pleasant outlook over the garden, and that if he had finally abandoned this plan it was not because he felt any hesitation to give up comforts for the sake of his son — for on the contrary he was approaching the time of life when mindless sacrifices could be considered wholly natural — but rather that, as he had discovered, and as he was taking the opportunity to convey now while the experience was still fresh in their minds, life in that house would require a certain humility, and a penitential habit to which his son might have difficulty, without the aid of material tranquillity, in accustoming himself. A quite peculiar combination of personal qualities was needed for a man to live on the scene of a past catastrophe; it was not enough to strike up an easy compromise with it. A man must learn to understand it, to see all the ways in which he had failed and, just as important, all the others in which he had done what was required of him. Now, had his son such qualities as these? Would it be possible for him to retrace the last moments of another's life, recounting to himself the manner in which he had failed, and that in which he had in part succeeded, but only to fail again more dismally, withholding comfort and sustenance in her hour of need? It was easy, and his son must surely know as much, to be parted from her in a place where she had never been. But to confront the familiar corners, the rooms and arbours where her ghost was lingering, this was the trial of moral stature. Of course there might also be a subtle pleasure in it, a kind of morbid sense that, being aware of one's failings, one also ceased to possess them. But the Colonel did hope that his son would be able to overcome and reconcile all the many conflicting emotions to which he had just alluded, and so settle in that house with the flexible but firm resolve to make a go of it.

'But father, I am due back soon in London. I cannot stay more than a few days. You presumably realize that.'

'That's as may be,' he replied, smiling more broadly, 'but there are certain matters which it is incumbent upon me to explain to you.' He referred to the Kid, whose education had proceeded with remarkable facility in the circumstances but whose future must surely be greatly affected by what had happened, and by nothing so much as his own refusal to believe it. The Colonel knew that it was difficult to love a creature who deviated so palpably from the norms of human conduct, and that it was difficult to overcome the repugnance one must naturally feel at a mind and a body neither of whose movements could be predicted with any degree of success. But he hoped nevertheless that his elder son would in time give the Kid credit for his pathetic if misguided love for Jennie, and come to recognize the harmlessness of his eccentricities. He himself, if he be allowed to confess it, had never loved the child, and would prefer all things considered to maintain only an indirect responsibility for his future . . .

'As indeed would I.'

The Colonel, moving towards the door, maintained the ghost of his former smile.

'Of course, and I am sure you will find some adequate solution. You are so intelligent and what you lack in application you will make up for in the perception of necessity. But now I really must be going and perhaps I may entrust to you this letter. There's no hurry to read it. Take your time. I wonder if . . .'

He had already opened the front door and, not finding a hand outstretched towards him, pushed the letter into the breast pocket of Fortnight's jacket. The old black Daimler purred on the drive,

Catherine Parkhurst sitting at the wheel. The Colonel slipped beneath the lintel. With renewed smiles and moist-eyed blinks, he shut the door behind him.

There was hilarity now in the laughing-room. Mrs Thurlow lolled in the arms of the doctor, receiving downturned condescending smiles. Aunt Kate stared before her with unconcealed distaste, while the Vicar mumbled general benedictions. They held their glasses forward for the wine. A ham sandwich had been pressed into the carpet and bore the imprint of a lady's shoe.

'One last glass, and I must be going. A sad business.' John Higgins fixed him with a mournful stare. 'So you'll be staying awhile, your father says. Apparently you might help on the legal side. We have a few developments coming up. Planning permission tight. Be good to have you in the office. Once you've got over this, this . . . Yes, very good.'

His white shirt was stained with wine, and the purple tie hung out above his paunchy stomach like a windless flag.

'Has my brother gone?' Aunt Kate asked, suddenly approaching. 'Has the cad scarpered with his whore?'

'I think he might have gone for a drive.'

'Ridiculous. He's scarpered, the fox.' She laughed abruptly. 'Serves you damned right. Teach you to realize that every change is absolute. The slate is clean, Kenneth. Start again.'

She got up and gathered her clothes about her, patting as she did so the scattered ornaments in her piled grey hair.

'I, for one, am going. My dear boy. Let me give you some advice. Have that child put away. Sell the house. Settle in London. Doesn't matter what you do, so long as you get out of this backwater. Also, you should keep the mind you were born with. Don't pollute it with education. Law is permissible, so long as you treat it with disdain. But beware of theories. Be especially careful of welfare economics.'

Aunt Kate vanished. Suddenly Fortnight felt the Kid's hand in his.

'It's all right now Kenny. It was nothing. I've cleared up the mess. Nothing to worry about. I'll be all right now. Now that they've gone.'

'I . . .'

'You don't *have* to say anything Kenny. Just go and lie down. I'll see to this lot. Have them off the premises in a jiffy.'

Fortnight crept up the stairs and flung himself on the bed. Almost at once there was a knock on the door, and Mrs Thurlow entered.

He pushed her roughly towards the bed, she yielding with a

quiet sigh. Some demon possessed him. He was aflame with a kind of anger. The ease with which Mrs Thurlow issued from her skin of clothes made an odd impression, as though he were about to plunge into her body the dagger of religious sacrifice. Drunk now, she was pretty again, speechless, waiting; her nipples tightened as he touched them and slowly, with strange composure, she opened her legs.

He began to undress. The room was full of imperatives, imperatives of grief, of rage, of desire. From whom they issued Fortnight did not know. They were not his; they were not hers. Her hands, as they loosened the belt of his trousers, responded to a summons more powerful than they could issue. Trembling explorations were compelled from them. Observing them, he felt pity for these creatures, forced to trade in decency for such small reward.

Mrs Thurlow pressed her lips to his legs and stomach, opening her eyes as she took him in her small uncertain mouth. Everything was silent, unuttered, like a moment of prayer. Fortnight tried to discard his jacket, but pleasure enraged him. Half-dressed he lay down; it was as though he were pushed into her by some pitiless hand. She let out a cry, and dug her nails into him, panting and biting her lip. They were on the floor, on the bed, lying, sitting, above, across, beside themselves and no sound but the sound of their unhappy panting as, with merciless attention to rule, the powers commanded them to die.

At the moment of climax, he noticed the Colonel's letter. It had fallen from his pocket on to the coverlet, and was now being crumpled by Mrs Thurlow's body. He had the thought that it was this letter which contained their orders. It was in obedience to the Colonel's closet imperatives that they made love. Clearly it was necessary to check the instructions. Mrs Thurlow lay muttering, eyes closed, one hand limp beside her. The expression on her face was of a restless sleeper, a will-less, dream-haunted face. Fortnight extracted the Colonel's letter from beneath her shoulder.

He thought he should make no noise while opening it. This was difficult; the Colonel had sealed the letter very firmly, and stuck it over with sellotape. Perhaps he had written it, sealed it, then opened it for some correction. But why not use a fresh envelope? Perhaps he was too lazy to re-address it, Kenneth Fortnight, Esq, *manu*. It was one of mother's blue envelopes. There was something odd in his speculating on these circumstances. When he got it open, he held the paper down on to the bed and began to read. Mrs Thurlow opened her eyes.

'Darling, delightful. Feel young again, drunk and young, alcoholic, beautiful, kiss me, tell me you'll do it again, every day, every mournful afternoon, adultery to order, behind the shelves

marked "Land Economy", super place, feel so young there . . .'
*My dear Kenneth, I doubt very much that you shall see me, or
want to see me, again. Both these circumstances are wholly
natural. You will find two sets of keys in the ice-making compartment of the refrigerator. The garden needs attention once a
week, in my experience, unless . . .*
'so young, quite drunk with lust and love, and other things, but
why are you not undressed? What's that bit of paper? It was super
you know, quite out of this world, or worldlet, *hors concours.*
Don't, if I may advise it, despise me; this is not the time to reflect,
au contraire, j'ai bien le droit, toi aussi, mon petit . . .'
She worked her blanched and blotched pommettes against his
shirt-front. For a while he fenced off her hands. Then she seized
one of the vague and valedictory wrists from the air above her and
pressed it hard into the harvest of her hair. She laughed with conditional fellow-feeling, as though at rest with another human being.
   *. . . you should choose to concentrate on the vegetables, which
may in the circumstances be more appropriate. The tools are
still in the shed, and only the lawn-mower needs restoring. I had
meant to get it done a couple of weeks ago so as to have it ready
for the spring, but things intervened. If you ring up Dimmock's
they will come to collect it. As for business you will no doubt . . .*
'. . . because everything in this town is so sad, and humdrum and
ordinary, and what am I, I ask myself, an immaculate, or fairly immaculate valetudinarian of cultivated tastes, to do without the occasional solace of foreign follicles around my body hairs? *Hein? Je
te demande. Bien sûr, il ne répond pas: il s'occupe de choses bien
plus importantes. Un morceau de papier, une feuillette inscrite de
mensonges; un monde sans moi.* How can I get my fingers on
it?'
Her sticky hands crabbed across him, undid a button, gained
access to his rib-cage and loitered there.
'. . . *te voila hors tes draps mon vieux.* But why still reading?
What . . .'
   *. . . wish to know about financial matters. The new solicitor is
Michael Oddle of 14 Prince's Tower, which is the block you see
from Jennie's window. He is answerable for most things, and
will have instructions as to funds. If you need to communicate
with me you can do so through him, or else through the
Voyagers Club, St James's, although that will be, of course, an
address of convenience . . .*
Mrs Thurlow had sent the advanced contingents of caresses into
the recess of his shirt. Somewhere in his left armpit the sticky
fingers were staking claims. He shifted across her body.
'. . . everything about you so enigmatic. Awfully likeable, I don't

know why. Genuine perhaps. *Tu l'as très bien fait, mon chéri: il faut bien que tu le saches. Tu sais arranger les choses — quant à l'amour, je me donne congé.* Why am I speaking French to you? *Ça ne me rend pas plus agréable.* What a silly word, isn't it, "sin"? It ought to be a preposition or something. Sin you come, I come too, or no ...

  ... and you would be advised not to seek me there. The child can continue at St Stephen's. Move him if you wish, provided it is to some similar squalid place. I don't suppose it much matters, except that they have got used to him there. Oddle will see to the fees. I'd be grateful if you did not touch the cellar. Higgins has a job for you if you're interested. I believe you could finish the Bar by correspondence course. I am sure you need time to consider things. I should imagine that you would do better with a woman in the house. Please do not hesitate ...

'... such a relief. *Les extases charnelles doivent suffir.* I wish I could stop speaking this silly language. Tell me all about yourself Kenneth, will you? *Mais pourquoi tu lis, qu'est-ce que c'est?* Not in your family to be quite so ungallant, but why should I care? *Je ne blâme pas les divagations d'esprit, nous y sommes tous susceptibles.* Why should a girl be offended? God I wish I wasn't so drunk, you must think I'm awful ...'

  ... to do whatever you think fit, bearing in mind what I said to you on the night Jennie passed away. And now I can only say that I hope that all goes well, and that you will not hold too much against your ever loving father.

  P.S. I have absolute confidence in Holtius. Do get in touch with him.

'.... but I think you're awful too, can't you speak to me? Oh do say something, *tu me traites comme un môme, tu sais?* ... But why am I crying? I wish I didn't drink. Please don't take it seriously Kenneth darling, will you? Don't think that I am always like this will you? But where are you going? Please stay ...'

It was clear. The Colonel had managed the whole catastrophe, from beginning to end. The Kid was right. There was no turning back. They had to discover the truth, to bring evidence, to accuse. Fortnight, recalling his own part in the catastrophe, was overcome by nausea. He looked down at the figure on the bed. Mrs Thurlow's make-up was beginning to melt under the pressure of her tears. She bit her lip, but still it trembled. 'I'm sorry,' she was saying, 'I really am sorry'. He wondered why she should apologize. At least *she* was innocent. He turned away, and staggered to the bathroom. He was sick for a long time, and when he returned Mrs Thurlow was no longer there. The Kid, instead, was sitting on the crumpled bedclothes.

'Hope you're feeling better,' he said. 'There was a lady in here a moment ago, looking for you. Seemed to have forgotten some portion of her clothing. Under the impression that you might have info as to its whereabouts. I said you were otherwise engaged.'

'Get off that bed, and bugger off.'

'You'd better put on your trousers, Kenny. And now sit down. I've got something to tell you.'

Chapter Four

PROTEAN CONTORTIONS were required before the Kid had
found the position from which to begin his lay. Fortnight listened,
conscious of their growing insanity.

'The true song of the battle between Fist and Finn, slayer of
heroes. Long had the monster's spirit lain upon the land of Flack,
and roamed at night, bane of warriors, in the mother-harbouring
hall of Fortnight . . .'

'For God's sake, Kid.'

'You mean it's the facts you want? Right baby. Where do I
begin?'

'Begin from the time I left here.'

'The time you left here? That is a very long time ago indeed. It is
approximately an aeon. But behold! I summon memory, and
unlock for your benefit its store of words. Here Ken, have a gargle.
Nunc est bibendum.'

He pulled a bottle of wine from within his jacket and offered it.
Fortnight shook his head and watched as the Kid drank copiously
from the bottle, afterwards smacking his lips.

'You shouldn't.'

'At my age. Bang right. But that's another matter. So let's begin.
And to your surprise we will begin with Miss Langley.'

'What's Barbara got to do with it?'

'Listen. She and I, as you know, are great friends, she being so
beautiful and me so incredibly bright. Now this grizzly thing that
has been happening, and about which I understand a fraction
more than you, began about the time that queer doctor came on the
scene and we decided to put you into care.'

'Who's we?'

'Myself and Miss Langley. It was quite obvious to anyone with
an ounce of brains that you were not coping, as Mummy would
say. Miss Langley had the idea that since *she* was going to London,
and since you were clearly not going anywhere *else*, then the best
thing was to put it to you tactfully that London was really quite a
good place to be. Theatres, opera, dances, excitement, youth, all
that twenties crap. So we packed you off, as you surely remember,
with some considerable success when you think about it. Anyway,
it was obvious that I would have to hold the fort, so I did. In fact I

was rather well-placed, having just completed my map and being hard at work on stage 2. It was all worked out and agreed between myself and Miss Langley.'

'What was agreed?'

'It was agreed e.g. that I would stay behind, although I was stupendously in favour of coming to London. But I had to postpone my career, the essential foundations for which had been so carefully laid.'

'What career?'

'You wouldn't understand. As I was saying, I was to remain here to do the dirty work. But Miss Langley promised to send you home once a month. Hardly very difficult I would have thought, probably rather a relief from her point of view. But there, she didn't, except for that one time when you were so hopeless I had to send you away. I don't know why, but she hardly ever wrote to me. So I had to face the whole thing alone. No hard feelings, of course; I expect there's an explanation. She's a good sort, as you will have observed. But not very grown-up, and I always expected her to go hippy and liberated and mess around with "attitudes", as Fist would say. Know what I mean?'

'You don't know what you mean, Kid, that's for sure.'

'Was I saying I understand these things? Honestly Ken, I am making every allowance for my age, my lack of experience, and my well-known mental confusion. You've no idea how hard it is to get all this into shape for you. Anyway, to continue. At first it didn't much matter, being cut off here; I quite enjoyed some of it. I managed to foil the Colonel's plans completely, over the question of Mummy's houses. But that's not to the point. As I say, at first it didn't matter much. Fist was away most of the time, and I was only half at school. I turned up for the Latin and the music, but they allowed me home when I wanted, since I had a letter saying I was prone to epileptic attacks, hallucinatory episodes, etc, etc, and while harmless, these could prove disturbing to the other boys. As though they cared! Once Miss Langley did write to me, but only to say you were not able to come home just at present, since you were going to be a barrister and so had to stay to eat dinners, which is apparently all that's required. It's only respect for my literary vocation that stands between me and such a career. Well — I have to explain this extremely carefully to you because you're so incredibly dim — Mummy had been ill, as you know, in hospital. She was back home, convalescing, I wanted you to come; she wanted to see you, saying you should be there, saying I should write to Miss Langley and ask her to persuade you. As you can imagine, that was not my line of country. You could almost have called it intruding. So I wrote to you instead. I got a silly reply, entitled 'statement of claim' or 'indictment' or something. I'm not complaining. Only it was lonely here, and Mummy became sad. When Fist returned there were awful drinks parties and dinners for pinstriped people, the whole world striated like a crazy banknote. I was going out of my mind. I couldn't concentrate on anything, and I knew I was letting Mummy down. A solution was required. I won't go into *all* the details, but you'll know what I mean when I say that there was a dinner party for various nobs in the middle of which, when I was trying to be on my very best behaviour and Mummy was looking really tired, Britchell appeared, stepping out of the steak and kidney pie and lifting the top off his head with a really horrific smile. I couldn't help it, I just screamed and threw my plate at him. It went all over Sir thingummy thingummy, VIP. Mummy started to cry, in front of everyone. I felt really terrible. After that, we were both kept upstairs, and she used to cry almost every day. She wouldn't speak about it, and the funny thing is that, although I am very perceptive, I couldn't discover the reason, apart from the obvious one of Fist being a monster and myself bonkers. But she should have been used to that. It occurred to me that she was bored. I suggested she work again — you know, back with Lord Gilroy, so that we could go over like we used to for tea and croquet in the summer, and she would feel important. She needs to feel important.

'Well, one day I met this peculiar geezer on my way back from choir. Despite his unbelievably vulgar manner, and his habit of wiping his nose on the back of one hand, he introduced himself as an important poet. He felt it appropriate to buy me a drink. This was last summer, and I could sit outside at the Brewers. So I said sure thing honey, make mine a pint of the best. We sat around for a while, and, since I was feeling depressed, I explained my situation. After all, you never know with poets, it may be true that they have some special insight. As likely for poets as for psychiatrists.'

The Kid refreshed himself from the bottle, and Fortnight went to the door. From the threshold he could see the empty stairway of the house, and the hall, lit by a beam of sunlight. Everywhere, on tables, on bookcases, and scattered over the carpet, lay bits of food, paper plates, overturned glasses, and empty winebottles. The sound of the Kid's drinking made him queasy, and he asked him to stop.

'Right. So I asked this geezer's opinion of my case, and he replied in a most poetical vein, a real earsore.

' "Look," he shouted at the top of his voice, "I don't know who you are or why I'm wasting my effing time listening to such an effing weirdo, but just watch it that's all."

'Naturally I was not very much encouraged by this response, so I asked him what I was supposed to be watching.

' "Watch what you're saying to me, see? I'm known round here. I have a taste for boys. Especially boys with specs. But I can't stand effing weirdos. I now see you're not my type. Bloody waste of a pint of bitter. But there's something I could tell you, since you think you need my advice".

'He snorted and slobbered and I reminded him that I was listening with great attention to his mighty words.

' "Shut your effing trap," he said. "Look, my advice to you is get her out of that house. Just get her out, that's all. And keep her out. And then crawl up your own arsehole."

'I asked him how either of those things should be accomplished, and he snorted.

' "You just bloody do it, that's all."

'Well frankly Kenny I didn't feel I had made much progress with my interlocutor. I communicated this observation to him, whereupon he got up, let out a positively cataclysmic fart and trundled off, shouting "effing weirdo", "waste of a bloody pint", and other remarks calculated to leave me in a state of some disillusionment. But when he had gone I began to think over what he had said.'

'About what?'

'About taking Mummy away. I stayed there, staring at the people, and it began to rain. It was heavy rain, big splashes of it, bouncing off the pavement like little fountains. The people started running, real people. I wasn't having a turn or anything. You mustn't think that. I am trying to tell you as clearly as I can about this so you will know what's been happening. I was watching the people, and the rain, enjoying getting wet, and thinking about the poet's words. You know how rain reveals things, wipes off the surface, divides the people with style from the oafs and the bunglers. You can see that clearly in the street. Some of them run in a kind of panic, holding newspapers over their heads and bumping into each other. The better sort simply narrow their eyes and change direction as if they had emergency instructions. I was thinking how stylish it was to sit there with my pint, getting really wet, and with this great plan forming in my mind. The beer began to get watery, and because a police car went by and sent out some kind of signal, I swallowed the stuff down as quick as I could. Then suddenly (I don't know how it happened and as you know I've always had difficulty in believing in miracles) the whole world became clear, with a special clarity. There was hardly anyone left in the street now, and I was still watching the rain splashing on the tarmac and drumming on the leaves of a tree across the road. When I looked along the street everything seemed normal, exactly as it was, only totally clear. I'm repeating myself, but the words "clarus et simplex" kept going through my head. It was like being part of the world for the first time in my loony life. I knew I was safe. I belonged. There wasn't a lusion in sight. I felt as if someone had just handed me a written guarantee that the world was real and I belonged to it. I could *see* the world, I could do whatever had to be done. I could decide straight off, there and then, to take her away, and it wouldn't matter a bean.'

The Kid paused to drink again. The house was still with an eerie stillness.

'Then, you see, the most perfect thing happened. Mummy appeared, coming down the street in her gardening togs, all alone, wet through, and smiling. She came straight towards me. It wasn't as if she saw me and then changed direction; but more as if she already knew I was there and was relying on me. She walked across the street and came right up to where I was sitting, with this angelic smile on her face, happy like I hadn't seen her since you went away. We didn't even have to say hello. I just came out with the plan I had concocted, and she agreed, saying they were her very own thoughts.'

'And what was this plan?'

'Simple. To go straight up to the Park and put it to old Gilroy that he should take her in. You know how he is, quite round the twist, and always in need of an amanuensis to twist him the other way. And since he had always liked Mummy so much I knew it would work; she thought so too. She had had the same idea herself. I noticed she was actually carrying her suitcase. I asked her why she was wearing her gardening togs, but she just shrugged her shoulders. I didn't suppose it would matter, so what was there to do but go straight up there, as we were? You should have been with us. There was such a feeling in the air. The rain had washed all these ghastly years away. It was the clearest day in my life. You know how muddled I can get with these doctors and their drugs. Well, that day I was not muddled one bit. By sitting quietly in the rain, letting the bother of it slip away, I had foiled them completely.. Of course, I realize the authorities need crimes, victims, guilty people. Naturally it is dangerous to make a move without consulting them. But it didn't bother me that we were acting irresponsibly. Once or twice Mummy looked nervous about it, but I managed to reassure her. "Look," I said, "there's bound to be somewhere in that house, some unused room, or even a whole wing where you could stay. And how can he mind? Everyone says he's been lonely since Lady G popped it." Well, I got her as far as the portico and I could see the old boy's head in one of the downstairs windows. It really pleased me. It had the look of a head that could be influenced; it was already on our side. We thought it best if I didn't go in, since I'm not very presentable and have quite a reputation as a lunatic. So I left her there, on the steps, wet through and holding her suitcase. I disappeared into the bushes and back to town. When I looked round the door was closing and she had gone inside. It was the last time I saw her.'

As he swallowed again from the bottle the Kid executed a convulsion with a kind of punctilious detachment, dribbling slightly from the corner of his mouth. The gesture suggested to Fortnight that he might be serious.

'The last time you saw her,' Fortnight repeated.

'Yes. But of course I don't expect you to believe it. In fact I know that you are tempted to believe in the version according to Fist.'

'And what is the Colonel's version?'

The Kid laughed. 'To be honest I don't fully know. There's absolutely no reason why I should know. But I gather he has been putting it around that she's dead. And of course he has arranged a suitable pantomime to give colour to the story. Closed doors, hushed whispers, sick beds, nurses coming, nurses going, this arrangement, whatever it was, in Mummy's room. . . . Look,' he shouted suddenly, 'just don't ask me about all that will you? It makes me sick just to think of it. You've had the opportunity to find out. You saw what was going on. I see absolutely no need to speak of it.'

'Well, then, we won't speak of it. Besides I need time to assimilate what you've told me. But first, perhaps you could clear up one small detail.'

'Fire away.'

'Have you been in touch with Barbara recently?'

'*Barbara?* Oh, Miss Langley. Well, it's funny you should ask that, because in fact I had a letter from her this morning.'

'A letter?'

Fortnight was not astonished. The world had slipped quite out of his grasp. It was as though the Kid and she were lovers, and he was receiving a condescending visit in a loony bin. Neither of them would heed his words; it was useless to tell them what to bring him, or how to get him out.

'Yes. A rather peculiar letter. I can show it to you. Or at least, I shall show it to you on one condition.'

'Which is?'

'That you hand over the letter from Fist.'

Fortnight hesitated.

'As you wish.'

'You are a fool, Kid. You play dangerous games.'

'These outbursts of yours are most awfully disturbing you know Ken. It's not that I believe in shrinks, but really there are times when a chap needs help. This Holtius, now. He is extremely expensive; but they say that he is quite an expert in his field. I wonder if, should I condescend to pay him a visit, I might ask you to accompany me. What do you think?'

Fortnight took the Colonel's letter from beneath the pillow and threw it at his brother. A crumpled sheet of airmail paper was extracted from the Kid's pocket and handed over in exchange.

Ave O puer!

This flat is very nice, and all the quieter for the absence of your brother. Why don't you pay me a visit? You won't want me to say how sorry I am over what has happened, but will it cheer you to hear some news? In case it might, I now disclose it.

Numero uno: I am a member of the Opera chorus. Numero due: I have joined the Communist Party. The meetings are chronic, stuttering auto-didacts and leather-jacketed queens from the university who speak about 'valid action' and 'revolutionary praxis'. You wouldn't like it, but somewhere there's a spirit and a cause. Both highly detrimental to the things that we disfavour. Will you come and see for yourself? Tell your brother to let me know soon what he is doing, and write to me if you have time.

Vale, B. Langley.

Fortnight sat back and tried to think about this letter. It was not Barbara's style. On the contrary, she never found reason to announce her intentions, and the deliberate childishness of the tone suggested that she wanted him (for clearly the letter was meant for him) to realize that she had something quite peculiar in mind.

He watched the Kid as he read the Colonel's scrawl. Fortnight felt sure that, from some celestial height, a cruel smile could have then been seen spreading itself like a contagion through his soul. It seemed impossible to love the monster that he was about to become, and yet nothing in him, at that moment, wished for any other fate. He began to think of spiteful, unseemly, even obscene things that he would write to Barbara. He would dwell on her wasted feelings for him. He would mention with derision the new image of party member and liberated female. He would describe with medicinal detachment what had passed at the funeral, and afterwards. He would make her hate him through love, taking elaborate vengeance for his own inability to act or feel.

The Kid interrupted his meditations with a sigh, throwing the Colonel's letter towards the open window. It fluttered to the floor, and he crushed it with his sandal.

'Passed away!' he said, 'What a phoney! Why can't he say died? Does he think he's going to hurt your feelings?'

Fortnight looked at the Kid, and tried to understand his meaning. Even in his monstrous state of mind, his soul could not detach itself from the Kid's. It wasn't love; all that had been repealed. It was rather that, despite all efforts to annihilate him, the Kid continued to thrive. He would not go away. He was unknowable, precisely because in everything he was himself.

'What are you thinking, Kid?'

'I'm thinking you're an ass.'

'Me, an ass?'

'You, that's right. Do you want to know why? I'll tell you. You believed all that cock and bull story I told you about Mummy, didn't you? Or didn't you? It doesn't matter either way, because, you see,' he went on, beginning to shout again and getting up from the bed in a state of great agitation, 'it doesn't even matter whether it's true. Nothing matters. I don't want to hear about it! She's dead, right, so she's dead. A big joke. I shall have to take a break in my studies. I shall have to divert my attention to more serious matters. And just one last thing, before I finally lose patience with you. You should never have gone to London, and you know it. You've made a mess of everything, and now you come back to disturb the solitude I was planning. It won't do!'

He had begun to stamp on the floor, in a frenzy rare for him, his limbs out of control, and sweat gathering beneath the mop of flaccid hair. Fortnight wanted to apologize. He felt sure that there were words that could convey to the Kid a deep sense of his own inadequacy. But strangely, the desire faded as soon as it had come. He found himself observing the Kid as one might a creature in a cage. The boy ceased his gyrations and began to let the tears flow in rivulets from his swollen eyes.

'Why won't you believe anything, Kenny?' he said through his sobs. 'Why can't you help me to believe things? Now I've as good as told you to go away, and I am sure you will. But you will stay? You'll promise? You must stay. You see, I am sure there's a solution.'

Fortnight muttered something. He couldn't speak. Too many images crowded into his mind. When he rehearsed the crazy yarn that the Kid had told him, it became so vivid that he too saw his mother disappearing through the door at Bramhurst Park, the bowed head of old Gilroy emanating its reassurance through the window of a downstairs room. Then this image was submerged in another. He saw himself, monstrous with borrowed activity, thrusting at the corpse of Mrs Thurlow on the bed. This second thought was so disturbing that he tried to banish it. He could not. His head ached, his body seemed to have rebelled and sunk into a bothered posture of its own.

The Kid stopped crying and suggested that they clean up the house. Fortnight nodded, and the Kid smiled a strange smile. Fortnight told him to go downstairs, saying he would join him later, and as the boy descended into the lower house he began to sing, falsetto, 'Who is Sylvia'. He paused at the line 'That all our swains commend her', and repeated it, an octave lower. Then he laughed, softly, gently, as though engaged in the most intimate conversation with someone dear to him.

This laugh, which Fortnight was to hear many times, affected him at once as something wholly new, something that had entered the Kid's repertoire as a kind of answer to the present crisis. Fortnight felt that if he could penetrate its meaning, he would know what was in his brother's heart. At the same time the thought of what the Kid really felt was terrifying, and it was not long before the laugh, as symbol of the Kid's secret, began to fill Fortnight with an uncanny premonition.

In the letter-rack on the Colonel's desk were sheets of woven paper, embossed in Gothic letters with *The Manor House, Ormley, Flackwell*. The village of Ormley had disappeared in the nineteenth century, bequeathing its church to the Parish of Flackwell; the address was really number 3, Vicarage Lane. Fortnight chose the paper in order to stimulate Barbara's hatred of social snobbery.

> *Dear Barbara,*
> *I am glad to hear that you have plans for your life, and that I am not included in them. It will interest you to know that your parents did not come to the funeral. I shall stay here, to plan the counter-revolution: do you really think that your side will win? . . .*

He stopped. He wanted to say bluntly: look at me, I cannot hurt you, because I cannot be loved. But he also wanted to hurt her. A colossal battle had to be fought, in order to make her suffer what he could not feel. He paced about the room and then tore up the letter and began again.

> *I am interested that you should be joining the Communist Party. I am sure you have the most respectable motives. You might even meet some working men. Perhaps you could introduce them to Delacroix and Courbet. It is time they understood the revolutionary potential of paint. But don't think that I mind. I have been pensioned off by the Colonel: my duties are here and now, and you can keep the future to yourself . . .*

It was of Delacroix that they had talked when first walking home. He remembered entering the Langleys' house. From the moment he passed the door he felt that some bruised part of him

was being softened and bandaged. There was an air of assuagement, a safety which reached out from the tapestries, the oatmeal
curtains, the rushwork mats and woven carpets, fingering his
tenderest parts.

'It is so nice of you to come in. And you know I don't mind the
least that you are a tiny bit drunk. I have seen you so many times
and wanted to talk to you. Does that sound forward?'

No. And anyway he wasn't drunk, only awkward: he repeated it
again in his thought, feeling how important it was to press the
point home.

'But you mustn't feel awkward. I know this house seems
precious and . . . arranged. But they made sure that nothing within
reach is seriously breakable.'

Why had it mattered so much?

'Of course it matters. Daddy, you see, is an aesthete.'

And he remembered the way she moved her hands as she said it,
seeming to type the word on the air before her. Her quick little
gesture warned him of an impossibility. She was thinking, even
then, of his future. There was no greater injustice than to pour
scorn on her, and, tearing up the letter, he walked down uneasily
into the lower house.

Slowly they picked their way through the debris, while the Kid
quietly sang.

For some reason the Kid's anecdote stuck in his mind, and always,
when he remembered it, he would be tempted to visit his mother's
haunts: the genteel coffee house in the High Street from which he
fled beneath the wan wailing of her wispy companions; the castle
gardens where she sat to meditate; the Conservative Association
jumble sale, where he incongruously purchased a bowler hat, a
copy of Wordsworth, and a set of ashtrays made from scallop
shells. Sometimes, during the course of his wanderings, he would
stop in his tracks, uttering some mindless phrase that had risen
into consciousness, or attempting to recapture a fleeting thought
that had seemed just a second earlier to explain his strange
perambulations. At other times he would be stopped by the
Colonel's friends; stockbrokers, architects, businessmen. They
would take him in their pulpy hands and stare long and manfully
out of regulation grey eyes until, observing his discomfort, they
changed the subject and invited him to a midnight sauna.

Then the day came when he could resist no longer, and he
walked the road to Bramhurst and the Fanning estate. He broke his
way through the hazel hedge into the wooded hill where once she
had taken him. She had been carrying some papers of Lord
Gilroy's, and had read them, exploding into laughter, her voice all

girlish, as though some chasm had opened and all the bells of childhood rang distantly within. 'I would recommend Her Majesty to study only after dark; it is not often realized that light refreshes the intellect and must be absorbed wherever possible through the eyes.' 'The decline in political consciousness that we have witnessed in recent times is due, not, as some would suppose, to the advance of democracy, but rather to the widespread practice among our public men of eating fish cakes and other artificially yellow substances.' Such were the former Minister's most intimate thoughts.

He sat down at the copse's edge and listened to a woodpecker hollowing the tree behind him. From this angle the house was shapeless, with the crenellated facade of the Gothic wing jutting out incongruously above a heap of gables. Outhouses and walls had been pierced at every period with contrasting apertures, and the zigzag path of the Victorian garden touched the corner, streaked off again, and rejoined the house on the other side. It looked as though a whole medieval village had been shovelled up behind a frail screen of cardboard. Beyond the house was the long row of elms flanking the drive, further still a little road which passed the gateway, and then, in the distance, a hill, the green drums of a gasworks barely visible behind. He sat at the edge of the rambling stretch of scrub, spotted with copses, which was known as The Park. It took off from the herbaceous border, petered out on one side into farmland, and was stopped dead on the other by a council estate, built on land given by a former earl to the people of Flackwell. No sound reached his ears, apart from the chunk of the woodpecker and the cooroo of a pigeon in the copse.

He took from his pocket one of his father's large cigars, and smoked it. He began to feel dizzy and his heart quickened within him. A wind sprang up and clouds spattered their moving shadows across the park. He shivered, and tried to control his thoughts. At one moment he thought he heard footsteps in the bushes behind him, and he jumped, strangely afraid. He searched the house for signs of life or movement, but there were none. The image arose of Lord Gilroy dead at his desk, a dribble of blood from his nose coagulating on his last unfinished manuscript. Then he envisaged his lordship's secretary, also dead, sitting in a leather armchair, her skeleton arms hanging at her side. He hid his head in his hands, overcome by the memory of her death.

Suddenly the silence was broken. It was nothing more than a soft 'hello', but he knew that the voice was hers. He held his taut body still and his eyes covered. She was standing behind him, had quietly tripped through the bush to where he sat. The sound of her girlish voice, its timid, plangent appeal, filled him with terror. He knew now that he was mad, madder even than the Kid; moreover there was nothing that could stop it.

'Hello.'

She sounded less timid now. There was even something proprietorial in the tone, as though she were so well settled on this land that she felt free to assert a right of ownership. He would have to open his eyes to see what she was wearing. She must have changed from her gardening clothes. Perhaps she had not recognized him, and was preparing to ask him to go. Perhaps she would vanish at once when she saw his face, before he had the chance to speak to her. He must find the right words. He must not fail.

His terror was concentrated into the effort of finding words for her. How could he, now, refrain from discussing Barbara? How could he not lay down the burden of remorse?

'Am I interrupting?'

The voice had changed again. Now it was bold, almost metallic in sound. It was not like her to speak so sharply; he could not bear it. He got up quickly and turned, wanting her to be what she had always been, wanting to look questioningly at her, and so precipitate the old self-deprecating laugh.

The woman who was standing at the edge of the copse was his mother, as she might have been some fifteen years before. Her neat hair and blue eyes, her pale and slightly freckled features, and most of all her mouth, full at the centre, disappearing into a Leonardine *sfumato* in the folds of the cheeks: all these were Jennie Fortnight's. So too was the motionless way of standing, and the frozen expression, which seemed to be waiting for the imprint of another's will. But there were points of difference. His mother would never have made the error of taste embodied in the yellow tweed suit; nor would she have carried about her person so many jewels and ornaments, certainly not a gunmetal pendant of Hollywood Aztec design.

It was some time before Fortnight could speak, but she waited patiently for his words, slowly narrowing her eyes. His mother would never have narrowed her eyes while looking at someone, nor would she have been quite so self-possessed before a stranger.

'I'm sorry,' he said at last. 'I rather think I'm trespassing.'

'If you apologize, it's because you rather think I'm not.'

She spoke slowly, distinctly, softly. The voice was entirely confident now, and Fortnight admired its cadence.

'I think I know you,' he said. 'I think you are Susan Fanning. We played croquet once and you beat me by a mile.'

'Susan Waterford. I've been married for seven years. You must have been a babe in arms. Whose, I wonder?'

'I'm Kenneth Fortnight, the son of . . .'

'Oh, the Colonel.'

So she did not remember his mother. Always it was the Colonel who made his mark. But there was a degree of uninterest in her voice that suggested that the mark had not been made on Lady Susan. To his surprise she came towards him, walking with the familiar girlish step, and smiling openly.

'Now I do remember you. You were the best person I ever did play croquet with: the only one that I ever beat. I think that qualifies you to stay.'

She indicated a log where they could sit. Her eyes became fixed on a point slightly beyond his head. He described his impressions of her father's house, with a vigour that in no way corresponded to what he could remember. He felt that he was pouring out all his pent up emotions, even though he described only a dim staircase, a great hall, and a long drawing-room with sheeted furniture and the blinds drawn down. She had been eighteen when they met: he remembered the butler bringing tea on to the lawn, and the Kid being convinced that the great silver teapot contained a bird.

'It was almost the last time I lived here,' she put in. 'I got married soon afterwards and went to London.'

She told him that she had worked with a fringe theatre group, acting small parts, but that really she wanted to write plays of her own. Did he like the theatre? Did he know people in that world?

'Yes,' he said, for there were friends of Barbara's who acted — perhaps there was one, a hairy sentimentalist, who claimed to write. But he had never entered that world; he had left it to Barbara. Lady Susan did not question him further, and seemed to drop the subject. Perhaps she too had met with failure and was seeking to hide the truth.

They talked of Flackwell, and of the changes there. Slowly he steered the conversation round so that he felt that he could mention the calamity that had brought him home. He had just broached the subject, feeling, though not knowing why, absurdly confident, and forgetting for the moment all the impossibilities that seemed to surround him, when, quite suddenly, she jumped to her feet and looked at him, holding a hand to her forehead.

'Look,' she said, 'it must be eleven at least. Let's go down to the house for coffee.'

Abruptly she swung on her heel and made down the path, without waiting for him to get up or accept the invitation. The gesture amazed and disconcerted him, but he admired it too. This was the saving egoism that he was seeking, and which always slipped his grasp.

'Will your father mind?' he asked, catching up with her.

'My father? But there's no need to see *him*.'

She laughed. Birds were singing in the garden, and a border of sweet-smelling herbs ran beside the path. Lady Susan reached out and snatched the spikes of a bush of rosemary. She held some out to him.

'This is what I'd have all our cooking taste of, if it was up to me.'

'Your husband doesn't like it?'

'I mean our family cooking. My father loathes the stuff. He loathes everything cosmopolitan, everything modern. Cooking with herbs he considers a sign of degeneracy, like long hair, printed T-shirts, and pinewood chairs. He would like you, because you wear a waistcoat and a pocket watch.'

Until she said this, Fortnight had not noticed his dress. He wondered whose was the waistcoat: certainly not his. And whose the pocket watch? He wanted to take it out and examine it; but he felt that there was derision in her tone and it would be better to affect a complete acquaintance with his own habits.

'The watch, I admit, is a little anomalous. But you see, it was given to me by a lady friend.'

She stared at him. 'Most people would have said, "a girl".'

He felt more uncomfortable. 'Yes, but it sounds so commonplace. I prefer to be utterly characteristic of myself.'

She looked at him, a light of cold assessment in her eyes. He was struck by her beauty, by the well-ordered Englishness of her pose, and by the sober dominion that she was beginning to exert in his emotions. She turned away and pointed to a door that opened from the wing of the house on to the garden.

'This is where we go in. Thank God Poppa has got rid of his political connections. The place contains no pie-eyed aspirants, no lecherous newscasters. Now that Poppa is so eccentric the house has returned to — to what it was. It became impossible for them in the end. It wasn't that he started to analyse and qualify the party slogans, though that was strange enough. Or even that he chose to explain the whole course of politics in terms of his theory of colours. What upset them was his complete indifference to policy. He spoke two hundred times in the House during a single session, and never showed the slightest interest in what to do. And each time it was only about trees. Poor Poppa: he has never understood that the centre cannot hold.'

As she spoke she conducted him quickly through a dark hall of Jacobean panelling, crowded with portraits in oils. A little door led off it into a small drawing room in the front of the house, in which Empire furniture stood on a pale Aubusson carpet. The light entered through tall windows to fall on a thousand functionless objects, to shiver into coloured fragments in a Venetian chandelier, and to scatter itself over a bowl of spring flowers that stood on the central table. They seemed rare and extravagant; early lilies poked their petals through shrouds of green, and bearded irises were scattered through the bouquet, some claret-coloured, with hairy scarlet tongues, others deep sienna or railway brown, with drooping petals and mouldering dust-covered hearts. Fortnight became lost in wonder, and when he raised his eyes to Lady Susan it was with a sense of utter submission to the mocking sexuality that had come to inhabit her face.

She reached across him as he settled by the fire. He thought that she was going to ruffle his hair; in fact it was to press a little brass button beside the marble fireplace, and so set a bell ringing somewhere behind green baize doors.

'I like you,' he said, just as the maid came in with coffee. She looked at him without the slightest trace of wonder.

'Good,' she said when the maid had left. 'That's as it should be.'

'I was afraid you'd think me impertinent.'

She laughed. 'Silly boy! You don't, I imagine, take after your father.'

'My father?'

'Oh well, you know, he was a friend of my mother's at one time. At least, his name was mentioned in that connection.'

Fortnight felt an impulse of distaste.

'I doubt, you know, that your mother would have known him well. He is an extremely disagreeable man.'

'But Mummy was an extremely disagreeable woman. It sounds like a perfect match.'

He got up and went to the window, to stare at the damp lawn with its fruit of crumbling statuary, lit by a yellow sun. On this side the sash windows descended to the floor, and the grass almost brushed against them. He thought of his mother, and her attachment to this place. She would have helped him now — but how could he lean his head on the picked ribs of a lifeless thing? How could they expect him to do that? He became suddenly angry.

'You sound like you're trying to find out my weak spot,' he declared.

'Now you *are* being impertinent.'

He turned. She was smiling at him.

'Well, you have the knack of making one feel foolish.'

'Not at all. You have the knack of feeling it.'

'Do you mean that kindly?'

'Of course I do, Kenneth. May I call you that? I like you too.'

'I wonder why.'

'These things don't have a reason. Have some coffee.'

She came close to him with the cup. She was entirely unruffled, as though she neither wanted nor did not want his company, nor any other thing. Everything was up to him. When, in taking the cup, he touched her, letting his hand rest for a moment against hers, she stood still, making no attempt either to encourage or to repulse him. It was as though inadvertently he had touched on a button that brought her to a halt. A look came into her eyes, like that of a child who does not know what is wanted. He withdrew his hand and sat down by the marble chimney. As he moved away she wrinkled her lip and lowered her eyes; he wondered whether it was by chance that her stare then faltered.

Fortnight described himself. He invented a life on the 'outsider' basis, his hands held low between his knees in a routine parody of awkwardness. There were trips as a merchant seaman to the Cape, and subsequent dealings in the East End, with a shipment of rotting fruit. The villain of those proceedings — one 'Oily Platter' whose reputation for taking the best of a deal was matched only by the fear with which the criminal community contemplated his invariable sense of outrage — was the very same Mr Platt who had brought Fortnight's career as a composer to an end, by eloping with the woman upon whom he depended. As the story developed, with the wan complicity of his better judgement, Fortnight imposed a strict discipline on his hands, which had become fascinated by the pocket watch. They were anxious to explore its properties. Perhaps it was gold. Perhaps it was an heirloom. Lady Susan, who had passed her thirty years in comparative ignorance of the banana trade, but whose sexuality seemed normal enough to be aroused by the savour of crime, listened to him with pale and mealy features. Seeing her half believing him, he half believed as well. If it were not for the enigma of the pocket watch, he thought, he would get through to the end with no problem at all to speak of. One of Barbara's friends had met Ezra Pound in Venice, and told of the sunken eyes, the shrivelled skin, the vacant expression of the extinguished poet. Fortnight mentioned this detail. It was important to realize that a merchant seaman can change ships in quite interesting places, and get to know the best and worst among people there. He described the particular balcony, the view over the Grand Canal, with the pennants of shadow fluttering beneath the water skin, and the yellow light of evening on the Salute's dome. He recalled the poet failing to recite some lines that he had often translated, turning to spit on to the head of a passing gondolier. This was a happy observation because it led her to discuss the works of Pound. Lady Susan seemed to have no conversation except about literature. Once she had fallen into her routine he could relax in the chair and watch her lips with varieties of sincere concern. It was a large watch, with an engraved back. Could it have been Uncle Jonathan's? Or his maternal grandfather's? It would depend on its being silver or gold.

Lady Susan complained of Pound's obsession with the trivia of dead occasions. Dark millet, Tchang wine for the sacrifice. What could it signify? On the contrary, said Fortnight, and you could see it in the poet's face all red against the yellow dome, chewing liplessly, hoping for words, it was that which was most important. Fragments, each of them hinting at its own completeness. So many images of fulfilment. Couldn't some of it rub off on us? She began to interrupt him. The watch was gold, with a rococo pattern engraved on its back.

'You see,' said Lady Susan, 'there are some people coming for lunch. I shall have to get ready. Can we meet again? Can I ring you? Yes? That would be nice. I shall look forward to it.'

She left him at the entrance to the drawing-room, indicating the door. Was that normal in this house? As he walked across the hall his steps faltered on the marble, and he felt again that someone was watching him. He turned. The door was already closed. Were those his mother's eyes again, china blue and varnished, framed against the panelling? Why had he told such lies?

A door opened among the bookcases, and Fortnight started. A figure came stooping from beneath the lintel, its head bowed beneath fine white hair. The scene was etched out with light like a Rembrandt; a bald patch glowed redly among the ashy streaks, and flakes of light fell across simulated bindings in the door. The old man wore slippers, a woollen waistcoat, baggy trousers and a polka-dotted scarf. He looked at Fortnight for a while and then smiled in a kindly, apologetic sort of way. He had the slightly ruffled manner of someone who, working alone for the betterment of mankind, is surprised to discover an example of the species. Fortnight remembered again his mother's descriptions of Lord Gilroy, who lived in the slack backwater of his self-inflicted isolation, rocking slightly from the wash of far-off politics, but for the most part disturbed only when he shifted his moorings from library to dining-room and then from dining-room to library. Fortnight began to apologize, having presented such an inescapable obstacle to his lordship's passage through the shallows. But Lord Gilroy forestalled him, narrowing his eyes in just the way that Susan had done.

'I believe you are Jennie Fortnight's son. Yes, that's who you are. As a matter of fact, although I don't know why you are here, I confess to you that you couldn't have come at a better time. I have put together the first volume of the manuscripts.'

'Oh.'

'Yes. Quite a business. I wondered, perhaps you would be so
good as to take it to your mother? She is one of those who follow my
thought processes, I really do need her help. I wouldn't want many
people to see it at this stage. There is a chapter on the colour green
for example, I finished it last week, and . . . your mother, she would
know how to improve it, to correct it . . .'

Fortnight studied the contents of the bookshelves beside the
door. His attention was caught by a large folio of the *Annales et
Historiae* by Grotius, marked 'Amsterdam, 1657'. His greatest wish
at that moment was to take it down and open it. To prevent this
catastrophe, he forced his eyes sideways into Baedekers, Army
Lists, Debrett's Peerage and Baronetage for 1950, and another folio
volume marked 'Fanning Accounts, Domestic, 1858-1862'. He
became aware that the old man was silent, watching him.

'My mother is dead.'

'But of course,' said the earl at once. 'How could I have forgotten? My dear chap! And all these months gone by. So sorry that
we missed the funeral. Abroad I'm afraid. Some manuscripts in
Romania. Such a sweet nature. Terrible business. How could I,
I, . . . most distressing . . .'

There was another shelf, this time of Camden Society books,
Burlington's magazine, isolated copies of Hansard, and Hals-
bury's Statutes. Then, lower down, the Eton School register, the
Eton school lists, *An Eton Anthology, Musae Etoniensis, 1869,* Sir
Edward Creasy's *Memoirs of Eminent Etonians*, Chattock's
Sketches of Eton. On the very bottom shelf, tempting and touch-
able, stood huge folio volumes of the Church fathers, their nut-
coloured spines glowing with neat's foot oil. When he looked up
again Fortnight saw a cunning gleam in Lord Gilroy's eye.

'I am sure you will find it odd of me to say this and I do hope that
you will take it as it is meant, which is that we don't now understand these things, death for example, and it is only one very small
example, we don't understand them as we should. They have an
illusory quality, I think that is the word I am looking for. I don't
refer specifically to your mother. But there. Very odd of me, and I
can only apologize.'

There was a pause while Fortnight avoided the fixed grey eyes.

'But you wouldn't know, would you, of someone else, someone
discreet, sensitive, like your mother, someone who . . . ? No? I
suspected as much. It is so difficult. I suppose there is nothing to be
done. How *silly* of me to have forgotten, I do hope you will come
again. Another time, when I am a little less busy. My daughter likes
you, you know. She likes you very much. I am sure of it. Goodbye,
and thank you so much!'

Lord Gilroy moved on with a half completed wave. Fortnight

went out through heavy doors held by a single latch. The west wind was piling up clouds above Bramhurst Hill, and the spire of the valley church pointed unwaveringly into the dizzy heart of them.

Fortnight had set the rice to boil and gathered into a single pan tomatoes, onions, herbs and madeira with which to make a sauce. Slices of ham lay ready on the dresser and doughy wads of white bread steamed beneath the grill. He took the spare set of keys from the ice-box and plunged them into hot water. There were keys to the house, to the potting-shed, and to the garden gate. But no key to the cellar. He made his way with patient gestures down the steps. As he began to kick, with uncertain movements, at the cellar door, he heard the Kid's uncanny, intimate-seeming laugh. Soon he was standing behind him.

'There is something amateur in your performance. Look, retire for a while. Let me stage-manage this. I have a deeper feeling for melodrama.'

Fortnight moved slowly backwards, and then the Kid, bundled up like a rugby player, launched himself from the third stone step towards the door. It gave way and he fell among the bottles chattering.

'Revolutionary Guards Storm the Winter Palace! Long shot of Guard with peasant features contemptuously breaking a cellar door. Close-up of same. A faint smile suffuses his noble features. Cut to close-up of second Guard, with depraved expression, eyes aghast . . .'

'Where should we start, Kid?'

'He used to keep the older stuff on the left. That means we go from left to right. He has a very linear mind.'

Fortnight took down two bottles from the left hand row.

'Château Beychevelle 1950', he read out slowly.

'Long shot of second guard, idiot face opening in a leer of anticipatory greed. Sudden cut to first guard, handsome features restrained and disapproving. "We will content ourselves with that", he says. "Although it was not such a very good year".'

'Why don't you get up?'

'My God Kenny, that's a corker! You are quite right. I *am* still lying on the floor.'

As the brown-coloured wine sped from the bottleneck its perfume rose to fill the room, annotating his thoughts with trite but pretty maxims, lending shine to sluggish dissipations, changing their gestures into a simulacrum of domestic life. Fortnight smiled at his brother, sniffed deeply in his glass, and then mentioned casually the third place at table. The Kid replaced the sheet of ham in its bath of orange sauce.

'It is a very strange remark that you have just made.'

His eyes shifted a little in their sea of opalescent lights, and his mouth remained open in admonition of this new *bêtise*. Fortnight drank deeply, closed his eyes, and lay still on the surface of wine.

'Yes,' he said at last. 'It is. Very strange.'

The Kid passed the plate to his brother, and sat down.

'I think I should speak to you seriously, Kenny. We are, if you want to know, in what Fist would call desperate straits. It struck me today: *at me tum primum saevus circumstetit horror*. Yes and *obstipui* too. Who wouldn't when the form of their father so-called rises before them? Enough to give anyone the jim-jams. Did you know the bugger telephoned? No you didn't know. I put the phone down. I fear his absence may be only temporary.'

'Is that all you are worrying about?'

'Isn't it enough? In any case, it isn't all. Ever since you went away things have been bad. Our civilization apparently is on the brink of disaster. Law and order are passing from the land. I wonder if you read the statistics in this morning's *Times?* No of course you didn't. Are you acquainted with the Labour Party's plan for education, or the Town Council's decision to allow houses on Wenbury Hill? No, of course you're not. You know as much about these things as about the Musician's Welfare Fund, or the Dutch Reformed Church, to name only two. In fact I would go so far as to say that you are wholly cut off from reality, perhaps even to the point of being mentally disturbed. This would explain many things. For example, your watch-chain. You are not going to say that there is a watch on the end of it. . . .'

Fortnight interrupted him. 'I went to Bramhurst today.'

The Kid, who had begun a series of compulsive movements, continued them for a few seconds, flagging out the news of revolution on the outstretched fingers of his large right hand. Then he stared at his brother silently.

'I went to the Park in fact. I met Lady Susan. And even — well, I met Lady Susan. She was very nice. We talked. About many things.'

The Kid made a little explosion.

'Does this have anything to do with me, I ask myself? Does my brother have some secret reason for intruding on my peace of mind? My few little pieces of mind?'

'No, I suppose not.'

'Them's my sentiments. Shall we open another bottle? After all, school starts tomorrow and I need to get pissed. Who is Lady Susan anyway? Could it be that you have been reading books?'

'Oh, just a daughter of old Gilroy's. I think there's another daughter too.'

'The existence of this other daughter is a great relief. Perhaps you will introduce us.'

There was a long silence. Fortnight noticed that the grandfather clock had stopped.

'We should wind up the clock,' he said.

The Kid laughed softly. 'No. I plan to have everything motionless in this house. It will take about two weeks. Go on about Lady Susan.'

'There's nothing to tell.'

'Then this whole conversation has been of an irrelevance remarkable even for you. Shall I tell you what I did? I delivered a speech.'

'A speech?'

'Yes. To the electors of Flackwell. Oh, not many of them. About twenty all told. Under the Cornmarket. A handy place for politics.'

Fortnight looked pensively at his brother, and saw that he was speaking the truth.

'Tell me more.'

'I was about to. The subject matter was "The Principles of Speculation in Real Estate". It was mostly fairly abstract, in the manner of Miss Langley. You know, the condition of labour under capitalism, exploitation, accumulation, the idea of common land. But then I got down to details. I was quite good re Wenbury Hill. You know it's one of Fist's little projects. If there had been a better attendance, and say one or two civic dignitaries, I think I might have swayed them. Then he wouldn't have an icicle's chance in Hell.'

'What were you trying to achieve?'

'Amusement. Said to be a harmless emotion. I wonder if you ever tried it? Also, to tell you the truth, I was rather hoping to get arrested.'

'Why?'

'Oh. Just a little plan I had.'

Fortnight left the table and went to the piano in the laughing-room. It was pleasant then, to remember that he was not mad. The proof lay in his meeting with Lady Susan, and in the proprietary interest that he now felt towards Bramhurst Park, and which he had heard in his mother's voice as she addressed him from the edge of the copse. Of course it had really been Lady Susan speaking; moreover the logic of his feeling was in certain other respects unsatisfactory. But on the whole and all things considered it was an encouraging sign. The Kid came in and told him to tickle the ivories with his fingers and not his feet; this made Fortnight think of the solicitor.

'What would you feel about a boarding school, Kid?'

'I would *prefer* prison, if it's all the same to you.'

Those were the last words that the Kid spoke to his brother, before their lives had been scattered and rearranged like pieces on a chess-board.

Of all the ghostly presence which the Kid's now almost silent laughter created, it was the Colonel who took precedence. He was king, minister and champion under the law of ghosts. He owed this virtue largely to the tactics of surprise. The implied involvement with Lady Gilroy was a small matter. Much else began to emerge. The Kid was adept in the art of discovery, and did not trouble to raise an eyebrow: it was sufficient to lay the evidence silently before his brother and wait for Fortnight to express astonishment for both of them. All the chests and boxes in the house could now be opened, every door held ajar, every threshold crossed where childhood had wondered and stood still. Fortnight wanted no part in it; he hated attics, box-rooms, the dust of discarded things. But the Kid needed no permission. Photographs of women appeared at the breakfast table, women whom they did not know, or did not quite remember, or about whose features an air of familiarity lingered, marking them as subjects of that kingdom where the Colonel reigned. Documents proved the Colonel's part in the development of Flackwell, in the projects for Wenbury Hill, in the establishment of a Marina on the West Midlands Canal. Others referred to a bankruptcy order dated two years previously, and spoke in masonic language of projects too secret to be legal. A collection of delft was unearthed from beneath the rockery and left by the Kid to speak for itself on the tablecloth. Fortnight recognized it as something whose loss his mother had often bewailed after the move from Blackett's. Some of the finds were less explicable: the buried Colt 45, the collection of flamboyant female clothes in taffeta and printed silk, the rolled-up handkerchief full of a colourless substance that smelled like snuff.

The Kid's silence about these and all other matters was exemplary. On the third day, Fortnight decided that it would be good to be angry. He found it difficult to be angry with his brother, and his momentary experiments in exasperation seldom succeeded. But it seemed almost as though a principle were at stake. Returning late from St Stephen's, carrying a jar of tadpoles, the Kid offered him the occasion. Once, at Blackett's, Fortnight had caught a lugubrious look of his mother's from the window where she sat, and became instantly aware of the barrier that had formed between them. He too had been carrying tadpoles, with just the air of precarious care for nature that the Kid struggled to simulate in jerky flickers of his arm. That was the first time that Fortnight had needed to interpret her features. Had this barrier come suddenly, or was he becoming aware of something that had always been there? Her face forbade him to question. She was withdrawn into some unfathomable ultimity, a bottomless abyss, where her mind darkly circled in the same protracted orbit of unthinkingness. He sensed an identical abstraction in himself. It came as a taste in the mouth, a fatigue, a hollowness: under its influence his whole experience changed. The afternoon by the pond, watching the brown insects on the water, the yellow turds of refuse nibbled by unseen mouths, the slimy edges where the tadpoles flicked their tails: the comfort of this was gone. The very smell was different, as though the gas which broke in bubbles was infected by a corpse. The completeness gave way, showing his existence as merely provisional. He had never possessed the love which would complete it. The effect was wordless, a simple impression of his mother's face in the kitchen window. But her ghost was now useful. He snatched the tadpoles from the Kid and emptied them on the grass. He saw them wriggle and die: now the world was *this* way. He smiled at his display of anger. The Kid stared mournfully, made the sign of the cross over the dying creatures, and then silently ascended through the house. Their mother's ghost returned to her place in the queue.

On the fourth day Lady Susan rang. She expressed surprise that he had not been in touch with her, and at once Fortnight began to feel guilty, as though he had broken a promise. He accepted (protestingly) her invitation to lunch, feeling he had no right. Whether it was this event, or whether it was the Kid's sudden return from school in mid-morning, tears flowing down his cheeks, or whether it was some other episode altogether unrelated to these, such as the milkman calling for money, or the arrival of a letter from Barbara which he at first left unopened on the floor and then, when the Kid returned, hid behind the poetry books in the hall — whatever it was, Fortnight decided that he must confront the Colonel's absence.

He was not surprised to find that this exercise should begin with a visit to his bedroom, although who was radiating the orders he did not know. He was comforted to find that everything had become wholly unfamiliar. Even the naive aquatint of Blackett's which his mother had composed, and later framed in an imitation tortoiseshell mount intended for a photograph, seemed out of place. He felt that had the photograph (which he had never seen, and which perhaps had never existed) been there, he might have belonged in the room. As it was, he turned his back on it with a smile of valediction. He went to her own room, smelt the smell of dust and the lingering aroma of female things. When he tried to imagine his last experience here, he recalled only the Colonel, striding across in his dressing-gown, his hands trembling with a simulated anger and his eyes aglow. Bit by bit he armed himself for the struggle. Finding the Kid silent in the laughing-room, he announced to him in a steady voice and with crisp military phrases the order of the day. It was not his own voice, but it served.

'I'm going to see that man Oddle. I'm going to sort things out. You're not happy at St Stephen's. I'm not happy here. We shall have to make a move. I shall find out what is possible, and then report back. You stay here. Right?'

The Kid rolled his melancholy eyes upwards and slid from the canapé on to the floor. His mouth quivered and his large pale hands slipped along the carpet.

Once announced, the decision could be made. Fortnight was no longer surprised by the accumulated evidence of perfidy; he looked at the pile of objects on the kitchen table with mingled distaste and satisfaction. They provided reasons for his move. The Colonel, who had intended surprise, was to be overcome by detachment. It was in this spirit that Fortnight left the house to begin his mission. The centre of Flackwell had gone. He was forced to weave towards Prince's Tower through an arcade of plate-glass shop fronts, listening to music and birdsong piped through hidden speakers in the potted palms. Fortnight remained indifferent to this, and ascended by the stairs to the fourteenth floor of the block which spoiled the view from his mother's window, so as to prolong the feeling of serenity and watch from the windows of each landing the pink and sienna houses spreading towards Wenbury Hill.

Even Mr Oddle did not unnerve him, strange though it was, entering the office of carpet and steel, to find only a young man in a calypso shirt lying on the floor with his hands behind his head and the telephone ringing beside him. The Colonel paid close attention to detail in campaigns of this kind. Oddle's claim not to have heard of Colonel Fortnight aroused as little immediate interest as the story — which the solicitor rose to his feet to deliver — of a client who had screwed a twelve-year old groupie after a rave-up in Wembley Stadium and was now doing porridge in the Scrubs. After ten minutes of impassive staring, Fortnight moved Oddle to extract a file from under the desk. It was empty, but it bore the name of Fortnight. Oddle was of the opinion that a letter had arrived; soon he had discovered among the disordered papers on his desk a short note from a hotel in Biarritz, in which the Colonel pointed out that there were *two* sons involved, and that income from a specific account was to be used only for the school fees of the one who was mentally deranged. This reminded Oddle of another client, who, after a bad trip, had eaten five hundred one-pound notes and then attempted to drown an old lady in the fountain. It had been in all the papers, on account of the fountain containing no water; had Fortnight not read about it? Dr Holtius had come in as witness for the prosecution, saying that he could find no sign of insanity. Of course everyone knew that Holtius was a fraud and a grass, and it was surprising to find instructions from Biarritz to pay whatever fees the doctor should require. Oddle became excited, and began to dribble on to his chin. Drops of saliva fell from the wispy beard into the crevice of his shirt, watering a golden pendant of Elvis Presley. He stormed about the room, upsetting papers and chairs, angrily describing all Dr Holtius's mannerisms, his affected culture and pretended wisdom, his lust for power, his stuffy attitudes and effeminate appearance, his tireless withering smile. Suddenly Oddle stared at Fortnight and asked 'Who are you?', as though seeing him for the first time. Fortnight received Oddle's apology with elaborately graceful gestures. The solicitor had had a bad scene with Holtius; he apologized again for firing off. He went so far as to offer Fortnight a job as conveyancing clerk, which was accepted, despite suspicion that it was part of the Colonel's plan. As he walked away from Prince's Tower, through barren spaces with concrete fountains raised above pools of slime, Fortnight summarized the evidence. It amounted to little. His father was abroad, there was no money to support him, and a court action would be necessary to place the Kid in care. Observing Oddle's failure to confuse him, Fortnight had felt a kind of strength. Once, staring from a window at St Stephen's School, he had seen a fat lady in a red jumper at a bus stop. He had studied her movements. They seemed both random and predictable. He had felt an upsurge of power; so too in observing the Colonel's natty little doll did he feel completely unthreatened by its movements. Moreover, in discovering the hopelessness of his predicament Fortnight began to feel free. Here at least the Colonel had extinguished his traces.

One of the Elizabethan houses in the High Street had been spared. It was the studio where a gentle photographer had lived with his model. The angle of those wide windows was such that, looking up at them from the street, you could see only glimpses of the life within. Dark shadows slipped behind the leaded glass like fish in a murky sea. Sometimes, when the sun struck from behind the clouds, a golden fire rose up in the apex of each panel, spreading as you approached, until every square of lead enclosed a dancing flame. He observed the effect, and smiled with pleasure.

The next step was to make love to Lady Susan. The idea struck him with such vivacity as he surveyed the photographer's windows, that he forgot to make a note of the reasons that supported it. All his sentiments rushed to the idea of conquest, like disordered troops heartened by the appearance of their chief. As he arrived home the sun again burst through a bank of cloud, irradiating the house and lingering in the bubbles of the fanlight. Soon he would be leaving here, and it did not matter that the fish and vegetables which he carried were all his remaining fortune. He went through to the garden. Language contained no meanings that would weigh its grade of reality. Everything in it seemed to be struggling for a completion that could not be defined. The patch of nettles had smothered the remaining herbs: soon you would not be able to see beyond it to the vicarage. The Kid's wooden chair sat unattended in a flood of vegetation, and even the oldest trees were beginning to struggle into complexities of leaf. The thought of Susan mingled with all this life and power. As he sank into the bath, hearing the good sound of water swishing in the tank, he rehearsed the possibilities which her seduction made available. Fortnight the victor stood somewhere on the path of time, flashing his sword in triumph, looking back over ordeals survived. The barrister played the part well, driving back rivals with a shower of brilliant words, gathering money in heaps from grateful clients, penetrating the mysteries of sin and crime, and finding on the underside of every human weakness a precious crock of gold. The professional dandy, the sly civil servant, the unmoved minister: all these stood behind him, and, somewhere in the distance Fortnight discerned a quiet novelist, recording in precise and poignant imagery the recondite struggle of his earlier years, ennobling suffering, redeeming time.

The sun poured in through the window, playing in the steam above the bath. His thoughts, having sheered against the side of true ambition, now shivered into coloured fragments and floated before his mind. He lay supine in the bows of a long canoe, as native boys steered him between clustering swamp weeds, a green shade round about him, monkeys chattering in the boughs above. He was astride a rough pony, the blue wind of the steppes endlessly sighing in the tufts of knotted grass, a wild Tartar picking old teeth at his side. His hand rested on the gunwale of a chugging boat, putting into port on a sun-drenched island; young widows eyed him from the shore, and fishermen looked up as they beat the live octopus lazily on the quay.

The Kid, who had been happy in Greece, interrupted Fortnight's ruminations. He seemed not to be home from school. Fortnight was surprised at the anxiety which this thought caused in him; as though he were still fighting to protect his younger brother from the bullies and teases who had once flocked about him like chattering crows. Soon he was running about the house again, with a renewed sense of its power to detain him. In the Kid's room the relics were beginning to accumulate. Many of Mrs Fortnight's boxes, jewels and scarves were arranged on the chest of drawers. Her favourite books — from *Little Women* to *Yoga for Everyman* — stood next to Ovid and Virgil on the shelves beside the window. The room had the air of a *proseuche*: it seemed as though one should kneel at the little desk, and bow one's head before the photograph of the family at Weymouth, now stuck with sellotape to the wall. The Colonel's figure had been eliminated with scissors, leaving only the dismembered hand which clutched eerily at their mother's shoulder. As he turned to leave, disturbed by that angry hand, Fortnight trod on something soft. He recoiled in disgust. It was another hand, this time the Kid's, which protruded from beneath the bed. Like a wounded creature it curled itself slowly, tremblingly, and then slowly, painfully, uncurled. A slight hissing noise accompanied its tortured movements. Fortnight went out quickly and closed the door.

He awoke late, with a dim memory of hearing his brother leave for school. He was light-headed, and nothing resided for long in the bubble of his mind, save only the thought of Lady Susan. After he had seduced her he would read all the books in her father's library, and — and yes, he realized, as he galloped past Barbara's house, he would devote himself to the *petits soins* of social intercourse, and to the refinement of his literary style. He would write the Colonel into non-existence, and then retire to linger on life's vine-wreathed margins.

She met him at the door of the house. With exemplary daring he kissed her cheek, and smelt her fuchsia-laden smell. The flesh was taut and unyielding; he bounced back like a figure on a trampoline. The hall doused him with the odour of daffodils, hyacinths and beeswax polish, and from somewhere far behind the green baize door came the deep vocables of a Neapolitan voice.

> *Dormirò sol', nel' manto mio regal',*
> *Quando la mia giornata è giunt'à sera.*

'I saw you on the drive,' she said.

'Ah.'

He wondered what he had looked like on the drive. It had been a mistake to pause by the laburnum-tree; nor should he have twittered at the robin, although the Kid had taught him how delightful it is to speak to animals. A faint smile played along her lips as she observed him.

'Do you know,' he remarked anxiously, 'you remind me of someone?'

'Oh?' Lady Susan's interest seemed to focus in a rush, as though every cell in her body had turned in his direction.

'Someone I knew.'

'Would I have liked her?'

'I think so.'

She relaxed and a vague faint smile replaced the temporary intent. As she closed the outer door he watched her unhurried actions. Her body possessed the space in which it moved. His own position could only be regarded as provisional; he held it in trust for the time when she would displace him. He had the impression, as they proceeded across the hallway, that she continuously edged him backwards from one unauthorized hold-out to the next. With every word and gesture she seemed to limit his being, and to remind him of the temporary nature of her interest.

From the three great windows of the dining-room there was a view towards the copse where they had met. A grandfather clock ticked against one wall, and the dark encrusted portraits seemed to speak in monotonous unison with its voice. A spirit lamp sputtered and flared on the sideboard, bubbling the soup in a silver tureen. A gong sounded somewhere and a maid with pinched unfriendly features came sideways in a black apron through the door. As the maid served them with soup, Lady Susan asked a question. Fortnight was so surprised by it that he could not grasp its meaning.

'My brother? How on earth do you know him?'

'I don't. You mentioned him, if you remember, the other day.'

'Did I? In what connection?'

'I forget. But I saw the article in yesterday's *Courier*.'

'The *Flackwell Courier*?'

Fortnight watched his reflection redden in a polished silver pepper-pot. Every highlight in the room caught the glow of his embarrassment; he had the sense of being squeezed out of this anciently occupied domain, into some darkly wooded periphery where he bayed among shabby masses of his kind.

'You didn't see it? An amusing little paragraph entitled "A new name in local politics". Apparently he gave a speech under the Cornmarket. I assumed you must have been there.'

Fortnight looked at Lady Susan with a careful imitation of old-world melancholy and dignified distress. She reached out at once to take his hand.

'Have I upset you? I am sorry. I am so clumsy; of course you don't want to speak about it.'

On the contrary, it was the topic he had prepared; a black pattern of unhappiness had been daintily etched along the steel of his conspiracy. But he said nothing. She continued to hold his hand, looking with soft expertise into his simulated eyes, while reaching with her free arm to press a button under the table. The distant Neapolitan, who had kept up his doleful sonorities through the soup, was suddenly extinguished. Fortnight raised Lady Susan's hand towards his lips. A diamond-mounted topaz rode upwards on her middle finger, and so large was it that he was forced to enclose it in his lips. He had the absurd image of Lady Susan as prelate, trailing her ring to a pious following. The door opened and a golden quiche on a silver plate conducted the maid towards them. Fortnight let go of Lady Susan's hand; only by a quick spasm of her arm did she arrest its progress towards his half-finished bowl of soup.

'No. You haven't. I . . .'

He stopped. The food was served, the maid withdrawn by whatever strings and levers were used to control her. They stared at each other in silence, and despite the mounting palpitations of an embarrassment that threatened to silence him completely, he knew the battle was won. Lady Susan was now in charge, and had her own reasons for submitting to him. She had issued him a licence to talk about his brother. For dramatic effect he made the illness recent, and found words from his scattered reading with which to render its incurability particularly sad. He demolished many popular superstitions about mania, depression, schizophrenia and sleeping sickness. He made a great point of the unimpaired individuality of the helpless victim, and, drawing on the stock characters of the psychoanalytic comic strips, he gave a plausible rendering of the oedipal ur-scene. He invented an episode in which the Kid had prophesied the Colonel's next adventure. The Kid pursued the woman with wild lunatic gestures, deflecting her from uncertain purposes. Fortnight's narrative concluded with an impressive tableau of the Kid's new silence. He emphasized the hand that curled and uncurled beneath the bed with such fastidious attention to detail that Lady Susan set down her fork and stared out of blue beneficent baptismal eyes that invited him to bathe.

As he reached for her hand Lord Gilroy entered, reading. He nodded to them absent-mindedly, took a piece of Caerphilly from the sideboard and shuffled, chewing slowly, towards the door. Then he paused, turned towards Fortnight, and lowered his book. His moist grey eyes flickered with intense emotion.

'My dear Mr Fortnight,' he exclaimed. 'You must excuse me. I have just heard. Your poor mother. It is too awful. What a fine woman: so gentle, so delicate. Ours is no age for, for . . . I shall always remember her particular way of sitting, her sweet smile, her — how shall I put it? — her ease with the world. And her extraordinary comments. Such an observer, such insight. Do you remember, Susan, the way she summed up that vicar at Flackwell, the enlightened one, what's his name, Appleton? Clothes without an emperor, those were her words. Wasn't that splendid? Poor woman. After such an illness, a mercy. But sad, terribly sad. You have my sympathy. I can say no more.'

The earl slid at once past the mahogany door, balancing book and cheese in one hand, and rapidly pulling the ivory knob in his wake, so as to forestall riposte. Fortnight turned to Susan, his intentions in disarray.

'Is he mad or what? My mother was — well, whatever she was, she was not a woman of insight. In fact she was downright commonplace. Does that shock you?'

'Not at all. Why should you tell yourself lies? I hate lies. But you know, don't mind Poppa. He is perfectly harmless. Tell me about your mother.'

It was true, she was next on the list. And Fortnight was proud of his cruel beginning. He felt himself move recklessly towards confession, helping himself to Susan's eyes, and closing his own. But almost at once he became aware that no real thoughts or feelings attached themselves to the idea of his mother. All was dark, inchoate, inaccessible. He would have to invent it; but how? Had he not been engaged since his mother's death in ordering his emotions, restructuring the past with the sharp clarity of a projected memory? He had even taken decisions in this light. For example, he was to be a conveyancing clerk; he was due to start tomorrow.

'I hardly knew her,' he found himself saying. 'She would seldom speak to us. I mean, the Kid, my brother, yes, she had words for him. But they were private words, without general meaning. My father was a social climber. She could never adjust to all the changes in social position, sailing upwards past balcony after balcony, always with a different party toasting each other in different kinds of drink. She had . . . she had the most beautiful blue eyes, like yours. The same complexion too.'

Coffee was to be served in the drawing-room. By the door he turned to kiss her. Her mouth was smooth with salad oil, fanned by a wine-sodden breeze. She watched him, and afterwards a cold smile rested on her lips. He apologized, since underneath his clothes he was naked, and disreputable. She returned his kiss in mute complicity. When they disentangled a faint colour had risen into Lady Susan's cheek. The cold stare of her eyes had retreated and now observed him from a greater distance, like an animal chased from its prey. She moved off, and he followed, eventually holding her wrist like a child's, as they fled towards the central stairway. On the landing hung a tapestry of Flemish work. A goddess in pleated robes strode out from a field of sea-green vegetation, gesturing with a fleshy arm towards a kneeling mortal, whose long blue robe trailed in the earth behind him. Fortnight wanted to linger, preyed on by the sentiment that some message was conserved for him in the bowed head and disordered locks of this kneeling subject. But she hurried on, past Romneyish portraits, past cases of dismal porcelain and majolica, past marquetry and satinwood tables on each of which stood some functionless oddment — an ivory box, a penholder, a cutglass, silver-mounted, bottle, a sculpted letter-rack. They rushed beside these things like clouds across a spangled sky, darkening with their passage the gleam of every little possession. Here was an Italian bronze of fighting centaurs, there a small gold clock hanging from an arch of ebony and tortoiseshell; here a seascape by Bonnington, with its sand and tidefall almost smelling of brine, there a vitrine full of silver-gilt. In all these things they extinguished, as they passed, the warm light of ownership.

At the end of the gallery, they turned into a passage, with dust-smelling bookshelves and rows of chairs with fretted backs. A little door opened at the base of a flight of stone steps, a mock Jacobean tower. Doors of heavy oak held them back for one second from Susan's room. It was imperative to implant as many kisses as he could during that initial second. She broke away from his parody of passion.

'At least let me close the door.'

He noticed a wooden angel, breasting out like a ship's figure-head above the bed. With one quick, almost angry gesture of the arm, Susan stripped away the coverlet, the blankets and the upper sheet; she turned to look at him.

'Why,' he suddenly asked, against all his own instructions, 'did your father say those things?'

'No answer', came the answer.

She put one hand over his mouth and the other beneath his shirt. Her face was flushed under its freckles, the cold eyes swooning in the middle distance. Seeing the lovely odalisque amalgamating itself with the linen sheet, he forgot even to remind himself to desire her. As she moaned in his embrace he had the impression of a distant spirit puppetting her body, watching its antics, jerking it into lascivious poses according to some uncanny etiquette. He focussed his mind on lustful abstractions. Through all the studied abandon with which she greeted his entry, and the frenzy with which from time to time she would seize his lip between her teeth

or squirm into some new position, he sensed in her an equal but
more mysterious detachment. It was the detachment of a superior
being, aware of social convention, yet indifferent to its sway. 'I am
going to come,' she announced, in well-bred accents, and it
sounded like a decision of policy which he was privileged to overhear.

They lay static, half touching, on the bed. Sunlight polished her
red, plumbaceous eyelids, and mingled with her hair. He looked
across the room: a grotesque mixture of antiques resting in a knee-
deep carpet of lichen green, interspersed with red, white and
orange chairs of inflatable plastic, spindly plants in flaking vinyl
bowls, books in low cupboards of steel and glass that spread below
the windows and stretched into the eight complicated corners of
the tower. A steely staircase on a central spine spiralled through a
hole in the ceiling. She opened her eyes.

'Do you like it?'

The voice of unconcern.

'No.'

'Nor do I. I come back here ever so rarely. It's my refresher course
in adolescence. Up there's my den.'

She lifted a long langorous arm towards the ceiling.

'What does it contain?'

'Secret things. Love letters, unfinished novels, things that I
never got round to. Torn up menus, invitations, sometimes the
spectre of a rose.'

She smiled, and then placed her body under a regime of playful
kisses. He began to remember what he should have said to her at
table. In fact he had had the whole speech ready days before, and he
could not imagine now why he had been tongue-tied when the occasion arose. He was not quite sure of the propriety of beginning in
bed what should have been concluded at table; but nevertheless he
half rose and delivered to the recumbent womanly form a sermon
on the death of women.

'It is not remembering the dead that is difficult. It is the presence,
of course I mean the absence, of a dead woman. We don't have
words for it; even the Kid, who has words for most things, can't
pull the right label from the hat. A man leaves his signs behind
him, things he had initiated, taken over, torn apart. You discover
him everywhere, in every corner of the house, in every street, every
alleyway, every place of business or pleasure, or pain. Documents,
photographs, records of crime and goodwill; and faces everywhere, faces still bound by his contracts, by his promises, by his
protestations of hatred or love. But a woman, nothing, only
absence. Unless the key is turned, the door unlocked, and the whole
thing stands before you just as it was. As when Marcel bent to tie

his shoelaces, or Aeneas glimpsed the dead Dido, and vainly tried to hold her in his arms. Why doesn't Hamlet act? Because his father still exists. Hamlet lives in a world created by the old King's will. Everywhere he turns he sees the signs and effects of it. He just can't believe that now it is up to *him*. He is angry with his father for being permanent. So he spites him by doing nothing. At the same time he knows that his father is watching him, out there on the castle walls, or inside in the most secret inner chamber. Hence Hamlet's self-disgust, like a thing that is too much looked at. He asks his flesh to melt away; because he would rather die than face up to his father. To face up is to take over. The death of a woman belongs to another order. It is as the stranger describes it: "aujourd'hui maman est morte, ou peut-être hier, je ne sais pas". Her passing from the world is like her stay within it, a secret, a surreptitious ploy. When she has gone, elided into a million images of vaguely wailing things, she is no longer discoverable. But at the same time, your experience undergoes a change, a slip from white to grey. Everything observed, felt, suffered, alters in character, but no detail emerges as particularly significant, not even, for example, that awful canary-yellow suit that you were wearing when I met you. I set myself sometimes to remember, and my mind goes blank. That's the way it's been for me, ever since my mother died.'

Susan looked at him, ran her fingers through his hair, and said, 'I know what you mean.'

'Do you?'

'Well, I think so. I don't agree, though, about the suit, although I admit that my taste is erratic. Besides it isn't *canary* yellow.'

He was proud of his speech, and sad that it had caused so little interest. For once he had not been lying to her; but she had refrained from attending to the subtle difference that it made. But when she sprang from the bed, opened a cupboard in one corner of the room, and stood before him, a bottle of wine in one hand and a decanter of whisky in the other, it made him laugh. There was a triumph in the sight of her naked body, waiting on him, the little medallions of cinnabar gently patterned on her wheaten skin, the pubic hair sparkling with recent dew as the sunlight brushed it from the window. She seemed younger than her thirty years, and although her beauty was straw beauty, her youth false youth, they seemed so much the more captivating than real youth and beauty, being products of the will. Susan was, in her way, responsible for them. Her thirty-year-old adolescence was her own creation, and, in admiring it, admiring, for example, her way of standing with such phoney impulses of innocent amusement in her hands and eyes, he was admiring not an accident of nature but a moral achievement.

'What I like in you,' she said, 'is the eccentric muddle of your mind. You have managed to avoid education, and yet still acquire a civilized confusion. My muddles took me so much labour: yours are almost natural.'

'You want me to lose my confidence.'

'Not at all, darling. I want you just a little bit to appreciate me.'

'Oh? Well, I do.'

She dropped on her knees beside him and slowly sealed his eyes with columbine kisses, secreting a store of saliva in his ear. They drank together from the neck of the decanter. The topic of her marriage was rehearsed and abandoned; lacking words, he began to take stock. In the pocket of his jacket was the rolled-up sheaf of papers on which he had been writing every day. It was the final proof of his existence. His triumph over the Colonel would be complete could he interest her in that. She was certain to enjoy his remarks on the appeal of madness, when untempered by the sense of crime. He reached for the papers, announcing his intention to read. Susan rested her head on the bed and looked at him.

But whose writing was this? A new sensation overcame him as he turned the crumpled papers: he felt as though he were encountering himself in a dream, or seeing himself grotesquely mirrored in a glass, and being forced to convince his image that it had made some mistake about its highly significant, though admittedly worthless, identity. It was a legal nightmare. Judges and juries stood up in angry bewilderment at his inability to manage his affairs. How had it come about, for example, that his thoughts, Fortnight's thoughts, if he were willing to admit at least that they were his, how come that they were written in this small crabbed hand that slanted sideways and drooped towards the bottom of the page? No answer? There was an answer, he protested. He needed time to find it. He wondered if they, if she, would mind waiting a second. He would not be long. He felt certain that it would be a matter of moments. He found the remarks on madness. They were executed in his normal hand; bold, upright letters, with large full stops punctuating the separate phrases (he thought that any other form of punctuation suggested compromise). And here, gentlemen, ladies, is the paragraph on freedom, written as I watched my poor brother vainly attempting to chain himself to an apple tree in the garden. It would not wash. In amongst the sober exercises were inserted the rambling unpunctuated passages in a tiny hand, his own hand, he could not easily deny it, but squashed, tormented, oppressed by a burden of unusual thought, dwarfish and sinister. Moreover there was a clear explanation of these verbal vomits. Each thought had been begun on a fresh sheet of paper: what serious writer would use an exercise-book? And of course, he turned the page face down when the thought was finished, regardless of whether the paper had been filled. These graffiti had been inserted always into the space remaining, so that Fortnight would not know that they were there. The other Fortnight, that one in the mirror who smiled in conviction at the evidence, had filled these pages. That is to say — he looked at Susan in deep consternation at what she could observe — he himself had done it, in some deep and unfathomable vacuity of consciousness that he could not recall.

'Just a moment. Just a moment.'

Her expression did not change.

Nothing moves and still the stillness of the house is unlivable at least I don't believe it except you can hear her creaking (occasionally)   they say she'll need new shoes (this must be some kind of joke) such noises belong to the refusal to appear a kind of political decision ...

Each page was crowded with such remarks. Now Fortnight knew that he was insane. Schizophrenia is a hereditary ailment: the Kid clearly had it, and what better explanation of her, of her abstraction, of her compulsive refusal to appear? He looked back at the page: the phrase was written there. Refusal to appear. Fortnight had written it. He rolled up the papers carefully and replaced them in his pocket. If, as he intended, a smile then came to his features, it was one of ghoulish acquiescence.

'No. I won't read. It's all very foolish stuff. Why don't you speak to me about yourself?'

He hid the offending smile in her flesh, where it was pocketed along with the other casual treasures of their acquaintance. After a while Fortnight walked to the window. For the first time he was facing the fact of annihilation. This is how it must have seemed to her. He hardly listened to what Susan was saying about her no doubt wholly admirable husband who in the interests of a merchant bank left her so very much alone. Even at this distance, he had learned, you can catch a faint murmur from the far-off hullabaloo of death. Some turnings block it off completely, and for miles there is silence, until an unpropitious corner brings you suddenly towards it, and you find yourself nearer than before. In the end, when you are properly on the run, you plunge wilfully into the darkest hollows, dead-ends, cellars, through which you canter inexorably, until the noise is all around you, roaring in the sound of your own voice.

He began to dress, while Susan, who in some vague way had apologized, spoke into the telephone. Bright sunlight played on the lawns, and in the middle distance, two groups of flaking statues, lichen spotted graces and a Laocoon, posed on a pair of sandstone plinths. Behind them a flight of stone steps mounted the gentle rise, and two great urns crowned them at the summit, emerging out of rhododendron tops, and lit by the slanting sun. Some beech-trees stood on that rise, their silvered branches sprinkled with green; to the side was a little shrubbery, where brown paths twisted between the clumps of bushes. It was the kind of scene his mother would have planned; he stared at it, filled with images of his own decay.

And then a terrible detail emerged. Crouching in a bush behind the steps was a young boy of awkward aspect, dressed in grey flannel, his mammoth glasses catching the sunlight and throwing it sharply across the lawn.

'Susan! There's my brother! In your garden! He's staring at the house!'

'Just a moment darling,' she said to the telephone, and, placing her hand over the receiver, 'what is it?'

'My brother. Down there. In the garden.'

'Your brother? How odd. But perhaps not so odd. I mean if one can trespass, why can't two?'

'But you don't understand.'

He did not know what it was that she did not understand, and so stared at her in helpless surrender. She took her hand from the receiver. 'Someone's just come,' she said. 'I'll speak to you later. Yes. 'Bye.'

Fortnight stared into the cork-lined bathroom, and felt the unseen impact of Susan's cork-lined eyes.

'I hope he didn't spot the joke. A white lie, though. Now, sweet, you are coming over all afflicted, as nanny used to say.'

'But you don't understand.'

'You've already pointed that out. Perhaps he came looking for you? Or maybe he came with Adrian.'

'Adrian?'

'A friend of mine. It's a good job you reminded me. He's due for tea.'

She swung from the bed and brushed her lips against his cheek as she padded to the bathroom. The sound of water drowned her voice. Emerging towel-tied she said 'why not go down, my love, and wait for me in the drawing-room? If your brother is there, invite him in. I'm longing to meet him.'

Susan promptly disappeared. It was clear that no one in this house could wait for answers.

He moved fragilely along the corridor and gallery, finding his way by instinct. On impulse he reached out as he passed the gulley of book-cases and, taking a small dusty volume from the shelves, slipped it into his pocket. The portraits followed him with their eyes. As he reached the stairs he began to run. He paused before the drawing-room door; Lord Gilroy poked his head from the library, waved cheerfully, and withdrew. Fortnight opened his mouth to speak, but since his voice seemed not to be obeying him, turned the handle and burst forward into the powdery air. A tall thin figure made willowy patterns against the window pane. Its hands were clutched behind it, the long, effeminate fingers clicking one against the other with a soft ivory noise. He turned and stared intently at Fortnight from black ballistic eyeballs.

'You must be Kenneth Fortnight. I don't believe we have met. My name is Adrian Holtius.'

And the doctor advanced, defining himself with delicate gestures of a hand which finally fluttered towards Fortnight's lap and fondled the dead fingers that were hanging there.

Chapter Five

THE MACHINE tore sheet after sheet of unlaundered noise. It clattered, squealed, and racked, its champing jaws swallowing the rows of upended bottles and opening always for more. Bodies moved in its ambit, as though they had served up its savage antics for the entertainment of a crowd. Crates clanked along squeaking rollers, and crashed against each other like the mock-up of a fairground tragedy. Hands reached into the crates, took the bottles, and pushed them into the jaws. With heart of steel the machine cried out for bottles. It was passionate for bottles; it had no other desire but bottles; the entire workshop was bent to the task of finding bottles for it, and yet by no quantity of bottles could its appetite be stilled. With rubbery frameless movements, the small figure dropped its hands into the splintered crates. Fortnight watched as the brown bottles upped towards the light, flared, and fell diminuendo to the bottle-holes, minutely, tragically softened by that touch of hands. The jaws closed; a friction-filled fracas acknowledged the donation. Human shouts were deftly inserted into interstices of quiet, like bottles into holes. 'Fuck you' was trumpet-tongued into every hesitation, and sometimes a cacophonous caw would answer from the larger figure at the machine.

Fortnight looked out over the russet-coloured roof beyond the window. The old brick chimney relinquished vapours from its rings of cornice, and through the open window came the soft sweet smell of rotting malt. Suddenly, the noise took on a new quality. He heard a faint but persistent ululation, like the cry of some living creature trapped in the deep machine. The hands faltered in their movements; the large black man who had been flinging crates ceased his movements, and stared with vacant features at the flag of steam outside. The jaws began perceptibly to falter; they closed, parted, closed again, and then rested in a grin that revealed the last despatch of bottles half masticated in their dark insides. The noise ceased abruptly, with the suddenness of death, and the hands fell from their task. The smaller figure staggered backwards into the light, and the white curds of its face slowly clotted into semi-human form. It turned and opened its mouth.

'Kenny! This is an unexpected displeasure. Do come in. Make yourself ill at ease. Allow me to introduce my colleague, Comrade

Phyllis, No Doris . . . excuse me, I have failed to remember your surname.'

The large fat woman shuffled her body round through a few degrees and exposed the other side of her head. Its apertures were closed up; it was not a face, but a piece of red flesh, skinned and dolloped on to a tray of shoulders. She wiped red hands across it and said spittingly:

'Aw!'

'Comrade Aw,' the Kid continued. 'My tutor. Do not omit to feel respect for her noble features, and compunction at our common lot. We — Comrade Aw and me — exemplify the late-capitalist proletariat. May we show you our machine? Lovely bit of metal this, built to last till doomsday. Look at the way the templates is nutted together at them corners, a bloody marvel, can't see the crack hardly 'cept you got x-ray eyes. Today specially it's prime, had its clean only this morning the lovely bleeder . . . What's that?'

'A notice to complete.'

'A notice to complete. Complete what? Myself? Are you going to — to serve it on me? What posture must I adopt?'

'When is it going to stop, Kid?'

The Kid looked apprehensively at his brother, and then shouted across the shop to a bearded man who was crouching motionless among the crates of empties.

'Keep it up then, Charlie! Don't let them get in your hair!'

'This fantasy of yours, when is it going to stop?'

'You mean my belief that you work for some kind of lawyer? I don't know. Maybe I could renounce it. Let me see. No. Doesn't work. I'll try harder.'

The Kid's hands were scarred and blistered with his new-found occupation, and, as he lifted them in mock puzzlement to the white skin of his forehead, Fortnight winced.

'I mean,' he said, 'this fantasy of yours, that you are some kind of honorary member of the working class.'

'I told you. I've got to earn my keep. You'll be going soon, and then where shall I be? Half way to the loony bin if I'm not careful. I've got to stand on my own two feet, my own two darling little spondees. I need the support of the English workforce. And you tell me this is a fantasy?'

'You are only fifteen.'

'Sixteen next week. And anyway, why should the buggers care? I've made my choice. *Perstat Echionides, nec iam iubet ire, sed ipse* how does it go *vadit?*'

'Why do you think I am going to go?'

'Because I'm driving you to it. Anyway Miss Langley wrote this morning to say I should send you to London. Back to scare one.'

'Barbara!'

Fortnight shifted his gaze and examined the figures of the bottle shop. They stayed fixed in their postures, as though attached to the machine and condemned to share in its stillness. Doris stood like a sack of rags, oddly crowned by her butchered head. The others were weedy and strengthless. Around the shop stood the rough unordered mass of things, the ill-matched elements which awaited the fiat of the stilled machine. All objects were at odds, and among them the ruined forms of people were cast about like lifeless dolls. Fortnight decided to be unmoved by the memory of Barbara.

'Is it my business?' he inquired, business-like.

'I cannot follow your train of thought, oh brother. But let us assume that it isn't.'

'Good. So let me tell you. There is no need for you to be here. Oddle gives me a fifty per cent cut. That's enough for both of us, if I work at it. You can go back to school.'

The Kid looked about him in an agitated way. He called out to Charlie, who failed to reply. Then, taking his brother by the arm, he led him away from the motionless Doris, to a corner where oily cloths were piled beside the shattered parts of spent machines.

'Kenny. I know it sounds crazy, but I like it here. Among mental defectives I am a king. I am the intellectual vanguard, the authentic voice of their despair. For the first time in my life (I exaggerate) I have felt in command. The more I am slave to that machine, the more I am in charge of the thoughts in this room. I can think anything, believe anything here. It is like being alive, almost.'

Fortnight nodded slowly. The Kid's desire to set his brother free created the deepest bond between them. The Kid could not perceive it. For him the clarity of each plan made it seem like an answer. But he had not framed the question.

The Kid was sad, and wearing in his features the washed-out look of the child labourer. Speculations concerning him began to run like nightmares through Fortnight's mind: whether he really did feel like a king in this place, and if so how did he express it to his comrades? Where he spent his breaks and in what kind of conversation? Whether it was right for him, as Dr Holtius said, to engage in mechanical tasks? Whether he was not going further out of his mind as a result of this new pretence at a decision? And as to the decision, whether it had been precipitated by advice from Barbara, and to what extent it was connected in the Kid's mind with his political ambitions and burgeoning social conscience? If Fortnight paused over any question the others instantly crowded it out, so that the Kid was a subject not of thought but only of a prolonged mental hesitation.

'Well,' he said, 'I had better be on my way. I was just wondering what you wanted for supper.'

The Kid laughed, clapped his chapped hands and then squeaked at the pain.

'I am not wholly averse to lobster *à l'américaine*, which I am told is really *armoricaine*. But it would introduce an element of disharmony into my life. So make it burgers and Branston. Where to?'

'Oh, just about the town. I have to deliver this notice.'

'And?'

The Kid was suddenly tense. Looking at his brother narrowly, he extracted from the front pocket of his boiler-suit a tin of tobacco and a briar pipe. Slowly he tried to fill the bowl, pressing it with ruined fingers. His hands were trembling.

'And then I stop for the day.'

'The charmed life of the bourgeoisie. And?'

'I was going to see Adrian Holtius.'

The Kid tried to light his pipe. The black man emerged from the crates into a ray of sunlight, pointed in their direction, and laughed.

'Adrian!' the Kid said with disgust. 'Adrian. What a name! A drain, Adrian. Why did I introduce you?'

'You did not.'

'If you mean that it was an accident, his meeting you . . .'

'Nothing in Adrian's life is an accident,' said Fortnight stoutly.

'Then I fail to see what you mean. But why should I care? You go your own way.'

'I wish I could explain to you . . .'

'Anything I would want to know?'

'What I owe to him.'

'Owe to that creep? You're off your rocker, Ken, round the twist, up the pole.'

'He helped me. He taught me to feel . . .'

'Look, this is a respectable place of work. I don't want you coming in here with that phoney crap. I am working with realities, look at them, hardened men with faces you could strike a match on, tough bags of female flesh with plenty going and more to spare. I don't need all this gaff. That doctor is a fraud and you know it. If you don't believe me — and I should know since I'm a real loony and you're only a pretend one — then ask Miss Langley.'

'I . . .'

'I don't want to hear about it,' the Kid shouted. 'You and all those people, all those effeminates and snobs. I can't influence you. So just keep it to yourself, right? and . . . saved by the bell.'

The hooter broke the stillness of the bottle shop, and almost at once the machine was in motion. The Kid turned back to it, gasping for breath; he picked up four brown bottles by their necks and swung them like chickens into the clanking jaws. Fortnight watched his hands for a moment, and then turned to go. Another surprise encounter failed. Yet the Kid must accept the doctor. It was only then that the nightmare of the diary would begin to end. He could not explain it, however. At table, at the piano, while reading, walking, while filled with domestic labours, the Kid refused to allow the existence of Holtius. Yet Fortnight needed to reveal how deeply, since that fateful day, he had fallen in hate with the doctor.

The doctor's methods were unorthodox. Having held Fortnight's hand for a few seconds limply, in the manner of one who is taking a pulse, he retreated to the far corner of Susan's drawing-room, and stared again from the window. Fortnight watched with astonishment the antics of those burning eyes, as they swept clean the little landscape of its old significances, and replaced them with phantoms of a more up-to-date design.

'You may have noticed your brother, in the garden.'

'No. Yes.'

'He insisted on coming. You do not mind.'

The doctor turned and made a gesture with the fingers of one hand, as though scattering petals of forgetfulness in the air.

'Insisted? How?'

'By way of forbidding me admission to his mother's house. That's what he said.'

'What were you doing in my mother's . . . in our house?'

The doctor watched him, bird eyes half eclipsed.

'I received a telephone call. From your father. He seemed considerably distressed. He . . . ah! Perhaps if you could come to the window for a moment.'

Fortnight came rustling past a bowl of desiccated plants. The dry noise sparked in his mind the tinder of dead emotions. At once he was aflame with fear. He rehearsed the evidence against himself. From the moment of his first imitation of a human being until the discovery of the diary, everything had conspired to deliver him into Dr Holtius's government. He perceived it at once. In those black pupils he was just the homunculus that he had sought to be. It was necessary. He must eradicate nature and begin again. The fear swept through him, consumed the last vestiges of resolve, and a charred foetus was dropped sizzling into the bottle of the doctor's eye.

'Yes. If you could stand just here, and appear to be engaged in conversation. That's right. Yes, he has seen you. He is off like a hare down the drive. Excellent.'

There was a silence, while Fortnight refrained from looking through the window.

'Is Susan in the house? I had the feeling that I was expected.'

'Yes. I think so.'

The doctor looked at Fortnight with an expression of penetrating tenderness.

'Your brother, you know, is quite passionate about Wagner.'

'Oh, yes, we both are.'

'Your father thought that he must have entered a clandestine phase. It seems that the telephone is never answered. I suppose your brother is responsible.'

The doctor turned and began to step ostrich-like about the room, his taut buttocks battling beneath the hands that gripped each other behind.

'That's unfair,' said Fortnight. 'Sometimes he doesn't answer it. At other times I don't.'

'I can't stand this room! So messily feminine!' The doctor's hands parted in order to flick at the bowl of lilies, and then were quickly reunited. 'The way it spills over! Anyway, your brother did agree to talk, provided we went outside. An intelligent boy. Hopeless of course. You must be very anxious. Just look at this dreadful Sèvres: so unnatural! The colour, I mean.'

His face creased into an image of a pussy's crinkled anus, and then instantly reverted to its old expression.

'I *am* anxious,' said Fortnight.

'It is true that you do not seem well. Have you known Susan for long?'

'Not really.'

'Do you find her interesting?'

The question contained an accusation; Fortnight understood at once.

'I don't exactly cultivate her.'

'More like husbandry than cultivation, in your view?' said Holtius, unperturbed. 'Personally I am very fond of her. She is absolutely of our time. Sometimes I think I invented her.'

Fortnight directed his eyes through the window and fixed them on the little Yorkshire terrier that was yapping soundlessly at the edge of the lawn.

'Probably I should be going.'

Palpitations filled him, as his eyes were drawn back to the doctor's tender gaze.

'Don't think that I judge you. I can see that you are worth knowing.'

'Oh, I shouldn't think so.'

'My dear boy. I am not a snob. None of my passions rise to that level of detachment.'

The door opened, Susan entered, and with the single cry of 'Adrian!' walked over to the doctor and offered her white cheek to be pecked. The sight of this sexless osculation against the flesh that he had decided to make his own aroused nausea in Fortnight. He wanted to leave, but the doctor and Susan fell at once into a kind of intimacy, laughing at affectations which they elegantly affected not to have. He felt unable to turn his back on them; only a kind word from Susan would justify his presence, and so permit his absence.

The doctor stepped back, and as he gossiped in an eldritch voice, concealed his eyes behind a spiral stand of brass, a vine on which electric fruit was clustered. From this vantage point he directed soft possessive glances. Their conversation was at last stilled by Fortnight's silence; Susan turned on him with vengeful looks.

'I yes it they . . .' he said. A question, statement or forewarning had been offered.

'Darling: where is your brother? I thought you said he was here?'

'No,' said the doctor, 'he went home again. It just so happened that he followed me.'

'What did you say to him?' asked Fortnight.

'I listened. It takes less time.'

'What did he say to you?'

'He was immersed in *The Ring* when I arrived. It was a useful starting-point. I made a suggestion about the significance of labour in the genesis of Wagner's characters. Labour is a good word. It has so many convenient meanings. He began at once to tell me a story about your mother. He called it "Cock and Bull". That, you understand, is the name of the story. I took it, from the name, that the story was really about your father. Susan, you really must do something about this appalling picture.'

'But I like it.'

Dr Holtius looked at her, and then at the excremental pigment that had been piled in ringlets on the canvas.

'That is why you should do something about it. This,' he said, tapping the surface with the nail of one finger, 'is without interest; your taste, on the other hand, is one of my lasting preoccupations.'

He turned back to Fortnight.

'The details are not significant. The fact is that he spoke. I do not hope for more. He referred, by the way, to a certain Miss Langley, who seems to be his authority in political matters. I wonder is she related to that dauber who lives out his cottagey pieties somewhere hereabouts? Perhaps she is. It would figure. He thinks, apparently, that you are a victim of this story called "Cock and Bull". I couldn't follow it. But he thinks . . . let's talk about it some other time.'

'How much do I owe you?'

For a brief second the doctor frowned. He repeated the words slowly, spearing them like fishes in a tank and holding them wriggling in the air for a moment before casting them at Fortnight's feet.

'How much do you owe me. Really, my dear Kenneth, may I call you that? Susan, may I call him that? I wonder what you imagine. How much do you owe me. A Socratic cock perhaps? A papal Bull? How should *I* know?'

Susan rang the bell, and, with muffled excuses, Fortnight left the room. He nodded to Dr Holtius, who stared through him with tight-lipped unconcern.

Susan followed him out. At the door, as he clutched the folded papers in his jacket pocket, and stared into the sunlight of the park, she held him back.

'Let me see you tomorrow.'

She did not smile, but only stared at him from inimical eyes, her well-trained hands unleashed in his trouser pockets.

'Tomorrow. I start work tomorrow. I . . .'

He turned and made his way slowly towards the gatehouse. The face of Dr Holtius filled his thoughts: it had become ageless, stony, Medusa-like, an abstract idea of blame.

The Kid was waiting for him in the hall, his features gauzed over with anxiety.

'I have decided to break the silence. Of course you're right, you've been right all along, we must face up to it. Life is too short. It was a strange thing, that creep coming round here; sometimes I wonder whether Fist isn't off his rocker too. But it was a clever move. If it hadn't been for the need to point out to him that he is an arse-hole of the first order, who knows, I might still be keeping silent vigil.'

They had proceeded to the laughing-room, and there, because the light was so strong on their grandmother's face, Fortnight watched her changing expression as it responded to his brother's words. There was nothing steadfast in her look, and whether it was the fault of the artist, or whether it was due to the ability, which perhaps she had passed on to her daughter, never to be wholly dead, not to make up her mind even about that one most important transaction, her vagueness now occupied the room. The lilac blue and silver fox of her outmoded evening dress and the folded hesitating hands sucked at their surroundings and continued to move. She had the Kid's blue-grey eyes, and lips like his: pale, large, blubbery, with indeterminate edges. As the Kid became agitated, her figure seemed to follow his failed aerobatics.

'My God you should have heard him on the subject of *The Ring*. Burble, burble, burble. The gold of nature bound in the ring of surplus value, alienated labour in the depths of Nibelheim, the forging of personality in labour, enough to give you labour pains in the arse, which I should imagine is his main idea. He didn't even know that Götterdämmerung opens on an E flat minor triad, and in fact I don't suppose he knows what a triad is, or why it has to move on to a D seventh in order to put a question mark in the music. No doubt he doesn't know that it *is* a question-mark. And those eyes! Those fingers! That positively porcelain pate! Trying to wangle himself into my unconscious as though the place wasn't bloody crowded out already with ids, yids, kids, whatever, all divided so as the better to be ruled. If I hadn't agreed to walk up with him to the Park I reckon he would have started coming over all mouldy with me, the filthy queer. By all that's hirsute and gashly,' the Kid continued, dancing through into the dining-room, his face red with embarrassment at his own discourse, 'I declare him to be the number one menace of Flackwell. Distil him, that's what I say, and flush him down the bog! Here, I've got dinner ready, not exactly galoptious nosh, but quite a decent bottle to wash it down with, and home-made almost except that they came out of a tin goosegog pie.'

With ceremonious gestures he indicated the table, at which, for the first time since their mother's death, her place had not been laid. So great was the Kid's agitation, that he began at once to dish out the stew of oxtail pieces, spotting the table-cloth and attempting simultaneously to straighten the knives and forks. He sat down, breathless, having succeeded only in transferring all the stew from the bowl to his brother's plate, piling up the cutlery at one end of the table. Fortnight quietly took over and measured half the food on to the second plate.

They pushed the food away, the Kid humming softly. Fortnight took from his pocket the roll of papers and laid them on the table.

'Do you know anything about this?' he asked.

The Kid shrieked with laughter. 'He asks me if I know anything about a heap of paper! This is wonderful!'

'What do you know about it?'

'Do you have your brains on the Kathleen Mavourneen system Kenny, or is there every now and then a real attempt at ownership? I only ask.'

The Kid's face collapsed into an expression of ineffable sadness and decay. Fortnight, afraid of silence, spoke rapidly about the masterpiece that he was presently writing — of which these scraps constituted a fragment — and which was to deal with the entire phenomenon of madness, in particular with its oracular character for those who were not afflicted by it. It was very useful to be able to study the Kid's own minor lunacies. But he was more interested, when it came to the pinch, in gerontology. He had read an article which Mrs Thurlow had dug up for him about the tendency of old people, particularly women, to focus on some incident in early childhood and to reinterpret it as containing characters from their later years. Thus they mythologized the past, sometimes resisting the most obvious truths out of duty to the myth which they created. He thought this the type of all admirable insanity.

'Who wrote your script, Ken?'

'Why are you being so rude today?'

The Kid's neck was trembling. His khaki shirt and loosened green-striped tie were dampening with the sweat that gathered in a smear beneath his adam's apple.

'Sorry. I enjoyed listening to you. I blame that creepy doctor. Let's eat something. Next week is a kind of mock-Whitsun holiday. I shall need my strength.'

'Your strength? Are you thinking of ascension?'

'No. Degradation. They need people at the brewery. Apparently its the kind of job a mental defective can do. I shall become a noble prole, like Siegfried.'

His ghoulish laugh as he left the table seemed afterwards to echo in an upstairs room.

It was arranged that Fortnight should collect the papers from Oddle and work at home. There were no deeds among them, only letters and printed forms.

Fortnight had not slept, but kept watch on himself through the night, lest he should rise from the bed to begin writing at the table. He heaved up his soft voice like an unmanageable pile of rags. It erupted into the air to compete with the blanket of cute harmonies with which the office was always filled, the solicitor being entirely predicated on the substance of radio noise. Fortnight made a vague enquiry about the rate of his commission, raising his eyes to the grainy snivelling face which spread in a yellow-fanged yawn behind its beard, and then found himself afraid. Memo: to telephone Susan. Also: to return to London. A puff of breeze made a flash of darkness on the green beech-tops behind the new town hall. It whistled in the steely windows of the tower, passed, and was forgotten. The faint sound of traffic returned. Oddle began to scratch himself beneath the candy-coloured shirt and to stare at Fortnight's hand.

'I know that scrawl!'

Fortnight looked down. Beyond the letter that he had brought with him he saw the white lambswool carpet, bejewelled by Oddle's lime-green shoes. His encounters with the solicitor had the condensed falsehood of the comic stage. Oddle in his dignity of conjuror, and Fortnight in his own peculiar motley as stunt man and clown, had only brief and histrionic need of each other. It was absurd to linger in this place, and surprising that the solicitor should repeat his statement.

'I know that scrawl.'

'Ah!'

'Holtius. Why's he writing to you?'

Fortnight assumed a disdainful expression. The letters, he said, were not addressed to him, and as for the Colonel, who was to say what arrangements he imagined himself to be making?

'*That* one. The one you brought with you.'

Fortnight stared at it. 'Yes, I brought it with me. It came this morning.'

He examined his name, carefully transcribed in italic flourishes. The ink was black, copious and shining. 'He that takes the raven for his guide will light on carrion'; it was one of his mother's sayings.

'The cunt writes to me as well. Look at this.'

Oddle sprawled on to a pile of papers on his desk and thrust his thin arms into the heart of it. The telephone began to ring. Lifting the receiver with his foot Oddle shouted in its direction before burying in lambswool the soft plaintive voice. He swivelled, attempted to arrest an avalanche of files, and then slid off the desk with a sheet of paper in his hand. He groped for the telephone while Fortnight read:

> Since our recent dealings I have noticed a change in your behaviour towards me. Our past association is not so insignificant that you should choose to ignore my feelings. To me such disloyalty is incomprehensible. It was with no little contempt that I discovered what you had been saying to Ninian Adaire. His affection for me being unshakeable, your attempt to undermine it is so much the more absurd. Indeed, it bears an uncanny resemblance to your conduct on another occasion of which I hardly need remind you. You will soon be making yourself ridiculous . . .

Fortnight glanced at the solicitor, who was pouring obscenities into the speechless telephone. The paper floated from his hand towards the carpet. Outside he became impatient to open the doctor's letter, and prevented himself only by arranging elaborate distractions at the shop-windows of the High Street. Who, he wondered, was Niñian Adaire? He sat down at the desk in the Colonel's study and extracted the stiff sheet of paper. 'Bramhurst Park', which was embossed on the letter-head, had been crossed out, and the doctor's own address neatly inserted beneath it. Fortnight noticed that the address did not name the street where the old Georgian surgery had been. Had the doctor gone up in the world, or down?

> My dear Kenneth,
> I was sad that we had to come across each other in this melancholy room and in circumstances which must have made it seem as though it were curiosity and not genuine feeling that motivated whatever interest in you I might have betrayed. Believe me, if my manner towards you was awkward, this was no more than an expression of respect, and of my sincere desire for your friendship. Could we meet again soon? I am at home all afternoon tomorrow, and would be delighted to see you.
>
> With every good wish.
> Adrian.

Fortnight stared for a while at the letter, and then at the few documents which he had to answer on Oddle's behalf. He noticed a letter over the Colonel's signature, asking for a contract of sale for Bramhurst Garage. The voice of his mother intruded into his thoughts, telling him to lay it up in lavender. He pushed everything aside and concentrated on the doctor's letter. He tried to understand the fear which it inspired in him. One half of Fortnight recognized the unreality of Susan and Holtius; the other half was drawn to the abyss from which they beckoned with such impatient gestures. What was it that they knew? Why did they lay claim to him? Clearly Dr Holtius was a master illusionist. He could veil himself in transfigurations; he had the secret of nothingness, that could endlessly transform itself into being. Fortnight was reminded of Britchell.

Britchell, as the Kid described him, was a small, neat personage, with a vellum complexion and soft, powdery hands, his flesh emerging at each point from waxy white starch. The wreath of hair around the rim of his cranium was regular and brilliant as a silver crown, and all about his person he wore the badges of respectability: a discreet but evident school tie, a watch-chain, the laundered corner of an absent handkerchief. He was the model of decorum. Generally he entered the room in some unusual way: through a wall, out of a table-top, or from the glassy orb of a wine-glass. He moved cautiously at first, circumnavigating things and people with apologetic bows. When he had thoroughly prepared himself, however, he would turn to the Kid and begin the monstrous attempt to prove (on a fine point of law) his actuality. He would raise his hand to his brow, to pass it around the top of his head, unzipping the scalp and lifting it free. Then another, smaller, Britchell would jump like a jack-in-the-box from the hollow skull, smile with just a shade more irony than its master, and, raising its hand to the exact simulacrum of its master's cranium, unzip again. With gathering momentum the *mis en abîme* careered towards infinity. And (so Britchell repeatedly argued) an illusion multiplied to infinity is real. Hesitantly, the Kid had revealed the secret to his brother. A doctor had been told; he prescribed stelazine. 'Useless,' said the Kid, 'I am a star already.' But Britchell appeared more rarely now. He existed mostly as an after-image of absolute terror, such as Fortnight himself had experienced, in Susan's bedroom, in the presence of Dr Holtius, and now in the lineaments of the doctor's handwriting as it summoned him to the interview which he had four years previously postponed.

The house was smaller than the previous one, a kind of shapeless cupboard of indeterminate age inserted between stone façades. He had expected a brass plate, a polished knocker, high cornices, and the brows of high windows. He had expected to be taken in hand and propelled through the rooms and corridors by hushed and hieratic priestesses, with smooth brown skin and disdainful eyes, dressed in white robes, walking with measured anxiety-free steps, and gestures redolent of winter skiing and the Bermuda surf. He expected to be systematically humbled, to feel graceless and neurotic, while led adaze along fields of soft carpet, around corners of grandfather clocks and beeswax-scented sideboards, over the thresholds of vacated rooms, through white-panelled doors, to be quietly told to mind his step by a voice that disclaimed responsibility, since whatever he did would be done deliberately, would be yet another ruse to draw attention to his case; he expected to be ushered across gleaming hallways sparkling with Venetian chandeliers, and finally allowed under the impulse of his previous movements to glide into an empty chamber, as the last nurse stepped aside for him and shut the heavy door.

However, the doctor opened the front door himself. He was wearing a silk dressing-gown and smelled faintly of talc.

'You must excuse me. I was taking a bath. Do come in.'

The hall into which Fortnight stepped was bare, except for two broken chairs and some cardboard boxes which seemed to contain documents or books. They passed almost immediately into a smaller room, with a table and a set of dining chairs.

'Would you like to go through to the study? Or shall we sit here?'

It was a strange question, and Fortnight immediately interpreted it as a kind of test to which he should have some ready answer. Instantly a host of reasons why he should choose the doctor's study presented themselves, and as instantly a host of conflicting reasons stood against them. It seemed the most important choice he had ever had to make, yet all along, as the balance of reasons tilted now this way, now that, he was aware that the doctor was profoundly indifferent to the outcome. It was precisely this that was disturbing: having presented the dilemma, Dr Holtius now stood back and watched him prevaricate, giving no encouragement, and withholding the authority that Fortnight craved. By the time he had made up his mind, or rather, not so much made up his mind as cut it short in the midst of reasoning with the answer 'it's all right here', Fortnight felt that he had committed his whole future with this choice. The doctor would now know what kind of man he was, and would gently fashion and reinforce the endless sequence of new decisions that followed on this first.

'Ah,' said the doctor. 'Probably on second thoughts we should go into the study. It has a nicer view.'

The study also was nearly bare. Too bewildered to read the spines of the few books on the shelves above the desk, Fortnight obeyed the doctor's hand on his shoulder and sat on the sea-green couch beneath the window. The monastic quality of the study contrasted strangely with the doctor's manner. It was like a magician's stage, bare because it could at any moment be folded away and resurrected in some other place, the rabbits and handkerchiefs mysteriously carried in some secret pocket.

'I'm so glad you could come. For a while I almost thought that you wouldn't.'

Fortnight wondered about the 'almost': it seemed to suggest that the doctor had approached the brink of something terrible and then saved himself by an act of will.

For a few moments there was silence, while the doctor sat back in the solitary armchair and gazed wistfully at Fortnight.

'I know that you are unhappy,' he said at last. 'It is written on your face. I know too that you don't know who you are, and that for some reason you want to find out. I am not saying that I agree with your ambition. But it is true that for two hundred years now mankind has been disposing of the idea of self, and a fashion that lasts as long as that is on the verge of becoming serious. Far be it from me to break with tradition. But you must tell me, if you don't think that I'm intruding, about your father, whom I slightly know.'

Almost at once Fortnight had the image of himself as sexless. The transfiguration was miraculous, a plunge from the cliff of his personality into uterine mysteries that for some reason (he guessed it was his mother's fault) he had always deplored. He imagined himself perched all sweat and albumen on the coral lips of his mother's wide vagina. The doctor wanted him to be ambiguous, indeterminate, driven back into the maw of creation and suffering there the illusion of total choice. To choose everything, one's life, thought, self, even one's sex. To return to that state of gelid unconcern and form out of protozoic nothingness a complete marvel of a real human being. That was what the doctor intended. Suddenly it seemed more important than anything else to show that he was a man, that he lived and suffered and would no doubt live again. But someone had deprived him of words. The words that he had needed for his mother he again needed now. He tried to fill the vacuum with a story. He recounted the dream of Blackett's that came to him each night.

He asked the doctor to imagine a bright March day, with a brisk wind hurrying the clouds across the eye of a low-lying sun. He walked at the edge of the field, a ditch of water trickling to one side. The bare trees flexed in the breeze and sparse flocks of seagulls rose from the dead earth and fanned in the sky before him. On the left was the little cottage of red brick and grey slate roof. It always grieved him, returning to this place, to perceive its littleness, and to see through the window the sparse landlady furnishings of darkened oak, the brown and green carpets, the mica-fronted stove and his mother's elmwood rocking-chair. He met the Kid, frightened, on the threshold, and, taking him by the hand, led him for protection through the kitchen door. The row of printed blue cups were darkening now with dust. The house too was darkening. The Kid cries 'don't go, don't go', but he has to go, in order to investigate the creaking on the stairs. He leaves the kitchen door open, swinging slightly on its rusty hinges. Upstairs he stands in what was once his bedroom, with the low ceiling that had seemed so high, the blocked sash window of leaded glass, the bed with its white coverlet of her crochet work. All is at peace beneath its veil of dust. He feels like the discoverer of Tutankhamen's sepulchre, having trod where no one previously had trod since death was catered for. And perhaps it is only a just reflection of the inadequacy of his arrangements that the dead return again and yet again, and always to molest him. For just then a voice sounds from below, where all that is unwanted is hidden away, crying 'Is someone there?'. Turning he sees his dead mother at the head of the stairs, observing him. 'Kenneth, is it really you?' He calls for his brother, who stays below, moaning that he will not come. So Fortnight alone has the task of finding words for her. 'I love you,' he thinks, but his throat is dry and he has to mould the words silently with trembling lips. She seems not to understand, although curiously she mouths the words back at him in distorted form. Fortnight sees the familiar folds of her flower-patterned dress, the little green brooch above her slender breast, the slightly greying hair and ageless features. He realizes that she cannot die, and that he should therefore never speak of love to her: for how can he risk it, except in the belief that she will soon be gone?

She descends to the kitchen to prepare his meal, and the Kid comes panting through the open doorway. Spring sunlight invades the room, striping the motes of dust and spreading a halo in the Kid's scattered hair. They go down quietly, hand in hand, though it is certain that she knows their every movement and cannot trouble over their escape, expecting nothing, except the eternity in this little house which she must fill. At the door the Kid goes safely to the garden and begins to run. But Fortnight hears something creak again on the stairs. He turns back, the house door locks behind him, and there on the stairway is Kenneth Fortnight, in the old alpaca suit, who rests his weight on the bottom step and watches him with eyes like Susan Waterford's, sober, cold, selfish and inscrutable.

'Of course,' he concluded, 'that's all a lot of lies I have told you.'

He crouched forward, his hands in lap, his head wrapped in vice-like bands of tension.

'One can be moved even when one disbelieves,' said the doctor softly. 'Especially then.'

Fortnight looked up. 'You didn't believe me?'

'I want you,' said the doctor, ignoring the question, 'to tell me everything about her, everything that you remember.'

Fortnight remembered only Susan's body as it moved on her linen sheets.

'There is nothing to tell. I remember nothing.'

'It's that nothing which interests me. That, and what will come of it.'

'You are not, of course, a real doctor.'

'I am not an illusion.'

'I mean, Dr Holtius, that . . .'

'Please call me Adrian. I have to be close to you.'

'But why do you need that?' said Fortnight, feigning surprise.

'Who spoke of need? My dear, I can help you.'

Fortnight swallowed. Hatred is blind, as well as love, he thought. It was one of his mother's sayings.

'What I mean is that if you are a doctor, it is in the style of Faust.'

'My dear, you flatter me. I am doctor of an unformed church. But I carry myself about the world in many shrewd disguises.'

'Tell me what you really are.'

'Just what I appear. A man without peace, a dreamer. A lover of strength.'

'Strength?'

'Strength. Such as you have.'

Fortnight could not forbear to smile. 'You must be joking.'

His mother's saws kept coming back to him, and he craved nothing so much as the sound of her selfless laughter. Must is for the king, she said.

'Only in the way that, yes, I am always joking. I am intemperate, irreverent, to a fault. Languorous, wasted. But you: you exist.'

'You have an awful lot of opinions about me,' said Fortnight. 'Get away with you!' his mother added.

'None that you do not instantly confirm in every gesture.'

'Well, this strength, let us consider it. What does it amount to, when I am like this, when I cannot breathe, cannot think, cannot remember, cannot decide?'

'You are warming, I see. Those, you will recognize, are the smallest things.'

Holtius rose in a rustle of silk, took a pace about the room and then went to a cupboard that stood in the corner. He stooped over it with a faint noise of cloth and a circumambient gesture of the right arm, and Fortnight watched his reflection in the glass over the gas fire. He was puzzled by the doctor's movements; the affectation of lightness had gone from them, and now they seemed random and incompetent, quiet only because the air of that room contained nothing that they might disturb. Where the doctor had come from, where he was going, how long he was resting in this brief posture of society, all these were mysteries, rendered doubly mysterious by the bareness of his surroundings, and by the unattached nature of the objects that remained within his reach.

'There's something else,' Fortnight said. 'I want to tell you about someone else. Someone who means, who would mean . . .'

'Ah, here it is, I thought I had remembered.'

The doctor rose with a bottle of champagne on which the rainbow-coloured droplets promptly settled out of the warm summer air.

'You have a strange way about you Kenneth, uncanny, evocative, like a memory of antiquated manners.'

What are you talking about? thought Fortnight, who was told by his mother that he knew good manners but used few.

'I want to make you linger over every word you say to me. You make me ashamed of the sentimental confections and titbits of gossip that I serve up to all-comers, and of course especially to people like dear Susan, spiced in my favourite sauces and done to a turn in a cunning cuisine of cynicism. But — I have forgotten the glasses.'

He jerked forward, placed the bottle on the floor beside Fortnight's couch, and went from the room, swishing his dressing-gown in a parody of domestic haste. The doctor's household was, like himself, unfathomable. He could be fetching glasses from the sink of a bachelor kitchen where coffee and cereal stood unaccompanied on a single shelf. Or he could equally be summoning from some cavernous recess a human face stiff with old proprieties.

The doctor appeared, two tall glasses slotted into his bony hands. He worked at the champagne cork, and then observed the white froth with a sniff of satisfaction.

'You were about to tell me,' he said, offering the glass, 'about Miss Langley.'

'How on earth do you know?'

The doctor shrugged his shoulders. 'This is first-rate champagne. You must taste it.'

Fortnight raised glass and eyes. In colour Dr Holtius was a faint primrose yellow, with dark hair thinning on top and curling about his ears. In the afternoon light that slanted in from a reflecting window, his raised glass glowed coral-toned against his chin. The liquid lapped towards his mouth and expired in quick clear bubbles on the strand of his upper lip. His eyes were alight with sudden jouissance.

'I am not often happy,' he commented, 'but now I am. Is that not strange?'

'Why should it be strange?'

'Were you going to tell me about Miss Langley? I think you should.'

An hour and a half later the last of the champagne was transferred into Fortnight's glass by a figure that had relaxed into the postures of authority.

'A vacuum,' said the doctor, 'abhors nature. But I adore you. Will you let me be your friend?'

The rumblings of terror were distant now, like thunder in a landscape. The doctor's eyes and words preceded them, a wondrous lightning which cast in Fortnight's sentience long evanescent shadows of inexplicable forms.

'You must let me,' the doctor continued.

Fortnight rose, his legs unsteady.

'But you do not have to go? Surely you do not have to go?'

Pain coiled itself deftly into the doctor's words and flickered its tongue at Fortnight.

'No. That is to say, yes.'

Across the street the little trolleys of normality wheeled past, doll-like women packaged in printed cloth, their prammed nippers commanding them with commissar looks to move on. The roman ochre of the sun on old stone walls canvassed their innocence, and Fortnight looked out from the doctor's study as though about to be cut off from such things forever. The old brick chimney of the brewery rose up among the stony rooftops and a scroll of white smoke unfurled from it into the blue. Fortnight prayed for the *nunc dimittis* which the doctor had arrested with a frown.

'But then, you will be coming again tomorrow. We must make that visit.'

'Visit? Oh, yes, the visit.'

It was true that they had talked of a pilgrimage to his mother's ash. Dr Holtius had painted it in the most vivid colours. There had been something monstrous in the literary allusions through which Holtius had so persuasively illustrated his meaning. The doctor had far outrun anything that Fortnight could have imagined. He had a tongue so sharp as to pass unhindered through every barrier. The fastidiousness with which he etched out his meaning in suffering flesh did not mitigate its cruelty, which was, however, so fine that there was no gainsaying it. The work of mourning required that Fortnight surrender to the doctor's judgement. He accepted the theory that Barbara was no more than a fantasy, an icon with which to blot out the *perspettivo* of the truly feminine. Out of loyalty to himself he was persuaded to disown her; the first result was to be a sight of the deceptive vista at the end of which his mother's tomb lay quiet and unattended. The doctor cited many authorities in his favour, from Dionysius the Areopagite to Yeats and Genet. It appeared that Fortnight was not only strong and brave but also endowed with a kind of genius that made him an honorary member of the club to which those celebrities belonged. This made it self-evident that he must agree in their joint opinion. Above all, Fortnight was invited to discover himself thinking, there is a knowledge of death that is acquired not through observation but through action. Sexual prowess was the form that this action had, initially, to take. The doctor was particularly delighted that his new-found genius had, as he put it, surmounted Susan Waterford. He looked forward to many such conquests, all of which must prove effective in annulling the Gretchen-imago of Miss Langley, and in making Fortnight the master of his world. They would also benefit his brother, who had come to accept the girl as an authority only because truth had been represented as whatever female chanced to be uppermost in Fortnight's life. A balanced approach to sexual conquest would no doubt dispel some illusions: even Britchell — who corresponded, it appeared, to the usual symbols of absent authority — would cease to be a threat.

These self-discoveries so emboldened Fortnight that he confessed for the first time to a shameful episode: Barbara's pregnancy and the abortion in which he had abetted her. The doctor listened with corrosive emotion, emphasizing each delicate point, and nodding in sympathy as his patient winced in pain. By the time Barbara had been disposed of and his mother summoned into court, Fortnight was clearly persuaded of his guilt, and desired nothing so much as the stiffest sentence in the doctor's repertoire. This took the form, at last, of a joint pilgrimage to the place where the vestiges of Mrs Fortnight lay interred.

'Yes, the visit,' Fortnight repeated.

He watched the sheet of smoke as it detached itself from the chimney and began to tear in two.

'You are apt to be entranced, I perceive, by foregone conclusions. Please say freely whether you would rather not.'

Fortnight relinquished his freedom with a nod. 'I must go. You are right.'

'We must go. Tomorrow.'

'Yes. Tomorrow.'

'And until then,' said the doctor, who took a sudden step forward and seized Fortnight's hand, 'I shall remember this conversation. I shall look on it as a station on the endless slope.'

'What?'

'The downward slope of my many indiscretions. Pay no attention to my words. Please go now.'

And the doctor so sighed over his final sentence as to transform it from permission to command.

They walked, slowly at first, but seized by a strange impatience as they went. There were few houses on this side of town, and soon they had left the white concrete roads behind them and were walking on a lane of tar, bordered by blossoming hedgerows. Between two white posts the drive of the crematorium wound away from the road. They observed the sign:

WAYSIDE CREMATORIUM
OPEN TO VISITORS 9 - 5
DOGS NOT ALLOWED

They walked the long drive between the young Christmas trees, bowed in silence. Fortnight knew that the doctor was observing him, and so affected to be much affected by what he could not feel. The serpentine drive diverged into two parts as they approached the building, allowing privileged arrival to the funeral cortège. The two lines converged again in an oval, with a raised pavement and yellow lines suggesting parking lots for cars. Fortnight turned his eyes to the building, seeing it for the first time. It was low, of flesh-coloured brick, with a line of white fungus like a water mark three feet from the ground. Of the six bays, one, with discrete but slightly blackened funnels, was blank. The others had windows and doors, with plastic lettering fixed to the wall above their lintels: Waiting Room, Main Chapel, Refreshments, Private, Enquiries. His attention rested on the blank bay, which brought the aluminium Gothic of the chapel to an abrupt conclusion.

'Courage,' said the doctor.

The tone was almost triumphant: Fortnight resented the intrusion so much that he was glad of it. He felt that if he could concentrate on hating the doctor, he would get through to the end of this mistake. Perhaps that was what Holtius intended.

From one of the funnels a thin string of sacrificial smoke went up. Fortnight imagined that he heard the organ playing softly, tremolando. He knew that it could not be true, but he recognized the melody: 'Praise, my soul, the King of Heaven', no. 298 in the book, with a D pedal, too low for the Kid to reach. Perhaps the organist was wearing a candle in her cap. He entered the office by its mottled green-glass door. The doctor minced at his heels, and Fortnight felt the sharp eyes focussed on him.

The solitary chair on the public side was occupied by an old man in a pale brown mackintosh, with parchment-coloured hands and sandy teeth. He stared open-mouthed at the clock on the facing wall. At the off-sales counter was a woman with an adenoidal face. Two officials in blue uniforms stood before her at a heavy ledger, slowly turning the pages. They uttered names and dates in self-important accents, as though rehearsing a lineage or citing referees. The woman seemed unwilling to disturb them. Fortnight too felt that their office placed them beyond communication.

'Speak,' said the doctor, in a venomous tone.

'Good morning!' Fortnight shouted, to no one in particular.

One of the officials looked up. His face was grey and oozing, like half-boiled meat, and he stared at Fortnight out of blank and cancelled eyes.

'Moody,' his companion said. 'Reginald Arthur. Thirty-first of January.'

'Yes,' said the first official, in a non-committal tone.

'I should like to know . . .'

Fortnight hesitated. What had he come to ask? Whether she had died? When? Where? He could already answer those questions, in a rough sort of way. The official went back to the ledger and read out another name.

'Speak,' the doctor repeated.

'Excuse me!' Fortnight shouted.

'Yes,' the man said.

'I have to know where my mother's ashes are.'

'That's better,' said the doctor, and Fortnight looked round at him with experimental anger.

'All in due time,' said the official, returning to his reading.

Fortnight stared for a while at the calendar on the wall, open for June, with a coloured photograph of an English village. Below it, on a chrome-legged table, were more ledgers, all with red plastic bindings. There was something that he should remember. It had to do with the sleeve of the second official. There was a long brown stain on the blue cloth, stretching in a thin line from the brass buttons of the cuff to the creases at the elbow. He felt certain that it was a burn.

The first official closed the ledger and, while his companion exchanged it for another, slowly looked up.

'Well, young man.'

'Speak,' said the doctor.

'I must know where my mother's ashes are.'

'You'll have to wait. We're still dealing with this lady.'

The new ledger was produced, and more names were read out.

'Yes,' said the woman. 'That's it. Potter. Thought it was Potter. Thirty-first of Janry. Thought it was.'

She smiled a gappy, shapeless smile, her eyes popping. The first official turned again to Fortnight.

'Right,' he said, 'what's the name?'

'Fortnight. Mrs Angela Fortnight.'

'And when did she pass away?'

Despite the euphemism the tone was crisp and brutal.

Fortnight hesitated. 'I'm fairly certain it was the 18th of March.'

'Eighteen March. And what year?'

The man raised a hand to rub the side of his large grey nose, which was covered with a glistering wetness that refused to go away.

'This year. Three months ago.'

'Then you'll 'ave to come back tomorrow. It's all being typed up. March was a bad month. Rushed off our feet we were.'

Fortnight was puzzled. For a second or two he observed the man's neck as it pulsed behind the soft collar of his grey official shirt. Fortnight could never feel comfortable with such people. They had a way of simplifying every situation, reducing it to the least number of variables, time, work, sleep, money, and by this device they always stole a march on him as he ponderously toyed with eccentric observations. He felt unfortunate in belonging to no definite class — straddled on the limbs of this social order he was pulled now up, now down, now at the head, now at the feet, by forces which he did not understand and which were deaf to every argument. That was why, he suddenly reflected, he had felt such pleasure in Mr Archer's grocery and, in another way, in the back room of Mrs Williams's sweet-shop. The peace was one of pure acceptance, such as the Kid was going to pursue in the brewery. Memo: not to telephone Susan. The man, he noticed, was beginning to turn away.

'This won't do,' said the doctor beneath his breath.

'Yes but you see,' said Fortnight, 'I only wanted to know where her ashes are.'

After all, it wasn't much to ask. It was not as though he had required an eye or a leg. He only wished that Dr Holtius would stop looking at him.

'How do I know?' said the man tetchily. 'I said you've got to come back tomorrow. Didn't you put a marker?'

'A marker?'

'A plack. With 'er name or a bit of scripcher or a 'ymn. That's what they usually do. Then you'd know what rose it is.'

'Rose?'

'Yes. Rose.'

'Rose.'

Fortnight meditated on his mother's most hated flower.

'No, it wouldn't have been a rose.'

'They don't allow nothing else.'

Fortnight thought for a moment.

'Where are these roses?'

'In the Garden of Rest,' said the man, slowly and impressively.

The rudeness seemed no more than a just punishment for his own confusion. If he had presented a picture of honest grief, no doubt he would have been dealt with accordingly. The doctor was breathing in an agitated way.

'And where is that?'

'Out the door, round to the left, straight down the bottom, turn right. March this year'll be on 'Hawthorn Prospeck' round about the middle I should think. Who's next?'

The man loudly addressed the room, but it was empty now, except for Fortnight, the doctor, and the old man in the mackintosh, who sat in silence, chewing with his mouth as though to induce the stretched skin to fit more comfortably on his tiny features.

'That man!' breathed the doctor, as they reached the air. 'How could he! What unfeelingness! What . . .'

'He was right.'

They made a few steps along a concrete path.

'I don't understand you,' said Dr Holtius.

'Oh? I thought you understood everyone.'

'My dear, I know you are distressed . . .'

'Just tell me one thing. Why did you pretend not to know me when we met at Susan's house?'

The doctor stopped walking and stood with a melancholy expression, facing the grey downs like a king surveying stolen territory.

'Perhaps you would rather I waited for you?' he offered.

'Oh no. Two's company.'

They crossed an alley of shrubs, with a notice advising them to take flowers to the Chapel of Rest. Glass jars, vases and jam jars not permitted. Visitors particularly requested *not* to lay wreaths on the rose-beds. Holly wreaths and similar tributes brought at Christmas-tide to be laid in an area near the chapel which will be specially indicated.

'You see. It's all well organized,' said Fortnight. 'They do a good job.'

They continued down the slope, facing the cool wind that started up the hillside. The doctor sighed with a great accomplishment of miserableness. A wiry entanglement of trees and bushes gave on to sloping lawns, with the small scimitars of rose-beds arranged around a central track. Most of the roses were beginning to bud. Here and there a red or yellow flower was opening. Fortnight looked at the small brass labels which gave the meaning of each thorny stem. 'To John; All that he came to give he gave and went again'; 'Love's last gift Remembrance'; 'Janet, till we meet again'; 'Good Night, God Bless'; 'Sadly missed'. Fortnight laughed, and at once he felt the nervous presence at his side, greedy for emotion. He must offer a scrap. He stopped and turned. There behind the doctor's yellow head stood the incinerator where his mother had been burned.

'I am . . . I am sorry.'

Holtius shrugged his shoulders, twitched slightly, and then tried to smile.

'I didn't want to upset your plans.'

'*My* plans!'

Some of the rose stems, he noticed, had no plaque, but only a metal ring bearing a number. 'It shall be well with them who fear God.'

'That's a good one,' he said.

'Why don't we look for the place he mentioned.'

The doctor's voice seemed very close, as though it were about to pounce into Fortnight's head.

'Yes. I'll look for it. Let's meet in a few minutes time. I'll come back here.'

'As you wish.'

Fortnight moved on. Almost at once he felt confident that he had put a distance between himself and the doctor. Soon he reached a turning: 'Acacia Walk'. Then another; then another. Only the sound of the wind as it stole through the rose-stems disturbed his complete failure to meditate. In front of him appeared the wooden sign for Hawthorn Prospect. He turned in the direction that it indicated, beginning to walk faster. Breathing seemed difficult; his eyes began involuntarily to close.

Suddenly he heard footsteps behind him. He stopped and waited. He could tell from the sound that it was a man, but a small man, bent forward perhaps, hurrying towards him up the slope. Soon he would pass. Would they greet each other? Would the man turn as he passed and stare at Fortnight curiously, revealing some terrible feature like a lopped-off nose, a tumour or a shot-away chin? Fortnight focussed his attention on the unseen stranger as though he would bring answers to every question. Now the man was at his side, sniffing, panting, gasping. Fortnight froze.

It was the old man in the mackintosh. He hurried onwards up the hill towards the chapel, occasionally flicking a tear from his right eye with a stiff parchment hand. Fortnight watched him and then furtively mimicked the gesture, trying it out. All at once he began uncontrollably to weep.

He sat down on a bench. After a while he was able to look at his surroundings. The bench had been given by musician friends in memory of Herbert Thorpe. It was inscribed *Kyrie Eleison*. In the distance a patch of sunlight splashed on the downs, crowning a sheep-spotted rise, and then was quickly erased by the hurrying rainclouds. A slight drizzle had begun to fall. Partly because of this, and partly because the form of the doctor had materialized on the bench beside him and was vainly endeavouring to take his hand, Fortnight rose. He followed the mackintosh towards the Chapel of Rest.

Before one of the roses was a wooden marker, with *Angela* inscribed on it. It was the place where her ashes were buried. If the doctor were not watching he would stand and reflect on it. Even so, he paused long enough to see another wooden marker, this time with the solitary name 'Jennie' painted in black on its slimy surface. It was likely that those in charge would have used her familiar name, the vicar for example, Aunt Kate, perhaps he himself had unwittingly put his signature to some forgotten document. On the other hand the Colonel would have preferred, as a gesture of studied realism, to call her Angela, consigning her to eternity under a name that he had never used. For a brief moment his eyes shifted between the two competing plots of earth. And then, annoyed with her, he moved on.

The chapel was small and round, sheathed in the same flesh-coloured brick as the other buildings. Inside it was bare, light, with perfunctory imitations of black marble in the walls. Pillars of pressed cement divided it into alcoves, in each of which a long narrow strip of glass descended from the ceiling to a pool beneath the floor. One of them contained a notice: 'Please put all flowers here today'; it was completely bare. The remaining alcoves were filled with gaudy flowers in varying stages of corruption. There was no altar, only a table overlaid with a laundered cloth of white linen. Fortnight lifted the cloth: the glass case containing the Book of Remembrance was exhibited beneath. The book was open at the page for 11th June. Barnaby bright, longest day and shortest night. He began to claw at the case, hoping to turn back to the 18th March — or thereabouts. Then he noticed one of the inscriptions:

Alice Gillian Bickerstaff 1900-1968: 'So brief her time she scarcely knew the meaning of a sigh.'

He began to laugh. Soon he was shaking the glass case, scratching his fingers as he tried to prize it open. He listened to his laughter as though it belonged to someone else. He was almost interested in the character who could make such a sound.

A shadow darkened the page, and Fortnight turned. He nodded to the old man in the mackintosh, whose blank grey eyes seemed unaffected by the tears that streamed from them. Fortnight released the little table, and the old man took it from him. He too began to shake it, addressing the book with an expressionless stare. His cries now filled the chapel. He rocked the little table, violently at first and then gradually more softly, until, as Fortnight backed from the door, his movements had assumed the rhythm of a lullaby.

Outside Fortnight felt a pain in his chest, and he reached one hand to where his heart should be. He found a bench on which to sit. He thought of his mother with anger. She was a waving of ribbons in a breeze. Once, at her death, the ribbons had formed a pattern. But he had missed the moment, and had no knowledge of the meaning that was contained in it. He could not be sure even that it had happened.

'My dear . . .'

The doctor pirated his masterless hand. Curious at the intrusion, Fortnight half turned towards the sky of oily greys. Behind Dr Holtius a blue monument of raincloud rose on baroquish bulwarks athwart the sun.

'This is no laughing matter,' he said.

The doctor's sallow skin tensed itself, and bore its droplets patiently; the eyes became sombre with emotions not lightly to be borne. Fortnight felt that he owed the doctor something, if not love, and so allowed his hand to remain enfolded.

'I am sorry,' said Dr Holtius, 'I wanted you to feel this. And now I see that I was wrong. Forgive me, please.'

Again the note of command strode through the hollow reaches of his sentence.

'Feel what?'

The doctor, relinquishing Fortnight's hand, stared towards the downs. A sort of acrimonious beauty entered his parakeet features. He jerked his coverlet of wispy hair and it erected itself like a cockerel's crest. The old man in the mackintosh emerged from the chapel, battling forward, infinitely ignorant of the present tense.

'Do not be cruel.'

'I am cruel. Look at the way I treat my brother.'

'It is better not to speak.'

Obediently Fortnight steadied his stare on an unclaimed rose-stem. After a long moment the doctor unfolded himself.

'We'll go now,' he said.

All the way back Fortnight struggled to contain his anger. He was particularly angry with his mother, for being its object.

He began his narrative with harmless details. He remembered a snippet of dialogue which the Kid heard with a show of patience as he washed.

' "No it's a marmoset", said one of them. "I prefer to regard it as an ape", said the other, to which the reply was "Who is getting between your sheets, I wonder?". I didn't hear any more.'

The Kid continued washing. His face wore a puddingy expression of after school, and his eyes were puffy and slow. Fortnight could see from his earth-marked trousers that someone had been kicking him.

'And then I moved on, as I said.'

'Second subject. Dominant key.'

'There is no second subject exactly.'

'Transition and variation. Does just as well. But in fact all we've had so far is the upbeat.'

'I was on my way to visit Dr Holtius.'

'*Noctes atque dies patent atri* . . . shall I translate for you?'

'By night and by day the gates of Dis stand open.'

'Go on then. You were talking of him.'

'He took me to Lees Hill. To the crematorium.'

'Characteristically ghoulish.'

The Kid followed with a loud blowing of water from his mouth and nose. The kitchen seemed, for a moment, hardly to contain his movements.

'We ought to eat some of that chutney,' he said.

'At the crematorium, I . . .'

'I've discovered, by the way, that Fist and Dis are in close communication.'

The Kid dropped the towel on to the floor, jumped on it, and then threw it into the laundry basket, where it lay on top of a pile of rotting cloth.

'We'd better get a cleaner too.'

'Why do you say that?'

'Admittedly, Kenny, I'm confused. My thoughts are balloons that I am packing through a window in a storm. But some of them are inside. Joining the Party was good for me. You know, there are some interesting people at the meetings. For example, Dis has his letters delivered by an Indian postman who has a degree in biology from the University of Bombay. Not a bad Latinist either. Promised to teach me Sanskrit.'

'Before the revolution or after?'

'The date of the revolution is not yet fixed. Or at least it has been mislaid. I have no note in my diary. Oh, and another thing. This man from Chattaways who also comes to our meetings is quite interested in the set of delft. Fist offered it for three grand a couple of years back. Apparently they now think its worth twice as much.'

The tension was mounting in the Kid's voice. Without his glasses he had to keep his eyes half-closed. His appearance was that of a face squashed against a window. A terrible wailing broke from him at last. Rushing at his brother, he beat him on the chest time after time with his large soft fists.

'Go away! Get out of this kitchen! Ghoul! Monster!'

The Kid prepared a meal of bacon scraps and kidney beans. They ate in silence. The third place had returned to the table.

During dinner Fortnight recalled a remark of Barbara's, to the effect that the nearest he ever came to love was the feeling of guilt that he could come no nearer. He wanted to do something to disprove it. Several times he tried to break the silence. And then, looking around him he suddenly saw a way.

The box of tools had been tipped over the scullery floor. He began to reassemble it. The Kid watched him for a few minutes and then, picking up a brush from under the sink, began to sweep out the corners. After a while a division of labour was silently established. The Kid performed their mother's tasks, Fortnight their father's. They continued wordlessly. Fortnight wiped all the box-wood handles of the chisels and sharpened their blades. He cleaned the metal planes, oiled the blade of the brass-bound handsaw, and slowly restored to each object the sheen of its old utility. When he had finished he shifted some of the furniture, and the Kid cleaned the floor with bucket and mop. They repaired the plug of the washing-machine, and found some detergent with which to begin soaking the dirty clothes. The Kid began to hum softly as he worked. Soon they had closed the scullery door and were working in the kitchen. When the telephone rang Fortnight went quietly into the hall, placed the clamorous object in the bottom of the chest on which it stood, and covered it with some of his mother's clothes that were hanging under the stairs. It continued to ring, but it mattered less when its appeal was so faint.

Their domestic life began again. They did not quarrel, but manoeuvred their feelings around each other with agonizing gestures. The Kid refrained from mentioning the doctor, and Fortnight refrained from passing comment on the Kid's experiment in not quite living. When Fortnight at last disinterred the telephone to ring Susan, the thing came out alive and shrieking in his hand. He answered. The doctor commanded him to visit. He put down the receiver, knowing he would obey. Then he telephoned Susan. He was at first surprised, and then gratified, by the news that she had gone to London. He decided to postpone his love for her, and to that end, he returned the telephone to the bottom of the chest.

Calling in at the brewery was his first mistake since the crematorium. It made him realize that he was as unfree in his hatred as a man in love. He lacquered the feeling with a sweetness of compunction, and then, carefully, carried it over to the doctor's house. Dr Holtius welcomed him with the look of an artist gazing on his work, deciding whether it had improved or spoiled since last he studied it. During the second or two of expert assessment Fortnight's soul burned again with panic. Together they conducted the blackened remnant to the doctor's study, to be bottled up in words.

'I am deeply offended,' said the doctor, 'for example, by your late arrival.'

'I looked in on my brother.'

'I looked in on my brother.'

'Why do you imitate me?'

'So that you can hear your voice. I hate it. I hate you to betray yourself. Also you do not smile at me. Why don't you smile at me?'

'I meant to smile at you.'

'That is precisely what makes it impossible to smile.'

'Then I can't help it.'

'Can't help it? My dear Kenneth, every expression is the shadow of an intention. Look at you.'

Fortnight wondered whether he should use a mirror for this

purpose. There were no mirrors in the doctor's study, and this was a relief because he felt disinclined to see his flesh hang bloodless on its cliffs of bone.

When he left it was only after a strange penance of tears had been exacted from him, tears which he could not understand, except that they sprang from hatred and not from love. The Kid was waiting for him, with a new episode of the story marked 'Cock and Bull'.

Chapter Six

'WHAT REALLY happened was this. When Mummy left she was extremely concerned about my state of mind. She had read a description in some cranky book corresponding exactly point by point to my case. Her lack of a classical education makes her vulnerable to that kind of stuff. So Fist, who was planning her departure pretty carefully by then, started to look round for some way to put her mind, or maybe, if I can use the word, my mind, at rest. He concocted the Dis idea. They are old partners in crime. I'll tell you what we've discovered, Mr Patel and I.'

'Mr Patel?'

'From the Post Office. First of all that Grabenaz is a friend of Dis. They were at Oxford together, and it is actually her house he's staying in at present: he moves into places as others move out of them. That's how he met Fist. I don't say that they immediately took a liking to each other. But they were mutually serviceable. Dis, of course, has no qualifications. I grant you that he took a degree with lots of Ps in it at Oxford and then went for a while to a place in London called the Tavistock, but it was only in obedience to fashion. His title is *Philosophiae Doctoris*, and he has no claim to be allowed to tinker with people's intellectuals. But that's neither there nor here. Apparently when this chap Ninian Adaire . . .'

'Ninian Adaire?'

'Yes, the architect who was working on Fist's projects, when he cracked up, and looked like giving evidence for the Flackwell Society, it seems that Dis got hold of him and brought him back to his, at least to someone's, senses. Fist has gone on believing in Dis ever since. He persuaded Mummy that I ought to be shrunk by him. That explains Dis coming here, although I admit he too has his motives if I am not mistaken. Well, as I was saying, when she was passing through the other day . . .'

'Passing through?'

'You didn't see her? It's true she didn't have much time. Well, she had heard I was working in the brewery, and dropped in to see me in the bottle shop, much as you did this morning. She was looking gorgeous in a summer frock and Doris came over all maidenly at the sight of her. I went to give her a hand with the suitcases, only she wouldn't allow it, saying I had better obey union rules. She asked me to stop working soon, now that I've proved my pointlessness, and maybe — she didn't say which doctor exactly, but maybe I should . . .'

The Kid sat down at the piano and played five loud chords, before beginning to cry.

Over the next weeks Fortnight began to make blunders in everything. Even the Kid reproached him for his lack of table manners. He could not concentrate on the conveyancing, much as he had been moved at first by the Land Charges Act. The Kid's attendance at the brewery was becoming irregular, and occasionally they would have to worry about money. Fortnight also wanted time to read, to write, to think even. But the doctor begrudged this time more fiercely every day. Because the telephone was not answered Holtius would come knocking at the door, so as to rage in the Colonel's study at the intolerable predicament in which he had been placed. It was of course unfair; Fortnight conceded as much to the doctor. But the Kid's employment was not only irregular, it was also illegal; he *had* to work for Oddle, there was no alternative . . .

'For Oddle?' squawked the doctor, whose outstretched fingers were conducting the massed choirs of the Red Army in 'Ride a Cock Horse'.

'Yes. For Oddle. I suppose that must be wrong.'

'That's for you to answer. How is it that you did not tell me?'

'Perhaps I forgot.'

'Oh, as for that, you will have known my feelings. You simply hid it from me, a particularly base form of perfidy.'

'This is tiresome,' said Fortnight, with the sense of one forbidding with his hand the advance of a hungry lion.

'Nothing concerning myself is tiresome.'

Bright echelons of angels beat their wings in the Colonel's study. Fortnight held his hands close to his beleaguered face.

'All right. I am sorry. I am to blame. It is deducible from incontrovertible principles of pure mathematics that I am to blame.'

'Make no mistake,' the doctor continued urgently, 'I have nothing against Oddle. In his small, preoccupied, lousy way he is a character. He has qualities of seediness and malice which are to be envied. You should not stop seeing him for my sake.'

It was always for his own sake that Fortnight was commanded.

That evening the Kid announced that the big discovery was imminent. To celebrate they should go to the fun fair which was about to close. When they came across Angela Williams, spick and span and turning like a doll in the hands of a large red man, she smiled, waving to them, and Fortnight waved back. But the Kid took him quickly by the arm.

'We must be scaramouching along, there's the ghost train to attend to, and, look, a whole tray of saucy underwear to win with three shots of the rifle, my, those slinky stockings in Costa Brava tan, and tantalizing directoire knickers, I just have to shoot them down for you, so that you can hand them over to Mrs T at the library with a stage whispery ceremony of devotion. . . .'

He fired wildly into the canvas and then, throwing down two shillings, wriggled away. They dodged through the crowd into a clearing, where stood a Guy Fawkes figure in Oxfam clothing, his straw hair sketched against the air like aborted lightning. He gestured towards a booth, and because the lips of his grey mouth married inexactly the Kid breathed a sigh of relief when the man began to speak.

'Come and see her! Come and see the alligator girl! Alone in a cage with two live alligators! Rubbing against her naked flesh! Blood curdling spectacle! See it if you dare! Come and see! Two bob a throw!'

They entered and stared for a while at the large blonde with crows-foot eyes and sagging flesh, who sat in a heated cage of glass. Two leather valises lay at her feet, and from time to time she would kick one of them, so that it momentarily revealed to the spectators one half of a sleep-sodden eye. Her lardy white skin clashed with the emerald green of her bikini. Her vacant eyes met the Kid's, and at once he began to cry. He was inconsolable over the alligator girl. 'How could they!' he repeated, 'How could they! For hour after hour after hour! What a dismal decorum! The shame of it!'

They restored themselves with two bottles of burgundy and some piano duets. During a Schubert silence the Kid cocked his head and let his hands fall from the piano.

'Do you hear it?' he asked.

'Hear what?'

'Listen!'

And indeed there was a noise, a faint low wailing somewhere in the upper reaches of the house.

'What is it?'

'Have you never heard it?'

The Kid turned towards him the two full precarious globes of eye-lymph.

'I . . . no . . .'

The noise began to swell. For a moment it seemed almost as though someone were sobbing up there. And then the sound dwindled into non-existence.

'Let's carry on,' said the Kid, with forced nonchalance. 'It's nothing. It only happens when you play lots of As and Fs together, and even then only sometimes.'

The grey clouds moved asunder and exposed a flash of blue. The wind rose, shaking the trees, blowing the cut grass from the petrol-mower across the borders of the lawn. Everything in the park seemed to be hurrying eastwards, and the two little Yorkshire terriers, Fons and Origo, ran yapping in the wake of scattered things, holding now a green branch, now a flowerhead, now a scrap of paper in their jaws.

'Don't let him get up your nose,' said Susan.

She was lying on the bed in the pose of the Maja Desnuda, wearing her nakedness as she would the latest fashion, with trained insouciance. It was another glass through which to show herself to the world. Susan was the high priestess of appearance, a glittering florilegium of aspects, a phenomenon with no material core.

'Can't you explain to him?'

She laughed, a high tinkling laugh. 'Explain! To him! As though he didn't know what he's doing.'

'What on earth do you see in me?'

She lifted herself half off the bed and looked at him kindly. 'I don't see anything in you. I just see, and desire. If you want a reason, I can invent one that is fairly near to the truth.'

She raised her voice in theatrical accents.

'Secretly I am very like you. I am a creature tormented by ambitions for which I have no name. I too have spent my life playing with rejected roles. I need now — now that I am married and fashionable — to have serious affairs with people who haven't made it. I need to feel that the real me reserves judgement on my social antics, that I am still exploring possibilities that most people leave behind forever. You see, your actual failure, your real incurable chump, is a *rara avis*. A drop-out is no failure; a bohemian is no failure. You've got to combine ambition and doubt; certainty and hesitation. There we have the essence of Kenneth Fortnight. But actually I love him — well let's not exaggerate — I like him for his looks as well.'

She got up and kissed him.

'I seem to have got myself into a muddle.'

'But darling, only you can get out of it. Because only you are in it. Adrian's not in a muddle. Far from it.'

The truth of this remark caused him to sigh. It felt like the eructation from some common grave, where unnumbered corpses have been bundled after a plague. Swallows were skimming low above the lawn, arching over the bank and encircling the urns. The mower had stopped, and now sputtered as the gardener pulled at the twisted starter-cord.

'It is going to rain.'

'Those poor little darlings.'

'What poor little darlings?'

'Fons and Origo. I must fetch them in.'

Susan dressed quickly and went out. He was beginning to feel angry again, and was pleased to have Susan to be angry with.

She took him rabbiting at the edge of the park. He was dazzled by her appearance. She looked so impossibly healthy with her fair skin whipped into points of light by the high west wind, her long legs in blue jeans striding through the grass, and her tweed jacket with a twelve-bore jutting from the armpit. From time to time she would turn to look at him as he stumbled in her wake. He felt happy, and when they opened fire on four little rabbits which were sitting up to nibble in the light of a smouldering sun, a curious elation overcame him. He ran up to Susan and took her by the elbow to kiss her ear. She looked cross.

'Oh do stop! Couldn't you go and kill them? I really can't bear the way they scream. It makes me feel quite dreadful.'

Fortnight limped over to the place where the rabbits lay. Two of them had been hit, and one was already dead, lying on its side with no sign of an injury except for a single tear of blood that slowly formed behind one eye and oozed on to its muzzle. The other rabbit was kicking and screaming. Fortnight felt sick. He hesitated to take it by the legs. But then he looked back at Susan who was walking away from him towards the house, and his anger renewed itself. He snatched up the rabbit and hit it again and again on its neck. As he did so his legs trembled and he said aloud 'wretched thing! poor damned wretched thing!'

He stayed late that day, feeding on his anger. All evening after dinner she was on the telephone, and, since Lord Gilroy was away, he stole into the library and began to browse. A numbness came over him as he approached the big partner's desk at which his mother must have sat. It was covered now with untidy piles of newspaper cuttings. He was puzzled to find that the one lying uppermost had been extracted from the *Flackwell Courier,* and described the Kid's brief sally into public life. When he returned to the drawing-room, Susan was still in battle with the telephone.

'What? Did you? My dear how uncanny! I have just had one myself — well, it isn't as though it were a hysterectomy. I should think so. Yes, that would be lovely. Oh, wait a minute. I've just remembered a beastly cocktail party of Hugo's for that American youth of his. One has to encourage it, if it is true that it *is* the real thing . . .'

Sometimes she would look across from her chair with an expression of mortal hatred directed neither at him nor at the telephone, but at some far distant point where all these ghosts were somehow projected in a conglomerate inhuman sprawl.

'Bye,' she said suddenly, and looked at him.

'Well, that's over,' she went on, 'and I'm glad. Please don't criticize.'

'I had no intention . . .'

'You were about to criticize, don't deny it.'

'Have you got anything to drink?'

'Good idea. Let's have a beano.'

'Just one glass of something will be enough.'

'Come upstairs.'

It seemed that Susan wanted him to sleep with her. He tried to concentrate on this fact, as she led him through the gallery. The faint glitters of ornamental objects were uncanny in the darkness: he could make nothing out, but it seemed as though eyes followed them everywhere. The house creaked. As they turned the corner, a brief snatch of song from the kitchen struck their ears. Then everything settled into silence.

'I think you are very strange,' he said to her as she undressed, 'very strange, and very hollow.'

'Oh yes?' she said, forming her face into a question-mark, 'is that what you think?'

'It's not what I *think*. The idea came to me.'

He stroked the grey cat that had followed them through the door until its fur was electric and its face wore a mask of swooning ecstasy. 'Nice cat,' he muttered, 'lovely little puss, lovely little oedipus'. Susan stared at him mockingly.

'And what more have you refrained from thinking?'

'I expect there's something more.'

He lifted his hand from the cat which jumped down suddenly and walked off with its tail in the air.

'I am sorry to irritate you. I irritate everybody.'

She said it as though to point out that a fault so widely distributed had the dignity of custom.

'I am to blame,' said Fortnight, doubtfully.

'Just wait, I am not the least bit angry with you for what you said. And I shall go on displeasing you to the point where I take pleasure in it.'

'*Le plaisir aristocratique de déplaire*.'

'Yes; it will be good for you.'

'And for you?'

'I've explained all that. Stop being neurotic and come to bed.'

He could not sleep. He lay awake thinking. He had slept alone on every night since he left Barbara. He thought about this fact obsessively, and from time to time turned to observe the static form of Susan at his side. He thought that there were three kinds of sleeper: those like Barbara who abandon their bodies at night and leave them thrown down and vacated like heaps of sacking; those like Susan who stay in their bodies, carefully, scrupulously, arranging their last positions before sleep overtakes them and even then keeping close silent vigil within; and those like himself who leave their bodies but, unable to be fully parted from them, stay beside them, locked in a childlike embrace. First he would lie on the left side, and then quickly roll over on to his right, hoping to seize the vanishing spectre of his former position. And so it would continue until far into the night, his anxiety mounting as the hope of success decreased. He watched Susan enviously, and, once, she opened her eyes, smiled, and closed them again.

Deprived of solitary habits he could neither sleep nor wake. He rose at daybreak, and prepared to go. Susan watched him.

'You must come back,' she said, 'every day, however much I make you cross. Will you promise? Please. And don't worry about Adrian. Will you promise that too? The best way out is through the French window in the drawing-room. Ring me.'

The doctor was walking on the road to Flackwell, staring wild-eyed at Fortnight as he approached. He did not greet his victim, but simply turned and fell into step beside him.

'We must start,' he said, 'from the assumption that every conceivable weapon against each other has already been used. I've thought about it, and I know that that is so. I cannot be angry with you, nor you with me.'

Having received these instructions Fortnight felt obliged to point out to the doctor that his anger was his own concern. The doctor, who had a quite different conception of the ownership of Fortnight's feelings replied, his head dislocated to one side, and his hands engaged in some urgent transaction at his back, 'My God your coldness is astounding. I actually don't believe that you are as you appear. It must be the morning air that has sullied my perceptions. I have nothing more to say to you.'

They walked on unspeaking. The doctor's sighs passed across Fortnight's soul like wind over a graveyard, giving voice to a thousand absences. Then abruptly Dr Holtius stopped.

'You walk on,' he said. 'I don't want to be with you. I don't want to have anything to do with you. Not just at present.'

After a few minutes Fortnight reached the outlying houses,

which he failed to recognize. The brocaded curtains, huge and formless from sleep, the few figures in the frames of kitchen windows, the grey squally cloud scudding over the unstoppered chimney-stacks: everything seemed oppressed, insane, unfathomable. Every form was wrapped with its individual ghostliness, and stood among its surroundings in untouchable isolation. Even his own house seemed distant and provisional, like a stage decor, as he stumbled through the garden. He approached the shed and his eyes refused any longer to stay open.

He found himself sitting on the step of the shed, having just been woken up.

'So it's you!' he cried.

The Kid stood before him in his blue dungarees. A plate of sticky beans was in one hand.

'I happened to be taking breakfast. Is that unusual? Not so unusual, I think, as you spending the night in the potting-shed, or elsewhere.'

And then, with an urgent expression, he cocked his head and listened to something. He let his plate tip so that the beans began to ooze on to the lawn.

'Did you hear it?' he asked.

'Stop it!' Fortnight cried. 'For heaven's sake stop it!'

He got up rapidly and stormed into the house. In the Colonel's study he stared for a while at the books: the red covers of the Army Lists stood out among the dignified old bindings. His eyes rested on one of the titles: *The Old Colonel and the Old Corps, with a View of Military Estates*, by a certain Lieutenant Gleig. Then the Kid's favourite: Grouard's *Stratégie Napoléonienne*, over which they had argued so acrimoniously. Now he was truly angry with the Kid, and he feared that this anger would not go away, that it would stay rankling inside him until it was at last able to leap out and destroy its object.

He took a sheet of writing-paper in order to break off with Susan. He imagined her expression as she read his letter, the quick way in which she would categorize his sentiments, understanding without condemning, since this, like every move in the game of love, was already too familiar to evoke any lively dismay. He wrote:

Having failed in my attempt to love you I feel dreadfully ashamed of myself. I am sure that you will understand when I say that I would rather not see you again.   K

He laughed a little at the 'K', but he felt less happy about confessing to shame. He had the idea that she would feel better if he did so; but was it true that he felt so ashamed? And why should he confess what he felt, unless it was by way of slyly continuing the very attempt that this letter was supposed to end? He said to himself that it did not matter. He would let the message stand. After all, it was an expression of himself, of Kenneth Fortnight, of the man he was, that is, of the man he wanted, that is to say, wanted to want to be.

On the way out he stepped on a letter. It was addressed to the Kid in Barbara's hand. He put it into his pocket and walked down the drive. Why was the letter so thin? It seemed more disturbing that they communicated briefly, since it implied that there was something definite to say. He turned back home, after a while, unable to reach the Post Office.

The doctor was waiting for him at the door.

'Do you mind, please, if I speak to you?'

Fortnight commanded his face to smile out a greeting. He knew that the whole safety of his being depended upon the corners of his mouth ascending to the right points on his cheeks. Not too high, for that would indicate indifference; not too low, for that would show weakness, cruelty, or pain. Most of all he must not be unhappy. He made welcoming noises, offered tea, tried to move about the laughing-room with calm hospitable gestures. For the presence of unhappiness of which he was not himself the cause made the doctor impatient, like a door slamming somewhere in the wind. If only Holtius were patient, Fortnight imagined, then the matter would be quickly and amicably resolved.

'Please be kind to me,' said the doctor at last.

Clearly he was annoyed that his command had been obeyed before he had time to issue it.

'But I do intend to be kind.'

The doctor's newborn susceptibility was held out on cradled bony arms towards him, fragile, in need of an oxygen tent. Fortnight dared not breathe on it. He made a half-formed gesture in the air, and smiled towards his grandmother's anxious portrait.

'You brute, you savage,' the doctor murmured.

The Kid would know how to deal with this, thought Fortnight. He would be able to laugh. The doctor got up and walked about that room which refused to contain him, which lay for the moment manifestly outside his usurpations. Fortnight studied the pockets of the black velvet jacket, and felt the doctor breathing the air of his weird ambitions, the self-appointed redeemer, desperate for a Judas kiss. Fortnight's perception of the pockets seemed to cut him off from their owner, through a kind of realism which the doctor — confronting the world as he did with demands of transcendent retribution — could neither achieve nor desire. Fortnight felt absurdly pleased with himself, and even began to smile. He recalled his mother's forsworn religion. Jesus, now, he had no fussy peculiarities; the New Testament contains no record of his way of standing, of the moving of his hands, the lineaments of his dress, the odd incidentals of existence. His dominion could not be upset, as the doctor's was, by the underhand observation of random parts.

Holtius bounded suddenly forward. 'And you can only smile!' he cried.

'Well, goodbye,' Fortnight replied, with an exhausting affectation of insincerity.

The doctor too smiled. 'I see that you want me to stay.'

Turning, he slowly drew the damask curtains of the laughing-room, shifting as he did so Mrs Fortnight's japanned workbox. Fortnight observed with fascination as the room, portion by portion, and against all his expectations, was turned against him.

'No,' he said, 'you can't'.

'You do not understand me,' said the doctor. 'I have to teach you a lesson.'

'A lesson?'

'Tell me first what you are feeling.'

'Feeling? About what?'

'About me, of course.'

Fortnight searched for an answer. A vast detour through the caverns of his breast yielded nothing. The brief triumph in the matter of the pockets had been stowed away, perhaps for future use, and the Kid's laughter was now inaudible. He received the information calmly and consulted Clausewitz in his mind. The best thing at this point would be to retire to a defensive position, some convenient moral vantage-point, and there erect a garrison.

'Is it the word "feeling" that confuses you? Feelings can be very embarrassing. *I* am very embarrassing.'

Since what was happening could not happen, least of all in that room, it was not happening, and so Fortnight made no move.

'My brother . . .' he said, after a while. It was the doctor's signal.

'Do I care about your brother? Forget your brother. Forget all these worn excuses. How can I go now, when it seems that you want me to? You are behaving irrationally. If you want me to go, then of course you have to be kind to me. It is no easier for me than it is for you, to come across such elementary truths in all their simplicity. But you do not trust me, so you struggle to reject me, and what can I do but resist?'

It was all very reasonable. Fortnight saw in that brief second, before the doctor clasped his hand and pulled at it in desperation, that there were methods whereby justice could be driven out. And what came to replace it — the severe, single, undivided will — shared with it so many attributes that only in rare moments of clarity could a man separate the two. Holtius created about the two of them a pure cocoon of reasoning, so that Fortnight wriggled and thrashed his feeble limbs, getting nowhere. Now the doctor was clutching him, and already his brief insight was slipping away, a detached part of himself, neutralized by their entanglement. He returned to thoughts of religion. So it must have been in the beginning, when God usurped the primeval right of punishment and reward; so near were the two that, even in His own eyes, God could make no difference between them, supposing that a redistribution of benefits would appease the outraged laws of nature. For no echoes of a pre-existing order could ever penetrate the cloud of reasoning that God at once flung around the created world. All was compelled to testify forever to His benevolence and power. Even the private vision of a finer world could find no expression in that universe, except as the putting up of false gods, less worthy usurpers of the same original force.

It was as such false divinities that he began to think of the Kid and Barbara, the doctor having insinuated that his feelings for them were insignificant. Holtius surrounded him with stratagems. Each session ended with a new idea — Fortnight should meet him for tennis, for music, for wine, for sexual initiation — which the doctor set forth as a test, having prepared him with the minutest examination of his failings in respect of things of this kind. Fortnight was compelled to agree, if he did not wish to add the crowning fault of obtuseness, that he *ought* to (play tennis, listen to music, drink some wine, go to bed) with the doctor. It was then not open to Fortnight to refuse, since his first experiments in hesitation brought the accusation that he principally feared: not only was he deficient in all these little kindnesses, but they were but a portent of that other and greater deficiency which, in removing love, removed the only reason for his existence. So Fortnight answered the doctor in the affirmative. What was done then became his doing. It was his choice, his decision, and if he did not go through with it, as the doctor neglected not to remind him, then this showed something yet more despicable in Fortnight, that he was prepared to lead the doctor on and then abandon him just at the moment when he had acquired (through Fortnight's voluntary actions) a helpless passion for tennis, music, wine, bed. Fortnight discovered the invisible hand of self-denial. He had committed himself for life through his own indecision, and the doctor was merely there to remind him of a duty to live up to it, an almost disinterested observer of his moral progress.

Moreover, the debt of gratitude had now become enormous, on account of Holtius's solution of the diary problem. The doctor had come across many similar cases, of people who, ignorant of their emotions, had conspired to give them furtive outlet. He showed that every passage implied some mute reflection on Mrs Fortnight's absence. The writing therefore had a quality of advance in retreat. According to the doctor the whole manner of the diary proved both the goodness of the writer, and the denial of that goodness. Likewise Fortnight denied his own goodness by paying such meticulous attention to his brother's moral views, or, for example, by not suggesting (as he ought by now to have suggested) that the doctor go to bed with him.

In reaction to these events the Kid became silent. He began to lose interest in the brewery, and only rarely attended the Communist Party meetings in the Guildhall. He spent most of his time at home, melancholy and alone, and when Fortnight handed over to him at last — having forgotten the matter for several days — the letter from Barbara, he simply pushed it behind the poetry books, and looked at his brother accusingly. On wild nights in July, when the trees in the garden shifted in the torn sheets of wind that squalled past the vicarage, the Kid would remain outside, sitting on his stool by the garden pond. Their mother had planted rushes there, but they had been overthrown, and the pond was choked with lilies and blown marsh marigolds. The few goldfish, extracted by the vicar's cat, had been replaced by a company of frogs. The Kid began to work again on his map, anxiously building a wall around the house, named Avernus, where Dr Holtius lived. Many lines had begun to radiate from Bramhurst Park, but they all sheered away from the wall and continued in some unexplored direction.

Only once did the Kid venture to express his feelings. Fortnight returned one afternoon, clutching his conveyancing papers, his face caked over with the dried remnants of anguish. The Kid burst from the laughing-room, his hands and face all grubby with bottle-washing, his glasses steamed over, and his hair, grown long now, greasy with sweat.

'Tell me where you've been', he cried.

'Why?'

'Because because because because.'

'I looked in on Dr Holtius.'

'And what did he prescribe? Orchestration?'

'He helped me, as always, to talk. Do you need to know?'

'Yes. How did he approach the matter? Lento appassionato? Teneramente? Con tutta forza? Mit Dämpfe?'

'I don't like these games.'

'Non troppo agitato, if you don't mind, Ken. It's me that should be seeing him, I've told you. Not you, at any rate. Why don't you let me go in your place? You know what she, what we ought to do.

We'd be better then. Allegrissimo harmonioso domesticato non troppo inteso, etcetera.'

He sketched in the air a proof of their future happiness, and then withdrew into the laughing-room, his small frame shuddering with emotion. That night it rained heavily. The Kid refused his supper and sat in the garden, motionless amid the warm patter of unceasing raindrops.

Fortnight decided not to keep his appointment with the doctor. He remained at home, and read to the Kid — who had caught cold and, after exhausting himself in the attempt to dress, remained on the floor of the laughing-room in his dungarees. The Kid spoke only to command another book, feeling dissatisfied until they had settled on Clausewitz. From time to time the telephone rang in the bottom of the chest; the Kid no longer even flinched at the sound. Fortnight added the Colonel's greatcoat to the garments that covered it.

The next day the Kid lay silent in bed, and Fortnight awoke from the appointed nightmare with the thought that he must visit Dr Holtius. As Fortnight passed the window of the study, the doctor's face registered great astonishment. No one answered the door, but it was open. Fortnight was able to pass unmolested to where the doctor sat.

'Adrian.'

The name filled his mouth with dust.

Slowly the doctor looked up. Then he extracted from his mouth a long string of intolerable pain. The sigh reached its blood-soaked root and jerked free.

'Ah!' he cried. 'It's you.'

'No,' Fortnight wanted to say. He could not. On the desk were three books, a bottle of ink, and a blank sheet of paper. Time had not moved in that room since last he was here.

'I cannot even be angry with you!' said Holtius at last, hitting his knuckles against invisible cliffs of air. Fortnight re-entered his nightmare through an open door, pondering the many points of exit which he knew he would not take. The only thing that came to mind was an implausible alibi involving Susan. He caught the doctor's contemptuous glance and petered out. The black eyes seemed full of hatred, of an unqualified desire to annihilate him.

'So you still have time to see Susan? That is good. That is very good.'

As a matter of fact Fortnight had seen her less and less. But he could not say this to the doctor, since it would imply that he felt accountable.

'Perhaps, my dear, I should introduce you to the doctrine of contrition. To apologize is not so difficult. It is simply a matter of accusing oneself. You must show an understanding of your fault, and humility before the fact of it. It needs only a small amount of courage, a minimum of manliness, to achieve this. Yet you will not. You seem to subscribe to the view that I am more interested in whether you will behave properly in future. But do you think that I am remotely concerned with your future? No. I want to be appeased here and now. I want contrition, and then the joy, the power of unconditional forgiveness. To forgive is to receive you back, regardless of those resolutions that you may or may not be making to yourself.'

The doctor began a discourse. It involved reference to many classical authorities, and was, no doubt, very persuasive. But Fortnight felt distracted. A few days earlier he had tried to tell Susan what was wrong, how sometimes, especially, as it seemed then, when listening to someone (yes, even herself, for example) whom he deeply respected, he would let his mind wander in a most appalling way, the words would seem to fade in the distance, and it would then strike him as a matter of supreme indifference whether he suddenly should walk away or not, or whether he should himself add some word or other to the hundreds that possessed the air. The meaning did not, as he saw it, exactly escape him. (He knew for example that the doctor was now commanding him to take off his clothes.) It would parade before his mind with a sense of independent purpose to which he had nothing to add. He would lose interest, not because his interest was directed elsewhere, but because suddenly his mind was blank. The parade distressed him, but in a secret inscrutable way that left him without resource.

He had looked at Susan, and she smiled, as she always did, with exemplary kindness, and total unconcern.

'Yes,' she said, 'I can see that. I know exactly what you feel.'

'Do you?', he said, but to himself. He wondered whether she did, and at once, wondering, ceased to care.

'No,' he said aloud, 'That's not it. I've got it wrong. That's not what I feel. It's something else.'

But he could not explain what it was. Always he seemed to be lying when he spoke to her.

He recalled this conversation as he walked with Dr Holtius to the bedroom. There too the doctor's sepulchral emptiness prevailed, as though he belonged to some other planet and was only passing through. The hideous furnishings looked untouched; the doctor's laundry lay on the floor in a brown paper parcel. There were few books, a single pile of papers which Holtius promptly removed from the bed to the floor, and four brown medicine bottles laid out on the dressing-table. The doctor lay on his back, still talking, and Fortnight, standing over him, began to take note of his surprising words.

'And if there is one thing that is perhaps even more lowering than your general inability to express yourself — an inability which even goes so far as to deprive you of the weapon of contrition — it is the petty bourgeois prudery of your manner towards me. I am not in general happy, you know Kenneth, nor do I need to be. But sometimes, thinking of you, I envisage a serenity which I believe is mine by right, and which you could provide quite easily at no cost to yourself. It is in moments like this, sitting with you quietly in this room, that I can forget the clamour of the world that surrounds us; I can feel my life, rich, still, shot through with meaning. You are the source of that meaning, and yet also the demon that would destroy it. Even when I caress your hand I feel a movement of withdrawal. And yet, if you came here today it was obviously with the intention that there should be more than idle caresses between us. Personally I consider myself fortunate in that I have never experienced disgust or outrage at any sexual act. Indeed, to tell you the truth, we live in an age when hesitation denotes only inhumanity or incompetence; in your case it is hard to know which. However, it really is absurd to go on yapping when there are better things to do.'

The doctor had risen from the bed, and now attacked with a commanding smile. Contrition, after all, had not been required. His eyes shone in the semi-darkness like black fruit on a bough, while outside the window the mid-afternoon stirred its sultry vat of meanings. The doctor advanced, his bony hands trembling and his mouth awry. He attempted to kiss Fortnight's lips, frowned, and then began to undress. Fortnight listened to the cicada-like sizzle of clothes peeling from the doctor's skin. He was horribly thin and soft-bellied.

Fortnight recognized the true meaning of the masculinity whose liturgy he had been compelled to master. But seeing it before him, in the dry form of the doctor's phallus, he saw also that it was a sophisticated fiction. In one moment Dr Holtius had obtained and surpassed his usefulness; it was only a lingering courtesy that persuaded his victim to stay. Fortnight looked at the object that was being pressed into his hand. This was not the familiar thing of the changing-rooms, the shy, excitable companion that shuddered and gushed amid ribaldry and laughter. It did not carry the marks of its owner's progress. It was not notched with conquests, had not been patted, nudged and nicknamed by all the gang. It had never suffered the magic change from stick to sceptre as idiocy gave way to tenderness in the first recognition of another, unknown world. Such things had nothing to do with the doctor's masculine principle, which had now translated itself from the highest moral rhetoric into a dry pulsating mushroom. Holtius was placing in his hand the abstract principle of judgement. Touching it, Fortnight's fingers burned, for it spoke neither of love nor of friendship, but only of unassuageable demand. The yellow pylon hummed between his fingers, transmitting doom-laden messages. He held the centre of civilization, a perpetual despondent Reith lecture on the subject of the moral good. It was the voice of the nation, a demand for sacrifice, a reminder of duty. But it called forth nothing except pity and mild disgust.

The doctor pulled at Fortnight's clothes, Fortnight's resistance was without urgency. He could not trouble himself to be violent. Holtius whispered words of tenderness, praised Fortnight's devotion, spoke of all the goodness that he was about to possess. And then, with surprising strength, he pushed his patient onto the bed, pinning back the arms with bony knees, and forcing his phallus between the teeth. He cried 'you must, you must', and his face was white with anguish. With a wild cry he filled the patient's mouth with sweet, salty fluid.

As Fortnight went home, descending the hill into town with automatic step, his memory preserved the strange sensation of the doctor's rough cheek on his. The trees along the roadside looked large and threatening, and the people moved on a kind of creamy vapour above the pavement. After a while he had to think actively in order to find his way. At one point he sat on a doorstep, looking towards an abandoned Methodist chapel, observing the afternoon shadows in its portico, where two women in blue and white moved soundlessly like figures in a dream.

The summer afternoon moulded the town, rounding off the tops of modern buildings, blunting the church spire, pressing wads of warm air into every street and alley-way. High overhead the stillness was broken, and silky-bosomed clouds slipped in a white wind. Inside the bubble there was little movement, only the paddling of limbs in viscous air. Deep in their embroidered winding sheets mummies suffered and writhed.

The hazy day mazed and muddled the hot houses on the green; figures sauntered townwards like slow sails on a sluggish tide. The gate of their house was swinging slowly, with a reiterated clicking of the latch. The Kid was astride it, and, approaching, Fortnight overheard the words of his mindless song:

> Keep your hans off my baby,
> She don' belawng to you,
> If you don' kip yer hans off her
> Ah'm gonna put my bran' on you.

He took the Kid by the arm and conducted him unresisting

indoors. Then he went to his room and remained there.

During the next two days the telephone would ring each day, twice in the morning and twice in the afternoon. He would hear it quietly singing at the bottom of the chest, and once considered cutting it off at the roots with a pair of kitchen scissors.

The Kid did not go to the brewery, but stayed at home, deeply despondent. The propelling and gyrating movements dropped from his repertoire, and his favourite thematic device became instead the long pause, during which he would stand balanced in the strangest postures, seeming to be listening to unheard voices from above or below. He gave to these voices all his attention, while the real and violent sound of knocking or ringing at the door did not trouble him. This real sound also occurred with increasing frequency, and caused Fortnight to retreat into the garden. Neither of them made any move to open the door, and during the long intermissions, when the silence was complete, Fortnight would pass his time in the exploration of the abandoned rooms upstairs. He did not go to Oddle's, since the thought of belonging to any circle of which the doctor formed a part was intolerable. A letter from Susan inviting him to a party in London cost him no more than an easy smile.

At last the Kid entered a period of true silence. Fortnight deeply regretted this silence, since he knew that the point was coming when he would need to speak to someone. But the Kid refused to respond to suggestions or questions, and ceased even talking to himself. Not a laugh nor a snicker emerged from him.

The silence developed naturally. Soon there was not a sound in the house besides the noises that Fortnight chose — with increasing spiritlessness — to make for his own peace of mind. When he approached the Kid, wondering whether to say something, or to hold out until the Kid himself became conscious of their terrible lack of sound and saw fit to do something about it, the boy would quietly withdraw from him. He did not look up, did not seem to be interested in his brother's approach. But whatever he was doing, he would inevitably leave it rather than allow Fortnight to come close. And there was something in his manner of padding away that showed him to be, not indifferent to the silence, but on the contrary totally aware of it, listening to its every turn of phrase, and appreciating it as though it gave off a kind of grave intelligence.

In the end Fortnight confined himself to studying his brother's ear. It blossomed from his body like a changeling flower. So concentrated had the Kid's attention become on that part of his head that it seemed to exhale an intense perfume. It was the Kid's soul, which released itself like a vapour from that orifice and wafted about the room, to be drawn in again on the other side. It played about the limbs of Fortnight as he slowly paddled himself from place to place, gently impeding his movements, and creating a sense of nausea that accompanied all his small resolves. At last he was stilled by it, and spent long unthinking hours at the Colonel's desk. His thoughts turned slowly round, circling like ravens about the facts of decay and death. The doctor he hardly remembered, but his mother was continually and vividly present to him. He thought of things that she had done and wished for; her sayings were always in his mind; her movements seemed to pass by him in his semi-sleep. It was inconceivable that she should be no more. Applied to himself the proposition was manifestly contradictory. As he sat he tried to appease his destiny with soft well-spoken phrases, ideas of death culled from dead philosophers. But nothing seemed to match up to the enormity of what was required. His body still lay stiff on the rails of the future, waiting his arrival on a one-way train.

One day, secretly, he slipped a razor beneath the skin of his forearm and spilt a quantity of blood into a glass. The wound was not deep; he was able to staunch it with a piece of cotton-wool and a tight bandage, neither of which gave rise to any visible swelling of his shirt-sleeve. But the blood he kept in a special place, behind the clothes in his own part of the airing-cupboard. Even the Kid would not venture there. Day by day he watched its transformation, taking out the glass when he was sure of being alone and holding it to the light to observe the slow rhythm of his own decay.

Almost at once the surface of the blood had become dark, sticking gummily to the side of the jar and traversed by deepening wrinkles crossing hither and thither on the black strand. They made a pattern which at first he had compared to his own face, but which very soon came to represent for him the secret writings of an undiscovered future. The next day, the liquid had separated into its two components, the red clusters, like Japanese flowers, rolling slowly in a clear yellowish water. This stage had about it a kind of fragile stasis — for several days there seemed to be no change, except that the water dried off gradually and, in consequence, the black film which covered it began to sag towards the middle. Each day, as he lifted it, he would rejoice to see the same red blossoms drifting leisurely on the bottom of the glass, mounting each other, rolling slowly off, playfully touching before sidling indolently towards another soft encounter. Sometimes he would experiment with lightly shaking the glass, and then the balls of colour would float up and brush against the surface, touching in the middle where the black scum reached down to them. At other times he would try not to disturb them as he lifted the glass from its hiding-place, anxious to observe their positions of rest one against the other, lest there should be some higher symbolism here.

At last the brief idyll met its end. One day, leading the glass — he thought with meticulous attention — into the daylight, he noticed that, whether through some jerky movement of his arm, or whether on account of its increasing fragility, the black veil was broken and dripped its ragged edges down into the liquid. Already the red petals in the garden had darkened at their edges and little bits could be seen floating in the yellow slime. By the next day the level of the liquid had sunk drastically, and the black skin, fallen to the sides, smeared itself in moist streaks over the glass. Now it was necessary to look down into the glass from above. From this angle the blown underwater roses took on a horrible aspect that he had not seen before: they seemed alive and seething, with a venomous life of their own.

The next day, the balls were black entirely, congealed together, and covered by a thin film of greyish-yellow scum. Soon mould had formed on the broken skin, and a smell arose from the putrid mass which obliged him to keep the glass covered with a metal cap. Within a week it contained a mass of green mould, beneath which could be seen, by looking up from underneath, a greenish liquid full of dark black globules. Finally the mould conquered, filled the whole glass with a puffy grey-green cloud, and then collapsed and died, forming a dead brown residue on the whole surface of the glass.

The experiment had failed, the mystery had eluded him.

In that final day the doctor's ringing and knocking were especially persistent. Fortnight waited for them to stop, and then gave himself twenty minutes, as he always did, before leaving over the wall and through the vicarage garden. He was able to persuade Oddle that twenty-five pounds were due to him, and also to obtain twenty-five on account, promising to work seriously at last.

As he approached the house, he saw the doctor standing by the gate. Fortnight made a long detour by the Bramhurst Road, and entered again across the lawn of the vicarage. He was pleased that for two pounds he could buy haricot beans, cooking tomatoes and bacon scraps to last a week. He left them in the kitchen, together with fifteen pounds in cash. The Kid watched him indifferently as he counted it out. Fortnight turned, opened his mouth to say something, thought better of it, and went out by the garden. He cried as he passed the Kid's signal-box, and gave a pound note to a tramp who was sitting against it, and drinking from a bottle of British sherry. He walked on, seeing the London train round the corner under Wenbury Hill.

Chapter Seven

THE YOLK of sun broke suddenly and ran across the sky. The west was tinctured with evening; above the ragged roof-tops it slowly cooked and hardened. Fortnight walked without knowledge of his whereabouts. There had been a reason for his coming here: he looked for it in every passing shadow. A hand was reaching from a doorway, and he touched the fingertips, peering beyond the startled face of its owner into the dull interior of a terraced house. There was gold wallpaper, and a dim light in the hallway, above the small bentwood table on which stood a bowl of flowers. Were they real flowers? 'Good evening,' Fortnight said, and walked on.

He tried to recall the purpose of his visit. He remembered the train journey to London. The image remained of a closed compartment in which two blacks were playing cards on the empty seat between them. There had been sun in the carriage. One of the blacks had said 'More where that came from, boy!' and then laughed in a strange way, clicking at the same time with his pink little intimate tongue. As they drew out of the station, he had seen Adrian Holtius, leaning over the parapet of the railway bridge, staring intently at the train.

He came across a complex of buildings, some very tall, many with plate-glass windows and bright tinsel displays. Perhaps this was his destination. He looked for some time at the concrete exteriors, the silent alley-ways, the plain white patios on which the scraps of paper circled aimlessly with a dry scuttling sound, and he saw that he was wrong. 'Good evening,' he said again, and this time a man stopped and stared. Fortnight watched him. He was middle-aged, small, with grey eyes that flickered uncertainly in a round fluffy face that had been touched with rouge. At one point it seemed as though the man were about to speak, and Fortnight could see the quivering movements of indecision extend themselves along his jaw. He had a mole on his neck. That too began to quiver. Fortnight was pleased, and repeated his 'Good evening,' only with increased force and determination. Then the man lost heart and turned away.

It was getting dark, and he began to feel chilly. He tried to recall his last meal. It must have been two days before, in the hotel near King's Cross where he found himself at night. He had bought a tin of beans, and opened it with jabs of his pocket-knife on the floor of the dirty room. The cold sweet nuggets lingered in his mouth like kisses.

He passed near the Inns of Court, and a faint remembrance stirred in him. He stood under the arch of Lincoln's Inn, wondering whether he should enter and buy a ticket for dinner. But, seized with revulsion, he turned away. More serious things had brought him to London. Thoughts and motives continued to rise to his mind during his slow perambulations: his body drifted on regardless, ignoring the call to arms when it came, as though moving under the impulse of notions of its own.

He stopped, and watched the traffic lights at a corner. After some twenty times he could make the lights change colour in response to his own permission, which might at any time be arbitrarily withheld. He was pleased with this effect and smiled to himself as he repeated it. It confirmed the contingency of insentient things, that performed their tasks forlornly, waiting to be victims of consciousness, to move at last from be to seem, and so enjoy for a moment the privilege of will. It was not true that he had no aims. Here, now, in this small encounter, he could infect the world with purpose. The exercise restored him and he walked on.

He passed the front of the British Museum; it seemed to be distilling shadows behind its capitals, and passing them secretly into the night. It proved again that the only freedom lies in man's capacity to infiltrate the world with consciousness. He looked up at the white façade of the Opera House, and then, all of a sudden, without warning, his legs took hold of him, and hurried him forward. It was there, her name, on the poster for *Der Zauberflöte*: Barbara Langley, Third Lady of the Queen of the Night. It was not possible, he knew. Unless someone with influence had been protecting her, and he discounted such a notion as self-contradictory. It must be another Barbara Langley. One of those coincidences which existed purely for the sake of distracting him. He walked down Floral Street. It was empty; the lights were dim and sputtering, like lights in a dream. He repeated under his breath the words that created and dispelled his fear:

When I went up Sandy-Hill,
I met a sandy-boy;
I cut his throat, I sucked his blood,
And left his skin a-hanging-o.

Still pools of shadow gathered against the long wall of the Opera House, crossed only by a bridge of light from an open door towards the end. The faint sound of music emerged, and Fortnight paused to look inside. On a distant platform, three glittering figures stood, singing into the auditorium. The door had been propped open with a brick; he saw a forest of dangling ropes, some of them shining with light from a distant source, others hanging in shadow. Above them steel girders encrusted with wheels and pulleys made a decorative tracery in the air. Each metallic object released a little gleam of reflected light like a star, and vague forms suspended in the black firmament beyond them gave the impression of clouds of galactic energy which might at any moment erupt into light. Beneath the cross-beams slots of scenery fanned the uneasy air.

Entering from night-fall the heat of this midday darkness astonished him. He tripped over a heavy metallic object. There was a tumble, a rustle of unconcerned clothing, a flutter of moths in his ears and nostrils. Then, steadying himself, he looked around him. A smell of sized canvas pervaded the place, and down each false corridor between the wings of scenery little figures moved on tiptoe, or loafed like schoolboys with no part to play. The music was everywhere; he recognized the three ladies of the queen of darkness:

> *Hiemit kannst du allmächtig handeln*
> *der Menschen Leidenschaft verwandeln . . .*

He turned to the stage. The three singers in green and silver had been sprinkled over face and hair with silver star-dust. The young figure who stood near to him settled on an F and then repeated it, catching the stage light on the slime of her lower lips, which was wet from the spray of saliva. He had seen that tremulous membrane before, had even kissed it in clammy moments that he would never forget, or which, if he had forgotten, would still exert their secret influence, cascading through his embarrassed mind, pouring muddily into cul-de-sacs, bubbling, spilling and dripping into bothered darknesses of the unexplored below. He remembered the way she sang, a full, surprising mezzo that seemed only to traverse the slender flute of her body on its way from somewhere else. How neat she was, neat as a new pin. It was not right that her life should progress so easily. He should be allowed to damage it.

None of the three figures moved, but each stayed open-mouthed, holding for a moment in their vocal cradles the infant parts of F major. The voices of Tamino and Papageno entered, hushed, and distant. The great moons shifted their silver light across the stage and her face was eclipsed. Now one of the ladies stepped forward, holding the box of chimes. The music had passed through G minor, swept away the claims of E flat, and urgently moved towards an F, first as tonic, now as dominant. Fortnight listened with rapt attention, and for a moment it did not matter that the girl on the stage, whose painted face was lost in shadow, was to betray him that evening — in the arms of a painter, probably, or of an angry poet, sodden with rhetoric. She stood there in the shadow, terse with otherness among props of gold and silver. He might have been watching one of the zany theatricals that the Kid and his mother would stage during the Colonel's trips away.

The scenery had begun to shake, a wheel was turning somewhere, sparks of light twinkled among the girders. Perhaps she was being wound away, to be jerked suddenly upwards by the neck and dangled above the stage. It hardly mattered. She was not Barbara: the arms, bent at the elbow, poised for some purposeless courtesy, were not Barbara's. The legs had none of her girlish wilfulness. He could not see the colour of her eyes. He took a step forward and was held by the shoulder.

'Who are you?'

The voice spoke from a pile of black felt; he turned, but saw only darkness. Through the doorway the light from the street invited him. As they led him out, Fortnight vainly tried to answer their question, drawing attention to its complexity, and denying all connection with the figure on the stage, who certainly was not Barbara.

In the street, he began to run. He found that he could move effortlessly at the speed of sound, in a noiseless world of his own. Cars stopped and barriers gave way before him. A policeman watched him as he swept along the Mall. Soon, like the Kid, he was to be arrested and charged. He began to explain matters to the court, which was fortunately impressed by the conspiracy of circumstances that had beset the accused. The young magistrate had read Sartre, dabbled in nihilism, was an expert in penal reform. It was pleasant to see him lean forward with a puzzled, sympathetic expression as Fortnight recounted his experiences. The magistrate began to nod earnestly at the part where motives expired and the accused stood motionless in command of a set of traffic lights. That was particularly significant, so it was felt, and many of those present in the court-room jotted a few notes on their empty pads. A policeman coaxed him away, and he was given a cup of tea in a little office, where someone in a donkey jacket was warming his hands above an iron stove. He spoke to them all about his experience, describing it from every point of view, showing an admirable sympathy for Barbara, for the Kid, even for the Colonel and Dr Holtius, and accusing himself punctiliously of faults that he hardly knew to be his.

After a while he noticed that he had slowed to a walking pace. He was by St George's Hospital, where Barbara had been taken after falling from her bicycle in Hyde Park. How terrible to see all that blood caking in her fine pale hair. He should have made that wound himself. He began to summon his anger against her. A flush, he imagined, was now spreading across his forehead, and he could distantly record the convoys of adrenalin as they took up the march through long and cavernous arteries. Soon they would have reached their destination, and battle orders could be composed, issued and modified as the need arose. But when the troops of jealousy were posted at last in the trenches of his face, he called them off with a laugh, and retired for tiffin.

Outside the white house in Eaton Square many cars of many sizes were arrayed, the small ones nosing the buttocky coffers of the large, the large growling toothily at the squashed backs of the small. A woman tipped from a taxi as Fortnight arrived, and preceded him towards the door. Her brown hair of jewels and powder was mounted like a Christmas feast on her carefully packaged head. She smiled at him, and the door was opened. The servant wore an expression that was blank but urgent, like the stop-press column of an evening paper on a day with no news. He allowed the woman to enter, vacantly surveyed Fortnight's features, and then stood aside, feigning to reprove a crease in his linen jacket.

Fortnight followed the lady. In front of them, barring the way, was a middle-aged man in a grey suit, and, with him, a youth with ringlets, who wore a velvet jacket lapelled with fur, and a blue butterfly tie of shimmering damask. They held out of danger their glasses of yellow champagne. For a moment it seemed to Fortnight impossible that any human face should convey such ineffable good-will as was to be seen in the red features of the older man, folded over like a jammy pancake to enclose ooze upon ooze of simper and smile. But then the expression shifted in the direction of a less committal state of mind, and he said:

'Margot darling!'

He bent forward to kiss the lady, who murmured her way forward with pouting lips. Finding a gap between bums, Fortnight began to move towards a door which he took to be that of the drawing-room.

'Evelyn,' said Margot. 'I have just met the most delicious friend of yours. A gorgeous old-fashioned gentleman, who quite swept me off my feet.'

'Should I know who you mean?'

'Of course, Evelyn darling, you know who I mean. One guess.'

Fortnight had gained the doorway and hesitated. Perhaps Margot's flame was an acquaintance — his father, say. Then he saw in a great Venetian mirror the face of Lady Susan. His heart or some similar organ jumped. It was as though he had not expected to find her; and perhaps, as he approached, she felt the same, for she looked at him as at an unwanted visitation. In his embarrassment he tripped over the extended legs of someone whose photograph he had once seen in a newspaper. Then a young woman in a sparkling blue dress, open to the waist so that the round brown breasts could be seen rising from the unmuscled valley of her chest, stood in his path and began to talk to him. He said yes several times, trying to divine the form of her attractions. Suddenly she stopped and stared at him. She had large brown eyes and a face that was not quite pretty.

'Do you really think that?' she asked.

'Yes, yes, I do,' said Fortnight emphatically. 'Very much so.'

'That they ought actually to be shot?'

'Yes. All of them. Tortured to death. I really believe that.'

'Good God! The brute!'

He thought it wisest to advance towards Susan, for courtesy's sake. Full of courtesy, full of craft. He begged his mother not to interrupt him.

Over the sideboard of onyx and ormulu hung a pair of bugles, and in front of the fireplace stood a long low table of polished glass, with absurd claws for feet, bearing the biographies of great dead men. Susan was statuesque and splendid, the translucent skin of her neck scarcely moving above the collar of an evening dress in sea-green plush. Her sleeves were trimmed with Indian embroidery in white and silver: it reminded him vaguely of the costume of the three singing ladies. He was struck dumb by her beauty and command; she was a queen of the sea, a cold enticing siren who had secret knowledge of men's dreams. Here, in her palace, it seemed easier to explain her. She was so obviously above and beyond him that their meetings at Bramhurst could have been no more than a holiday. He must try to match her, to rise up to regions colder and clearer than those where he had dwelt, to a place where the distinction between self and other is absolute, and where you stare down from a lonely promontory on the sea of commingling failures. 'Barbara!' he muttered to himself, by way of an experiment. What must be above all satisfying to a man in his predicament was to see himself the victim of tragic circumstances, maintaining a cheerful countenance for the sake of those around him, but inwardly debating as to when he should call the show to an end. Calmly, and with the faintest of operatic smiles, he stepped towards his hostess and made a half bow, stumbling as he did so against the leg of a tripod table which wobbled precariously and caught Susan's eye.

'Kenneth!'

She looked at him, wreathed in smiles of a purely social nature, but with something dark in her eyes that made him want to be alone with her, on his knees, in confessional posture, begging forgiveness for faults all the more serious through being unknown.

'Susan! I didn't know, I am not sure, I was wondering whether you were expecting me.'

'I never *expect* anyone. But I invited you. And I have been longing to see you.'

She held on to him almost affectionately. He cursed the incompetence of his class, that could neither speak its own meaning nor pretend to a meaning that it did not have. If the gods have a gift, it is the nectar of insincerity, which sours to resentment unless swallowed at once.

'In fact, Kenneth, I have some things which I must say to you. I have been worried: yes, believe me. What with phone calls every day from Adrian and only silence from yourself.'

'Adrian?'

'*Il est bien épris, mon pauvre.* I was wondering how to help.'

'To help him?'

'No, you, silly.'

'But why should you help me?'

'Do you think me without remorse?'

'Remorse?'

'For ignoring you, for going away.'

'Did you?'

'I had to be in London. Adultery is an unstable thing. One must be prepared for surprises.'

Since Susan looked at him directly, he felt unable to study her features. Her meaning eluded him. Was she referring to their adultery, or to another? Then he smiled, for some proof had been given of his existence. He could not understand by what miracle he had arrived at this place, but clearly some benevolent spirit had been guiding him.

'I say, Susan . . .' he began, and then looked down at his shoes, which were scuffed and dusty, at his trousers, smudged with the dirt of the opera backstage, at his tattered cuffs and threadbare jacket. He had a vague memory of washing and shaving that morning, but he felt sure that he was no longer presentable. A music-hall duchess was looking scornfully in his direction, and because her cheeks were rouged carmine, her greying hair dyed a copper colour, and because moreover she wore a toque trimmed with stuffed pink bullfinches which was no doubt going to the absolute limit even in this milieu, he felt in her frown the whole authority of her class. A weight of superciliousness was being brought down on him, and, making an excuse, he left for the bathroom.

The faint aroma of *Calandre* arose from arty men on whose denims every speck of dirt had been the subject of meticulous arrangement. Two women followed him with their eyes. The old lady he would discount, but the other, who stood by a chased silver urn idly rearranging the slipper orchids that poked from it, had something urgent in her expression which made him take mental note.

In the bathroom were photographs, cartoons, headlines and cuttings, all of which recorded the fame of Mr Waterford, or the notoriety of his Susan.

LADY SUSAN IN MINISTRY SCANDAL
GOVERNMENT ACCEPTS WATERFORD SCHEME
BREAKFAST WITH THE FANNINGS

Through these notices Susan displayed to her guests a well-bred indifference towards every kind of scandal just so long as it involved herself. It was while reading one of them that a disturbing thought occurred to Fortnight. Somewhere in this party was Barbara's seducer. It was not an older man, but someone young, like himself, only with definite convictions. Neither a painter, nor a poet, but a slogan-mouthing socialist, who filled the flat in South Hill Park with committees of mirthless students and grey unemployables. Someone vigorous too, who moved in society, conquered elegant ladies, wrote pungent articles for the *New Statesman*, and spoke his mind on the wireless. Barbara would appeal to him, with her poetic soul, her neat bourgeois gracefulness that translated itself into a tableau of revolutionary good manners. He had persuaded her to work for the destruction of men like Fortnight: that was why she wrote so often to the Kid. The instructions even included procedures for planting bombs. He was Irish, an angry republican, with a store of sentimental ditties, a deceptive folklore with which to inspire in men allegiance and in women desire. Every now and then, when drunk, which was not often for like all passionate men he was abstemious, he would rise from the table, strike it with his fist and shout aloud in memory of some great-uncle driven from his farm by a tyrannical landlord, to die in the Central Post Office on that grand heroic day.

It was with a great effort that Fortnight brought this episode to a close. In the end he had to summon his hatred for the doctor. Only then did he find strength in his anger. He feared that something real might be trying to break through, and he washed out the salt from his eyes with a strange apprehension. He was roused by a gentle knock at the door.

'Kenneth.'

Susan's voice was soft with vagrant tenderness.

'Kenneth. Are you all right? You seemed ill.'

'I am fine,' he replied, and looked at the mirror. A bottle of

Cologne stood on a glass shelf and beside it a canister of hair-spray, on which was written, in large red letters: KEEP AWAY FROM EYES.

He stared at this message for some time, and then went nervously into the hallway.

Susan was alone in a concealed recess, like an icon designed for solitary meditation. But the icon was alive. She pulled at him, covered his face with stinging kisses, pricked his skin with the point of her tongue.

'I've missed you, silly boy. Silly boy.'

'I don't understand you.'

'What is there to understand? I am as I appear. I have no depths. I make a point of filling them.'

'How did I get here?'

'Oh please! I can't stand metaphysics. You're here, and I can kiss you.'

'Why should you?'

'Why not? Besides, if you meet my husband you must bear my signature.'

'Is he here?'

'Of course. Did you think I keep him in the attic?'

'And who else have you got for me?'

'I have not arranged this party for your benefit, but for mine.'

She laughed her silent crumpled laugh, and tickled him gently.

'Where were you?'

'More metaphysics?'

'I mean these last weeks.'

'Here mostly. Oh, and Paris for a few days. I'd promised to be at a *vernissage*. And then one has to stay a little, and stare at all those books in exciting white covers, each pretending that it's the one thing you absolutely *must* have read. And why did you come to London?'

Far from home, near thy harm. Fortnight was angry that his mother's interruptions were so underhand. He had stood it long enough, and as she said, forbearance is no acquittance.

'I'm afraid I don't know.'

'You don't know?'

'Of course it's absurd. All I can say is that I'm not in Flackwell. I left. Perhaps to see you.'

'Don't lie. Villain. Was it to escape from Adrian?'

'Could be.'

'Wrong move, my dear.'

They were interrupted by a harlequinade of festive costumes, which suddenly surrounded them, took them up, and transported them to another room. The ghoulish faces opened in laughter as they rifled each other's eyes. Evelyn stood deep in conversation with a younger man, who wore a silk shirt and a gold-embroidered jacket. Susan took Fortnight by the hand and guided him across to them. Releasing him, she gently slid her amorous fingers along the reaches of his own.

'Darling, let me introduce you. This is Kenneth Fortnight, a friend from Bramhurst. Part of the family. Kenneth, I don't believe you have met my husband Peter.'

She said it as though her husband Peter was sharply — though perhaps not too sharply — to be distinguished from her husband Paul.

'You must be Julien Fortnight's son.'

Fortnight mumbled agreement; his mumble was taken up anti-phonally by Evelyn, who had begun to stare out of sellotaped eyes. Fortnight was less interested in his father's range of acquaintance than in the memory of the Colonel's sudden grief on the landing, the rasping sound of which returned to him with unexpected force. He began to remember the purpose of his visit. He had to prove that the Colonel felt nothing.

'You know Julien Fortnight, don't you Evel? Something to do with Flackwell Properties, isn't he? Very thick with Diane Forster.'

'Oh,' said Susan. 'I expect Diane will be here.'

'Good,' remarked her husband indifferently, 'so fond of her. Got a drink?'

'No,' said Fortnight. He noticed that Susan was leading Evelyn, who seemed reluctant to depart, into another corner of the room.

'Here. Here's the man.'

Mr Waterford put out one hand, and the servant, a young man dressed eccentrically in tight black trousers and a tapered shirt, with a silver medallion at his neck, stopped in front of them. He handed Fortnight a glass and filled it with champagne.

'Can't drink the stuff myself.'

Mr Waterford looked at Fortnight. His hair was receding, his face slightly lined, with a cultivated steadiness of look, and arching eyebrows that probably contained a small menagerie of perse-cuted body lice.

'Are you a writer perhaps? Susan collects writers. Did you see that poet, what's his name, Cecil Armstrong, next door? No?'

'I'm nothing as yet,' Fortnight answered. Presently he added, 'I am reading for the Bar.'

'To tell you the truth, I'm not so fond of intellectuals myself. I am sure we'd get on rather well. How did you meet Susan?'

The question was casual, and Fortnight held back a moment, suspecting the tone. He noticed a sly look sideways as though things not altogether secret need not at this juncture be referred to.

'I know her from Bramhurst.'

'As I say, a barrister is a better thing to be than half a poet. I wrote poetry once. That's how *I* met Susan. Published a volume, don't suppose you'll have seen it. All about time, rivers, allusions to naiads, dryads, maenads, self-ads, the usual stuff. Susan says she likes it, though frankly, I'd rather she didn't. Her reasons are sure to be the wrong ones. I'm not that kind of man now. Nor are you; I can see that.'

Mr Waterford was looking at him with mingled kindness and curiosity. In an unexpected daydream Fortnight saw Mr Waterford dancing a slow foxtrot with the Colonel, in a hushed clinch of Hollywood aspect, while the Kid played lugubriously at the grand piano. He swallowed the champagne and his glass was promptly full again.

'All that stuff is dead anyway,' Mr Waterford continued. 'I mean, who is going to pretend, since the invention of the television commercial, who is going to pretend that poetry can speak to the human heart? The human heart has been remaindered and sold off. A job lot. These people,' he gestured vaguely into the drawing-room, 'they know that as well as we do. Please don't let me bore you to death.'

Fortnight noticed a pastel portrait of Susan, hanging in a gilded frame above her husband's head among unmeaning pieces of tasteful modernism. A giggle of women passed them, kissed Mr Waterford, and fluttered on, leaving a rich fug of hyacinth, and beneath it a faintly ammoniac smell.

'It is not quite right,' Mr Waterford continued dreamily, 'to generalize. There is a great difference between men and women in this respect — and perhaps in other respects as well. A man seldom lives in penny-pinching isolation. He doesn't balance his accounts, or try to live within his moral means. On the contrary, he promises everything, he contracts everywhere, he mortgages to the limit every one of his powers. I sometimes think your father is like that.'

'My father?'

The woman whose eye he had caught in crossing the drawing-room was making towards them with slow deliberate gestures. Mr Waterford continued to talk.

'He may even mortgage his soul, like Faust. No woman could have done that. A woman might sell her body to the devil, but she would become a devil before she could sell her soul. Ah, here's . . .'

The woman had interposed herself and was kissing Mr Waterford, fertilizing the deep runnels of his gritty face. Fortnight was introduced. Her name was Stefania Marmelade. Mr Waterford touched Fortnight affectionately on the shoulder.

'Nice to have met you Kenneth. I wonder whether it's true, what I said about your father. I don't know him well.'

'Neither do I,' said Fortnight, who caught Mr Waterford's arch expression and turned to Miss Marmelade with a plaster-cast smile.

Her dark hair and dark eyes reminded him of Mrs Thurlow, as did her Majorca-coloured breasts popping at the lip of a low-cut dress. He thought of Mrs Thurlow with sadness; like himself, she had been badly cast. They had both suffered, moreover, from the director's choice of locale. He should never have returned to Flackwell. But wherever he went the Colonel preceded him, taking the leading part.

'I'm not going to ask who you are,' said Miss Marmelade. 'Or what you do. I'm sure I won't understand.'

'I'm grateful to you,' he said, with feeling.

She adjusted the points of her fingers against each other and observed politely, 'I think we shall like each other. You have a pleasant face, a decorous manner, a derelict appearance, and a virginal smile.'

'What?'

'Don't look at me like that! Those are Susan's eyes!'

'What's wrong with Susan's eyes?'

'What's wrong with Susan's heart!'

'Has she robbed you of a paramour?'

'What a question!'

The lady leaned towards him and said, in a confidential whisper: 'Tell me quickly the answer to this riddle: if a boy loves a woman whose husband's mistress loves a man who desires the boy, can they each be satisfied while being jealous only of one?'

'Is it mathematical?'

She laughed like broken glass, and touched his sleeve.

'Or mechanical?'

'Don't be vulgar.'

'Then I give up.'

'Yes,' she said glumly, 'so did I.'

Their glasses were filled, and by a process of which he was only partly conscious they were again on the move. Miss Marmelade's touch was light, masterly and thrilling with sophisticated lust. From time to time the face of Barbara interrupted him, always accompanied by some ironical maxim of Mrs Fortnight's. Faint heart never won fair lady.

They had transferred their guilty badinage into another room, with silky red wallpaper in Renaissance patterns, red leather chairs with globular feet, red books in red mahogany bookcases on the wall. The people were more heavily choreographed here, slow, drunken, as though they had got through the initial frenzy of self-advertisement and were now preparing to settle into habitual solipsisms. He entertained Miss Marmelade with his impressions of tribal life in Matabeleland.

'. . . and from time to time the river would widen,' he caught himself saying, 'the trees recede, and a torrent of vertical sunlight comes beating down, driving the breath back into your body.'

'To think!'

But before he could press his advantage they were interrupted. A young man with a puffy face, half-open urgent mouth and square tinted spectacles, placed his physiognomy suddenly at their disposal. He defied them to deny that all of Shakespeare is irrelevant beside the early films of Harry Watt.

'Take *N-night M-mail*, for example. There is a great film. A m-masterpiece.' He poked Fortnight in the ribs, at the same time holding Stefania by the hand and playing with her fingers. 'It contains the saddest, s-sublimest m-most sp-sp-splendiferous lament that our civilization has ever enjoyed. What could be m-more r-relevantly m-moving than steam?'

'Yes darling,' said Miss Marmelade, 'but you are being rather a bore.'

'Am I?' he asked, brightening, and continued with renewed vigour.

'The p-power, the n-noise, the continual ph-phallic action of the spoke, smooth lovely oily b-baby-b-bercing m-movement; clouds of m-magic steam, shrouding the engines like g-gods. The s-symbol of the inevitable, of the straight line, of endless, un-unmi-unmitigated boredom. The ingredients of m-modern life. What could be m-more ecstatically d-dull, my dear, what could be m-more quintessentially this and us and here and n-now? Art. I say art. The only art that m-matters. The documentary f-film.'

He let go of Stefania's hand and slid to the floor. Someone trampled on his face, at which he raised himself a little, and then sank again. A bystander offered help. Fortnight took one of the limp arms and they placed him in a chair. At once he woke up, turned to his immediate neighbour, and began to explain in urgent tones the architectural merits of Robert Cromie's Odeon in Hammersmith.

'Poor Mark,' said Miss Marmelade, 'I'm afraid he's rather a failure.'

A piano belled distantly. Someone was playing 'These Foolish Things', slowly, lugubriously, adding sevenths and ninths to the skeleton harmonies. In the early hours, when people were considering how best to slip from their social roles, he himself would play. The scenario was brilliant: a forties interior, lit by silk-shaded lamps on tables of wrought iron and marble, the women in their evening dresses spread in a sea of crushed cloth across the floor. Somewhere, on a raised platform, just discernible in the half light and flattered by a backcloth of dark but faintly iridescent green, sat Fortnight. He played the B flat minor Prelude from the Forty-Eight, so returning those laden harmonies to their proper place. Lady Susan raised herself, glanced meltingly in his direction, and stayed there, poised most uncomfortably in tribute to an emotion which she divined but probably could not feel. There was no applause, only a hushed appreciation that some significant experience had hovered for a moment in the room, seeking embodiment, perhaps somewhere finding it, in the breast of this woman, or of that woman, not revealing itself even to her. They directed at Fortnight yearning and expressive gestures, seeing in him the life which they had missed. Cruelly nonchalant, he chose only Susan, exploiting her sudden insecurity so as to take revenge. But revenge for what? His train of thought was abruptly halted. He looked down at Miss Marmelade.

'I asked, have you ever slept with Susan?'

Fortnight stared; clearly he had let things get out of control.

'Don't be shocked. You can always lie. It is never possible to trespass on another's privacy, unless he wants it.'

'Of course I'm not shocked, Stefania.'

'Sonia, actually, Sonia Marmaloff.'

She laid her hand on his sleeve.

'But why do you want to know?'

'Imagine,' said a bald man in a spotted bow-tie, who had been slowly bearing down on them, 'a world shortage of toothpicks, or of toilet rolls. In what way, do you think would our lives be changed? I ask because I believe that neither of you have faced up to these questions.'

More champagne was poured into their glasses. Because there was no reason, he decided to confess the truth to Sonia Marmaloff. But as he opened his mouth to speak he caught sight of the loveliest girl he had ever seen, adrift like a white swan in the hallway, with pearly skin, a chignon and dark lustrous eyes cast this way and that in feigned timidity. The advertisement poses of her upturned oval face, the expensive fragility, achieved amid such strife, like some windborn seed caught high up on a faceless building and one day, briefly, opening into flower ... Sonia caught his gaze.

'I suppose you know Julia, Susan's luscious little sister? Wouldn't you like to eat her up? Listen! You can hear the crack of cold hearts thawing as she passes.'

Fortnight listened. And sure enough he did begin to hear a kind of cracking sound. But his attention was interrupted by Evelyn, who laid a hand on his shoulder.

'Ho! Hoh-ho!' he cried. 'I've caught you at last. I am not going to let you get away with it.'

He fixed his victim with a basilisk stare and began to squeeze his shoulder painfully. Then, at a carefully premeditated moment, he relaxed his grip and broke into a toothy smile.

'Evel, please leave him alone,' Sonia protested.

'I, leave him alone? My dear, it is no longer possible. He has been baiting me.'

'I do not know what you are referring to, Evel. You are not a judge of character.'

Evelyn cackled. 'Character my dear Sonia? You sound like Henry James Junior. The modern specimen has no character. The only real man is the characterless man: here he stands before you, in all his palpable absence. All face and phallus, attracting and attracted, repelling and repelled, without respect to code, authority, principle, without . . . how did it go?'

'I'm afraid . . .'

'Come young man. You wrote it, you are not going to deny that you wrote it. I know you. I know your style. Think yourself a theatre critic? Think you can write me off with gobbledegook out of existentialist comic-strips?'

'I'm afraid that I do not know what you are talking about.'

'You awful tease!' Evelyn exclaimed, and flung out his hand. It rose in a considerable arc, turned flat, rocked once to port and once to starboard, and then, with a quick flutter, tumbled down again on Fortnight's neck. Evelyn pulled himself closer and peered from bold unshifting eyes into Fortnight's own, assumed a serious attitude, slightly raised an eyebrow, revealing a black smudge on the upper eyelid, and then backed away again, laughing raucously like a crazy cockatoo.

'I know your father too,' he went on. 'You will not, I trust, deny that he is a bonnet laird, a whisky-soaked ignoramus with a weird taste, to be observed only rarely in winter, for ballooning ladies with elegant manners and itchy drawers. You, the offspring of one dull afternoon's mortally moribund exertions on a gay spinster from Brighton in the Glasgow Railway Hotel, you, young man, in deference to the colossal undistinction of your ancestry, have turned away from all that is natural and good, have not held a shotgun in your hands since you were six, took up masturbation in gentlemen's lavatories, of which the village had but two, advanced to French impressionism and thence, don't deny it, to Elizabethan love lyrics, and, sneaking your way, following Dr Johnson's advice, as far as London, on a ticket to Berwick-on-Tweed, have pawned, yes pawned, your father's sporran, bought a bottle of epicene after-shave, and presented yourself, as yet an unmolested virgin, and with all the ruthlessness of a chastity as self-exciting as it was self-imposed, presented yourself, I say, if "present" is what you do with a thing so undesirable, presented yourself at the back door of that manufactury for pink bum-paper, and . . .'

He sneezed unexpectedly, with cyclonic force.

'Evel, you really have got the wrong man,' said Sonia.

'Have I? Have I really old sport? Most frightfully sorry. No but really. How could that have happened? I could have sworn. Kiss me. No? More champagne?'

He poured the contents of his glass into Fortnight's, and began to talk quite amicably to Sonia about the structure of the vagina, and its relation to the gates of Hades as Virgil and Milton describe them. Sonia kept her eyes on Fortnight who was drinking rapidly. Reminded of the gates of Dis, he fought hard to abolish the thought of his tormentor.

'Imagine,' said a grave voice in his ear, 'a world shortage of chewing gum, of prunes, of harpsichord quills, of charcoal biscuits, of French intellectuals . . .'

'We've just been on tour,' a female voice declared, 'like a circus. Jonathan was so thrilled. I had to restrain him wearing tarzan underwear.'

'So you are not a theatre critic? I am glad, since I was beginning to like you. Now we can explore the more fruitful possibilities of animosity. You may not believe it, but from birth I have been a lesbian. I am also a bicycle thief.'

Evelyn's remarks seemed less urgent now, and after a while he ceased to attend to Fortnight, and drifted away. He took hold of the arm of Mark, who was adamant that there is more invention in Cripple Clarence Lofton's left hand than in all the ground basses of Purcell. The room cleared at once, and Mr Waterford's voice could be heard from the hallway, loudly booming instructions. Fortnight lingered until he and Sonia stood alone behind a door.

'You wicked boy,' she said sharply, as she moved into a position from which he could lever a breast from its pocket. 'I am not your type.'

'I think you are. I really do think you are.'

Fortnight was so angry now that he would have killed Barbara, he thought, had she suddenly entered the room. But it was not Barbara whose nipple he was assiduously squeezing.

'That hurts!'

'I know.'

'Please. Desist.'

'Give me your address. And your telephone number.'

'Ruffian!'

Sonia reached quickly into her handbag and extracted a piece of paper on which the information was already assembled. And then she looked at him with a certain ferocity.

'But you had far better stick to Susan.'

'Susan?'

'Isn't it for you that she's celebrating? She has been at it for weeks. I can't see anyone else here who is sufficiently unknown to attract her.'

'I see.'

'Not that she ever falls in love. I mean she is always falling, but only like an angel into hell. She gets further from love every second.'

'You don't like Susan?'

'But I adore her! What makes you say that?'

Mr Waterford thrust his head around the door, asked whether he could join the plot, and then withdrew. Evelyn reappeared, took hold of Fortnight's collar, and shouted.

'You must believe! You must have faith! Allow me to baptize you!'

With his hand he divided crosswise his glass of busy champagne.

'*Qui hanc aquam regenerandis hominibus praeparatam arcana sui numinis admixtione foecundet. . . .*'

'Really Evel, can you . . .'

He made the sign of the cross three times over Fortnight's head, mumbling continuously, and then suddenly cried out 'My God, I have forgotten to absterge the podex!' Fortnight hit him, but hesitantly, and as he crumpled to the floor, Evelyn raked the laughter along the rough griddle of his throat. He lay rolling gently from side to side on the carpet.

'Oh! Oh!' cried Sonia enthusiastically. Fortnight helped her to replace the offending breast.

'I can see you. Little Evel can see you. Naughty things!'

With theatrical gestures Evelyn flapped and groaned, and then crawled out into the hallway.

'No respect for the cloth,' he murmured.

Sonia followed him, and Fortnight found himself alone. He heard Mr Waterford's voice from the hall, saying 'Oh well done! You're a hero!', and then the sounds of general merriment. He began to read the titles of the books, but for some time his drunken eyes would not focus. On the bottom shelf he discovered a paperback copy of *King Lear*. It was marked inside: Susan Fanning, London 1960. He noticed that Regan's part had been annotated with a red pen. He smiled to himself:

> *No Regan, thou shalt never have my curse,*
> *Thy tender-hefted Nature shall not give*

Thee o'er to harshness.

Fortnight replaced the volume and glanced down, still smiling, at an agate table bearing a silver paper-knife. The cracked ivory handle was engraved with a coronet, and in the haft a little blue jewel was sunk, chased round with mottled gold. It was the kind of object that the Kid delighted in, and Fortnight played with it for a moment meditatively. Then, on an impulse, and with a tiny thrill of prohibition, he placed the knife in his pocket. He recalled the book taken from Bramhurst Park; that too must still be in a pocket of his, like the gold watch that he had been wearing on that, or was it some other, day.

He turned to find Susan watching him from the doorway. She entered the room quickly and closed the door.

'Don't be embarrassed. You must keep it. Something to remember me by.'

'I . . .'

She cut him short with a smile.

'You never see when I am serious. I really don't mind. Though, while we are on the subject, I think that Poppa is rather missing vol eleven of Madame de Sévigné.'

A drunken pulse of feeling flushed his face, and he leaned towards her. Susan received the smear of Sonia's saliva with rigid sang-froid. He noticed through a crack in the curtain that a policeman stood motionless beneath a lamp-post in the square. His hat did not sit straight on his bullet head.

'You are so phlegmatic, Susan. Do try to make a scene.'

'I have no desire to make a scene.'

'I wish I could explain how confused I've been. I wish . . .'

Tears came to his eyes, and he was vouchsafed a vision of himself being handed over with gestures of exquisite tenderness and sympathy to the waiting policeman. Susan, confident but smiling, squeezed his hand in a reassuring way as he was guided to the Black Maria, where other policemen, equally decent in their confidential gravity, led him into the half-lit interior. One of them dusted the bench before politely inviting him to sit down.

'You need shaking. I want to shake you.'

And in a sort of way she did shake him, though her unskilled hands, which probably had never held a child except to put it somewhere out of the way, lost all sense of intention. After a while, catching sight of a fat cigar butt smoking in an ash-tray, she stepped over to extinguish it. Her fine hand seized the butt squarely in the middle, and she began to stub it up and down with a chopping movement, watching her hand at its work with a puzzled, girlish expression. The line of her neck was beautiful, and her hair shone with a reddish lustre of henna. A half-empty glass of champagne was murmuring quietly on the mantelpiece. Fortnight swallowed its contents.

'What actually are you going to do about Adrian?'

'What am I going to do about anyone?'

'Why did I invite you?'

'Did you invite me? Did you invite any of these monsters?'

'Let us admit that they are monsters. Will that make you believe that I am not?'

In her anger she was like an angel, every gesture accurate, immortally pointing to a place past change. Now he had to recognize her strength. The way she held her left hand against her hip, for example, and the way she slowly twirled her right foot so that it moved like a guardian creature secreted in the depths of green: her limbs became the avatars of Susan's sovereignty. They stood posted about her body, parcelling out the room for governance. When she came to life this way, or, if not to life, to that brilliant approximation which she practised, Fortnight could only desire her. No doubt that was his destiny, to be granted visions only to put them forever beyond his reach. At the end of things, as he was bowing himself out, some beam would slip sideways and reveal the centre all aglow. It was there that he should be burning, in the fire that she had made for him.

'Of course Susan, I fully intend to change. I want to belong where you belong.'

She looked at him for a moment with constitutional tolerance.

'Adrian is coming. He rang a moment ago.'

Somewhere a little Fortnight went down on its little knees and smally howled. The flap of batty air oppressed its little head and its delicate foetus fingers pawed at the unoffered succour.

'Help!'

'When I was a bairn my mama gave me a piece of advice that I shall now pass on to you. Not that I believe in advice. Courage, she said, is an acquisition; but it goes to the root of being, and changes every act.'

Fortnight laughed.

'So courage is your answer?'

'I have no definite answer.'

'England expects that this day every man will be in two minds about everything.'

Susan relaxed her pose, pirouetted spiritlessly, and said, 'I am going to Italy on Thursday. Will you come with me?'

'To Italy?'

'Sonia Marmaloff has a castle there. She told me to come.'

'Told *you* to come.'

'She mentioned, a moment ago, that I should bring you.'

'Away at last. Away from them all. From fathers, mothers, brothers, sisters, away from moral turpitude, from vice and sin, law and order, the prospects of safe employment, the Derby, the State Opening of Parliament, away from Bramhurst and Flackwell, oh yes and Adrian too . . .'

'Well,' said Susan with an exasperated sigh, 'you can't say that I haven't tried.'

'You tried. I failed.'

She gave him yet another forbearing look. The supply seemed inexhaustible.

'Say you'll come.'

'You'll come.'

The door opened as Susan backed away from him. Still she did not seem angry. A short bearded man, with electrified hair and black obsidian eyes, entered the arena. Fortnight stared at the hairy belly, gossamered over by a veil of transparent silk.

'Angelo! How nice!'

'Susan you bitch!'

The man laughed, was introduced, snatched at Fortnight's hand, and said: 'Pleased to meet you. I like your work.'

'My work?'

'Yes. Wonderful. You're the one who paints girls in cinnamon and sepia, little doe-eyed ballerinas, conscripted circus waifs, that kind of thing. I've studied them. Let's have a drink.'

And again he laughed, a red rag of dog's tongue panting from his jaws. Holding Fortnight's arm he began with his free hand to excavate the foul deposits of his nose. He exchanged a few pleasantries with Susan, and then led his protégé from the room, administering an inexplicable pinch of fellowship as they squeezed through the door.

People were standing with plates of food in their hands, cold salmon and slices of spiced Suffolk ham. Angelo snatched a plate from the sideboard and thrust it into Fortnight's hand.

'I am not a painter,' Fortnight said. 'I am not a theatre critic. I'm not a poet. I . . .'

'What else are you not?'

'Everything. Everything. Everything.'

'No need to be so breathless, baby. What's eating you?'

Fortnight looked at Angelo, who was smiling and waving to the room.

'I just want to go. Away. To Italy. To think.'

Angelo roared, throwing back his black beast's head.

'How about it! Going to Italy. To think. And so young. Really, I blame the Queen.'

Evelyn was beside them, begging Fortnight's forgiveness for his act of anabaptism. Angelo began to praise the body of a prostitute called Maria whom he had enjoyed behind a sarcophagus on the old Appian Way. He raised his fingers in the air and moralized at Evelyn.

'No doubt about it, Evel old boy. None of your Grand Tour sentimentality. None of your light of the Campagna. None of your Piranesi, your Augustus Hare, your German professor's Renaissance man, none of your Russykin, your Bussykin, just the old pussykin. And seldom worth the candle. Allow me to introduce Childe Harold.'

Taking Fortnight's fingers, he entwined them with those of Evelyn, who remarked, 'strange, but I have felt these members before. It must be love.'

Fortnight began to cross the room.

'Who *is* that young man?'

'Theatre critic. *Financial Times*. Frightful chap. Bores like a corkscrew.'

'No Evel, he's a painter. Promising too in his way.'

'Actually he's a famous welter-weight boxer Julia picked up outside the cinema in Ealing.'

'I think he's private pilot to a Scottish duke.'

Fortnight did not know why he was limping, but it was quite involuntary, and the few mental efforts that he made proved ineffective to control it. Someone had poured claret into his glass, and he drank it. Angelo had managed to get hold of Sonia, and now propelled her after Fortnight, panderously pinching her plump bum.

'*Amore!*' he cried, '*amore: fate la bestia a due dossi*, which is, being interpreted, how's your father. Go to sirrah, go to.'

He roared with laughter, drowning the coy squeaks of Sonia. Fortnight fell out of the hallway into a room with a piano. It was empty, and no one attempted to follow him. He played a few chords, and then sat down and began to spin on the piano-stool. After a while he felt queasy; ceasing his movements, he raised his head in a meditative stare. A woman was sitting on a long sofa of heliotrope velvet. She was dressed in eau-de-nil and her green eyes popped from her blanched and powdered face. The combination of colours was appalling, and Fortnight began to pile cushions on top of her, with the noble intention of saving the appearance of Susan's room. She smiled at him sadly, and then rolled off the sofa on to the floor. Then she sat up, and said very slowly: 'I wants go bed with shoolie For'night. Must go bed for for'night.'

'My name's Fortnight.'

'Don't tease, young 'un. Don't ease. You not For'night.'

He stared at the brown mole on the side of her nose. He wanted to rub it. Feeling dizzy he got up from the piano, knocking, as he did so, a silver-framed photograph to the floor. He retrieved it, and recognized the young Lord Gilroy, dressed in Oxford bags, with a silk kerchief beneath his jacket pinned high under the chin. His lordship stood in the garden of some country house, and next to him was a black labrador puppy. The photograph bore the inscription: 'Poppa, with Epsilon, and no smile.'

'You,' said the woman at dictation speed, 'are not For'night. I want him. Go to bed for whole for'night.'

After a silence she resumed.

'You don't know what slike *want* someone. You never wanted someone sbody.'

Fortnight observed both of her bodies, one sitting up dazed on the floor, the other mimicking the posture half a foot higher. The little frieze of plaster cherubs on the ceiling had begun to dance and sing. It was something from *The Magic Flute*, and one of them had the face of Barbara. He was glad she took no notice of him.

'Pillicock sat on Pillicock Hill,' said Fortnight, 'Alow, alow, loo, loo.'

He chuckled quietly and then looked furtively towards the door. There, beneath the lintel, eying him with confusion, stood his father.

'Shoolie!' crooned the woman in green, vainly trying to levitate her hundred bodies. 'Shoolie darling! Thish boy, young shwipper-shnapper, spretending syou. Naughty raschcal, rapshcallion, taking 'vantage. Knock 'sblock off. Knocksblock off shoolie please?'

'Kenneth,' said the Colonel, looking beyond his son to some feature on the wall, 'Oh dear. How nice to see you. I should have known. I might have guessed. Anne sweetie, do get up. Here . .'

He stooped. His fine legs slightly trembled in their velvet trousers, but his hand reached from a velvet sleeve with old-fashioned manliness. He took the lady by the waist and effortlessly swung her upwards.

'Come and meet my son. Kenneth this is Anne Shadbolt, a friend of mine. My dear boy, I won't ask how you are. Perhaps we might have a little talk. Anne darling you won't mind will you, if I propel you into another room? We have a few business matters to mull over.'

'You can't repel me in nother room, no,' said the woman faintly, as the Colonel steered her into the hallway. Fortnight fell on to his knees before the piano, pressing his chin on to G, A and B. He craved in that moment to be cast even in the most melodramatic part, only so long as there were instructions attached to it. 'In one blinding flash of understanding,' his creator wrote, 'I felt the fullness of my calamity. At last, oh powers of darkness, you had delivered my soul into the hands of him whom most I dreaded. Now, after all these weeks of waiting, my fate was taken from my hands. As I reflected on this fact, a minute might have passed, a day, a week, or a thousand years, so lost was I in the dark cavern of my meditations . . .' He who bewails himself has the cure in his own hands. He smiled at his mother's interruption, accepting it. Fortnight rose to greet the Colonel. But it was Susan's figure that stood in the door.

'You're still here. I wanted to warn you. Don't go into the Red Room. Adrian has come, I have trapped him there.'

'I shall see you, when was it? on Thursday, yes, on Thursday, at the airport, or are we to go by train?'

But Susan had disappeared, jostled in the human flotsam that was awash again around him.

'. . . of drawing pins, buttonholes, iambics, can you imagine it? What would you *do*?'

'. . . and even if I was wrong about your name, occupation, date of birth, circumstances, paternal origins, I think I have a story or two about your mother that will prove entertaining . . .'

'. . . the best thing is your actual contadina: a tight-cunted little virgin with titivating preludes of priest-nurtured shame: that's the ticket. No but really, I do blame the Queen. . . .'

Fortnight found the Red Room, entered, and walked straight over to the shelf of books. A glass of champagne was again bubbling lazily on the mantelpiece; he swallowed a couple of mouthfuls, before his mother remarked that it would never do to be drunk as a wheelbarrow in the devil's presence.

He knew that the figure in the chair had glanced at him and was now taking stock. It was best to allow a minute's silence, so that the strength of his intent could be demonstrated. He fingered the silver paper-knife, and after a while took it from his pocket and returned it to the table. The atmosphere of the room was impoverished, as though a sacramental candle had sucked out the air. In the paucity of true emotion every gesture sketched a moral. Once he would have stolen out into the darkness, his hand in Barbara's, enjoying her catlike noiselessness as she steered him through the swamp of unwanted passions. Now he had lost his guide. He turned to his tormentor in a state of such anger that for a moment he imagined the doctor had raised his hands to shield himself.

But the explanation was implausible, for the hands were pinkish, mottled, and far too large. Eventually they were lowered, revealing two little tears that made their snail's tracks down the Colonel's greying cheeks. Fortnight saw that they were alone. For a second he recklessly experimented with laughter. Then there was a silence, and as with every family gathering, the world fell away, leaving the protagonists to fend for themselves in the circle of emotion. It was as though Fortnight had trodden on a weak board in some sparkling drawing-room, and falling softly, found himself settling at a cellar table, where by candlelight all the familiar faces had solemnly gathered, awaiting his return.

'If you can manage not to hate me,' the Colonel said, 'it will make things easier. But of course I recognize your rights in that as in everything.'

Fortnight snorted. It is a dear collop that is cut out of thine own flesh.

'I had no intention that we should meet,' the Colonel continued, 'no intention whatever. It serves no purpose. No purpose whatever.'

'I don't agree. In fact, I came here to see you.'

The Colonel looked up for a moment with a light of surprise in his eyes. But at once it was replaced by a cunning expression.

'Yes. That might be the case. Tracking down the old Charley James. Well, you do get around.'

'As you say, we must discuss . . .'

'No. I must speak. I owe it to you to speak. My dear boy, you look so unwell. I have just met Holtius. He tells me he sees the Kid often, that he is making progress. Is it true I wonder? What can he possibly mean by progress? A dirty word. Perhaps you too should see Holtius from time to time. I know of course that. . . .'

'I do see Holtius from time to time.'

Again the Colonel looked surprised, but this time he disguised his emotion by pressing his thumbs against his mouth and rocking back and forth as though accepting his punishment like a man.

'Of course I am selfish,' he said, in a firmer tone. 'I am a monster, I am everything you accuse me of being. I have failed, failed, yes, failed.'

The Colonel smiled to himself briefly, and then straightened his lips.

'Yes, failed in my duty. To you, to your brother, to her. You see we were not suited, your mother and I, not suited in the least. I needed someone lively, sociable, full of fun, and Angela was none of those. She was frail, ephemeral, childlike — why am I telling you this? — timid, most damnably timid. She was a burden, a burden that I had to bear unaided — why can't I say the truth? — yes, unaided, for twenty-five years. And bear it I did, after my fashion. I planned everything, saw to everything, made us comfortable, filled the house with people, actions, prospects. Didn't I do that? Yes, I did that. I wanted life. Was Angela going to give me life? Of course not. Never. But I failed in my duty.'

The Colonel had risen and was speaking now in a rapid whisper, grasping his son by the sleeve. Fortnight peered into those greenish-grey eyes, slimy with tears, and in their middle distances seawaves signalled to him of childhood holidays, little patterns of brown seashells in the pupil ringed round the image of ancient pains and pleasures, and the discreet tobacco smell of transcendent competence came back to him with a release of fear. Why had the Colonel used her proper name? Was this 'Angela' just one more seal on her official certificate of non-existence?

'You hated her,' he said quietly.

That was better; he saw the Colonel flinch.

'Sometimes, yes, I did, I hated her.'

He added, recovering: 'Why should I deny it?' and raised one hand to check that his lacrymal ducts were open. 'No I won't deny it. If you neglect someone, then unless you also hate them you go under. I am not made to go under, Kenneth.'

'How did you fail?'

'Towards all of you, everything, Queen, country, the whole caboodle. Goes against the grain too, believe me.' He intoned: 'Most heartily we beseech thee with thy favour to behold our most gracious sovereign Lord stroke Lady King stroke Queen Edward stroke George stroke Elizabeth oh yes I've seen quite a lot of them with the grace of the Holy Spirit that he stroke she may always incline to thy will and walk in thy way, etcetera, and make no mistake about it,' he added, 'I would have followed the whole thing through, been the perfect soldier if it were not for one thing, and what was that one thing you ask?'

'I don't ask, I am not asking. I don't want to hear your beastly confessions.'

'Oh but wait a moment, there you are wrong, quite wrong, you do want to hear them. You have tracked me down, and despite what your mother used to say, you can have more of the fox than the skin. Let me tell you. The one thing to which I refer is your mother's faintheartedness, her habit of sprinkling anaesthetic on everything painful, on me, on my career, on my business, on the few women in whom I have been privileged to elicit the moral support I needed, on that child who might have been normal had she conceded that he wasn't, yes, on her own illness too, sprinkling morphia indiscriminately on the quick and the dead. Oh I was encouraged to believe in it, don't get me wrong, in the Holy Ghost of oblivion, in the holy Carbolic Church, in the communion of pain-killers. Blame me if you like for these words, but it is dog's truth I utter.'

Fortnight watched his father slip away on a cloud of self-complaisance, resplendent like a rococo Jupiter floating above the remnants of his crimes. Books and glasses seemed to cascade towards the floor. Someone entered at the door, hung there upside-down, and dropped with a clatter into some hidden aperture.

'And now what of me?' the voice persisted. 'You may beg me on your knees to come back; of course I will not come back. It has never occurred to me to come back. I will not come back. I have donned the shabby frock-coat of indigence. I have made myself bankrupt. You'll see, perhaps you already know? Oddle will have the news by now. You'll have to sell the house. You might earn some money drafting the conveyance. I am told it's your line of country. So you'll have to fend for yourself. Do I care? Don't think that I care. Just stand there and take it, as your mother would. Take every blow. What more can I add? No money for Holtius, no money for St Stephen's. No roof over your head. Both of you on your mettle. That's what you bloody need!'

The voice shouted, and the Colonel, who exercised only a nominal control over it, staggered back towards the chair, the tears flowing more rapidly now, and the chin trembling. Hardly expecting from his soft body any such sudden impulse, Fortnight observed his hand swing through the air, sending the empty champagne glass against his father's brow. It broke in two, a point of glass entered the paternal forehead, causing a fluxion of blood from which consanguinity, had the occasion permitted, might have been proved. As is normal in such cases, the culprit promptly reconsidered his rash action, and extracting a handkerchief from his pocket, applied it with unconcealed repugnance to the punctured flesh.

At this point the Colonel, holding the red-spattered ribbon to his brow, chose to rise once again and smile tenderly at his offspring. Fortnight reported to his biographers the unworthy commotion in his spirit, and begged them to find some portion of charity, dignity or whatever other nameable virtue might justify his disgust. While acknowledging the difficulty of the case, his biographers nevertheless undertook to provide a provisional guarantee, and there was even a certain optimism when the Colonel went so far as to invite, with an elegant gesture, a second blow, which was, however, courteously withheld. Their client began to exert himself in the direction of self-control, and when the Colonel began to protest at the silence, did nothing except reach into his pocket to extract three bus tickets, a gold watch-chain, and a photograph of Barbara Langley. How this last item had insinuated itself among his most private possessions he was at a loss to understand. Nevertheless, when held before the Colonel's hungry eyes the snapshot, which showed a young girl of enticing aspect ardently caressing a dog now several years deceased, had the desirable effect of inspiring an indelicate observation. Such a girl, said the Colonel, should be married. The photograph, which remained in Fortnight's possession thanks to a push in the chest which the wounded Colonel was ill-situated to parry, made its way back to the pocket of its owner, who promptly gave way to feelings of admirable forgivingness towards his former love. His biographers, however, interrupted this flow of emotion, in order to record the Colonel's observations, which, delivered in a less raucous tone, were to the following effect: first, that the Colonel was a tolerant man; secondly, that tolerance must be distinguished from the mindless lack of principle; thirdly, that his own principles were distinguished from the common doctrines of marital obligation primarily through being the fruit of varied, painful, but on the whole well-directed experience. From the height of this tolerance, which he symbolized by returning the handkerchief to the pocket of its owner and allowing the now darkening blood to accumulate in stalactites below his eyebrows, the Colonel was able to survey his son's heart and pronounce it wounded, guilty, and in need of womanly amendments. Wifeless at sixty, the Colonel had carved from his own heart a section that would be useful to his eldest son, fashioned on his own preoccupation with the idea of loyalty, the obeisance which the soldier, the stylist and the dissembler must all make before the single-mindedness of feminine commitments, as before a sacred fact like the sudden transubstantiation at the altar. Against the advice of his biographers Fortnight broke silence in order to ask if the Colonel had lately seen Miss Langley, to which the answer was yes indeed, he had met her here and there, and been on no less than four, perhaps even five occasions, to *The Magic Flute*, an opera for which he had little patience, in order to appreciate the charms which had in some measure been appropriated by his son. It had made the Colonel, who hesitated to confess it and testified to his hesitation by stylized defensive movements of the hands, heavy with impermissible desire.

Fortnight wished it to be recorded that, during this exchange, he entertained towards Barbara no feeling other than one of tender admiration. It is true that he doubted his ability to provide for her. His worldly possessions consisted of a change of underwear, thirty or so books of semi-permanent value, and about fifteen jars of chutney made from apples which fell while his mother was making up her mind to follow them. The rest, he supposed, belonged to sundry creditors of Flackwell Properties, Bramhurst Holdings, and similar concerns. But Barbara could look after herself, and while Fortnight's material circumstances were, for this reason, of no public concern, he could not forego giving utterance to the thought that the Kid ought to have been better provided for.

The Colonel replied that he had always preferred to keep disaster in the family, and that there was comfort in the fact that in his collapse, he had not scattered a constellation of disorders through the public skies. On the contrary, now that he had shed his responsibilities, he was more or less at ease, and would be able to live on whatever back was offered him with the bovine self-assurance of a military gentleman put out to grass. Fortnight, who had derived a few happy though pensive seconds from the thought of the Kid's predicament, caught sight of the histrionic twitch, originating in the Colonel's lower lip and ascending to his ear-lobes, and was assailed by a violent loathing. Fortnight was not wholly satisfied with this loathing, and while he acted on it in a fairly sporting way, causing the paternal wound once more to discharge its gobbets of ketchup on to Lady Susan's carpet, he hoped that his biographers would find elements of compassion in his gestures that he himself was unable to discern. At last, doubled up with laughter, the Colonel sat down.

'My dear Kenneth, this is really too grotesque. You may of course attack me, but neither confounding the persons nor dividing the substance. For there is one person of the father, another of the son, and another, so we are told, of the holy ghost. The father incomprehensible, the son incomprehensible, the HG likewise.'

Fortnight looked at his father's shaking form, and then turned away. He sensed that the Colonel was preparing new weapons, and thought it only fair to allow him time. Besides, so much was becoming clear to him that he preferred to meditate. He focussed on a large portrait that furnished the wall. The lady encased in it was a sumptuous piece of Mayfair magic, with wan forget-me-not eyes, and a wide white mouth almost sensuous in its air of self-denial. The superficial resemblance to Mrs Fortnight struck him less than the splendour of the ebony dress, the deep accumulation of which rose about her in buttressed shadows; the train, rambling through a vista of ivory-coloured arches, was carpet-thick. She seemed to be expecting a visitor who, stepping from the room into the painting, would take her by the hand and lead her in a heedless waltz for the sake of some memory that she contained.

His father was now quite recovered, and had once more risen to his feet.

'I came to Peter Waterford's party, with a woman who was somewhat drunker than myself. Anne Shadbolt if I am not mistaken. I intend to go away with another woman, a certain Diane Forster. What have you to say to that?'

'I have nothing to say to that,' said Fortnight.

'Not made, nor created, but begotten. Strange,' the Colonel commented, surveying his son with a look of appraisal. Gradually the look became wild, and the blood that covered the upper part of his face took on the aspect of phantasmagoric make-up, like an expressionist clown. He began to talk again about Mrs Fortnight, continuing his quotations from the Prayer Book. Fortnight listened for the trail of falsehood that ran through the words like the name in peppermint rock.

'Once, when we lived at Blackett's, before you were conscious of these things, we would listen to those words each Sunday. Remember not, Lord, our offences, nor the offences of our fore-fathers; neither take thou vengeance of our sins. Angela used to pray on her knees at the bedside, in a white cotton nightdress, her hair piled up for the night, so high in those days, it reminded me of those ladies on the big Fanning tomb. Very modest, very demure.'

The Colonel took a step forward, the index finger of his right hand pointing to his son. His shoulders, even in the paroxysm of his feigned distress, remained conscious of the braid and tassels of promotion which in family proceedings he always invisibly wore. In his eyes the tears slowly took up their stations.

'She prayed aloud. She even prayed for me. I laughed at her, because I had a passionate desire to be included in her innocence. By reviling, I worshipped, in my own way. But of course I intended her to stop. She was obstinate. Honest, but obstinate. It got on my nerves. Once, no don't go,' he continued more urgently, and begin-ning to pluck at the lapel of Fortnight's jacket, 'once, there is no harm in my saying it, I remember it as though it were yesterday, she told me that you should learn to pray. I decided to put on a display of anger. Enough is enough; the household of a man with a career cannot be too sodden with righteousness. You must have been four or five at the time,' he added. Fortnight saw that, in the deft usury of his confessions, the Colonel had withheld the principal gesture until the moment when he could double his returns.

'I dare say you have some fleeting memories associated with that display. In any case, she chose to disregard my instructions. One day I found those little tracts in her workbox. Jesus books, with pictures of children from every nation and social class being suf-fered to come unto him, provided they were not overtly deformed or putrescent. Do you remember them? Don't answer me, it is of no significance. I took them out into the little garden we had then and burned them by the lawn, in her favourite patch of Chinese gentians, while she watched from the kitchen window. It was important to make her understand. It was I who needed faith, do you see? It was I,' he continued, with whispered laughter, 'who needed her assurance. Why should she give that simplicity to you, when I stood in need of it? I wanted to take hold of her suffering little body and shake out the piety that she hid from me. That night, when she was kneeling down to pray, and said something silent to herself which I took to be a specimen of Christian charity, as though I wanted her morbid forgiveness, I leant across the bed and hit her dear face, not once but twice, so that she fell over, and — what are you doing? My dear Kenneth . . .'

Fortnight received Susan's impassive glances from the doorway. There was something masterly in the way that she refrained from pressing her hand to her mouth, refrained from stepping forward, refrained from seeking help, redress or punishment, refrained even from looking at the Colonel. She fixed her eyes on Fortnight with a light of pure understanding and almost disinterested support. She was a marvel, and with her help he steered the paper-knife clear of his father's features and returned it to his pocket. He thanked her warmly, while she, with all the fortitude of her race, handed him swiftly to the door, telling him to move with whatever rapidity seemed suitable. She was even strong enough to hold back the doctor as she closed the door. Fortnight shouted through the letter-box: 'I will telephone about Thursday. I want to lie on a sheeted balcony with Sonia Marmaloff.'

He ran to the corner, where the Kid was waiting.

'Jeepers Creepers, Kenny, you take your time. Having to track Dis all the way from the Garrick Club is bad enough, but then you keep me shivering outside until the three of you have just about had time to plot the counter-revolution. We've got twenty minutes till the last train. Holy mackerel,' he added as he hailed a cab, 'that hotel of yours was sordid. And they even tried to charge me for your meals.'

Chapter Eight

'THERE WAS enough type came with it to set up a full length book practically.'

The Kid waved towards the platen press that had been screwed to the top of the Colonel's desk. Its brass and nickel parts seemed smooth and ancient, while the iron handle had lost its black paint and caught a metallic sheen from the morning light in the window.

'Owing to a penetrating awareness of cracks and flaws, and a precocious skill in mirror-writing, I shall be the world's greatest typesetter. In fact,' the Kid went on, picking a handful of italic *e*s from a case on the trestle-table, 'it would have been better on the whole had I always been encouraged to observe the world in mirrors. It favours contemplation over action, a stance which the philosophers instruct us to prefer. Trouble is, I can't see so very well these days. Everything has to be eighteen point or bigger. This,' he added, gesturing to the right hand part of the study, in which the pine-wood table from the scullery had been placed, 'is the composition room, while this is the print room itself.'

On the scullery table were cases of type, together with tins of printer's ink, a roller, bottles of paraffin and rubber-solvent, blocks of wood and metal quoins, all arranged with a craftsman's concern for order, only with something more absolute, more untouchable in the arrangement than was compatible with any serious exercise of craft. Little tables culled from the house bore their burdens of mallets, bodkins, brayers and tweezers; on the shelves were stacks of paper of various shapes and styles, and driven into the wall in pathological straight lines were nails bearing cloths, blocks, and instruments polished with use.

The Kid ran his hands through a tray of type. 'My sortees Fortnightiana', he called it, and picked up letters which spelt 'marjplop'.

'The oracle is dum.'

He began to work, slowly inserting the type into a composing-stick. His hand, subject to customary trembling, caused him frequently to stumble in the operation.

'But how much did it cost?'

Fortnight studied with an unconcluded motion of acceptance the iron god that stood on the altar that had been consecrated to it.

Its handle reached before it like a hungry tongue, and above the mouth to which all the parts progressed was a round disc of blackened aspect, a kind of sightless head which seemed to possess occult awareness of their intentions. As he lifted the type into the stick the Kid moved with a reverential gravity, rehearsing for the millionth time a ritual that would always be miraculous. At last he seemed to bring his task to some temporary stasis.

'Oh, not much,' he said. 'Not much at all considering.'

'Considering what?'

'Considering history, first. What I am doing was done by Gutenberg. In the intervening five hundred years the world has seen many significant developments so I am told, but none that has changed the art of printing. Considering market prices, second. Thanks to Bill, one of our members who was actually in the printing trade himself at one time only he did the opskop on a kaffir that had tried to be umfundisi in the chapel if you get my drift so being out on the proverbial ear, who told me to put up my hand; thanks to Bill the hammer went down just as if I had offered my fragile clown's head for a battering, and there it was: a mere three hundred in coin of the realm. Considering our future third: this, you don't realize, is an investment of the highest kind. For example, it reinforces my position in the party. Although you may think it a trifle odd to see "Workers of the World Unite" in Gothic lettering it's the best I can do at present until the Perpetua titling comes in and besides it adds tone to what would otherwise be a vulgar declamation. It also makes us into a business: you director, me secretary. Considering finally the literary community, to which an institution like Fortnight Frères is indispensable. Kymbelin — that, believe it or not, is the name of the poet . . .'

'Which poet?'

The Kid returned to his work, transferring type from galley to forme, and surrounding it with blocks of wood and quoins that he tightened with an iron key. His clumsy movements were so swathed in hieratic gestures of the head and torso that the work, by divine dispensation, remained in place, making the procession to the altar without mischance. The Kid stroked a flat part of the inner machine.

'This,' he said, 'is your actual platen, and I am about to dress it with board and tympan prior to inking up. You know perfectly well which poet I am referring to. How many poets are there in Flackwell? I met one once, didn't I? Am I likely to meet another? Oh, I admit, he behaved badly. But for the sake of his art I am ready in my magnanimity to forgive. Now, here she goes.'

The Kid began to spread ink on the face of the machine, pressing it with a palette knife and then adjusting rollers, spindles and other inscrutable parts. He pulled the handle several times in succession. The noise was deafening: each cry of the machine was accompanied by a hundred little squeals from its moving parts, which ran against each other in a frenzy of half-revealed activity. It became clear that the Kid was succeeding in his task. Even now, when his eyes were weaker, his hands less controlled than ever, a sombre intelligence made meaning in all his actions, refusing to allow the world to slip beyond the grace of his failing participation.

'It was odd him turning up at the brewery, just on the last day, when I had decided to throw in the towel, but there it is. Naturally he didn't remember me. I had to remind him who I am, which is a joke in itself, given the permanent necessity of reminding myself. Well, he needs a publisher, as is not surprising, given the mediocrity of his verse. I thought begin with him, and then ascend, ascend. Poetry is what matters. It's the thing we've neglected.'

'We?'

'All right then, you.'

The Kid began to place a sheet of paper in the machine.

'My own pioneer experiment in that direction is about to receive its first impression. I should be honoured if you would peruse it for mistakes of punctuation, grammar, and morality.'

Fortnight realized that it was of the utmost importance to hold on to his new clarity of vision, and he delayed for a moment looking at the Kid's poem, until he could gain some sense of the real importance of this enterprise. Ever since the journey home, during which the Kid had begun to unfold his plans, Fortnight had perceived the need for delicacy. He had even suggested, when they had passed Oxford on to the home stretch, that the delft, which made three thousand in cash, had perhaps not been theirs to sell, and that their mother might have wished to keep it in the house.

'Oh no, Kenny,' was the prompt reply, 'she doesn't mind at all. She came round just after you left to pick up some things. It so happened I caught her as she was sneaking through the garden. She had a train to catch. But I explained that you had left home again. I pointed out that, being but a *rudis indigestaque moles etcetera*, I need a plan of action, with which *propositio* she entirely agreed. I *had* been tempted to sell the stuff. But it was her idea actually to do it. She said I should use the money to track you down and start home again. On which subject I must say, if it hadn't been for the thing Mr Patel intercepted . . .'

'What thing?'

'Well, perhaps you were not in your right mind when you wrote it. Though it *was* your writing.'

The Kid got up, with redundant circumspection, slid the compartment door, and surveyed the semi-darkness of the empty corridor.

'It was very short, as you know. But sufficient.'

'What did it say?'

'Your question is rhetorical.'

'No.'

Sick and ungainly, Fortnight weaved through the crowded ghosts of the corridor. He leaned from the window. The moon followed the train above ruined fields and towns, casting shadows into mouldy sidings, scattering highlights in factory roofs, dragging its trash of revelations into each familiar place.

The Kid was rolling on the long seats like a circus clown, in the belly of a great mother, exercising still his forfeited right to play. He chuckled, but with the sad, grim chuckle of one who recognizes that it would be more polite, were it possible, to laugh.

'It did not actually begin 'Dear Adrian', or 'Dear anyone', but its being in Mr Patel's postbag suggests it was intended for Dis. All it said, as I remember — here, Mr Patel made a note of it' — he held out the scrap of paper in order that Fortnight should acquiesce in his brother's finer version — 'all it said was "I don't understand it. But I will be there as requested on August 17th." As luck would have it you used the hotel writing-paper, though how such a hotel could *have* writing paper is beyond me.'

'I sent that from the hotel?'

'Apparently. Dis was there all afternoon looking for you, being awkwardly polite to everyone, trying to conceal his Borgia look behind a stiff collar and a trilby. Quite a bother trailing him: kept me outside the Garrick Club for two hours with a bag of chips while he noshed and poshed: if I'd had a bit of warning I could have looked in back stage at the Garden and said howdy. Still, *non si pasce del cibo mortale . . .*'

Fortnight looked up slowly lest there should be clues of a visual nature. But there were none. 'Well, then,' he said, 'that's it.'

'What, precisely, is what?'

The Kid jumped across to the opposite seat, and assumed the spruce posture of a competent analyst.

'Please don't move about so much, Kid.'

'Relax. Imagine I'm your friend. Excuse me while I adjust the photograph of my wife and child. Just tell me how it seems to you.'

'It's that I keep writing things, and not knowing what I have done. This is another example.'

'Can you elaborate? I think I have failed to grasp your senselessness.'

Fortnight decided that it would be tactful to join in his brother's game. He lay back on the seat, and stared upwards at the ceiling light.

'Once I kept a diary. It was written on loose sheets. I tried to convey all my thoughts from my head to paper without disturbing them. But when I read them, I could not recognize what I had put down. Even the writing seemed different.'

He waited for a moment, but, feeling that the Kid's silence had an unusual quality, turned at last to look at him. The Kid was blushing; Fortnight observed him in astonishment. 'Did *you* do it?'

After a silence the Kid replied in a voice filled with urgency: 'Let's not talk about it. It was a — a mistake of mine. I'm clearer now. I don't need to pretend that you believe, when I know.'

Nothing about those constantly mutating features surprised Fortnight so much as their colour. Only through calling on some great reserve of strength could the Kid have put himself in the moral position to blush. This blush became at once far more interesting than the trick of which Fortnight had been, he now realized, the willing victim. The Kid had created certainty from perpetual inquisitions. This certainty was like the motionlessness in the midst of a playing fountain, an untouchable simulacrum of absolute calm. The blush was the aspect that slowly moved on the surface of synthetic stillness.

Fortnight sat wondering at his brother's achievement. Panicked by no self-observation, he now remembered the bitter moment when he had wished on himself the evil of Susan's party, and sought to complete it by arranging for Holtius to be there. He smiled to think that his note had brought so much good. He decided to thank Mr Patel for his criminal dealings with Her Majesty's mail. The Kid reached out, held his arm for a moment, and said: 'It was my fault that you went away. But now you see, I know.'

Fortnight judged it most delicate at this juncture to fall asleep.

He awoke with a start, the Kid shaking him to announce their coming home. The air outside was light, feathery, and in his sudden assuagement, Fortnight wept. They sat together at station two, by the Baptist church, in silence. Then Fortnight pulled from his pocket the mementoes of his stay in London: the bus tickets, the address of Sonia Marmaloff, a piece of tinsel from the props at Covent Garden, a handkerchief caked with his father's blood. All these were explicable, and he threw them to the ground in contempt. Others, dating from several days back, caused him more trouble, and one in particular — the cloth-covered button strap of a woman's suspender — suggested that he was still hiding something from himself. He made a mental note to look for volume

Eleven of Madame de Sévigné, and to return it to Lord Gilroy. At last he found the paper-knife, which had made a hole in his pocket and slipped into the lining. The Kid took it in silence and then led his brother home.

The régime of tact endured through the next day, permitting the folly of the printing press, condescending to the Kid's elaborate pastiche of human industry, joining in the new efforts to put order into house and garden, concealing the disabling fact of the Colonel's bankruptcy. Under this régime no impediment to Fortnight's clarity could survive; it fanned into the reaches of his mind, dispelling all that had festered there.

Each law and ritual of the Kid's new kingdom was carefully studied, and Fortnight had to slow down the constitutional process in order to understand its successive turns. When he was prepared at last for the enterprise which the Kid described as 'poetry' (but which no doubt was something familiar under quite a different name) he was glad to find that there were extra minutes for reflection. The Kid had muddled the formes, and lifted from the press not the verses that he had promised, but a nostalgic memento of the *ancien régime:*

WORKERS OF THE WORLD UNITE!
YOU HAVE NOTHING TO USE BUT YOUR DRAINS!
Meeting: Tuesday, 4th August, Guildhall, 7.30 p.m.
Topic: Application by Flackwell Properties Ltd to
demolish workers' cottages under Wenbury Hill
FIGHT THE SPRAWLING MONSTER OF CAPITALISM!
'Sorry. My fault. Start again. *Non omnia possumus omnes.* Go farther and fare worse, say I, and, oh ye waters that be above the firmament (what can it mean?) bless ye the Kid in this his final transformation. The key, fasten it, yes, and under the friskets with you, down you go, there! My first published work, just let me fetch up a bottle if Kym has left any...'

He paused in the doorway while Fortnight held the smudged page of irregular print. The Kid's features seemed crammed into the locket of his outline, so that flesh, teeth, glass and hair commingled like the effects of a car crash.

'I have something to tell you, Kenny. It isn't easy to say.'

The tone was more of an invitation than an admission. Fortnight decided to take his chance. 'I have something to tell you, Kid, and it isn't easy either.'

'Then the only question is, who goes first.'

'As the older perhaps I can claim the right.'

'As the more intelligent, I concede it.'

'The Colonel is bankrupt. This house has to be sold.'

'Yes, but what did you have to tell me?'

'That.'

The Kid laughed. 'But how could you think that I didn't know *that?*'

'I . . .'

'Or that I hadn't taken precautions?'

'I don't follow you.'

'We stopped the planning permission for Wenbury Hill, the creditors moved in. He had to do what a gentleman does. He secured his assets and went underground. According to Mr Patel the payments to Dis were stopped. Naturally I concluded that this house would be next to go. Fortunately that man Addle is true to his name. He did not act.'

'Oddle.'

'Yes, him. All you have to do, as you probably realize, is register a charge under the Matrimonial Causes Act 1967, a statute which, according to your book, bristles with difficulties, being so new on the books, and another way in which marriage constitutes a blot on the title.'

'But what could you do?'

'Well, it stands to reason, Mummy not being here, that I should make an application for her. Addle let me steal some forms, I forged signatures, I wrote cunning letters to confuse the powers that be. For the moment the house is safe. I have registered what is called a caution.'

Fortnight, unable to refer to the major impediment, kept silent.

'Anyway, let me tell you *my* news. There is a poetry festival, to take place in the halls of Fortnight. On Tuesday to be exact. Prize, publication by the Fortnight Press.'

'And who will come?'

'Kymbelin plus one. Myself. You. Mr Patel. One or two old literary ladies, maybe even Mrs Thurlow if you don't object. Oh yes, and Mummy.'

Fortnight attempted to receive the news as a commander sure of victory listens to the announcement of a temporary reverse. He looked past the curtained windows to the vicarage, beyond which the afternoon was beginning to throb on the lake of green. The whole town was quiet now for the hours of work, before the home-ward-urging panic burst its way through office doors, snapping shut files, extinguishing the clamour of the senseless telephone. They too were to be incorporated into the rage of regulated days. Images of order stood over the old town of Flackwell; shiftless concrete obliterated the two children who had played among those buried stones. Turning to the Kid, he asked: 'How much of the three thousand is left?'

'I kept what I could. But you know, there are, in that adult world to which you belong, many incidental expenses. It even costs money to keep a telephone ringing at the bottom of a chest. Still we can survive. It is on deposit at the Midland. Enough of business. In a few weeks Fortnight Frères will be launched. Why aren't you reading that poem? It is a palindrome.'

'A what?'

'I forgot your lack of sympathy for Byzantine man, of which I am an example. Something that reads the same backwards as forwards, or forwards as backwards, depending on your priorities.'

Fortnight looked down at the paper and read:

Night, whispering to Morning, said:
"Have we death? Is life
Unlimited by prolonged persistence?"
"Birds have nests, as absurdity
Made new for long life,"
Said Morning. Morning said:
"Life longs for new-made
absurdity, as nests have birds —
Persistence prolonged by
Unlimited life is death"; we have said
Morning to whispering Night.

The Kid was singing quietly in the lower reaches of the house. Fortnight saw in the poem an allusion to the certainties that now governed him. The plot had turned full circle; his mother's eternal recurrence had received its constitutional guarantee.

On the day of the festival the house was in turmoil. Fortnight had been assigned a variety of minor tasks. All traces of the Colonel were to be removed from the print-room, from the laughing-room, from the dining-room, from the kitchen. Each of the Edwardian objects which had accompanied the Colonel from a half-gentlemanly past, laden with their masculine futilities, was to be removed: hair-brushes, lotion bottles, leather pouches and brass-bound cigar boxes; military swords, canes, ships' decanters and hip-flasks. All had been stationed sentry-like about the house and kept speechless vigil in his absence. Now a common grave was made for them out of a tea-chest in the scullery. Fortnight was given money and told to buy ham, chicken, eggs, gherkins, bread and cheese.

He visited Oddle, saying that he would like to return the advance. The solicitor listened without interest to his narrative.

'I don't know anything about the law,' he said. 'Your brother had it taped. It's the Land Registry's concern. As if I hadn't got enough on my plate without taking on Flackwell's most dangerous loony.'

Fortnight observed the solicitor twisting his face through its shabby disguises, turning like a yogi on the metallic grid of sound. As a boy Fortnight had envisaged the law as something majestic, beyond reproach, a golden chain of offices filled successively by family friends. It was like the church, the mayoralty, the institutions of state, the peerage: each claimant was embossed with the seal of office, his character subdued, the identity of things local left in a sacred pall of changelessness. Flackwell existed for him now as a kind of nightmare, an aftermath of revolution, in which peasants sat on judges' thrones, honours and offices were betrayed or held to ridicule, the small buttresses of rural life replaced by cardboard effigies: doctors who were not doctors, solicitors who knew neither custom nor law. All this was vivid in Oddle's features, as he swayed to the music. In a serene gesture of farewell, Fortnight placed his packet of food on the metal chair and fastidiously urinated on to the carpet.

'Whatever my brother did,' he said to the speechless solicitor, 'it is sure to have been right.'

He picked up the food and left.

Unfortunately the demolition of the old photographer's house had blocked the High Street. He was forced to enter a part of town still unafflicted by the dynastic requirements of expendable things. Here he had often walked with Barbara, and it was always here, precisely here, as he turned the corner beyond the chemist's shop with its blue glass phials raised in the window on fluted columns, that he felt the acutest anguish. It did not matter whether the street was busy or deserted, whether it was the time of day when the great lorries rolled by, head to tail like animals seeking in a troupe some rare but indispensable commodity, or whether it was the quieter time, when lights flickered into whiteness in old shop windows, and the last few walkers were brushed out quickly towards their homes. It did not matter whether the street was as it had been when he last came home, or whether some building had been pulled down, or a new one erected. None of this mattered as he reached this corner. He felt like the protagonist in the Noh play, stumbling on a haunted place to watch as his integrity is tried. This corner was the turning-point; here the public Fortnight, the man of leisure, means, ambition, sentiment, became the private playmate to a fool. He apologized to himself profusely as he negotiated this unchanged and changing place. But it was to no avail. He might have used this excursion to think of some stratagem; but he had thought of nothing. He had allowed the Kid to cast him in another desperate theatrical. But what would happen, when, as was certain, Mrs Fortnight failed to appear?

He ran quickly past Mrs Williams's sweet-shop, and, when he caught sight of a form that reminded him of Barbara, he did not stop, as at first he was inclined to, but hurried on at an unseemly pace towards the garden gate.

The dining-room had been arranged as for a séance, with candles set in terra-cotta vessels that Mrs Fortnight, in an arts and crafts whimsy, had thrown on a wheel at the evening college. The wax spilled in murky rills across the table-top. In semi-darkness the piled up sandwiches and uncorked bottles awaited the stirrings of hunger and thirst. Fortnight took his place, recognizing among those assembled only the Marchesa di Vespicci-Valeta, an antique woman with thin nervous hands raised winsomely to a face still young with untried aspirations. The Marchesa, having extinguished the petroleum flame of her fortune in the pool of another's noble blood, eked out the rest of her naivety in a series of commitments. She believed in the stars, in table-turning, in nature conservancy, was an avid collector of superstitions, and wrote a kind of rhymeless poetry that could be read only with the eyes raised to a distant light visible to none but her. The Kid had invited the Marchesa, he said, for the sake of business, since there was still a dollar or two secreted in those knickers.

A small courteous Indian bowed as Fortnight sat down. His liquid brown eyes rested for a moment on his new neighbour, and then were lowered to the long-fingered hands that enclosed his papers. Apart from the Post Office badge which he wore in his left lapel as part of the insignia of protest, Mr Patel was immaculate with a stiff collar, and a fine tie in navy-blue silk, which looked as though it bore the coat of arms of an Indian university. He said, 'It is with much pleasure Mr Fortnight that I am coming here. Alas, it is but to listen. To read my Sanskrit dialogue of the soul and body would not I think be fair.'

Two old ladies in bell-like dresses were perched at the far end of the table, and the Kid sat next to them. Four more places had been laid. The Kid was smiling serenely, and watching the hand of the clock as it crept towards nine.

'These places,' said the Kid, with the air of one who wishes all questions to be closed, 'are for Kym.'

A long interval followed. The Marchesa stared dreamily at the ceiling, while the Kid drummed with his fingers on the table. The two old ladies set to each other and pivoted like pigeons; their tiny clockwork movements accompanied little speechless yawns from half-open mouths, but at every word or gesture from some other guest they would look up simultaneously with an expression both affable and pointed, as though about to inflame the company with a spark of wit. Soon the gathering was on edge with anticipation.

Without a knock, the hall door opened and Kymbelin, tall, hirsute and with an air of thunderous vulgarity, marched into the dining-room. His first companion was a large teddy-bear in white washable dralon which he carried under one arm. The second, who followed behind, was a youth with a drag queen's jammy lips, and piled-up hair like a nest of chortling birds, wearing midnight blue trousers of some shiny artificial stuff.

'This,' the Kid announced, 'is the great poet, Kymbelin Fisher, OM, in the company of his necessary acolytes, Toot, an inarticulate bear, and Ekhnaton, keeper of philtres.'

The great poet stood in the door of the dining-room, pushing the fringe of black hair away from narrow eyes, which darted from left to right as though expecting a secret attacker. He wore a tousled beard, in which his lips lay long and protuberant, basking beside each other like coils of a buried snake. His clothes were various shades of soiled grey, and hung in disorder, with inexplicable strata revealing themselves at neck and belt. He resembled nothing so much as an unmade bed of stale sheets, with discarded hairs and spots of dry detritus scattered among the creases.

'We are delighted to meet you,' said the Marchesa, pushing her thin lips outwards as though the air were an apple and she was about to bite on it.

'Yes, yes,' said the old ladies.

'It is, I am sure, an honour,' added Mr Patel more circumspectly.

'You will be sure in a little while, by Christ,' the poet said, and sat down at the table. 'Shift your bum,' he added, addressing the Marchesa, 'Toot has to sit next to me.'

With a courteous inclination of the head the Marchesa rose, her hands disposed at critical junctures about her clothes, as though the whole contraption were in danger of falling apart. The poet turned and held out his hand towards Fortnight. Although the hand grappled the air before it like some challenging weapon out of a tank, its embrace was surprisingly limp, as though existing for no other purpose than to gauge the quality of another's grip. Should he press hard? Or should he respond with equal weakness? Fortnight was certain that there must be some intermediate pressure that conveyed exactly the right amount of hesitant animation and grateful acquiescence, but he was not sure that he had found it. When the poet had sat down Fortnight occupied himself for a while in studying Ekhnaton, who had begun to chirrup merrily and ask for wine. Fortnight noticed that the Kid looked anxious now, and applied himself to his hostly duties without commitment, as though standing in for someone else. The empty place at table was next to the Kid's, and Fortnight knew that Mrs Thurlow could not be the one that was expected to sit down in it.

Ekhnaton turned to the company and said,

'So this is the other Fortnight. He's fine-looking. Don't we think he looks fine?'

The poet forestalled all agreement by saying,

'I think he looks like a star-spangled arse-hole,' in a deliberative tone that left it uncertain whether the remark was intended as a compliment.

The Marchesa proved equal to the occasion.

'There has never been a day,' she remarked, 'when epithets of a glorious nature have not been appropriate.'

One thought must be driven out by another. With the poet, therefore, ideas were peculiarly tenacious.

'A moon-spattered bum-hole,' he said experimentally.

'Wonderful!' shrieked Ekhnaton, clapping his slender white hands. 'It's time to start.'

The Kid turned quickly from the sideboard.

'No. Not yet. We're expecting someone.'

'A glow of reflected light upon an orifice,' said the poet slowly.

There was a silence, during which Fortnight poured for himself a glass of wine. A low murmur of conversation began among the two old ladies. Mr Patel said quietly, 'I regret very much the intrusion of these exceedingly vulgar personages.'

The Kid controlled his nervous movements by transferring the wine into an earthenware jug, which he placed on the table. He himself drank nothing, but sat and watched the clock, which had now crept round to nine fifteen. The great poet remained silent, except for the occasional tender remonstrance at Toot's table manners. Ekhnaton bubbled and after a while the Marchesa looked round at the company and said, 'It won't be exactly beginning if I speak, since speaking is not reading, is it?'

Her eyes wandered, and then rested on a distant point. She re-arranged her clothes so as to be able to lean slightly forward, her delicate hand resting on her breast. The Kid shook his head but said nothing.

'It was summer,' the Marchesa continued, slightly exaggerating her Bostonian accent. 'My sister proposed that we make for the woods and camp there, picking berries. To a wild place one morning alone I came, my heart all open with the wild water sound, and he, he followed me unseen. It was the foam and froth of my song he said had mastered him, as I sang on unaware...'

'Great torrents of sperm!' cried Kym irrelevantly. The Marchesa ceased with the sweetest of smiles and continued to commune with the distant source of inspiration. The Kid rose from the table and took a turn about the room.

'What was that?' he cried. 'Kenny, did you hear it?'

Fortnight had also got up, thinking that he heard a footstep on the stair.

'The wind under the door,' said one of the old ladies.

'The slow terrible tearing of the veil of Maya,' added Mr Patel.

Fortnight went out into the hallway, and stared into the darkness of the upper house. A tap was dripping in the bathroom. He ran to tighten it. Then there was silence. The Kid was standing where he had left him in the dining-room, his hands to his face, his small body bent, frail, ruined. Fortnight took him by the arm and led him back to the table, where Ekhnaton was beginning again to overflow.

'This evening, ladies and gentlemen, you are to overhear the absolute honesty and completeness of the poem itself. Everything that is in our minds must be poured into crucibles, mingled, heated, replaced in our skulls. I am the impresario, and I shall ask the great Kym to begin with his letters to Rimbaud. Then perhaps one of the older generation could oblige; we shall work to a climax until the insane genius our host throws down his electric vomit from astral regions, and we howl like wild dogs so sweetly that the moon dissolves in a long slow drip of Chartreuse.'

Fortnight noticed a smell of marijuana in the room. What if Kym were Barbara's lover: the thought struck him just as Ekhnaton was interrupted by a tapping on the window from the garden. Everyone froze, except the Kid, who jumped from the table and ran into the garden.

'Hello!' he cried, 'Hello! Are you there?'

No answer came, and the wind, which had risen in the last hour, suddenly caught the door of the kitchen and slammed it behind him. Again there was a tapping at the window: Fortnight followed his brother into the garden. The ground seemed unsubstantial: the dark air buffeted about him, and he whirled in pools of blackness, at sea in the tumbling shapes of clouds and trees and hollyhocks, his feelings, phosphorescent, not quite distinguishable below him. The garden seemed full of hands, some out of reach, others brushing against him with a wistful tenderness.

A lamp was burning in the shed. He opened the door. Above the Kid's silent form her green gaberdine was hanging, and next to it, on the shelf, her gardening gloves, her little fork, her trowel and pruning shears.

'Please come back,' he said.

'I was a fool to invite them. Of course Mr Patel is right. They are vulgar, preposterous, disgusting. She will hate them. But why Kenny, why so late?'

'We'll go back now, Kid. Remember what she would say: nothing is certain but the unforeseen.'

'Trust me, Kenny. I'll behave.'

The great poet was bombinating, kneeling on his chair, taking sheets of paper one by one from the left-hand pocket of his jacket. He would read a line or two, and then transfer the sheet to the pocket on the right. Fortnight envied the gesture, which was one of purest self-containment. The high charivari of his voice shook the glasses on the dresser, and the Marchesa listened with half-closed eyes as though she would swoon away.

> *And the man with the green camel whose head of jewels*
> *come mad out of the chloroform alembic into the bleeding*
> *night*
> *And the teahead who was laid by holy motorcyclists on the*
> *unfinished highway crying 'Set me alight, oh Jesus, set me*
> *alight!'*
> *And the hotrod mastermind that signs at the bottom of the*
> *absolute insurance scheme,*
> *And the bald killers in regiments, with broomsticks and*
> *haloes, melting with smiles the eternal ice-cream...*

'Oh do stop,' said Mr Patel, 'it is most unseemly.'

The Kid removed the poet's glass, and sat down, patting the air with sad Palialic gestures. Kym had turned on Mr Patel and was screaming: 'I'll push your teeth so far down your bleeding throat you'll have to stick your toothbrush up your arse to clean them!'

'Bravo!' said Ekhnaton. 'Hurt him!'

'Ladies and gentlemen,' said the Kid, 'I apologize. I have made a horlicks of it. Let us begin again.'

'You effing weirdo, I don't take interruptions,' said Kym, his neck emerging from his many collars to its full extension, and looking like the stringy chard of a bluish artichoke.

'To begin again is not to interrupt,' the Kid replied. 'Shall we begin again?'

There was a murmur of assent, a snort from Kym, and all except the Kid quaffed from their glasses and replenished them.

'Of course,' said one of the old ladies, 'one should go everywhere naked. For Western man the erogenous regions have become objects of curiosity and therefore of shame. To reveal them is to say "I trust you".'

'Madame,' said Mr Patel, 'I am an Eastern gentleman, and I would trust you with my life, my daughter, my fortune, but not with those zones to which you refer.'

'Remember the prize,' said the Kid. 'Do not squabble. As our absent guest would say: a poet in adversity can hardly make verses. Let us return to Kym and ask him to rhyme some rats to death.'

Kym looked round uncertainly, with a kind of provisional menace in his eyes, and then reached again into his left-hand pocket. Suddenly the doorbell rang. Fortnight started up and held the Kid by the shoulder.

'Don't go!' he cried.

'Leave me alone.'

'You mustn't go!'

The bell rang again. It was followed by a timid knocking. It was faint and tiny, as though the hand were constantly reaching back in hesitation. When his mother had kissed him it had been like the pop of a fish at the surface, timid, unemerging, straightway plummetting for refuge in the depths. The knocking had just that quality of retreat into safety; but there was an urgency in it, a repeated drumming as of a creature shut out in the cold and begging admittance. The wind outside had risen and now rattled the panes in the dining-room window: even Kym was silent, and all the faces at the table turned to the brothers and watched them as though they might begin to dance. The Kid released himself and ran to the door of the room.

'No, Kid! Come back!'

The knocking began again, soft, urgent, saying let me in, let me in. It laid timid claim to a right of admission. This was its home; it had returned after long wanderings and they could not shut it out. It was full of that whimsical insistence, that quiet feminine obstinacy which the Colonel had wished to kill. They must let it in. Fortnight called again after his brother, and got up from the table. The Kid would be at the door now. The bell rang again. And then, before Fortnight could move into the hall, he heard the front door being opened.

There was a terrible scream. It was not a human scream, but the cry of the night, that had torn itself asunder and now released its black noise of pain, anguish and violation. Fortnight stood listening to it, his hemlocked legs bound to the place allotted them, his eyes and hands fixed in gestures of prayer.

'It must not be,' he said.

Little yelps of terror sounded from the hallway as the scream fluttered away. Fortnight turned to the company: some ghost was trying to clamp a look of puzzlement on to their self-complaisant faces.

'Stay here!' he commanded. With a sudden jump he freed his legs and gained the hallway.

In the half-light of the porch, stood Dr Holtius, who smiled into the house, pushing back the love that had been reborn there and which excluded him. The Kid had backed down the hallway as far as the poetry bookcase, and now stood his ground by the door of the laughing-room, seeming to be mastering himself against the corrosion of the doctor's smile. He trembled slightly, but he had ceased to cry out, and there was about his small tensing body a kind of resolve that astonished Fortnight and alerted him to the extreme danger in which the Kid had put himself.

'I came to see your brother,' said the doctor. 'I happen to know he's at home.'

'I happen to know,' said the Kid, in a deadened voice, 'that he does not want to see you.'

The Kid and the doctor looked at each other intently, silently, permeating the air between them like spiritualists hungry for ectoplasm.

'It is not a question of what you think he wants,' the doctor said at last. 'You must either let me in or fetch him to me.'

The doctor took a step forward into the light. He had a strange, tousled look, and his velvet suit was in disarray as though he had been brawling. His wild eyes continued to direct at the Kid their venomous anathema, and he tapped his feet slowly, like a snake-charmer. He took another step forward, and the Kid shouted: 'Get out of my mother's house!'

There was in the Kid's intonation all the moral unassailability of despair, and the doctor flinched slightly before resuming his smile.

'It would be sacrilege for me to intrude, I take it.'

'She doesn't want you here. Nobody wants you here.'

'You are deceived. I have spent many pleasant hours in your father's study; I know the dining-room well, and in that other room, the drawing-room, where you are standing, I once kissed your brother. I say that only for your instruction.'

The Kid drew in his breath and tottered. For a moment it looked as if he were going to fall. Then, mustering his strength, he shouted: 'You are full of shit!'

'About this and about many things you deceive yourself,' said the doctor advancing again. The snake-like menace of his face and gestures intensified. He re-created the fury of Hera seeking vengeance for her slighted couch. His hands came forward from behind his back and began to jab at the air of the hallway, as though each pulse of a finger propelled his claims further into the interior of the house. The Kid began to shift from one foot to another, uncertain whether to advance or retreat. He faced the doctor with an expression which seemed to involve the production of more saliva than his trembling mouth could hold.

'Keep back,' he said quietly.

'For God's sake, Francis — may I call you that — will you allow my relations with your brother to be my concern?'

'You may not call me anything: and your relations are a load of hocus pocus. Go away! My mother is coming.'

The doctor suddenly smiled and took two related steps forward.

'My dear Kenneth. You are there! Your brother has chosen to embarrass me.'

'Go away!' shrieked the Kid.

'You are the small change from my feelings for Kenneth. I would happily throw you away. As for your mother, I gather that you are expecting her. That makes it difficult to allow me in.'

'That, and many things.'

The doctor suddenly adopted a look of remorseful tenderness.

'My poor Francis,' he said. 'All right, I will not call you that, or anything. My dearest Kenneth, please don't stand there in the background. Let me speak to you. I can say what I have more easily if I say it to you. Your mother . . .'

'Please go away,' said Fortnight. He found that his voice was trembling.

'*Et tu Brute?* I have no intention of going away. I wanted to say that something terrible has happened.'

The Kid was alert and listening, and Fortnight, who had come forward, saw his expression slowly changing to one of acute anguish. Something in the doctor's manner had affected him: as the doctor was moved, so was the Kid moved in an equal and opposite direction, the one towards falsehood, the other towards truth. The Kid had begun to cry slowly. But now the tears stopped like stone tears on his sculpted face, a face ossifying itself into the incontrovertible exclamation mark of a tombstone. The doctor surveyed him with joyous disdain.

'Yes,' the doctor continued, 'it is true that she was expected. In the way that light is expected by the man who sleeps. Yes she was expected. But I am afraid that she will not come.'

'What have you done?' asked the Kid in a frozen voice.

'Adrian!'

'My dear Kenneth, you must not interrupt me. I do not tolerate interruptions. I am the bearer of ill news. But I offer myself. It is for your sake, Kenneth, that I do it. But that is of no concern. My dear Kenneth, dear Francis, your mother will not come, because she cannot come. She is dead. It is pointless for me to give you proof of it. I know what happened. But there . . . I am monstrous, I should not say it as I have said it. I am much to blame.'

And the doctor, smiling trimphantly, continued to accuse himself in tones of deep compunction. He repeated his message in the fullest repertoire of idioms and voices; whatever accident had snatched away the unfortunate Mrs Fortnight was a force, he showed, with whose operation he was secretly familiar. His voice dropped an octave, and, in broken snatches, he revealed what this death had cost him, by way of vacancy in a crematorium, symbol of all other vacancies that had recently been his. He wept a little, and snaked his fingers like a temple dancer apostrophizing deep affliction. He sneered in self-contempt and self-abasement. And then the Kid, with white and stony features went upstairs towards the printing press. Ekhnaton, who had been observing the performance from the threshold of the dining-room, gave voice to a loud acclaim:

'Here it is! The true electric death machine! Making foetid mole-hills out of golden mountains, dead eyeballs out of juicy pumpkins, turning upside-down the painted cake-tin, putting crumbs in the pubic hair. What a performance! You've translated the genius into inter-galactic languages, he's floating in a chrome-steel syntax way out in the freezing void!'

The Marchesa also appeared, said 'I count such forms this night in night's wide universe,' and then remained on the threshold poised untouchably.

Fortnight went forward, took the doctor by the arm, and drew him into the laughing-room.

'Why did you do that? Why?'

The doctor was on his knees, weeping. He shook his head from side to side as though swarms of bees tormented it.

'My darling! My darling! I had to see you! You must forgive me! I have forgiven you, did I not forgive you? Permit yourself to live!'

Fortnight saw his own corpse, rolled beneath a sea of the doctor's dominion, rising up, sinking down, floating forwards, scraping towards him along the shore. He kicked it in protest.

'Leave this place!' he cried. 'Leave it! Don't return!'

The doctor laughed and got to his feet with a sudden spring.

'You think you can dispose of me so easily? You are much mistaken!'

Fortnight drew back a pace.

'Is it forbidden to me,' the doctor continued, 'to rescue you from this? Am I condemned to stand by while you flounder in your uncomprehended feelings? Don't I understand you? I first showed you this catastrophe. Didn't I, in a sense, create you?'

His eyes shone with the brilliance of polished stones. A radiance of lust played like oil on the unyielding surface of his being. He was a self-effigy, ludicrous like a piece of gossip etched in travertine: the indestructible inane. When the Kid came through the door and discovered him in this pose Fortnight greeted with glee his brother's defiant posture. The doctor's face, as it raised itself to their grandmother's portrait, carved in itself the epitaph which fitted it: a sneer of self-hatred spread across its mouth, while the high forehead arched in indignation and the black eyes fixed unwaveringly the blue moonbeams of the watching woman. The Kid held the Colt in both hands and fired. For a second the sneer lingered on the doctor's features. Gradually a doubt seemed to spread through his body, and when the Kid fired again, the doctor, who had already lifted his sneer to an altitude where it seemed to breathe only with the greatest difficulty, rose higher and higher, like a mad puppet, like the superclown, pulled ever higher by secret strings, as though he would imprint his leer on the ceiling, leaving in bloodmarks the proof of his kiss in the laughing-room.

The doctor telescoped downwards, his hand pressed to a purple patch on the clean prose of his cotton shirt. Fortnight seized the gun. The Kid relinquished it without a struggle, having fainted away at the second shot.

'Oh!' cried the doctor, 'Oh! What will I do? What has he done to me? Oh! It burns inside! It's gone inside!'

And with ludicrous gestures of indignation he flapped towards the door.

Fortnight ran to the chest in the hallway. His mother's clothes impeded him. First her scarf, then her winter jacket, wrapped themselves around the telephone. Then the fur coat for army functions slipped from his left hand and stifled his movement. At last he threw the clothes backwards into the dining-room, where the two old ladies, who seemed to be alone, picked at them with curious expressions as though discovering an impromptu jumble sale.

For a second he looked at the telephone, which was cracked, showing a tiny red glow inside. The doctor made a noise in the hallway, intended, perhaps, as contemptuous laughter, but sounding like the vomiting of a dog. In his heart Fortnight wished for children and knitting, and he recorded this in Barbara's favour. But there was something he should do with this instrument which bore more directly on his brother's predicament. He knelt for several seconds staring at the tiny glow.

Then, unexpectedly, the telephone began to ring. He lifted the receiver and held it a few inches from his head. A voice like Susan's murmured from a distance. 'What's that you say?' he shouted.

He tried not to look at the doctor, who fixed him with eyes of burning accusation, adopting the privilege of the dying so as to give ultimity to his claim. Insensibly, Fortnight's eyes strayed to the hand at the doctor's side, which was now rose carmine against his shirt, like an outrageous flower.

213

'I have booked the ticket. You must be here tomorrow. Darling, are you there?'

'Where?' he asked. It was Susan's voice, muted by giggles.

'Here. Italy. I assumed that . . .'

'Will you get off the telephone, while the doctor dies?'

'Darling, are you all right? I . . .'

He cut her short. The operator could not understand his demand. He repeated it. 'Catalepsy,' he shouted, 'tell them catalepsy.' He went into the laughing-room. The Kid was lying on the carpet, the whites of his eyes visible beneath half-closed lids. Fortnight took the limp hand, shook it, felt the pulse, the heart, the cold, damp forehead.

'Kid!' he cried, 'Kid!'

There was whispering, a shutting of doors, a figure standing above him, its red hand dripping on the carpet. Fortnight was in a boat on stagnant water, gliding quietly through cave upon cave; his brother lay at his side. Occasionally he looked up and saw the running figures projected on the ceiling of the underworld. He was struck by the comic zeal of the two old ladies, one of whom was wearing his mother's fur coat, as they panted and ran. Soon the noises were muted; only the Kid's heavy breathing disturbed the silence. And then the siren tunnelled towards them through navigable reaches of twilight.

Through the fanlight the blue signal splashed the white ceiling of the hall. He saw the Kid's white arm like an abandoned thing, lying across the floor of the laughing-room and touching with its fingertips the bottom of the canapé. Grey uniformed men listened quietly to his words and then advanced towards the body. As he watched them lift the Kid on to a stretcher and bear it aloft, Fortnight felt a transformation of experience, as though all these things were being enacted in some separate sphere, and he was glimpsing them down a hollow shaft from another space and time. With the straightforward gestures of practical men the ambulance attendants simplified the Kid. The doctor they found by the gate crying, 'It's inside me, it's gone inside.' Fortnight watched as the wounds were inspected and the doctor invited to take his place in the ambulance opposite the boy. The Marchesa who, in her terror, had taken refuge in the lavatory, was included in the freight, and the double doors closed upon her ululations.

The two policemen were more concerned by the footprints of Kym and Ekhnaton in the garden than by the blood on the carpet, although one of them, who had an amateur interest in weapons, had much to say in praise of the Colt 45. He thought that the box from which it had been taken, which they found among the scattered type in the composing-room, was a work of art. He was much displeased with the Kid for scattering its lovely burden of accessories across the floor. Everything had to be left as it was. The constable stood and observed the disorder with the natural grief of a mind dedicated to beauty. Fortnight looked at the bowed head of the printing press. Then, on an impulse, he pulled the iron handle, and peeled off a copy of the Kid's poem for the constable to read.

Fortnight took the purple bus that went every hour from Flackwell to Harrisham, stopping by the long grey wall of the Mount Pleasant hospital six miles out of town. He particularly liked the colour of this bus, which belonged to a Harrisham company and stood out strangely among the red and green buses of Flackwell. He liked, too, the walk through the old part of town which took him to the bus station. He had become familiar with run-down streets and patches of untidy greenery which brought back to him the image of Mrs Fortnight's world.

It was a hot August day, and two droning bees were trapped in the upper deck of the bus, where he sat alone, staring at the thick-leaved chestnuts and oozing lime-trees that brushed the left-hand side. The constant hum of the bees filled his thoughts. He listened to it advance and then recede, advance and recede, like a busy petitioner seeking admission to the closed office of his skull.

The hospital was large, Victorian, classical, surrounded by parks and gardens littered with terrapin huts. The patients were free to walk as far as the great Roman arch of the outer gate, and their silent stares followed him as he entered the drive of fuchsias and laburnums, at the end of which the baroque chapel, modelled on a German village church, closed its old doors on the world. The blocks of the hospital surrounded courtyards with wrought-iron benches, on which cartwheel-patterned eiderdowns and dun-coloured schizophrenics were being aired. Wrought-iron fire-escapes spidered over the walls, caged in a filigree of suicide-proof wire. Patients mooned about the doorway, and high above them on the cornice sat a man in a ginger coat. His face was old and sad, brushed by a few grey wisps of hair. With his hands he distractedly cracked the shell of peanuts, and the broken husks dropped on to his coat, or floated downwards onto the heads of the patients below, who took down the remnants from their hair and stared at them with scientific intensity. As Fortnight approached, the old man began to cheer in a low voice, 'hurrah, hurrah, hurrah,' slowly and tonelessly. He did not move, and from below it was impossible to discover how he could have got to where he was sitting. His feet dangled into the frame of an upper window, and once a male nurse in white hospital livery pressed his nose to the glass, glanced upwards briefly, and evinced no surprise at the sight of a pair of legs hanging from the cornice.

Fortnight recognized many of the faces now, and had become accustomed to the two voices of the hospital: the indiscreet confessional, and the loud bellow of disappointed rage. Already as he passed beneath the glass dome of the antechamber a lank young man with greasy hair and sallow skin had accosted him and begun to whisper: 'You must realize Mr . . . Mr . . . You must realize the lengths they'll go to. I've had four ball-bearings shoved in my ears this morning. It was that nurse Harris is responsible. How am I supposed to live I ask you? Have I got to go round all day with ball-bearings in my brain? And do you see that one over there, that loony one? I want to tell you . . .' Fortnight had reached the main corridor and the young man, whose sense of boundaries, as with all the inmates, was greatly exaggerated, ceased to pursue him, standing instead at the door of the antechamber in order to bellow obscenities into the void.

The path to the male observation ward lay across a low-walled courtyard, reached from the corridor. On the benches blankets and cheerful eiderdowns were airing, with big blobs of flowers in emerald and royal blue. At the far corner stood the laundry, with its high chimney emitting black smoke. The door swung open as he passed. In the steamy interior were green enamel boilers, steel sinks and a long deal table on which clucking women struggled with horrid shreds of cloth. The sight of their industry reassured him, and he stood in the doorway for a moment and breathed the atmosphere of soap and steam. He looked down at the books in his hands: Cicero, Sallust and a translation of Chrysostom. A doubt entered his mind as to whether the Kid was able to read. The hospital report had mentioned degeneration of the optic nerves following an epileptic crisis, diagnosis uncertain, prognosis impossible. He stood in the door, watching the aproned stomachs of the women grooved by the edge of the bench. His own stomach tightened, and for a moment he could not move.

Dr Bishop tapped him on the shoulder as she passed. Together they walked down the alley of conifers that led to her ward. Dr Bishop was a tall New England beauty, fair-haired, blue-eyed, with the tiredness of pregnancy adding to the wrinkles around her eyes. Her chirpy conversation was designed to get him moving, and although he resented it, he admired the effect on the patients with whom she exchanged civilities as they passed. The inmates seemed to understand the egocentric patter of a pregnant woman, perhaps because it so perfectly matched their own, pregnant as they also were with amazing conceptions. They whispered to her confidingly, leaning slightly forward so as to navigate her belly, and she smiled at them her repertoire of bland agreements.

'Many of our patients,' she said as they approached her ward, 'come from the airport. Several a week. It is sometimes difficult to discover how they get there. Some want to go to Los Angeles, to be among angels. Others consent to get off the plane only because they know that a prince is sending a squadron to escort them to Moscow. Some come to watch the metal birds which snatch people's souls away.'

Fortnight nodded and looked up at the sky.

'As for your brother, we still don't know. Dr Fist thought at first it might be Wernicke's encephalopathy. But . . .'

'Dr Fist?'

'Yes. Apparently he treated your brother once before, years ago, when he was too young I expect to remember.'

'Is there a Dr Grabenaz?' Fortnight asked cautiously.

'I remember the name. He, or maybe it was she, is no longer here. Cheer up. We'll work something out. He needs to rest.'

Requiem aeternam dona ei, Domine. The words went through Fortnight's mind like a chill wind. It was true: that was his mission. He looked at Dr Bishop in anguish. He wanted to ask her to forbid him to enter. But he could not make such a request to someone used to cutting the knot of every contradiction. He followed her into the annexe. The patients here were women and gave off a smell of fear, a smell of the zoo. They moved in a furtive, bird-like way, picking inquisitively at various parts of their own flesh. As lunch was announced they rose slowly, coming forward to the tables like mechanical dolls, and fixing the food with mournful and suspicious eyes. Some pushed it away, knowing it to be poisoned; others lifted it to the mouth as though it were made of some dense substance which weighed down intolerably on the fork.

Fortnight hurried to the stairway. The male observation ward was on the second floor. None of the windows opened by the sash. Instead a roundel of glass could be turned in each one like a kitchen ventilator, to let in the air. Fortnight paused to wipe the sweat from his brow. He greeted a middle-aged man who sat in a deck-chair by the office door. The man replied, as he always replied:

> *Thus spake the gay old major*
> *With his face as bold as brass:*
> *'I won't have no more of your Christmas pud,*
> *Because I couldn't get rid of the last.'*

The ward doctor approached, twirling in his fingers the tuft of smoky hair with which he habitually excused himself.

'He asked to see you: I think we should be encouraged by that.'

Fortnight nodded, looked into the doctor's rimless spectacles in search of eyes, found none, and moved off towards the annexe. Here the Kid was kept in isolation, by high barred windows which faced the sun.

A nurse pointed to the only bed that was occupied. The Kid lay back on his pillow, eyes closed, mouth open, a faraway gurgle trapped in his throat. A transparent tube was strapped to his colourless arm, joining it to a bottle of fluid that stood a few feet from the bed. Fortnight stepped forward. The Kid wore no glasses now, and the plumpness of his cheeks had gone. In Fortnight's thoughts it was his mother's face that he saw distorted on the pillow, and it was as though he had come at last to beg forgiveness.

The Kid opened his eyes and caught sight of his brother. He tried lethargically to smile, opening his mouth on one side in a pear-shaped grimace.

'I'm dizzy,' he said in a thick voice. 'and there is two of everything. Dead.'

Fortnight searched for words.

'Here. I don't know if you can read. I brought some books. Cicero, and . . .'

'*Timeo Danaos donaet ferentes.* No. Not you.'

The Kid sat up slowly and rotated his head with an air of concentration, as though he were listening to something move inside it.

'I'm sorry, Kenny. You're not dead. The voice keeps getting stuck: it's driving me dead. Always dead. I have to make such an effort. It's in the corner of the room. Don't listen to it. Fist is in control. Maybe you could write to him. Dead. Don't cry. Not your fault.'

Suddenly the Kid began to move violently, tossing about, and pulling at the drip as though he sought to detach it from his arm. Gurgles and shouts accompanied his movements.

'Look at him!' he cried. 'The ten-stone weakling! Coming into the house without a licence, send him dead away! Strip him off! Call that a body, in its Mr Snugg V. Knutt boxerettes from Jules and Rodney fashions! Pure filth!'

Fortnight held the Kid's hand to restrain him; after a few seconds he fell back on the pillow, sweating and moaning. Slowly the nurse detached herself from the far corner of the room and drifted towards them, with a gentle susurration like a sail in a summer breeze. She fussed about, adjusted this and that, and departed as quietly as she had come.

Slowly the Kid roused himself.

'Who pulls the strings, that's what I want to know: who makes this puppet Kid go dead out of its mind? Funny that. I used to blame the dead, blame the doctors. You see they took all my blood away and replaced it with peppermint from this dead tube thing. I feel very peculiar. Honestly Kenny I reckon I must taste like an After Eight. They can do what they want with this dead body: you see, it's got no blood in it. Not your fault. Did you say you brought some books? Did you print them? No, that's dead, *kaput*. Cheer up Kenny. I've thought of some methods, get it under control. Needs time. Only time. So many muddles here. Other dead prisoners a frightful bore. Absolutely uneducated. Can you bring me the paper-knife?'

Fortnight stayed by the bedside for as long as he could, suffering the Kid's metamorphosis, his frenzy, confusion, and lucidity by turns, across all of which the word 'dead' came again and again with a hard blocked sound, a sudden unfocussed stare, as though the Kid had momentarily been stopped by a bullet, and then inexplicably revived. Fortnight felt that he understood everything that was said to him, understood the finest details of the Kid's despair, and wanted to reach in to where he lay and offer some consoling gestures. But his efforts were unavailing. A glass screen divided the Kid from the outer world, which he addressed only in soft pitying tones, as though it were the world and not himself that needed healing. Fortnight left the hospital exhausted in heart and mind.

Over the next five days the Kid remained the same. He refused to eat, describing his food as exhibits from Belsen. The fever settled deeper in his brain, and although he would revive at the sound of his brother's voice, even this could cause anxiety. He talked of the house, which he had precise plans for redecorating as soon as possible, as a matter of the greatest urgency. He also took an interest in Fortnight's career. He felt sure that there was a particular set of chambers, if only he could remember the name, where Fortnight would be well received. But certain subjects were taboo. The Kid mentioned the doctor only when screaming in pain or delirium. And their mother, who until that time had been implicit in every reference, was now consigned to the underworld, the word 'dead' thrown down like a charm before every point of entry. Fortnight rehearsed in his mind the days when he too had played with that word and found it meaningless. Now he lay at home at night, sleepless, his knees drawn up, unable to cry. That, he knew, was grief.

On the sixth day the Kid's speech became blocked. His few press communiqués took on proverbial form. 'The comforter's head never aches', he announced as Fortnight entered. Once or twice he tried to speak, but his sentences always ended prematurely, marking time on certain words beyond which his thought would not progress. Then there came over his expression the symptoms of the most intolerable terror, of which Fortnight felt some painful reverberation, and from which the Kid could be stirred only by the chance word or gesture that set the world in motion again.

During his fits the Kid would scream, shake, and move convulsively, pulling at tubes and pushing over trays of instruments. He cried out that he had forgotten his Latin, that someone had stolen his Latin, and then took refuge in a proverb: 'If the doctor cures the sun sees it, but if he kills the earth hides it.' He screamed again. He said that Britchell was sitting there. Then he fell back on the bed, exhausted, withered, with a twisted, pickled look and a vacant gaze.

One day early in September Fortnight saw that the Kid would die. The doctors made vague pronouncements. There were drugs, they thought, that could yet be tried. But the Kid dwindled inexorably in body and mind. His skin became yellow and leathery, and his eyes stared from their sockets as though something else had taken up position at the lack of them, and was peering through them at a distorted world. Fortnight went weeping from the hospital.

He tried to write to his mother's relatives. For a long time he sat at the dining-room table with paper before him. He imagined again the pinchpurse spinsters as they questioned cupboards for a misplaced joint of meat, the mustachioed bachelors with their model boats and medicine bottles, peering from windows that gave on to crazy paving and orange nasturtiums. In extremity, he realized, only the Colonel's tactics were allowed.

A card came from Susan. It was post-marked Agrigento and said: 'Darling, having a lovely time, but how tempus fugits, don't you think?' Holtius, who was recuperating on an East Anglian farm, also wrote, beginning with one horrendous sentence that caused Fortnight to burn card and letter together. After reflection, he retrieved Barbara's letters from behind the poetry bookcase and added them to the fire.

The time came to consider his father. A message was left at the Voyager's Club. There was no response. He decided to telephone Aunt Kate.

'My dear young man,' she said, 'the whole set up was screwy from the start. I've given you my advice. I really don't see why you have to trouble me now, when I am expecting six guests for dinner. Your father, by the way, is living with a whore called Diane Forster, who lives in Earl's Terrace. You will find her number in the book.'

Fortnight replaced the receiver and then went to the print-room. He gathered up the remnants that the police had carefully photographed, and restored the tables, trays and implements to the image of the Kid's arrangement. He took the runner from the spare bedroom and covered the bloodstained carpet in the laughing-room. And then he noticed that one of the bullets was lodged in the frame of their grandmother's portrait, just to the right of her wide astonished eyes.

That afternoon, when he called at the hospital, he learned that the Kid could not be visited.

The garden in the twilight was blue and silver; the soft rain pat-tered on the leaves, and on the long stalks of grass, with the noise of whispering children. Outwards from the house went the battalions of volition, worming their way through the jungle of azaleas, hollyhocks, foxgloves and begonias. They pulled him in their wake towards the shed. They took her gaberdine mackintosh from the hook, and cloaked him in it for the road. A little footpath took a plunge towards the railway cottages, and then up on to the bridge across the line. From there he reached the Bramhurst Road.

Seeing him approach, Barbara got up from the verandah, swiftly swirled her cotton dress and disappeared through the French windows. Her father sucked at his pipe, sending small puffs of smoke into the twilight air. He watched Fortnight dither with the gate, and said nothing until they were standing side by side. From time to time a drop of rain fizzled in the bowl, and Mr Langley would inhale just a little more strongly to keep the tobacco burning. Then he took his pipe slowly from his lips and spoke softly of the late summer rain that had come and gone so suddenly. Mr Langley adjusted his beret, and then moved out further into the whitish air. If you visited earlier you were rewarded with sherry, in exact and specified doses, as a rat is rewarded with a pellet. Mr Langley was prepared to enquire whether Fortnight had eaten but it was too late for him to concern himself with the reply.

Eventually they sat at the metal table. Mr Langley set down his pipe and stared at the remaining food. Fortnight watched as Mr Langley took a small pork pie, removed the pastry top and a great deal of the sides, laying them in a paper napkin. And then, with a dainty gesture of finger and thumb, he reached inside, seized the small knuckle of shrivelled meat, and popped it quickly into his small moist mouth.

'One of our few remaining Flackwell delicacies,' he com-mented.

They spoke of operatic music, for which Mr Langley did not care. He said how proud he was of Barbara. After a while there was a silence, which Mr Langley broke by saying: 'It seems that you are no longer quite so friendly.'

Fortnight felt himself shrink to the dimensions of a child who had jettisoned a playmate.

'I hadn't expected to see Barbara. Is she home for the holidays?'

Mr Langley nodded. 'Why don't you go and speak to her?' he enquired. 'She was talking of going back to town tomorrow. It would be nice if you could prevent that.'

Fortnight looked at Mr Langley and then hesitated. Over the artist's face a gentle smile wreathed itself, threading the dark eyes, the wrinkles and the reassumed pipe on a single string, and sucking itself up through the shiny volutes of his nose. He tapped out his pipe and said:

'To fighten for a lady: *benedicite*
It were a lusty sighte for to see,'

and then stood quietly, studiously vague.

'Have you been painting much?'

'On and off. On and off. It has been a particularly beautiful summer, and I have been studying flowers. The wild orchid, for example, no doubt soon to disappear from our meadows and woods: but for some reason astonishing this year. There are three varieties of helleborine in our copse. Which reminds me, I have left volume six of Horwood in my studio.'

He took a step off the verandah.

'Do excuse me. I must fetch it while there is light.'

Fortnight climbed the pinewood staircase that plunged from the punctured wall of the drawing-room. He entered a modern section. Everything here was bare, grey concrete, rough-cut stone, and unstained hardwood sticky with beeswax. Meandering passages suddenly contracted into cupboards or opened into airy rooms, and to gain the safety of the barn where Barbara was, it was necessary to cross a music-room with a dulcimer, a sitar, a set of Javanese gongs, and a collection of Turkish flutes in pierced bamboo. Nothing here was ever taken from its careful arrangement on the walls, and it was only on rare occasions that Mr Langley entered, to sit with exposed head on carpeted cushions, silently fermenting like an egg that would at any moment split open and release some black bedraggled bird. At last Fortnight touched her door. The handle seemed to move of its own accord.

He had the feeling he had opened the wrong door, entered where he had not meant to enter, but there was hope in this unexpected world, and he did not want to go to that other one where the game of self is played, and where he had agitated on his own behalf for seven months without reward. He moved to Barbara where she stood by the window, grasped her by the waist with hands shaking from tenderness and hardly knowing yet what he should do. Barbara was crying, but she made no gesture of resistance, and for a long moment he stared with her eyes from the window, watched with her pain the small form of Mr Langley cross from the studio to the house, and breathed gently into her hair with its soft familiar unperfumed smell.

At last he spoke, quietly, accusing himself, quite happy with the role he had regained, relying on Barbara as he had always relied on her, to respect his feelings once he could present them as sincere. She listened, nodded, was silent; nothing in her frame resisted him. He was astonished how easy it was to confess at last, to give himself up entirely to whatever of love and punishment had been reserved for him.

'I remembered always the other time, when I would have welcomed chaos, howling, priests in their long robes — anything but the sense of her impending nothingness. I was ashamed in front of you, as I had been ashamed in front of Adrian Holtius — do you remember him? I stupidly wanted you to allow me to be silent. And it also seemed easier to you: that way I made less havoc in your life. But don't mistake me. I love you for your neatness. I want it still, although I have lost the right. But the Kid! The Kid, Barbara. He took it on himself. He has done everything for me. And now he is dying.'

He began his story. The rain increased, pattering down on the glass skylight of the barn with a noise like a thousand tiny immaculate locks, opening and closing in synchrony, to prepare the passage that they now must take. Barbara turned silently, and went to move the books from a pair of stools. He looked at the score of *Dichterliebe* lying open on the maiden bed, the half-finished tapestry that she had begun the day before he left; he let his eye stray over her shelf of books, picking out the ones they had read together. He looked at her, and saw in her glance that she cleaved to him still. But she played with her fingers as in moments of unkindness.

'I heard all about you and that dreadful Susan Waterford.'

She caught her breath as though the sentence was spoken at the end of a marathon and in order to extract a prize.

'Dreadful?' he asked.

He remembered Susan with unsullied affection. After all, she had given him the knife which the Kid had asked him to smuggle into the hospital, and which was now concealed in his damp pyjamas.

'Dreadful.'

'Did the Kid tell you?'

'The Kid! Of course not. He wrote often, but only in order to praise you and ask for patience.'

Fortnight bowed his head.

'So how, then, did you hear?'

'From your father.'

'The Colonel!'

'He has been quite shameless in his denunciations of you. He has plagued me day after day with your dissipations.'

'Why?'

'Why do you think?'

Fortnight hid his head in his hands. He needed Barbara to be strong. He knew that she had resisted the Colonel, but not because she had not hated his son.

'I know you are resilient,' he offered.

'It is a mistake to ascribe resilience to people who won't be baulked. Resilience is the power to hope for some different thing. I simply hope incessantly for the same. You know that.'

'I do know that.'

Fortnight directed his sob now this way, now that, to his mother who deserved it, to the Kid who needed it, to the great nothingness in front of which Barbara still stood. We insist on grief. Her voice, her dear voice; she should speak again. He got up, sat on the bed, and again shielded his eyes, as though from a blinding light. Hours seemed to pass. She came and perched beside him on the bed, tucking her legs under her so that the long dress billowed up in a spangled dome and brushed against his elbow.

'Do you remember the way you left me, Ken? Do you remember your words? Do you remember?'

He nodded bountifully.

'Actually do you remember anything? Anything of our life together? I doubt it. I seriously doubt it. Do you realize what your mother's illness did to me? But, as you say, the Kid had suffered most. You exaggerate, of course, when you say he's dying.'

'Oh no.'

He turned to her in surprise. He tried to explain to her. Her eyes widened in amazement. He could not think. There was a great number of moths in the room, and as though startled into activity by his story, they began to haunt with maniacal persistence the unkempt corners of his head. She tried to speak. Her tears impeded her. He noticed that whenever she uttered the word 'actually' — which was often, because it was a favourite word — giving it a special emphasis all of her own, he felt consoled by the familiarity of this and of all her mannerisms. This intimacy seemed also to justify him. It seemed to show that he had observed her, slinkingly, passively, but with interest and affection. Raising his hand in the fluffy air to brush away a moth from his earlobe he happened to glance sideways at Barbara and saw that her mouth, which had been open in astonishment and grief, was now to be kissed. He attempted to strain into that kiss every drop of the tenderness he felt, and then to suck back an equivalent in love. The bargain led to a new exchange. Her hands trembled on his face and neck. Slowly the agony of appeasement wormed through him, and his grief, unlocked at last, crawled out and shook itself on the surface of his face.

That night they walked back to Flackwell together, the rain running through their hair, their wet hands twisted together, their voices silent. If his mother had not died, she would have taught him how to interpret the strange flashes of blue that lay now along the horizon. She had observed all nature from her window where she sat as though receiving instructions for her future moods. Soon he would sit there too. He was glad that he had put the house in order. He showed the scene to Barbara, speaking in hushed tones of what had happened. At the door of the Kid's room he shrank back, unable to enter.

Soon they went down to the laughing-room. Fortnight left her at the piano, playing with her right hand alone the rushing arpeggios of the last movement of the Moonlight Sonata. She had asked for wine, and he lingered over every step to the cellar, relishing the peace and tension that now inhabited his being. In all their gestures, this mixture sought expression, so that they asked themselves, would it last, or would it die?

On his way back from the cellar, the telephone rang. His chest constricted and he dropped the bottle on the floor of the hall. Every one of the nurse's words was expected, and he stood with a dry throat as the sentence was passed. The Kid was dead. The matter was closed. Quietly he went into the laughing-room, tried to open his mouth, gave up, and fell forward into Barbara's arms. Together, then, they sat down to wait.

London, 2 January 1981